DEATH NEVER LIES

ALSO BY DAVID GRACE

DEATH NEVER LIES

David Grace

WILDSIDE PRESS

Copyright Information

Death Never Lies

CHAPTER ONE

The newspapers later said that they were high on meth or crack or some other drug with a name that sounded like a line from a movie. But none of that mattered. When Franco Herrera and Ricky Bazzel took over Sam's Speedy Mart they were just two crazed gunmen waving assault rifles and screaming orders.

"Give me the money!"

"Don't look at me!"

"Nobody move!"

"Open the safe!"

Franco thought that the woman in the red sweater was moving around too much so he sent a burst of fire into the shelf of dish soap a few inches above her head. Green, orange and purple goo splattered like greasy rain. Franco smiled and fired off an extra couple of shots just to see more stuff blow up.

Barely a hundred yards from the store, Detectives Greg Kane and Ralph Amoroso were on their way back to Robbery-Homicide when the All-Units call came in. Ralph glanced left just as the Speedy Mart's front window exploded under another burst from Franco's AR-15. Theoretically, the guns should have been restricted to single-shots but Ricky had paid an extra hundred each to convert them to fully automatic. The fifty shot clips had cost another hundred on top of that but as he watched the glass fly across the parking lot Ricky figured that it was all worth it. He loved the AR-15. It made exactly the right statement: *Nobody better fuck with me.*

Amoroso mashed on the brakes and the detectives' Crown Vic screamed as it went into a sideways slide. Both men jumped out and turned toward the building before the car had stopped bouncing on its shocks. The store's front door shattered to another burst and a second later Franco jumped through the empty frame. He paused for an instant at the edge of the parking lot and, wild-eyed, stared at the two cops in cheap suits who were aiming pistols at him in apparent slow motion.

"Fuck!" Franco screamed and pulled the trigger before he had even raised the muzzle. A stream of slugs skipped off the asphalt like stones across the pond. At the same instant Kane and Amoroso opened fire. With a bewildered look Franco suddenly paused then tumbled backward, emptying the rest of his clip into the sky.

"Ralphie, are you hurt?" Kane shouted.

A trickle of blood ran down Amoroso's cheek. The detective ran his hand across his face and stared at his palm.

"No, it's just a scratch," Ralph said then looked up into the face of death.

As if by magic Ricky Bazzel had materialized on the sidewalk, rifle raised. He held the trigger down and a line of slugs marched across Ralph Amoroso's chest then crunched through the Crown Vic's windshield toward Kane. From the corner of his eye, living in some odd universe where time had slowed down, Kane saw Amoroso fall and the bullets walk their way toward him — THUMP - THUMP - THUMP . . . .

In an instant Kane stopped thinking about ducking or running or curling into a ball underneath the car. Rage flared inside him like a spark hitting a mist of gasoline. Kane raised his gun straight out in front of him and ran toward his partner's murderer, firing as fast as he could pull the trigger. As if buffeted by a sudden wind Bazzel staggered back, half turned, and fired one more round before collapsing. The last bullet hit the top of a cement parking-stop, skipped upward at a shallow angle and smashed into the side of Greg Kane's head.

Kane stared at Bazzel's body and the growing red-black pool creeping away from it then everything started spinning. While he was still trying to figure out what had gone wrong Greg Kane fell over and, with sirens screaming from someplace far away, he watched the world go black.

CHAPTER TWO

Washington D.C.
Two Years Later

A year ago Travis Sawyer had been the general manager of his father's Chevy dealership but a promise to "Clean Up Washington," a bland but clean-cut appearance, and a half-million dollar campaign contribution from his grandfather had turned him into "Congressman Sawyer." Normally Frederick Immerson wouldn't have wasted his time on a freshman congressman but the Chairman had asked him to give Sawyer the dog-and-pony-show and since the Department of Homeland Security was looking for a seven percent increase in their next appropriation Immerson was willing to oblige.

Immerson and Sawyer reached the squad room where the GS-13 Investigators were based and Immerson paused at the entrance to give his standard speech about the important work performed by the Department of Homeland Security's Office of Special Investigations. As instructed, everyone was at their desks busily flipping through files or pounding their keyboards. Everyone except Gregory Kane who was notably absent. Immerson forced his gaze away from Kane's vacant desk and pasted on his most sincere smile.

"We call this 'the bull pen,' Congressman. Each of these agents—"

"What I don't understand," Sawyer broke in, "is why we need all these people in the first place. Shouldn't the FBI be handling whatever it is you do here?"

"The FBI is a fine organization but—"

"I mean, all these people pushing papers at taxpayer expense just to do the same sort of thing that the FBI is already doing. It all seems like bureaucracy run amok to me."

Immerson made a conscious effort not to let his irritation show.

"Actually, Congressman—"

"You're completely wrong," Gregory Kane interjected, appearing from Immerson's blind side. Sawyer turned toward Kane and looked as if he had just noticed a bad smell.

"Congressman Sawyer, this is Agent Gregory Kane." Neither man offered to shake hands. "Kane the Congressman is—"

"Confused," Kane said. "The FBI is organized into various bureaus and departments whose funding and manpower go up and down like Paris skirt lengths depending on the crime *du jour*. Right now that's terrorism and human trafficking. Next week it might be industrial espionage and bribes to members of Congress." Kane gave Sawyer a hard stare. "What never gets much attention or funding are threats against non-elected federal employees."

"So, if my mailman gets mugged you spring into action? Is that it?" Sawyer snapped.

"No, we usually leave that to the Postal Inspector and the local police. We're more concerned with something like an attempt to blackmail the chairman of an FDA review panel into approving a multi-billion dollar drug or bribing a testing lab to pass defective medical equipment destined for a V.A. Hospital or the theft of the access codes to the copy machines installed in the executive offices of the Department of Energy. If you think the FBI is going to give top priority to anything like that you're . . . ." Kane finally noticed Immerson's wild eyes and sweating brow. ". . . mistaken."

Sawyer's lips were pinched into a tight line. None of his employees ever spoke to him like that. Nobody, not waiters, not store clerks, not even bank managers spoke to him that way. He was a millionaire and a Congressman and, according to his deacon, one of God's chosen for Christ's sake, and this bureaucrat thought he could call him out? Sawyer very much wanted to do something about it but the investigator's broad shoulders and big hands and most of all his hard eyes made Sawyer pause and think again.

"Kane, aren't you supposed to be finishing the report on the Jeffers case?"

Kane turned to Immerson as if surprised to see him still there, then nodded contritely.

"Yes sir, I'll get right on that. Congressman, a pleasure meeting you." A polite nod in Sawyer's direction and Kane was gone as quickly as he had appeared.

"I'm sorry, Congressman," Immerson said in almost a whisper. "Kane is a great investigator but, well, you have to understand his history. He was a senior detective on the Baltimore PD when he and his partner ran into two gunmen high on drugs. The thugs killed his partner and tried to kill him but he charged into their fire and shot them both. He saved a store full of people but," Immerson sighed, "he was shot in the head." Immerson's hand described a path along the left side of his skull from front to back just above his ear. "He recovered, he has a mind like a steel trap actually, and he's a terrific investigator. Sometimes it's almost like having our own little Sherlock Holmes, but, aaaahh, he's a bit short tempered and he has a tendency to say things out loud that he would be better off keeping to himself. The doctors assure us that it's temporary. In the meantime, well, he was a hero and we make allowances. And he closes cases. I'm sure you understand."

"A hero you say?

"Charged right into automatic weapons' fire to take out the criminals. They gave him a medal."

"Well, wounded in the line of duty, I suppose you have to cut him a little slack," Sawyer allowed.

"I'll tell you what — why don't you let me take you to lunch? I can fill you in on some of our more interesting cases. It's pretty exciting stuff and it never makes the papers. All 'need to know' you understand."

"Sure, I wouldn't mind getting something to eat," Sawyer said, giving Immerson a weak smile.

"Through that door," Immerson told him, pointing, then he gave Kane a quick, nervous glance before heading for the exit.

Greg Kane tried to focus on his work but his brain continued spitting out data points — Sawyer's watch was a $3,000 Tag Heuer but the $60 shirt and off-the rack suit and shoes screamed Macy's. That meant that the watch was likely a present which meant that there was money in the family someplace but it wasn't his. Either the parents or the wife, Kane decided, which likely made Sawyer a man who craved a lot more than he had. Based on him shooting off his mouth about something that he should have known he didn't know anything about, it was pretty clear that Sawyer's ego surpassed his intelligence. Kane absently categorized the Congressman as someone who had been born on second base and felt that he'd been robbed of a triple. That bulge in his tummy and the little veins around his nose told Kane that Sawyer was drinking too much and exercising too little.

The way he cinched in his belt and sported a red-silk tie signaled that he was concerned with his appearance. And Kane didn't miss Sawyer's sideways glance at Marjorie either. The Congressman was on the hunt for some action, Kane figured, while the wife and kids were back home planning church suppers and organizing prayer breakfasts. *Useless sack of shit!* Kane decided then sighed and tried to control his anger. *Focus on the file,* he ordered himself. *Focus.*

Everything had been so much easier before COV, Clarity Of Vision, had descended on him. His old life had been soft and fuzzy and half a blur and then Ricky Bazzel skipped a bullet across the surface of his brain and everything changed. When he came back to his senses he found that the world had suddenly become bright and sharp and hard-edged. He felt like a man who had lived a lifetime with poor eyesight and then had been given his first pair of glasses. And there were the dreams. He used to dream like everybody else, confusing, jerky little scenes in misty places where people appeared and disappeared without reason or warning. Now his dreams were detailed, crisp and clear, with all his senses intact and the most crystalline of them all were the recurring dreams involving his dead brother, Tommy.

Had people been this stupid, vain, petty and clueless his whole life and he had just never noticed before? Kane was reminded every day that the world was heavily populated by idiots and that most of the ones who weren't morons were psychopaths, egomaniacs, bastards or crooks which was even worse. If he were in charge — *No, stop it!* he ordered himself. *Stop bitching, stop complaining, stop imagining how much better the world would be if only people were smarter and better. You drove away your wife and ruined your job. Wasn't that enough?* Kane scolded himself. He closed his eyes and took three slow, deep breaths.

Greg opened them again and looked guiltily around the bull pen. No one seemed to have noticed anything. Kane forced himself to concentrate and paged through the Marilyn Jeffers file. Two minutes into the first interview he had known that she was up to something. It hadn't taken him long to find out what. She'd started out by leaking the Mine Safety and Health Administration's inspection schedule to the Tip Top Coal Company and then had branched out to supplying half a dozen other mines with not only advance notices of safety inspections but also the personnel files of the inspectors. She'd created a dummy LLC in Virginia to receive the payoffs but had foolishly listed her brother as the LLC's Manager on the form she filed with the bank when she opened the account. *Stupid, stupid, stupid!* But stupid crooks were a good thing. *If they weren't morons it would be a lot harder to catch them,* he reminded himself.

"You find something good, Agent?" Danny Rosewood asked, noticing Kane's smile.

"The suspect put her brother's name on the bank account where the payoffs were being deposited."

"Score!" Danny said and raised five fingers up high. Greg hesitated then awkwardly raised his own arm as well. "Get you a cup of coffee, Agent?"

"No, Danny, thanks. I'm good." Rosewood nodded and Kane watched him wander toward the break room. Officially Danny Rosewood was a GS 10 support tech but his actual job was doing whatever the investigators wanted that they didn't have the time or energy to do for themselves, everything from subpoenaing bank and telephone records to reviewing surveillance footage to making coffee and ordering another box of file folders. Danny was a glorified gofer, but a gofer with a dream. Rosewood wanted to be an Agent. He wanted to carry a badge, which wasn't unusual but, unlike most wannabees, Danny had a plan.

Rosewood constantly scanned the Internet for classes on police sciences. If some college was offering a night-school seminar on interrogation techniques, Danny was there. When the Government Printing Office issued a new manual on investigative procedures or forensic protocols, Danny was their first customer. He made a pest of himself to the investigators like Greg Kane, always asking questions, always wanting to know how they did what they did. Half the Agents avoided him and the other half competed to see how ridiculous a war story they could con Danny into believing. But not Greg Kane. Danny Rosewood was the only person in the office, except for maybe Fred Immerson, whom Kane actually respected.

Danny wasn't especially smart or creative. He certainly didn't have a charismatic personality and he wasn't a deep thinker. But Danny Rosewood had one quality that Greg Kane admired — Danny worked harder to make the most of whatever talents he had than anyone Kane had ever known. Kane was sick of nonentities like Travis Sawyer who were mediocrity personified and were too arrogant to even know it. At the other end of the spectrum were gifted people who wasted their talents or drifted along, doing just enough to get by when they were capable of so much more. Danny, on the other hand, knew he wasn't the smartest guy in the room and that he never would be, but every day he made a hundred and ten percent effort to be the best person that he could possibly be and that determination earned him something beyond price — Greg Kane's respect.

Kane turned back to his computer and started typing the Jeffers report which Immerson would forward to the U.S. Attorney. Just as he was about to hit "Send" Kane's cell buzzed. The caller was one of his oldest friends, Professor Martin Fouchet. Marty's wife was sick and Greg could tell from the way Marty's eyes darted away when he talked about Caroline that she wasn't doing well. Kane said a little prayer that Marty wasn't calling to tell him that Caroline had died and tapped the "accept" icon.

"Marty, what's up?"

"Greg, I think I need your help. I think something's wrong."

"Wrong?"

"I was supposed to have a meeting today with the Senior Deputy Director of the Department for the Control of Dangerous Biological Agents and Toxins and he wasn't there, hadn't been there since the middle of last week."

"Hadn't been where since last week?"

"The Department of Health and Human Services. He's disappeared. Gone. No one's seen him or heard from him since last Wednesday. No calls. Nothing. He's not answering his phone, not responding to emails. A man with his responsibilities doesn't just wander off. I think something may have happened to him."

Half a dozen questions raced through Greg's head.

"You said biological agents and toxins? What are we talking about?"

"Chemicals, drugs, things that could be used to make poisons or illegal substances, precursors. I filed a request for an exemption for . . . well, the name wouldn't mean anything to you, the short version is ACX. It's on the prohibited list. I have to have a supply of it for my research. He was going to approve my request for an exemption, Greg! He told me that last week. Today was just supposed to be a formality, one last interview and he was going to sign off on it so I could get the ACX past customs. But now he's disappeared and nobody wants to do anything."

"OK, Marty, I understand—"

"Greg, you've got to find him. As long as he's just missing I'm stuck in limbo here. I've got to get permission to import the ACX in order to complete my research."

"I understand. Give me the missing guy's name and contact info."

"Albert Brownstein, Senior Deputy for the Health & Human Services Department for the Control of Dangerous Biological Agents and Toxins. His office is on Independence Avenue."

"OK, Marty, I'll go over there and see what I can find out. In the meantime, email me Brownstein's contact information and anything else you think might be helpful."

"You'll let me know what you find?"

"I'll call you this afternoon."

Kane hung up and looked around for Immerson but his boss was still at lunch with Congressman Asshole. *Shit*! Greg sent Immerson an email on where he was going and retrieved his gun from his bottom desk drawer.

CHAPTER THREE

The Department of Health & Human Services filled a six-story concrete building on Independence Avenue across the street from Bartholdi Park. Washington's bureaucracy was still struggling with the reality that the farther technology advanced the more mayhem a handful of people could unleash. Back in the days of black powder and brass cannons half a dozen determined malcontents might have managed to take fifteen or twenty lives. Now with C4 and step-by-step instructions on how to make nerve gas just a few clicks away, a couple of nut-jobs could kill thousands and shut down a city of millions. Looking at the endless warren of cubicles that stretched out in front of him Kane wondered if the Government's efforts to prevent a disaster weren't little more than a replay of the Dutch boy madly trying to plug the holes in an already collapsing dike.

Brownstein's subordinate, the Senior Assistant Deputy for the Department for the Control of Dangerous Biological Agents and Toxins, was Sandra Cray. Kane found her in a packing-crate-sized office on the Department's fourth floor.

"Ms. Cray? I'm Agent Gregory Kane, Department of Homeland Security," Kane announced, holding up his creds.

Sandra Cray's chair was jammed between a steel desk mounded with brown folders and a windowless gray wall. Her complexion, already sallow under the fluorescent lights and the glow from an ancient Dell monitor, now paled even more.

"What? Homeland Security?" Cray looked at Kane with an expression halfway between confusion and fright.

Greg took that as an invitation and squeezed into the lone chair with his knees almost bumping against the front edge of her desk. With a long stretch of his arm he closed the door behind him.

"When was the last time you saw Senior Deputy Brownstein?"

"What's this all about?"

"It's about the last time you saw or talked with or communicated with Senior Deputy Brownstein. Is there some reason you don't want to answer that question?"

"What? No. Of course not!"

Frightened people usually talked more than was good for them which was just what Kane wanted. He stared at Sandra Cray and waited for her to begin babbling in an attempt to prove herself innocent of a crime of which she had not yet been accused. It didn't take long.

"Ummm, last Wednesday, around a quarter after five. I usually stay later but my daughter had a cello recital and I, well, anyway, I said goodnight to him on my way out."

"And after that? Any calls? Emails?"

"No, I mean, I don't think so."

"You don't think so? What does that mean?"

Cray looked helplessly around her tiny, steel box as if searching for a way out. A picture of a palm tree against a setting sun was stuck to the wall behind her. Kane calculated that she had just enough clearance to swivel around and stare at it during those moments when she felt the room closing in on her.

"I got a text, a partial text, from his cell around eight o'clock Wednesday night. I had my phone turned off for the recital so I didn't see it until Thursday morning when I was getting ready for work."

Kane stared at her for a heartbeat then snapped, "Am I supposed to guess what it said?"

Sandra gave him a chastened look and answered with exaggerated care. "Two words: 'Sandy, I'm' and that was all." Kane stared. After another heartbeat she continued. "Albert was the only one who called me 'Sandy' so I'm sure it was from him."

"You don't like people calling you 'Sandy'?"

"I'm not a beach!" she snapped, then continued in a forced-calm tone. "My name is Sandra, not Sandy."

"But Brownstein was your boss and if he wanted to call you 'Sandy' you couldn't stop him." Sandra just stared at Kane. "When he didn't show up at work on Thursday did you call him?"

"Of course. I called his home and his cell. He liked to keep his work calls separate from his personal ones so he had two phones, but they both went to voice mail. I also emailed him, several times, but I never got an answer. *And* I texted him." Cray gave Kane a "so there" look.

Greg stared at her and conspicuously made a note in his pad. "What did you do next?"

"What do you mean?"

"What do I mean? Your boss goes missing. You can't reach him. You've got an interrupted after-hours text from him. Are you telling me that you just ignored it and decided that eventually he'd show up dead or alive?"

"Are you saying that Albert is dead?"

Jesus, how stupid is this woman? Kane thought but somehow managed not to say it out loud. Instead he took a deep breath and tried again.

"Was Mr. Brownstein having any problems that you were aware of? Money trouble? Disputes with anyone?"

"No. Our relationship was strictly business."

Why would she go out of her way to add that? Kane thought. *Does that mean she's trying to cover up the fact that something was going on or that she would be insulted if anyone thought that she had become involved with Brownstein?*

"You didn't socialize?"

"No." Sandra gave Kane a hard look. *OK,* Kane thought. *You wouldn't touch him with a ten-foot pole. Got it.*

"Has anything unusual happened in the last few weeks? Was Mr. Brownstein upset, nervous, preoccupied, different in any way?"

"No, he was the same as always, but as I said, we didn't have a personal relationship so I wouldn't know anything about what was going on in his private life."

Yeah, I got that loud and clear, Kane thought.

"Did you do anything in response to Mr. Brownstein's absence?"

"I called Albert's boss, our boss, the Deputy Assistant Director and I told him that Albert hadn't come into work."

"When did you do that?"

Cray glanced at the ceiling as if trying to remember the formula for calculating the circumference of a circle.

"Friday afternoon," she said finally with a hint of pride. "Well, I didn't want to get Albert in trouble if he was just, well, I don't know, enjoying himself a little too much."

"Did he do that, sometimes miss work because he was enjoying himself too much?"

"Albert? No, never. You could set your watch by him, but, well, there's always the first time, isn't there?"

No, there isn't, Kane thought but just nodded for her to continue. She just stared at him.

"What did the Deputy Assistant Director say when you told him about Mr. Brownstein not coming to work?"

"He checked Albert's file and said that Albert had six weeks accrued vacation so he was entitled to some time off." She paused but in response to Kane's stare finally continued. "He said that I should keep the office going until Albert returned and that I should keep a record of the number of days he missed so that his vacation time could be adjusted when he came back. He told me that if I hadn't heard from Albert by the close of business today that I should call someone and file a report and to keep him in the loop."

"So, you're planning on filing a missing person's report this afternoon?"

"If Albert hasn't contacted me by then, yes, well, tomorrow actually. I've got a PTA meeting tonight and I won't have time to sit around some police station filling out forms."

Sandra glanced at a watercolor of a cat in an overstuffed chair taped to the wall. A juvenile hand had printed "Mr. Bonkers" in purple ink at the bottom.

"Your daughter's work?" Kane asked, pointing at the picture.

"Olivia. She's ten." For the first time Sandra Cray smiled.

Within thirty seconds of entering her office Kane had been frustrated to the point of wanting to strangle Sandra Cray but now his anger melted in the glow of her smile. He hadn't missed the lack of a ring and the cheap drugstore makeup and her hair going brown at the roots. Sandra Cray was a single mother stuck in a prison cell of an office pushing papers from one side of her desk to the other for forty hours a week all in order to build some kind of a future for her child. Cello lessons and PTA meetings and a boss who called her by a name usually applied to a beach.

Jesus, what's wrong with me? Kane thought.

"Is that what you want me to do? File a missing person's report?"

"No," Kane said, feeling empty inside. "I'll take care of it. I need Mr. Brownstein's numbers, his email and his home address."

Sandra punched a few buttons and a few seconds later handed Kane a page ejected from the printer.

"I'm going to check out Mr. Brownstein's home. I'll have some more questions for you after that. Call me if you hear from him." Kane stood and gave her his card: *Agent Gregory Kane, Department of Homeland Security, Office of Special Investigations.* Cray gave it a disinterested glance and dropped it face-down on her desk.

"Open or closed?" Kane asked as he maneuvered himself out the door.

"Closed."

Kane nodded, then took a quick, final glance at Mr. Bonkers before locking Sandra Cray back into her cell.

CHAPTER FOUR

Kane almost made it to Brownstein's apartment before his boss caught up with him. For a moment Greg considered letting the call go to voice mail. A host of excuses — dead battery, dead zone, heavy traffic — flitted through his mind but they were all stopgap measures at best. Eventually he'd have to deal with Immerson and he figured that he might as well do it now.

"Kane."

"What do you think you're doing? You're not supposed to be in the field without your partner."

"Useless is attending a seminar on Transformative Political Correctness and Advanced Paper Pushing."

"His name is Eustace, not Useless! I've warned you about creating a hostile work environment, Kane."

"I guess I confused his name with his job performance. I suppose that's why he's taking the Political Correctness seminar. Sorry, it won't happen again."

"You know it's not . . . ." Immerson paused, familiar by now with Kane's habit of getting the other person so irritated that they lost sight of what they wanted to talk to him about in the first place. "Just get back here until your partner returns."

"I would but this is an emergency. Lives are at stake."

"Lives are at stake?"

"The Senior Deputy Director of the HHS Department for the Control of Dangerous Biological Agents and Toxins has gone missing."

"What?"

"42 USC 351A," Kane answered knowing that the cryptic reference would raise Immerson's frustration level another few points.

"What the hell are you babbling about?"

"That's the Public Health Security and Bioterrorism Preparedness Response Act section that deals with the control of biological agents and toxins. The Department of Health and Human

Services oversees the importation of potentially dangerous biological agents and toxins. Albert Brownstein is the HHS administrator who handles importation permits and exemptions. He's the guy in charge of keeping bio-weapons out of the country and he's gone missing. Obviously this is a job for Homeland Security."

"That doesn't mean it's a job for you. Come back here, now. You can open a case file and it'll be assigned to the next team in the rotation."

"Sure, I could do that but what if at this very moment someone is using Brownstein's stolen credentials to bring in some kind of a bio-weapon? I mean, how would it look if hundreds of people died and then the press found out that we could have stopped it but that you pulled me out of the field because you were afraid that it was too dangerous for me to be alone on the streets of Washington D.C. without an armed escort?"

Immerson waited five seconds before he trusted himself to speak.

"Kane, I'm giving you a direct order. You have until six o'clock to get back to this office and file the proper paperwork on this supposed case." The line went dead.

Greg smiled and went looking for Brownstein's building manager.

* * *

"I have to have keys in case there's a fire or something," Henry Appel said defensively as he opened a battered file cabinet.

"It would be irresponsible not to," Kane agreed.

"Ummm, 506 . . . 506 . . . 506," Appel muttered as he leafed through a drawer of manila folders. "Yup, here it is, 506, Albert Brownstein. Do you want the lease app?"

"I just need access to the apartment for now."

Appel toyed with the key.

"I'm not supposed to give these out, you know. Not without a warrant I mean."

"It's all right, Mr. Appel. I'm authorized." Kane bent forward and lowered his voice. "It's a matter of National Security."

Appel stared for half a second then almost forced the key into Kane's hand.

"I won't tell anybody," Appel whispered.

"Good man," Kane said giving Appel a little nod. Washington was a city obsessed with terrorists.

Warrant? I don't need no stinkin' warrant, Kane thought as he moved from Brownstein's bedroom to what Kane named the "hobby room." Originally it had been a second bedroom but now it contained a high-end photo printer, a Win 7 computer and a top-of-the line 23-inch high-def monitor.

Brownstein hadn't bothered to enable password protection and when Kane pressed the "Start" button he saw that Photoshop was the last application that had been used. It didn't take long to discover that the hard disk was filled with photographs. Kane found a two-thousand dollar DSLR and four extra lenses in the closet. A sampling of the computer's images — trees, flowers, leaves and waterfalls — boiled down to one word: boring.

An hour later Kane finished his search of Brownstein's emails, web browser history and address book. He found nothing even remotely interesting. *You could set your watch by him,* Sandra Cray said and it looked like she had been right. Albert Brownstein was as boring as they came. If there were any clues here about what had happened to him or where he had gone Kane wasn't going to find them this afternoon.

Greg copied Brownstein's address book, email folders and his on-line phone bills to a flash drive more out of habit than with any hope they would help him find the missing bureaucrat. Whatever had happened hadn't had anything to do with this apartment or any of Brownstein's friends or acquaintances. Kane was sure of that. No, something or someone out of left field had caused Albert Brownstein to go missing and Kane didn't have the slightest idea of what or who that could have been.

When Greg returned the key to Henry Appel he put a cautionary finger to his lips. Appel gave Kane a little wink and silently closed his door.

CHAPTER FIVE

Kane had quickly learned that the key to successfully dealing with Fred Immerson was knowing how far he could push things before his boss snapped. Kane returned to the office at twenty after five, waved cheerily at Immerson and started the paperwork on Albert Brownstein's disappearance. Most of the other investigators had already left but Kane noticed Danny Rosewood pounding away on Stan Ewald's computer.

"Agent Ewald said it was OK to use his machine," Danny said when he noticed Kane watching him.

"Good."

"He gave me a tip on interrogation techniques and I wanted to put it in my journal." Rosewood gave Kane a weak smile.

"Good," Kane repeated and turned back to his own machine. After a few more seconds of silence he heard Danny's fingers back on the keys. *He wants to talk about being an Agent*, Greg thought, then corrected himself. *He wants a friend.*

Greg had just finished the case-intake notes when he felt a hand on his shoulder.

"Hey, partner, having any fun?"

"Barrels and barrels," Kane said, refusing to look up.

"Word is," Grant Eustace grabbed a chair and rolled up next to Kane, "that Dad might be able to get us a piece of the Supremes Case."

Kane turned away from the monitor and tried to figure out which of Useless' irritations to respond to first. He wouldn't have minded Useless calling Immerson "Dad" if he had had the balls to do it to the boss' face, but, no, whenever Immerson was around Useless was all "Yes, Mr. Immerson" and "No, Mr. Immerson." As far as Kane was concerned calling Immerson "Dad" only behind his back was the hallmark of a coward and a suck-up.

Useless' second transgression was referring to the threat on the life of Mr. Justice Hopper as "the Supremes Case" as if it had anything to do with the Office of Special Investigations, which it absolutely did not. Thirdly, it was just plain stupid to think that anyone was going to let the Office anywhere near that investigation.

The Marshals, the Secret Service and the FBI were already engaged in a full-scale turf war over that one. The job of protecting federal courthouses and the judges in them belonged to the U.S. Marshals. The job of protecting high-ranking government officials was historically the province of the Secret Service and the job of investigating attacks on federal judges belonged to the FBI. Since this was still only a threat the Marshals and the Secret Service were claiming jurisdiction. Since it had the potential to become an actual attack the FBI wanted in. It was absolutely idiotic to think that anyone was going to let their little office get involved.

Eustace took Kane's silence as interest and bent closer, lowering his voice.

"Whoever has a piece of catching the nut-job will get a big gold star on his record," Eustace said. "I wouldn't mind getting bumped up to GS 14. We could both use the extra money, right partner?"

Typical magical thinking, Kane thought. *Just wanting something badly enough will get if for you. Glory-seeking moron!* Greg bit his tongue and started typing.

"You're a pain in the ass sometimes, Kane," Eustace said, "but you do good work. I'm thinking that you can do your Sherlock Holmes voodoo while I keep the bosses off your back and together I bet we could break this thing. Division of labor, right?" Eustace gave Kane a friendly slap on the shoulder. Greg had been typing "searched" and scowled when it ended up "swarhed."

That did it. Kane's control snapped and he spun around.

"Grant, you're a moron. And not just an ordinary moron. You've raised the bar on moronhood so high that if you got paid for it you'd qualify as a Professional Moron."

"See, that right there," Eustace said, laughing and slapping Kane's shoulder again, "is why we make such a great team. You can get all your grouchy bits exercised on me instead of somebody who'll take it personally. If you pulled that stuff on some FBI SAC you'd end up investigating people who put Canadian quarters in parking meters, but me, it just rolls off my back like a duck." *Like a duck?* Greg thought. Oblivious, Eustace babbled on. "Then, once you've gotten it out of your system, you can go back to solving the case while I handle the bosses and type up the paperwork. Well, I won't personally type it. The girl will handle that. Or, Kid Wannabee over there." Eustace tilted his head in Danny's direction.

Kane struggled to unfreeze his brain. So much stupidity, so little time.

"Grant, they're not going to let us investigate a threat on Justice Hopper. It's not going to happen."

"Well, not with that attitude. Me, I prefer to think positive."

Positively, Kane screamed inside his head. *It's an adverb!*

Eustace glanced at Kane's monitor. "What are you workin' on? We got a new case?"

"Yes," Kane answered through clenched lips. "The Administrator in charge of the HHS department that monitors importing potential bioterrorist materials has gone missing."

"Missing, huh?" Eustace said, peering at the screen. "How long?"

"Since last Thursday morning."

"Too long for your usual bender or shack-up. Any chance that he drove his car off a cliff or something?"

"There aren't any cliffs between his apartment and the HHS building."

"Into the Potomac maybe?"

"Unlikely," Kane said with an edge that could cut steel.

"OK, well, we'll find him I guess, sooner or later. Hope it's sooner in case Dad can get us a piece of the Supremes Case."

"Grant, go home. Please. Go home."

"Yeah, good idea. It's been a long day."

Eustace smiled, gave Kane a last friendly pat on his shoulder and sauntered toward the door. Kane closed his eyes and took five long, slow breaths, holding each one for a count of two before exhaling, just the way he had been taught in anger management class. When he opened them again he and Danny were alone in the room.

"Is there anything I can help you with, Agent Kane?"

"What?"

"You were in the field all afternoon and now you're working on your report so I thought that if you needed any records checked or something I could do that for you."

"I can't authorize any overtime."

"That's OK. I'll do if off the clock. Maybe I'll learn something, you know, for when I get to be an agent."

Greg mentally did the math. Marty Fouchet needed Brownstein found ASAP. Technically he had a partner to help him but there was a reason he called Eustace "Useless." Then there was Rosewood — no law enforcement experience, average intelligence, but friendly and anxious to please, essentially the human equivalent of a one-year-old Labrador retriever. It was a no-brainer.

"I need all of the surveillance tapes for the block around Albert Brownstein's apartment for the entire week before he went missing.

If that doesn't get us anything then we'll have to widen the search to the HHS building. I'm sending you my notes." Kane pounded a few keys and copied the file to Stan Ewald's machine.

"What should I look for?" Rosewood asked, apparently unfazed by the huge amount of work that Kane's request entailed.

"If somebody grabbed Brownstein they probably would have cased his apartment. We're looking for any person or vehicle that shows up too much, anyone who might be watching the building or Brownstein. He had a car but I followed up with his personal assistant. She told me that he took the bus to work unless the weather was bad so we're looking for anyone who might have followed him from his building in the morning or from the bus stop back to his building at night. Maybe we'll get lucky and be able to spot their car and get a plate number."

Kane waited for questions or an excuse to get out of a job that was a lot bigger than Rosewood had expected but instead Danny said, "That's a good idea, checking the area for the days before he went missing. I'm going to add that to my journal under 'Things To Do When Starting A New Case.' Thanks Agent Kane."

Hmmmm, Kane thought. *I wonder if there's some way I can trade Useless for Rosewood? I just need to find the right lever. What would it take to get Useless to request a transfer?*

CHAPTER SIX

Kane grabbed some take-out Chinese on the way home and ate it at his kitchen table. With his marriage long gone the apartment seemed especially empty. ESPN was probably running a basketball game from someplace but Kane couldn't work up much enthusiasm for the idea. Before he got shot he had loved watching sports but now it mostly irritated him. He saw too many mistakes, too many missed opportunities, and he just ended up shouting at the TV.

On the other hand before he got shot he hadn't been able to play a musical instrument. Like every kid he'd picked away at an old guitar but he never seemed to be able to coordinate the left-hand fingering with the right-hand plucking. But when his brain healed something must have gotten re-wired.

It had started almost as an accident back when he was still married. He'd fled the house after another of his shouting matches with Elaine and taken refuge at Malloy's Pub, his new home away from home. Along the back wall Kevin had a battered upright piano on which had been played more renditions of *Danny Boy* and *Born In The USA* than Kane cared to remember. On his way to the can one night, half in the bag from self-medicating on shots of scotch, he had bumped against it, trilling his fingers across the keys as he passed. The sounds pulled at him like a child's eye drawn to a shiny toy.

Greg plinked his fingers across the keys, first the right hand then the left, and something seemed to click. He couldn't play it, of course. It was all just a series of random notes, but he had this feeling that he almost could do it. He fiddled with the piano for several minutes until Malloy yelled at him to "Stop torturing the elephant."

"Nobody uses ivory for keys anymore, genius!" Kane shouted back then wobbled into the john. The next day he bought a USB keyboard, a set of headphones and a $90 program called "Piano Suite." To his surprise he found that he not only could learn to play but that he had a talent for it. When he tapped the keys his fingers felt like they were remotely controlled by some higher, soothing power. A month later Malloy was giving him free drinks for as long as the customers shouted out requests.

The music helped soothe his otherwise constant sense of frustration. On the other hand the booze and the long nights at Malloy's Pub and his hair-trigger temper ended up destroying first his marriage and then his job. Now, he had a certificate of completion, not achievement, from an HMO-approved anger management class and playing still soothed his nerves.

Kane plugged in the keyboard, slipped on the headphones and let his tensions drain into the keys. Eyes closed, the music swelling in his ears, Greg let his mind drift off to the Brownstein case. He hated missing-persons cases. Why did this have to be a missing person's case? Wasn't one enough, more than enough? As a detective he had always despised them — kids gone, everyone knew they were dead, chopped up, buried in some hole, dumped down some well, but you had to keep looking, always looking for something you knew you were never going to find. It was bad enough when you were just the cop. It was ten times worse when you were involved, when it was your own blood. Like everything else in his life these days it all looped back to that morning at Sam's Speedy Mart, back to Franco Herrera. . . .

* * *

"How're they doing?" Tony Canaro asked Sergeant Ed Helburg, the first uniform he saw in the ER.

"Amoroso didn't make it. Kane took one in the head. The docs are operating on him now."

"What about the perps?"

Helburg pulled out his pad and flipped a couple of pages. "Ricky Bazzel, two-time loser. Got out of the joint three months ago. DOA at the scene. Kane," Helburg nodded vaguely toward the operating rooms, "took him out after Bazzel shot Amoroso. Perp number two is Franco Herrera. We should call him 'Mr. Timex,' takes a licking and keeps on ticking." Canaro gave the Sergeant a hard stare and Helburg quickly glanced back at his pad. "Shot six times, both shoulders, two in the legs, one in the arm, last one in the gut. Apparently none of them hit anything vital. The docs say he's gonna make it."

"Jesus wept!" Canaro muttered and pulled out his phone. "Terri, it's Tony. I'm at the hospital. Kane and one of the perps are still in surgery. It's going to be awhile. I'm going out to the scene. I'll meet you back here in two hours."

Six hours later a nurse whose brother was on the job let Canaro and his partner, Theresa Quinn, into Franco Herrera's room. They paused just inside the door and stared at the man who had helped kill their friend. Herrera looked like a half-wrapped mummy except that his left wrist was handcuffed to the bed. The prisoner gave them a distracted glance as they approached.

"Where am I?" Herrera asked.

"Hospital, moron," Tony told him.

"Hospital Moron? I never been to that one. Do they take Blue Cross?" Herrera's laugh turned into a cough.

"You killed a cop," Theresa said in a voice like ice cracking.

"Me? I can't remember a thing. Man, those drugs, they really mess you up. It's all a blur." Herrera smiled. "Hey, don't you got to read me my rights?"

Canaro glanced at his partner then at the door. "Terri, you should call your mom, let her know you're all right." Quinn looked from Canaro to the prisoner and back to Tony.

"Are you sure?" she asked.

"Dead sure."

Quinn paused for two heartbeats then turned and wordlessly left the room.

"Hey, where's Cutie Pie going?"

Canaro ignored Herrera and started going through the cabinet on the far side of the room. He found a plastic-wrapped insulin syringe in the back of the third drawer down. He stuffed the cellophane wrapper into his pocket and pulled the plunger all the way back.

"What are you, a doctor now?" Herrera asked, eyeing the needle.

"I don't have a lot of time here, Franco. You killed a cop and my friend. You're either going to go to the joint for the rest of your miserable life or you're going to die from your wounds. It's up to me which one you get."

"What's that supposed to mean?"

"It means that you need to convince me that I should let you live."

"How am I supposed to do that?"

"Actually, I don't think you can."

Canaro fingered the injection port on the IV tube.

"You think if you pinch off my medicine I'm going to get all upset and cooperate?"

"I'm not going to cut off your drugs, Franco. I'm going to add to them, not much, just a little bubble of air. Right in this line. Once it's inside you it's going to block up your plumbing." Canaro made a fake choking noise then laughed. "Shot six times, nobody's gonna be surprised that you didn't make it." Tony stuck the needle into the port.

"Hey!" Herrera shouted, "Somebody—" Canaro slapped his hand over Herrera's mouth.

"Live or die, Franco, it's up to you. What's it going to be?" Tony paused for a second, then reached for the syringe that was still inserted in the injection port. "OK, die it is."

Herrera tried to break free but with one wrist handcuffed to the bed and wounds in both shoulders he had no chance. His eyes stared wildly as Canaro fingered the plunger.

"Arrrugh aajllltlk!"

"You want to say something, Franco? You want me to take my hand off your mouth?" Herrera nodded as best he could. "OK, but no shouting or I'm going to finish you real fast." Canaro lifted his palm a couple of inches above Herrera's mouth. "You've got five seconds. Make it good."

"Man, you can't just—"

"Four seconds. . . . Three seconds. . . ."

"Wait, wait, OK. I'll give you the Randies."

"The who?"

"The Randies. The guys who sold me the guns!"

"Busting some two-bit gun dealer isn't worth keeping you alive."

"It's not a dealer. It's a gang and they're into everything — guns, explosives, dope. Man, they're big-time. That bomb at the DMV building — that was them. That meth lab the feds busted in Fells Point — that was theirs."

Canaro paused for a moment, then shook his head. "Naw! Meth cookers are a dime a dozen. I'd rather see you dead than them locked up."

"No, No! There's more. You heard about those two Feds who went missing last year? They killed them both. These guys are serious, political."

"What do you mean, 'political'?"

"Their name is from some book or something about getting rid of the government. No government, that's what they're after."

"Randies? After Ayn Rand?"

"I don't know. Is that a book?"

"You bought your guns from them?"

"Yeah, that's right."

Canaro thought for a moment, then shook his head. "No deal. So they sold you a couple of automatic weapons. Even if the jury believed you, even if we got a conviction, all they'd get would be a slap on the wrist. That's not worth keeping you alive."

Canaro reached again for the plunger.

"No, no! I can give you the head guy. His name's Ryan Munroe. I know where he keeps his stuff."

"What stuff?"

"Everything — guns, C4, hand grenades, the chemicals he uses to cook the meth." Herrera gave Canaro a crafty look. "I'm not supposed to know but I was fucking one of their bitches and she let it slip. I got a way with the ladies," Herrera said with a smirk.

"I'm supposed to believe that you just asked some girl and she gave up this Munroe's storehouse?"

"I had to convince her a little. Ricky and me figured we might rip the place off. Hah! We were stoned at the time, you know. Once we got straight we thought it over and decided that maybe that wasn't such a good idea."

"What happened to the girl?"

"Oh," Herrera said, glancing away, "she's around someplace." It was all Canaro could do not to shove the plunger down right then. "You watch the place, like with a telescope or something," Herrera continued, "and when Munroe shows up you bust him with the stuff. With all that dope and guns he ain't gettin' out of that." Herrera smiled.

"What's the address?"

"Hell, man, I don't know. It's a big barn on a farm out on Wittetca Road near Freeland up by the Pennsylvania border. The girl said that Munroe liked the name, Freeland, you know, Free Land."

Tony fingered the plunger and tried to make up his mind. One monster dead or another monster locked up? Bird in the hand or bird in the bush? After about ten seconds he looked down at Herrera.

"Here's how it's going to go. I want you dead. I want you dead real bad. I'm going to bring a video camera in here and you're going to make a statement on tape about everything, Munroe, the barn, the guns, the drugs, the explosives, the girl, everything. Then we're going to get a warrant and bust him. If that doesn't happen, if the barn isn't there or the stuff isn't there or we can't tie it to Munroe, then you're gonna die. If I can't get to you, some other cop will. If none of us can we'll promise some con in the joint a pass if he takes you out. There are a lot of guys locked up who'd kill you for a carton of cigarettes. Just think what they'd do if we promised to help them get an early parole or we agreed to trash the evidence against them so that they'd get a walk. Do you understand me?"

"Yeah, I got it."

"I don't think you do. If anything goes wrong, if you change your story, if Munroe gets away, if this bust fucks up in any way, you're not going to live long enough to go to trial. Period. End of story."

"OK, OK. Him for me. Fine. Hey, I don't owe the motherfucker anything."

"You remember that if you want to live. It's his life for yours."

*   *   *

Ryan Munroe was thirty-eight years old and boyishly thin. His face was all angles and planes, unsoftened by a wispy mustache and close-cropped auburn hair. Watching Munroe slouch into the steel chair Tony Canaro thought, *I let Franco Herrera live in order to get him?* Then Tony noticed Munroe's self-satisfied smile and the glitter in his pale, blue eyes.

"You've been read your rights. Do you want to do yourself some good here?"

"Form without substance," Munroe answered.

"Excuse me?"

"The trappings of freedom where none exists."

"With all the drugs and weapons we found in your barn, you're not going to have any freedom for a long time unless you've got something to trade," Quinn told him.

"I don't recognize your right to imprison me. I am a free man, not some puppet of your totalitarian government."

"You're a prisoner who's going away for a long time unless you can convince us to cut you a break. Give up your suppliers and help us round up your customers and you can do yourself some good."

"I'll do myself some good all right."

"What's that supposed to mean?" Tony asked.

"I've committed no crime. Free men take what they want and keep what they take."

"Do you have a couple of screws loose? Do you think you can beat this on an insanity defense?"

Munroe looked around the interrogation room then turned back to Tony Canaro. "When does the Federal Gestapo get here?"

"We don't need the feds. You've broken more than enough state laws."

Munroe smiled and clasped his cuffed hands.

"I'll only talk to the Gestapo."

"Prisoners have access to a payphone. You can call the FBI yourself if you want."

Munroe stared straight ahead and refused to say another word. Two days later Canaro was told that the following morning Munroe was being transferred from the Intake and Booking Center on Madison Street up to the Central Maryland Correctional Facility in Sykesville.

"Why isn't he going to the CC on Greenmount?" Canaro asked the clerk but no explanation was forthcoming.

* * *

Kane returned to consciousness a day and a half after he'd been shot. His head hurt like hell and everything seemed vaguely disconnected. His doctors spent most of the rest of that day testing his vision, hearing, memory and speech centers. His memory had some holes in it and they wouldn't let him out of bed for fear that he would fall over and do more damage, but by and large they were highly encouraged by the results. That evening they let him have a couple of visitors. The first was his wife, Elaine, who alternately fussed over him and complained both about his rotten job and his reckless bravery. Kane was secretly pleased when she left. His second was his Lieutenant who told him to take all the time he needed and that his job would be waiting for him when he was ready. Then it was back to more tests and lots of rest.

It was four days later when they removed all visitor restrictions. The first person in line was his brother Tommy's son, Jason.

"Hi Uncle Greg," Jason said beginning a high-five and then pulling it back to a sedate handshake.

Greg noted the change in Jason's uniform and pointed vaguely at the boy's shoulder.

"You finished your probation."

"Yeah, I'm a real cop now just like you, Uncle Greg."

"Well, not just like me, I hope," Kane said touching his bandaged head.

"How do you feel?" Jason tried not to stare at the dressing.

"My head hurts."

"Well, yeah. But uummm . . . ."

"The doctor said the bullet mostly skidded along the inside edge of the skull and popped out the back. One in a million. He said that with luck like that I ought to be buying lottery tickets."

"I'll buy one for you," Jason volunteered.

"Good idea. My wallet's in that drawer."

"No, I got it, Uncle Greg."

"It won't be lucky unless I pay for it. You want me to win don't you? Go on. There's a single in there someplace. . . . What are you going to be doing now that you're off probation?" Kane asked while the boy searched for the money.

"I don't know. They've got me partnered up tomorrow with a fifteen-year guy, Mearle Farber. You know him?"

"No. Detectives and deputies, you know."

"It's kind of an interesting assignment."

"Oh, what's that?"

"We're, Farber and me, transporting the guy who sold the scumbags who shot you the guns they used."

A couple of guys from the squad had managed to sneak past the nurses and Tony Canaro had come by personally to give Kane the details on Ryan Munroe's arrest.

"You're transporting Ryan Munroe? Where?"

"Sykesville. I guess they figure he's too big a fish for Greenmount."

"That doesn't make any sense to me. Does he have some kind of juice?"

"He's just some nut-job anarchist as far as I know. He won't get away with any shit on my watch. Don't worry, Uncle Greg. I'm going to make sure that he's locked up tight."

They talked a bit longer about Jason's Training Officer, Paulie Siamone, and Jason's latest girlfriend, who he seemed to be more serious about than any of the previous ones, and then Kane's eyes began to droop. Jason noticed Greg's fatigue and stood up to leave. Halfway out he stopped and gave Greg a formal salute.

"You did good, Uncle Greg. We're all proud of you," Jason said, smiling.

That was the last time Kane ever saw his nephew. Someplace between the booking center on Madison and Central Corrections on Buttercup Road in Sykesville Mearle Farber, Jason Kane, Ryan Munroe and the cruiser they were riding in all disappeared. None of them were ever seen again.

For the last two years Greg Kane had been searching for some clue about what had happened to his nephew but he had found nothing. The boy had vanished without a trace.

* * *

Kane glanced at the clock. Almost ten-thirty. It felt like midnight. He put away the keyboard and went to bed.

CHAPTER SEVEN

Ryan Munroe watched the front door from a booth half way toward the back of the room. He had set the meeting for a little after three, a time when the only people in bars were either hard-core juicers or men like himself who wanted to conduct their business away from prying eyes. A flare of light washed over the first few tables each time the door opened then died out before it reached him. His man arrived at about a quarter after three and paused at the end of the bar to allow his eyes to adjust to the gloom. After a moment he spotted Munroe hunched in the corner of his booth and signaled him with a flick of his index finger.

"I don't like sitting with my back to the door," the man said as he slid into the seat opposite Munroe. Today the name on his driver's license was "Paul Conklin," the latest in a series of aliases he had used over the last few years. Once Conklin had gotten into the crook business full time he changed his name with the same regularity that traveling salesmen changed their cars. Ryan Munroe had switched names a couple of times in the last two years as well. It was a normal part of the outlaw life and men like Munroe and Conklin didn't think about it twice.

"The next time we're doing this in my car," Conklin said, glancing nervously over his shoulder.

"All the cop cars have license-plate readers," Munroe said shoving a bottle of Bud across the table.

"I didn't say we'd meet in a stolen car," Conklin snapped. "My plate won't raise any red flags."

"The plate numbers all go into Big Brother's database. If some traffic camera gets a picture of me in your car and they match my face to their wanted list they'll end up grabbing us both."

"Nobody cares who's in my car. It's clean. I've told you that a hundred times."

"And I've told you a hundred times that the G is looking for me. You ever hear of facial recognition software? This place," Munroe glanced toward the bar, "doesn't have any cameras. They're bad for business."

"OK, fine, whatever," Conklin said, sneaking another quick glance over his shoulder.

"Relax. I'm watching the door. Nobody's going to sneak up on you. Jesus!" Munroe took another pull from his beer. "Any problems with the job?"

"If there had been a problem don't you think I'd have told you? Believe me, I wouldn't be sitting here if there'd been a problem." Conklin gulped down half the bottle and wiped his mouth on the back of his hand. Munroe frowned but said nothing. "It was textbook," Conklin continued, lowering his voice. "I held the stun gun under a map of D.C. and asked him for directions. When he bent over I gave him a blast to his chest. He didn't make a sound. I had him in the van in three seconds. No muss, no fuss, no witnesses." Conklin gave Munroe a hard stare. "And no surveillance cameras."

"What'd you do with the body?"

"Don't worry, they're never going to find him."

"I'll decide that for myself. Where'd you put him?"

"You ever heard of the Luray Caverns?"

"You stashed him in the Luray Caverns?"

"Yeah, I'm an idiot. Jesus! I'm just saying that Virginia is lousy with caves and caverns and holes in the ground. I found a nice home for Mr. Br—"

"No names!" Munroe snapped.

"Fine. I found a nice home for our friend at the bottom of a hole where nobody's ever going to find him."

"Where?"

"That's need to know and you don't need to know," Conklin said in a flat, dangerous voice.

"Good, that's good. Don't tell anybody your business. I just need to know that he's going to stay missing for the next two or three months."

What's supposed to happen in three months? Conklin wanted to ask but didn't. Questions like that made Munroe nervous. Questions like that got you killed.

Munroe pulled an envelope from under the newspaper on the seat next to him and held it beneath the table. Conklin grabbed it and slipped it into his pants. After another quick look around he asked: "You got anything new for me?"

"There's a clean phone in there. Keep it charged and wait for my call."

"What's the time frame? . . . I've got to pay my bills you know," Conklin added in response to Munroe's silence.

"There's going to be plenty of work for us, don't worry about it. Take a couple of weeks off and enjoy yourself. I'll be in touch. And don't use that phone for any outgoing calls."

"I'm not an idiot," Conklin snapped then glanced down at the newspaper. "What do you think about that?" he asked, nodding at the headline:

New Threat On Justice's Life

Conklin was curious if Munroe's people were planning on whacking Hopper but knew better than to ask.

"If the son of a bitch thinks he can take our guns away from us he deserves what he gets."

"That would be like assassinating the President or something. That's a lot of heat," Conklin said in a harsh whisper. "The guy who did that would have to leave the country."

"Only if they knew who he was."

"They'd never stop looking for somebody who killed a Supreme Court judge."

Munroe smiled, then shrugged, as if imagining what might have been. "Whatever. Anyway, we have our own business to worry about. Big money's coming our way. Real big money."

Conklin paused for a moment but Munroe didn't volunteer any details. Conklin studied his employer for a heartbeat then slid out of the booth. The thing you had to remember when you worked for Ryan Munroe was that the guy wasn't afraid of anything and that he was bat-crap crazy, as he had already proven to Paul Conklin on more than one occasion. *But then*, Conklin thought, *most of the jobs I've done for him aren't exactly your normal sort of projects either.*

Munroe slipped out the back door before Conklin even reached his car.

CHAPTER EIGHT

Kane had planned on spending the next morning searching for Albert Brownstein but Immerson would have none of it.

"How was the seminar, Eustace?" Immerson asked when Kane and his partner entered his office.

"Thrilling, sir," Eustace said, straight faced.

Immerson gave him a sour look and turned to Kane.

"Good news. The U.S. Attorney sent down the warrant for Marilyn Jeffers." Immerson handed Kane a stack of stapled pages folded in thirds. "Bring her in and see if she's willing to cooperate then take her down to detention."

Kane glanced at the arrest warrant and calculated that the odds of getting Eustace to serve it alone while he tracked down Brownstein's car were about the same as those of a starving fat man not grabbing the last jelly donut in the box.

"I'll drive," Kane said, tossing the papers at his partner.

* * *

Marilyn Jeffers and her husband lived in a four-bedroom mini-McMansion just outside of Laurel, Maryland. It was one of the first things she had purchased when the payoff money had started rolling in.

"A lot nicer than that dump she and her hubby had before she became a criminal mastermind," Eustace smirked as Kane pulled in behind a black Range Rover at the top of the Jeffers' driveway. "I guess crime does pay, for a while," Eustace said, laughing as he fingered the arrest warrant.

Kane led the way up the walk but when they neared the door Eustace pushed ahead. "Let me do it. I love this part." Eustace pulled the glass storm-door out of the way.

"Federal Agents!" *BAM! BAM! BAM!* "Open up! Federal Agents!" Eustace gave Kane a kid-on-Christmas-morning smile and turned back to the door. *BAM! BAM! BAM!* "Open up!" Eustace paused, listening, then looked uneasily around. "You checked right? She's home, right?"

"She called in sick Monday morning and she hasn't shown up at her desk since."

"You don't think she's skipped do you?"

Kane just looked from his partner to the seventy-thousand dollar Range Rover in the driveway and then back again.

"Well, fuck this nonsense." Eustace shoved the edge of the storm door into Kane's hand and took a step back. He had just begun to raise his foot when they heard the clacking of a deadbolt followed by the sound of a security chain being released. A slice of pale face peered through the four inch gap between the door and the jam. "What is this—" Marilyn Jeffers began but Eustace didn't let her get any farther.

"We have a warrant!" Eustace shouted and shouldered the door out of the way. Her mouth gaping open, Jeffers stumbled backward and landed hard on her ass. Her look of astonished fear energized Eustace and he jogged past her into the living room leaving Kane to deal with the terrified woman. By the time Greg had her on her feet Jeffers' face was filled with tears. Firmly gripping her arm Kane led her into the living room just as Eustace returned from the kitchen.

A veteran of hundreds, maybe thousands, of arrests Kane, unlike his partner, knew how this was supposed to be done. Before Eustace could screw things up any farther he quickly patted Jeffers down and then asked, "Is there anyone else in the house?" Jeffers stared at him blankly, so disoriented that she couldn't reliably have told him how much you got by adding two plus two. "Ms. Jeffers, I need you to focus," Kane told her in a surprisingly gentle tone. At this point shouting would have only made things worse. "Is there anyone else in the house?"

After half a second Marilyn nervously looked over her shoulder toward the stairway.

"My husband's upstairs, working. He works from home," she babbled, her words coming out all in a rush. "He's a corporate travel facilitator. He—"

"Call him. Tell him to come downstairs."

It took Jeffers a moment to process Kane's order then she turned toward the stairway and shouted in a voice on the edge of tears, "Charlie! Charlie! I need you to come down here!" Eustace started fingering the butt of his weapon and Kane feared that at any second his partner was going to race up the stairs like Teddy Roosevelt charging up San Juan Hill.

"Grant," Kane said then repeated his partner's name a second time. Eustace shifted his attention and Kane gave his head a little shake. Eustace stared for a moment and that was long enough for them to hear footsteps from the upstairs hallway. Eustace gave Kane a smile and a nod. A moment later a man somewhere between his late thirties and early fifties appeared at the top of the steps. He froze when he saw two strange men surrounding his wife. Eustace held up his ID.

"Federal Agents! Please come down here, sir." On paper the words might seem polite but it was anything but a friendly request.

Charles Jeffers was wearing a long-sleeved, burgundy polo shirt over black slacks. His hair was cut short above a face as tight and flat as a plastic mask. His shoulders back, arms loose, Jeffers descended the stairs with his eyes glued on Eustace whose left hand possessively gripped Marilyn Jeffers' arm.

Watching Charlie Jeffers Kane felt a tingle run up his spine. Eustace's smarmy smile told Kane that his partner wasn't taking the husband as any kind of a threat. Kane had seen that kind of blindness get men killed.

"Let go of my wife," Jeffers ordered in a cold, flat tone as he neared the bottom of the steps.

"You don't give me orders, pal," Eustace replied, his smile turning mean.

Oh, Jesus! Kane thought and raced forward just as Jeffers' hand darted beneath his shirt. Kane grabbed Jeffers' wrist and pushed up while simultaneously punching him in the balls. Jeffers tiny, five-shot revolver made a noise like a balloon popping then he groaned and tried to curl around his throbbing groin. Kane's right hand grabbed the gun by the cylinder and tore it loose then he released Jeffers' wrist and allowed him to slump to the floor.

Open-mouthed, Eustace stared at the gun, now in Kane's hand then down to the little man squirming on the carpet.

"You want to search him in case he's got a second gun?" Kane snapped.

While Eustace roughly patted Jeffers down Kane pulled Marilyn's hands behind her back. His cuffs made a *clack-clack* sound that caught Eustace's attention and he quickly looked up.

"Marilyn Jeffers, you are under arrest for bribery, unlawful disclosure of confidential government information and obstruction of justice. You have the right to remain silent . . . ."

Eustace watched Kane recite the Miranda warning and, for a moment, was irritated that he had lost the chance to slap the cuffs on the wife, but, he consoled himself, he still had the husband. Eustace hauled Charles Jeffers to his feet and cuffed him so tightly that Jeffers skin went white from lack of circulation. Eustace began reciting his own version of the Miranda warning: "You have the right to remain silent, *asshole*, and anything you say may be used to put your sorry butt in jail. You have the right to hire a scumbag lawyer . . . ."

"He's ready to go," Eustace told Kane a moment later. "Is she clean?"

"That was the only weapon." Kane pointed at the little revolver lying on the carpet. "Why don't you see if you can find a Ziplock bag that we can put it in?"

Eustace knew that Kane was pissed but angry was Kane's default state so Grant didn't know if Kane was mad at him, at Jeffers or at the world in general. He trotted into the kitchen to look for a plastic bag. A few moments later they had the Jeffers and the gun ready for transport. Kane motioned for Eustace to follow him to the far side of the room.

"Thanks, partner," Eustace whispered, shifting his gaze between Kane and the handcuffed prisoners huddled near the front door. "I owe you one."

"You owe me one!" Kane exploded. "That's all you have to say? You owe me one?"

"Uhhh, thank you?"

A dozen thoughts chased each other through Kane's head. The fucking moron had scared the wife half to death just for the fun of it, then he'd baited the husband in his own house, AND he'd done it all to people he didn't know, people whose emotions he obviously couldn't read and whom he hadn't bothered to search for weapons. He'd put both of their lives in danger and if things had gone a little differently Kane would have been forced to kill a man. And what did Useless have to say for himself? *I fucking owe you one?*

Kane closed his eyes and held his breath for three seconds but anger-control tricks can only take a man so far.

"You never threaten a man's wife or kids in his own house you moron and if you're going to do such a stupid, boneheaded thing, you certainly don't do it to a man you don't know and whom you haven't searched! That's Police Work 101!"

For a moment Eustace looked confused as if confronted by an elevator whose buttons were printed in Arabic then he smiled and gave Kane a friendly slap on the shoulder.

"Hey, you got it, buddy. You see, that's why we're such a great team. I'm the guy who goes balls-to-the-wall and you're the brain who straightens me out when I go over the line. So, what do you say? Let's get these mopes into a nice, cozy cell."

Eustace gave Kane another happy grin and headed back to the prisoners.

Son of a bitch! Greg thought, but couldn't think of a single thing to say that would do him any good whatsoever.

CHAPTER NINE

Since they had to interview Marilyn Jeffers before booking her and they didn't want to make two trips to the detention center Kane and Eustace brought both prisoners back to the office. They left Charlie Jeffers shackled in one of the interview rooms. At least in one respect the turmoil at the Jeffers house had worked to their advantage. Marilyn was so unnerved by it that by the time she was handcuffed to the steel table in Room Three they couldn't have shut her up if they had wanted to.

"Please don't take this out on Charlie," she babbled, tears running down her cheeks. "I'll tell you everything if you'll let him go."

"You think your husband can pull a gun on federal officers and then just waltz out of here, no harm, no foul?" Eustace growled. "He's gonna spend more time in the joint than you will. I'll see to that."

With any other agent Kane would have assumed that Grant was only playing "good-cop, bad-cop" but Greg knew that Eustace meant every word.

"Grant, let's talk outside for minute," Kane said. Irritated, Eustace looked away from Marilyn then shrugged his consent.

"You want me to work on hubby while you handle her?" Eustace whispered once they were outside. "Just let me scare the hell out of her a little longer and she'll pop like a—"

"Grant," Kane interrupted before Eustace could complete some disgusting analogy, "I don't want to spend all day on this. Why don't you get started on the paperwork while I finish up with her."

"You're freezing me out of the kill? Hell, watching them cop to it is the best part of the job, next to slapping the cuffs on 'em."

"You've scared her enough. If you work on her any longer she'll be too terrified to sign her own name." Eustace cocked his big head to one side. Kane thought he could almost hear gears grinding. "You do the paperwork, Grant. I'll get her statement. We'll share the collar and with any luck we'll be able to close the file by quitting time."

"Hmmm," Grant murmured.

"I'll tell you what," Kane said. "You do the paperwork and I'll take them over to lockup."

Eustace thought about that for a moment then broke into a smile. "Sure, I guess I've softened her up enough for you. If I went back in there she'd probably wet herself and nobody wants that." Happy again, Grant patted Kane on the shoulder and sauntered back to the bull pen. Kane stared after him as if watching a wild animal casually disappear into the trees then returned to the interview room. Seeing that Eustace was not with him Marilyn Jeffers looked at Kane with both fear and hope.

"Here's how it's going to be," Kane said, his expression flat and cold. "You're going to tell me everything you did, all the details, how much money you got and what you did with it, every penny." Greg put a digital recorder on the center of the steel table. "I'll tell the U.S. Attorney that you cooperated and sentencing will be up to the judge."

"What about—"

"And in return, your husband will be charged with one count of misdemeanor assault on a federal officer. We'll call it a scuffle in the heat of the moment and we won't mention his little popgun. Given the circumstances and his clean record he'll probably only get a fine and probation. I need your answer right now."

Marilyn stared at the recorder then looked at Kane. "How do I know you'll keep your word?"

"How do you know I won't? Look, I've got you dead bang on the money you took from the Tip Top Coal Company and I've got your husband dead bang on the attempted murder of a federal officer. If you both want to go to court on those charges be my guest. This is the only deal you're going to get. You've got ten seconds."

Marilyn Jeffers looked at Kane as if through sheer concentration she could read his mind. She might as well have been staring at a stone wall. After a few moments she sighed and slumped in her chair. Kane pressed the "record" button.

"This is Homeland Security Agent Gregory Kane with detainee Marilyn Jeffers. The time is . . . ." Kane glanced at the clock. Twenty minutes later he stood and turned off the machine.

"What happens now?" Marilyn asked, spent.

"I'm going to take you and your husband over to the detention center to be processed. They'll give you your phone calls. Tomorrow morning the judge will set bail and then your lawyer and the U.S. Attorney can arrange a plea."

"What about Charlie? Are you going to do what you promised or are you going to screw us over like the government usually does?"

"It's the government that screws people over? Really? Let's see, the government went to a lot of trouble to protect coal miners from being blown up or buried in some cave-in half a mile down and you took money from the coal companies to undo all that. But what the hell do you care if some miners in West Virginia choke to death with a cup of coal dust packed into their mouths? Hey, you've got that Range Rover to pay for and those babies use a lot of gasoline. What do you care if some asshole executive making half a million a year uses the personnel files you stole to blackmail some poor schmuck of a mine inspector into ignoring the fact that the exhaust fans in his tunnels don't work right anymore? You've got mortgage payments to make on that four-bedroom house of yours out in the suburbs. So what if a bunch of miners get blown up when a spark touches off a pocket of methane. Screw them, right?

"Don't play the poor innocent being abused by the big, bad government to me lady!" Kane's face had turned mean and Jeffers scrunched back in her seat. Bitterly, he shook his head and turned to leave, then paused. "And unlike you, my word means something. For what it's worth I understand what your husband did. It was wrong but at least I understand it. A man protects his family," *and his partner*, Kane thought but the words did not reach his lips. Marilyn stared at Kane as if he had been speaking gibberish. He left her cuffed to the steel table and tracked down Grant Eustace in the coffee room.

"She give it up?" Eustace asked between sips of something the color of melted caramel.

Kane held up the recorder. "Everything."

"Even the money?"

"What's left is in a safety deposit box over at Alliance West Bank in Silver Spring."

"My man!" Eustace tried to high-five Kane but only ended up sloshing coffee on his shoes. "Son of a bitch!" he cursed jumping back and spilling more coffee in the process.

"You finish up here," Kane said, glancing at the mess on the floor, "and I'll run them both over to detention. Print out the report and leave it on my desk. I'll go over it and sign it when I get back."

"Son of a bitch," Eustace muttered, checking his cuffs for coffee stains.

CHAPTER TEN

Getting Marilyn Jeffers locked up was no problem since the U.S. Attorney had already filed the arrest warrant but her husband was another matter. For him Kane had to go through the booking process which meant generating a completely new set of documents. By the time both Jeffers were safely in their cells and he'd gotten something to eat and returned to the squad room it was half past four and Useless had found a reason to be someplace else. *Just as well*, Kane thought since he had to go through the paperwork his partner had created and remove any references to the gun.

It's not like I'm filing a false report, he told himself. *I'm just leaving out a couple of details*. Pretty damn big details he admitted but at least everything in the amended report would be technically true. Eustace would blow a gasket when he found out but Kane could live with that. Thank God Useless had long since given Kane his password and screen name. Knowing how lazy he was Kane began to wonder if Grant would even check the file at all. After a moment's thought Greg figured that it was fifty-fifty that Eustace would never know what he had done.

Greg had just returned to his own terminal when Danny Rosewood materialized next to his desk.

"Hi, Agent," Danny said.

"Hi, Danny," Kane answered, barely glancing up. Five seconds later Kane felt Danny's eyes still on him. "Something you need?"

"Uhhh, no," Danny said continuing to stare. A moment later Rosewood glanced meaningfully toward the door then back at Kane.

What's that, Lassie? Greg thought. *Has something happened? Do you want me to follow you?* Danny gave Kane another stare then headed for the door, glancing at Greg over his shoulder halfway to the exit.

Oh, shit! Kane thought. *Timmy's fallen down the well.*

Greg caught up with Rosewood in a parking lot leaking the stink of wet tobacco and motor oil, its surface littered with cigarette butts from the nicotine addicts who gathered there to get their fix.

"What's up, Danny?"

Rosewood looked around then stepped in close. "I got the surveillance tapes from around Mr. Brownstein's building, like you asked me." Danny paused and glanced uneasily toward the doors.

"OK, good. And . . . ?"

"Well, I went through them. At first I didn't notice anything but I looked for people who were there more than once and who didn't seem to have any business in the neighborhood. That's when I saw him. At first I didn't notice him but then I realized that he was changing his appearance. One time he was wearing a parka with the hood up. Another time he had on a wool coat and a baseball cap. It was the same guy in four different outfits. I figured that was suspicious."

"You figured right but why couldn't you tell me this upstairs?"

"You remember. . . ." Danny began then shut up and nervously led Kane around the corner when a man in a black overcoat paused just beyond the glass doors and lit up a smoke. "You remember that special job you gave me?" Danny asked in a whisper when he was sure that they were alone.

Kane's skin began to tingle and he bent in closer. A year ago he had asked Danny to help him in his search for his vanished nephew. It wasn't Kane's case. In fact, he had been told by two different law enforcement agencies to stay out of it, as if that was ever going to happen. But he needed help with the tech stuff. He needed someone to run credit card checks, to get copies of bank records and phone LUDs, all of which was exactly what Danny did more or less all day long. And the kid had been more than willing to do the work even though it could mean his job, or worse, if he got caught.

"What do the video recordings from Brownstein's neighborhood have to do with that?"

"You know I went through the file you gave me and it had pictures of that Ryan Munroe and the two transport officers in it. At first the man from the street outside Mr. Brownstein's apartment building just seemed familiar somehow but when I blew up the pictures, that's when I recognized him."

"Wait a minute!" Kane snapped. "You're saying that Ryan Munroe was casing Brownstein's apartment?"

"No, not him. The other one."

"Jason?"

"No, the other officer, Mearle Farber."

"The man on the Brownstein video was Mearle Farber? Are you sure?"

"All I can say is that it looked like him. I ran a facial rec analysis. It came up 61%. Given the low resolution of the ATM camera that's pretty good, so, I think it was probably your guy, and, well, I'm at least 61% sure."

My guy? My guy is Jason Kane, Greg thought, but if Farber was alive . . . . If Farber was alive and casing a citizen who it looked like was the victim of foul play then the math was as simple as simple could be. With an almost audible click the pieces fell into place inside Kane's head. If Farber was alive then Ryan Munroe was alive and if they were both alive then Jason Kane was dead and Mearle Farber was the person who had killed him.

* * *

As a rookie Deputy Sheriff barely out of probation Jason Kane expected to be told to drive while Mearle Farber took it easy, so Jason was surprised when Farber held onto the keys and settled in behind the wheel. Jason almost asked "Don't you want me to drive?" but since Farber was already shoving the key into the ignition it seemed like a pretty stupid question.

Jason had put Ryan Munroe in the back seat and fastened the chain shackling his ankles to the steel ring welded to the cruiser's floor. Munroe's wrists were locked in a set of long cuffs which, in turn were attached to the chain binding his legs. There was enough play in the lines so that by bending forward the prisoner could scratch his nose and he could wiggle his ass a foot or so left or right on the vinyl seat but that was about it. Remembering that this man had supplied the gun that had almost taken his uncle's life Jason had double checked Munroe's restraints before locking the rear doors.

Sykesville sat halfway between State Highway 26 and Interstate 70 and you could get there by either route. "Which way are we going?" Jason asked as Farber gave the driver's seat one final adjustment and then idled the cruiser out of the lot.

"You just relax, kid, and leave the driving to me," Farber told him, never taking his eyes off the road. A few minutes later Farber gunned it up the ramp onto the I-70 and Jason had his answer.

"How come you got this job?" Jason asked once they were on the interstate. "Don't you normally work out of the Northeast Division?"

"How about you just shut it and watch the scenery," Farber snapped.

Asshole, Jason thought, then twisted around and checked the prisoner through the wire screen. Eyes front, Munroe sat like a statue in the center of the rear seat. Jason turned away and decided to put his brain in neutral for the rest of the drive.

It took them about twenty minutes to reach the exit for State Highway 32. Farber drove like a robot the whole way. *Thank God I'm not partnered with him*, Jason thought as they turned onto the two-lane and headed north.

It had been a wet winter and patches of snow grew thick along the highway where it skirted Patapsco Valley State Park. Above them the sky had congealed into a gray foam and it was cold enough that Jason wondered if what came out of the clouds was going to be rain or snow. A few minutes later they were enclosed by walls of trees, on the right side from the state park and an even denser forest from the Wildlife Refuge District on the left. After two miles Farber tapped the brakes and began to drift them over toward the shoulder.

"Feels like we've got a flat," he said slowing carefully on the damp road. Jason straightened up and strained to detect a tremor from a soft tire.

"I don't feel anything," he said.

"It's the right rear," Farber answered and pulled onto a dirt track that disappeared into the trees. Jason closed his eyes tried to heighten his senses but now they were on the dirt and the cruiser could have had two flat tires and he wouldn't have known it. Jason glanced at the dashboard but didn't see a red, "tire low" warning.

"Are you sure? I didn't notice anything," Jason said, nervous now that they were into the trees and the highway was almost out of sight behind them. The dirt road took a jog to the right and Jason saw a silver Jeep Cherokee parked at a wide spot fifty feet ahead. "What the hell is—" Jason began, staring at the Jeep, but stopped when he heard the *CLACK* of Farber's weapon being cocked.

"Change in plans, kid," Farber said, his nine-millimeter pointed at Jason's head.

"How much did he pay you?" Jason blurted out. It was a dumb question, he knew. What difference did it make to him anyway? But a man tends not to do his best thinking when a loaded gun is being pointed at his head. Farber answered anyway.

"Enough. Take it easy and you'll live through this. You'll be a little cold back in the trunk but we'll tell them where to find you once we're safe. Now, slowly, put your hands on the dash."

This was the most dangerous time for both men. Jason still had his weapon. If he managed to get it out and started firing inside the car anything could happen. The odds were that Farber would blow him away before he ever got off a shot but there was always the chance that he might get lucky. Comply or fight? If Farber was going to kill him anyway one chance in a hundred was better than no chance at all.

"I'm not going to screw around with you, kid. You've got until I count to three. Then I pull the trigger. One."

Jason tried to find some hint of fear or uncertainty in Farber's face. He might as well have been looking at a mannequin.

"Two."

Jason put his palms flat on the dash. Farber reached all the way over and used his left hand to snap a cuff on Jason's right wrist.

"Keep your hands straight out in front of you and slowly turn to face me."

Still using his left hand Farber snapped the other handcuff on Jason's left wrist, then he backed out of the driver's seat, never taking his gun off Kane. Once outside Farber grabbed the chain linking Jason's cuffs and pulled him across the seat and out the driver's door. In an instant he had Jason pinned face down with his knee on the young man's neck. Strong hands quickly removed Jason's weapon. A moment later Jason heard the THUNK of the trunk being opened.

"On your feet." The pressure on Jason's neck relaxed and he felt himself being hauled upright. A shove sent him stumbling toward the back of the car. "Get into the trunk."

He's not going to kill me after all, Jason thought and released a breath he hadn't realized he'd been holding. The cruiser's steel floor was cold as he clambered over coaming and curled down into the trunk. Twisting his face up he saw Farber silhouetted against the dirty sky.

"Sorry, kid," Farber said. "Nothing personal," then he centered his gun and fired a bullet through Jason Kane's brain. Farber took a breath then switched to a two-handed grip for the next two rounds. Guys had lived with a bullet in their heads. Look at the kid's uncle, still alive and kicking after taking one to the noggin. But no one was coming back from three shots in the center ring. Farber shut the trunk then opened the rear door.

"Clothes, ID and money are in the Jeep," he said as he unhooked Munroe's shackles. Munroe stepped out and took a long, deep breath.

"Free air. It's good to breathe free air again." Munroe held out his right hand. "Keys."

No smile, Farber noticed. No *thanks* either. A cold fish. No emotion. All business, which, Farber figured, was just as it should be. In the real world life didn't pat you on the head and give you a free lollipop. You did the job and you took what you wanted.

"I'll be in touch," Munroe said. "I'm going to have a lot of work that needs to be done."

"Contact me through the email address that I left with your new ID. And don't forget the rest of my money."

"Don't worry about your second payment. Like I said, I've got more work for you." Munroe turned and walked to the Jeep. Farber had located an abandoned barn where he planned to stash the cruiser until nightfall but first he drove it to within half a mile of the prison where he disconnected the GPS. As far as the Department was concerned he and Kane made it to Sykesville before the car went off the grid.

He had considered and discarded several scenarios for dumping the cruiser from just leaving it parked someplace a hundred miles away to bribing the night-shift guard at a junk yard into crushing it into a cube of scrap iron bound for China. But simpler was always better. He'd found an isolated spot not far from where Liberty Lake turned into the Patapsco river where he could sink the cruiser in thirty feet of water without any witnesses. Yesterday he'd called in sick and stashed a clean car a two mile walk away. He had one of Munroe's guys pick him up a mile beyond that. He didn't like involving other people but getting a ride back to town was safer than taking the bus. Besides, even if the guy ever talked, the junker Farber has stashed would be scrap metal long before they started looking anywhere near the place where his ride had picked him up.

Half a million dollars, Farber thought, assuming Munroe paid the second installment, and Farber figured that Munroe would pay it. That was another of the differences between them. If he had been in Munroe's shoes he would have skipped the country and never looked back. What could he, Farber, do if he didn't get the rest of his money? Sue? But Munroe wasn't built that way. He wasn't an ordinary crook. He had a Cause. He was a man on a mission. Farber had no idea what that mission was beyond some vague grudge against the government, against the idea of there being a government at all, but who the fuck cared? Mearle Farber was a quarter-millionaire and, he thought, he'd soon to be a half millionaire. Whatever crazy schemes Ryan Munroe had were of no interest to him as long as the money kept rolling in.

Farber checked the darkened highway down the hill from the barn where he was parked then quietly pulled the cruiser out into the night.

* * *

"Agent Kane? Agent Kane?" Danny repeated. "Are you all right?"

Kane blinked and the vision of Mearle Farber murdering his nephew faded but did not completely disappear.

"Yeah, I'm fine," he mumbled, still in a fog.

"What do we do?" Danny asked.

"Do? About what?"

"About the tape, about this Mearle Farber maybe having something to do with Albert Brownstein?"

"We find him," Kane said, staring into Danny's worried face. *And then I'll kill him*, he whispered only to himself.

CHAPTER ELEVEN

Kane planned the events of the following morning as if plotting an affair. Step one was getting Useless to cooperate, which wasn't very difficult as long as Kane dangled the right bait.

"Grant," Greg half-whispered followed by a "come here" wave. Reflexively Eustace glanced toward Immerson's office then rolled across the aisle in his chair. *Typical*, Kane thought, *too lazy to even stand up and walk over*.

"What's up, Big Guy?" Eustace asked. Kane hated Useless' little nicknames — "Big Guy", "Chief", "Boss", "Killer" — but this morning he struggled to keep his displeasure off his face.

"I'm on to something. It could be big," Greg said. Eustace would be suspicious if Kane flat-out said it *was* big. Paranoid by nature Grant responded more readily to the hint of a big score than the actual promise of one.

"What's up?" Eustace asked, cocking his head to one side.

"I think I may have stumbled across a terrorist attack in the offing."

"A bomb?" Eustace asked, clearly interested.

"Probably a chemical or bio-weapon. You want to help me shut it down?" He might as well have asked a German shepherd if it was interested in a free steak.

"I'm all ears." Eustace hunched forward a couple of inches.

"The HHS director responsible for keeping out toxic chemicals and bio-weapons has disappeared. It could be that somebody's trying to coerce him into bringing some bad stuff into the country. We need to find him before that can happen. You up for a little legwork?"

The only legwork Eustace liked was kicking down doors and he flinched back a couple of inches but Kane knew that he was still hooked. The thought of grabbing a bunch of terrorists was Useless' wet dream. Kane could tell that Grant was already imagining the press conference where he received a personal commendation from the Attorney General.

"What do you need me to do?"

Kane pulled out the Brownstein file and dropped it in Eustace's lap. "We need to find the victim's car. If we can figure out where they dumped it we might be able to get some video of them, maybe even catch their plate. Plus, that'll firm up our time line about exactly when they grabbed him."

"Did it have a GPS?" Eustace asked. *If Brownstein's Volvo had GPS I'd have found it an hour after getting the case, moron!* Kane thought.

"No, that would have been a $2,500 option."

"Cheapskate, huh," Eustace said with a little laugh and flipped open the file for no purpose other than having something to do. "You want me to put out a BOLO and check with parking enforcement?"

For a split second Kane thought about actually playing it straight then gave it up as a waste of time. The old saying, *Pearls before swine*, ran through his head.

"Sure, those are good ideas but we need to dig a little deeper. I think that they might have dumped it in one of the Metro lots or at the Amtrak or the airport. We need to contact airport and Metro Security and get them to run the victim's plate through their systems and then send us any video showing when it clocked into their lot. Are you up for handling that?"

"What are you going to be doing?" Eustace asked suspiciously.

"I thought I'd take Rosewood over to HHS to try to get a line on the kind of chemicals that we should be on the lookout for."

"The kid? What do you need him for?"

"Do you know anything about chemistry?"

"Yeah, right!" Eustace snorted.

"There you go." Kane stood and waved in Danny's direction. "I'll catch up with you in a couple of hours." Eustace stared at Kane, his lips pulled into a tight line. *He smells something wrong but he isn't sure what*, Kane thought.

"I hope we don't end up having to shoot it out with them."

A shoot out? Eustace thought. *With terrorists? Holy shit!*

"Yeah, we wouldn't want to get into something like that," Grant agreed.

"You've got this covered?"

"I'm all over it, Big Guy."

Kane stretched his lips into a semblance of a smile and motioned for Rosewood to follow him. With Danny in his wake Kane stuck his head into Immerson's office.

"I'm borrowing Rosewood to help me retrieve some surveillance tapes," he told the boss. "We'll be back before lunch."

Immerson looked up from the manpower logs barely in time to catch a glimpse of Rosewood's back heading toward the exit. He could have stopped them but he found the vision of himself standing in the doorway and shouting at Kane undignified and bad for morale. Kane was going to do whatever he wanted anyway and so long as he closed cases without pissing off the FBI or some federal judge Immerson was willing to give him a little slack.

* * *

Kane got behind the wheel of a four-year old department Crown Vic and a second later Danny piled into the passenger seat. The truth was that Greg didn't need Rosewood but Immerson had a bug up his ass about allowing Kane out of the office alone. Greg figured that if he had to spend every trip into the field with Useless, sooner or later he was going to lose it and kick Grant's ass. At least he wasn't likely to end the day breaking Rosewood's nose.

Danny clicked his seatbelt and stared thoughtfully through the windshield. They drove a block in silence. Kane liked the fact that the kid knew when to keep his mouth shut. Even though Danny was no genius Kane decided that maybe he could be trained.

"I know you read the Brownstein file," Kane began. "What's your take on what happened to him?"

"The guy I spotted on the tapes grabbed him," Danny answered.

"We don't know that the man on the tape had anything to do with Brownstein. Maybe our guy just ran off."

"You think so?"

"Why do you think he didn't?"

Danny looked around as if the answer might be written on one of the storefronts sliding past their windows.

"Well?"

"It doesn't seem like something he would do," Danny answered as if asking a question.

"People do things for a reason. Half the time it's a stupid reason — they're pissed off or arrogant jerks or insecure or whatever but there's always some reason. Brownstein had a month's accrued vacation. If all he'd wanted was some time off he didn't need to disappear. All he had to do was pick up the phone. You checked his financials. Degenerate gamblers and drug addicts don't have $19,000 sitting in an IRA earning a big one-percent interest. No agency had any open cases on him. He wasn't running from the law or an ex-wife. So, why would Brownstein have run away?"

"I guess he wouldn't have," Danny said.

"So, if he didn't run away it stands to reason that he was taken away. Why do people get grabbed?"

Danny parted his lips then clamped them shut.

"It's not a rhetorical question."

"Uhhh, ransom?"

"Is Brownstein's family rich enough to make him a target for kidnappers?"

"His father's a dentist. His mother's a retired school teacher."

"So, that's a 'no' on the rich family question?"

"He wasn't likely kidnapped for ransom," Danny agreed.

"Do you see him dealing coke and failing to pay his supplier or sleeping with the wife of some guy in a biker gang or something like that?"

"No. That's pretty unlikely," Danny agreed.

"It's more than that. If someone had a personal motive to hurt him they would have just killed him. If you stiff a shylock then they leave your body in front of your house as a warning to other would-be deadbeats. If you fool around with the wrong guy's wife he just blows your head off. But somebody went to a lot of trouble to make Brownstein disappear. What could be the motive for something like that?"

"The only reason I can think of is that it has something to do with his job," Danny replied.

"OK. Let's see if we can narrow that down. Maybe somebody had the idea that they could slip some coerced paperwork into the system, get a shipment through customs over Brownstein's signature, but we've already had ICE flag anything with his name on it and nothing has shown up. If that was the plan they'd have run the bogus paper and gotten their shipment in before anyone noticed he was missing. The longer he's gone the more likely people would start looking for something like that." Kane glanced at Danny and almost asked, *So, what does that tell us about why they grabbed him?* but the blank look on Danny's face killed that idea.

"Here's the thing that stands out — it's easy to kill a citizen. *Bang-bang* and he becomes another statistic — a drive-by shooting, he runs into a drug addict desperate for some cash, he becomes part of a gang-banger initiation — that stuff happens every day. So if someone wanted him dead why would they disappear him instead of killing him on the street?" Danny just stared.

"Because the point wasn't to get him to do something but rather to prevent him from doing something. If you kill a bureaucrat another one steps in to take his place. If a bureaucrat disappears then the system freezes up. Everything has to wait until they're sure that the guy is really gone. Then they have to process a ton of paperwork to declare his job vacant and then they've got to go through all the civil service mumbo-jumbo to bring in somebody new. In the meantime everything's in a holding pattern. It could take months to get Brownstein's department back on track. We need to find out what projects were on his desk for the next few weeks, what was in the works that someone might have wanted to keep from happening."

"So, we're going over to his office to talk with his assistant?"

"First, we're going to check the bus station."

"Why the bus station?" Danny asked more curious than confused.

"If you want people to think that a guy has just run off you dump his car someplace that'll make it look like he's still alive but hiding out. Airports and train stations are no good because you've got to show your ID to buy a ticket and the first thing we'd discover is that Brownstein didn't get on a plane to New Orleans or hop a train to Florida. You don't need to show any identification to take a cross-country bus so if you're smart the bus station is where you'll dump the car to make it look like the guy is on the run."

"What if they're not smart?"

"That's why Eustace is checking the train stations and airport parking lots. Just in case." Kane pulled into the bus station and began to cruise the aisles. "Keep an eye out for Brownstein's Volvo," he told Danny, secretly figuring that they had maybe a ten-percent chance of actually finding it.

Five minutes later Danny shouted, "There it is!" and pointed excitedly toward the end of the row. "Gee, Agent Kane, you must be some kind of a genius."

"Yeah, I'm a genius," Kane agreed, all the time thinking of his failed marriage and his shattered Baltimore PD career.

CHAPTER TWELVE

Grant Eustace's happy vision of himself knocking over balaclava-clad terrorists like tin ducks in a shooting gallery quickly faded into frustrated tedium. He stopped counting Metro stations when he got to fifty and that didn't include the Dulles and Reagan parking lots and the separate Amtrak lots at each airport and the ones around Union Station. *What the hell kind of crap job has Kane stuck me with anyway?* he grumbled. Still, Eustace reminded himself, Kane closed cases. Grant picked up the phone and made the next call on his list. *What kind a cheapskate jerk buys a Volvo S60 and doesn't get the GPS package?* Eustace muttered then stood and tried to untwist the kink in his back.

Eustace looked at the clock. *A quarter to twelve and Kane and the kid are still farting around in the field while I'm stuck here getting blisters on my fingers from punching so many fucking numbers into my phone.* Eustace glared at the dog-eared list of Metro Station security offices then his eyes slipped down to the Washington Post's front page peeking from beneath the Brownstein folder:

COURT TIGHTENS SECURITY
MORE THREATS IN GUN-LAW APPEAL

Now there was a case that had "career advancement" written all over it, provided that you caught the guy *before* he shot Mr. Justice Hopper. *Fucking gun nuts!* Eustace thought, though his sentiments were neither politically nor ideologically motivated. For him it was much simpler. Grant Eustace was an "us versus them" kind of guy and on a tribal level he wanted his own gang to be the only one with weapons. It was in his self-interest to keep all other groups, gangs and organizations that might challenge his tribe as powerless as possible. Not that Eustace was stupid. He could understand the ideological arguments. It was just that he didn't care. In that, as in many other ways, he was different from Greg Kane. Kane was a firm believer in the dictum: "Know your enemy" whereas Eustace's philosophy was "Get him before he gets you."

The court battle over the guns had started with the death of a child, but like World War I sometimes the murder of a single person can ignite a far vaster conflict. Nine-year-old Lyla Masterson had been standing in line with her mother, Sonya, at the Baskin-Robbins when the shooting started. Two gang-bangers with AR-15s had decided to rob the Elite Jewelry & Gold Exchange two stores down. One of the jewelry-store's customers was a twenty-two-year-old carpenter named Ronnie Dubois who held a firm belief that everyone should carry a gun "just in case." Today Dubois was convinced that his foresight was finally paying off.

Ronnie pulled his Sig Sauer Model 228 from the special holster he wore on his belt at the small of his back, shoved in a clip, and started blazing away at the closest robber. He missed. The gunman fired back and caught Ronnie in the right calf. Ronnie tried to crawl behind a counter and was rewarded with another swarm of bullets and a hail of shattered glass. Now with his adrenalin really pumping, Ronnie popped up and blasted away as fast as he could pull the trigger, soon emptying his entire fifteen shot extended-load clip.

Having planned on a nice quiet stickup rather than The Gunfight At The OK Corral the robbers hustled out the door while randomly blasting away until their fifty shot clips went dry. It took the crime scene techs twelve hours to catalog all the spent shells and bullet holes and splatters of blood. The final tally in human terms was surprisingly light: the store owner, Frank Shapiro, was hit twice by the robbers but was expected to survive. Ronnie Dubois had taken one bullet, also from the gunmen. The wound hurt like hell and he had lots of cuts from flying glass but he would recover.

The sole fatality was Lyla Masterson. One of Ronnie's nine millimeter slugs passed through the jewelry store's sheet-rock wall, through the adjacent dry-cleaner's wall and came to rest in Lyla Masterson's brain, staining her pink dress with blotches of red. She was dead before she hit the floor. When questioned by the police Ronnie explained that he had merely been exercising his Second Amendment rights and contended that he was a hero who had succeeded in driving off two "bad guys" before they could steal anything. When asked about Lyla Masterson Ronnie replied that he was sorry that the little girl was "hurt" but sometimes when you're fighting crime there's "collateral damage."

Since state law allowed an adult to carry an unloaded handgun so long as it was "in plain sight" Dubois could not be charged with a crime. Of course he could be sued in civil court but since he had no substantial assets, even if they won Lyla's parents would likely never collect a dime. Two weeks after the shooting the NRA put Ronnie's picture on page one of their *America's First Freedom* digital magazine. That's when the offers started pouring in.

In some circles Ronnie Dubois was a celebrity. Now the inconvenience of having to deal with a civil suit coupled with the possibility that his interview fees and endorsement money might be seized motivated Ronnie to declare bankruptcy which would wipe out any debt that some bleeding-heart jury might see fit to award Lyla's parents. Hell, he got $10,000 for posing with his Sig on the cover of next year's *Guns And Freedom* calendar and he intended to keep it. The text beneath his photo read:

Bad Guys Beware,

For Lyla's parents this was a million miles beyond too much. They created their own poster, a picture of their smiling child superimposed over her gravestone and captioned with the words: **"Collateral Damage?"**

Thus began the ballot initiative for what was called "Lyla's Law." The measure contained nine provisions:

1. Except for sales or transfers to (1) sworn law enforcement officers and/or (2) members of a state or federal government-sponsored militia or military organization, no non-clip-using firearm shall be sold or transferred that is capable of firing more than six rounds without reloading.

2. Except for sales or transfers to (1) sworn law enforcement officers and/or (2) members of a state or federal government-sponsored militia or military organization, no clips for firearms shall be sold or transferred that are capable of holding more than six rounds.

3. Except for (1) sworn law enforcement officers and/or (2) members of a state or federal government-sponsored militia or military organization, it shall be illegal to possess any fire-arm-clip with a capacity of more than six rounds.

4. Except for (1) sworn law enforcement officers and/or (2) members of a state or federal government-sponsored militia or military organization, it shall be illegal to possess

any non-clip-using firearm that in its then present state is capable of firing more than six rounds without reloading.

5. Except for (1) sworn law enforcement officers and/or (2) members of a state or federal government-sponsored militia or military organization, it shall be illegal to possess any non-clip-using firearm that can be readily modified to hold or fire more than six rounds without reloading.

6. Except for (1) sworn law enforcement officers, (2) members of a state or federal government-sponsored militia, (3) duly licensed sellers of ammunition (4) duly licensed shooting ranges, (5) officially accredited law enforcement agencies, (6) state or federal militia or military organizations, and/or (7) recognized delivery, transport or shipping services when possessed in connection with shipping the same, it shall be illegal for any person to buy or possess more than 100 rounds of ammunition of any one caliber and it shall be illegal to sell or transfer more than 100 rounds of ammunition of any one caliber to any person during any continuous period of seven days except for those persons exempted in subsections (1) through (7) above.

7. Except for (1) sworn law enforcement officers, (2) members of a state or federal government-sponsored militia or military organization and/or (3) persons duly licensed to do so, it shall be illegal for any person to carry a loaded firearm in any public place.

8. Except for (1) sworn law enforcement officers, (2) members of a state or federal government-sponsored militia or military organization and/or (3) persons duly licensed to do so, it shall be illegal for any person to carry an unloaded clip-using-firearm and a loaded clip for any firearm in any public place.

9. No person may purchase or possess a firearm unless and until that person has taken and passed an approved firearms safety class.

The Mastersons and their supporters might as well have suggested that Sunday church service be replaced with a free-for-all orgy topped off with a complimentary double-shot of cocaine. Nevertheless, to everyone's amazement the initiative passed by 1,127 votes. It was instantly challenged in Federal Court. After almost a year of legal wrangling the District Judge ruled that Lyla's Law was constitutional. The NRA members challenging the law appealed. Nine months later, by a two to one vote of one of its more conservative three-judge panels the Ninth Circuit Court of Appeals overturned the District Judge and struck down Lyla's Law.

The Secretary of State requested a rehearing *en banc* by the entire 9th Circuit. Recognizing that no matter what they did the case was going to end up being decided by the Supreme Court and desperately wanting to get out of the line of fire of the already overheated dispute, by a two-vote margin the 9th Circuit refused the *en banc* petition. The Secretary of State quickly filed an appeal to the U.S. Supreme Court.

For weeks prior to oral argument waves of protesters on both sides surged around the Supreme Court Building like rip tides preceding a storm. When the case was heard on a freezing mid-January morning a blizzard driving in out of the Midwest threatened the city. Snowflakes like fragments of shaved ice peppered the crowds in the plaza while inside the chamber every judicial twitch and blink was noted and pondered.

The attorney for the citizens challenging Lyla's Law began by reading the text of the Second Amendment:

"A well regulated militia being necessary to the security of a free state, the right of the people to keep and bear arms shall not be infringed."

"On its face," he told the Justices, "the so-called Lyla's Law prohibits citizens from owning or keeping, a wide range of firearms and also from bearing or carrying an even wider selection of guns. All of the provisions of the law that restrict the right to own certain types of firearms are in violation of the clear and unambiguous provisions of the Second Amendment. All of the provisions of the law restricting the right to carry firearms are clearly in violation of the Second Amendment. If the proponents of this law want to enact such a statute then they must first amend the Constitution before they can do so."

Mr. Justice McCoy noted that the stated purpose of the Second Amendment was to insure the existence of a well-regulated militia. "Don't the law's exemptions for members of a government-sponsored militia save the statute from being in violation of the Second Amendment?" he asked counsel for the Respondents.

"Militias are historically drawn from ordinary citizens in times of crisis and are, in fact, usually organized on an *ad hoc* basis after the emergency has become apparent. There are often no members of a militia in existence until the threat arises. For that reason the Second Amendment does not protect the right of the members of a *militia* to keep and bear arms but rather the right of the *people* to keep and bear arms. So, no, Your Honor, the exclusion of members of an organized militia from the provisions of the statute do not save it from being unconstitutional."

Mr. Justice McCoy frowned but said nothing further. Spectators quickly marked McCoy down as favoring upholding Lyla's Law.

Sensing that the "Militia Argument" wasn't going to win the day, when his turn came the attorney for the State took a different tack. He began by reading the text of the First Amendment:

"Congress shall make no law respecting an establishment of religion, or prohibiting the free exercise thereof; or abridging the freedom of speech, or of the press; or the right of the people peaceably to assemble, and to petition the Government for a redress of grievances.

"The text of the First Amendment is clear," he began "that the Government may not prohibit the free exercise of religion. Yet, it is without question that it is constitutional for the government to prohibit the practice of bigamy even though multiple wives are one of the tenets of a recognized religion. Without question members of a religion who wanted to practice human sacrifices or have sex with children or do any number of other actions which might well be a part of their religious beliefs may constitutionally be prevented from doing so in spite of the fact that the First Amendment says, with absolute clarity and without exception, that the Government may not prohibit the free exercise of religion.

"The First Amendment says with absolute clarity and without exception that the Government may not abridge the freedoms of speech or of the press, yet it is without any doubt constitutional to prohibit the publication of a person's private information and it is constitutional to prohibit making statements that are defamatory and that it is constitutional to prohibit shouting 'Fire' in a crowded theater.

"The clear language of the First Amendment guaranteeing freedom of speech, the freedom of the press and the freedom of religion is nevertheless constitutionally subject to reasonable, rational and common-sense limitations when the same are enacted in support of a compelling state interest. And so too is the Second Amendment's right to keep and bear arms also subject to reasonable, rational and common-sense limitations when they are enacted in support of a compelling state interest.

"Even though the text of the Second Amendment does not include an exception for machine guns, flame throwers or rocket-propelled grenades, counsel for the Respondents would admit that laws prohibiting private citizens from owning machine guns, flame throwers and rocket propelled grenades are nevertheless constitutional. The Second Amendment does not include any exception allowing the government to deny convicts and mental patients the right to own a gun but it is unquestionably constitutional to deny convicts and mental patients the right to keep and bear arms.

"The question is not whether the government may constitutionally prohibit some citizens from owning some weapons. That question has long since been settled law. The government may constitutionally prohibit some citizens from owning some weapons. Period. The only question before this Court is which people and which weapons may be constitutionally prohibited. The only question before this court is: Where can the line be drawn between the constitutional and the unconstitutional regulation of firearms?

"At one end of the spectrum it is clear that the government may not constitutionally prohibit all firearms other than the single-shot muzzle-loaders that existed when the Second Amendment was adopted. The respondents argue for the other end of the spectrum when they demand that the government may only constitutionally prohibit fully automatic machine guns and nothing less. Both are extreme positions. Somewhere between those two extremes is the proper line, which is to say the common sense and reasonable line between the constitutional and the unconstitutional regulation of firearms.

"It is the Petitioner's position that the Act in question is reasonable and rational, that it is in response to life-threatening conditions, that it is a proper exercise of government power, and that it draws the line between the two regulatory extremes in a reasonable place and that therefore the Act is constitutional."

If the Petitioner's attorney harbored any secret fantasy that when he concluded his remarks the Justices were going to nod sagely and say, "Yes, of course, clearly you're right" he was instantly disabused of that idea. Three different Justices immediately took turns challenging every point he had made.

At the end of the day savvy court watchers concluded that there were four votes against the law, three in favor, one Justice who would likely uphold several but probably not all of its provisions, and one jurist, Mr. Justice George Hopper, who, if not on the fence, was at least in the "unknown" column.

The Lyla's Law opinion could be delivered anytime between a month from the date of oral argument and the week of June 23rd, the last week of the term. The actual date that the decision would be rendered was unknown. One thing that the legal pundits seemed confident of was that if Hopper supported the law, it would stand and if not, it would fail.

As the man in the middle Mr. Justice George Hopper came in for threats from both sides. Supporters of the law warned that the lives of all victims of gun violence would be on Hopper's head if he voted to affirm the Court of Appeals and strike down Lyla's Law. Opponents warned that Hopper would be responsible for the eventual imposition of a police state on the American people if he voted to uphold the law.

Of course, there was no shortage of citizens whose threats went beyond mere warnings of moral responsibility. "If you take our guns away you will die," was a common theme in the hundreds of anonymous threats that poured into the Supreme Court's mail room.

Down in Jackson, Mississippi Carl Feeney did not concern himself with threats of retribution. His concern was more immediate — Should Hopper be killed before the case was decided? If Hopper voted to affirm the lower court's decision it would form a precedent that would block any gun legislation for decades to come. If Hopper voted to overrule the 9th Circuit and uphold Lyla's Law it would open the floodgates for similar legislation in cities, counties and states all over the country. But if Hopper died before the vote was taken the Court would likely be split four to four meaning that the decision of the 9th Circuit striking down the law would stand and, for a while at least, the threat to gun ownership would be averted.

Feeney had been told that a patriot in Silicon Valley had hacked the computer of one of Hopper's clerks and found material indicating that the justice was probably going to vote to reverse the Court of Appeals and uphold the law. Feeney couldn't be sure whether that was true or not but the risk was high enough that he felt that he had no choice. Mr. Justice Hopper needed to die, the sooner the better. The only question was how to do it. Feeney thought he knew a way.

* * *

None of these theoretical issues troubled Grant Eustace as he pondered how he might get himself involved in investigating the threats against Mr. Justice Hopper. He just figured that there were a lot of nut-jobs with guns out there and that if he was able to grab one of them in the act of trying to knock off the justice his career would get a rocket-ship kick in the ass. The question was, how could he get a piece of the Hopper case? After five minutes of thinking about it as hard as he could he had nothing. *I bet if Kane put his mind to it, he'd be able to find us a way in,* Eustace mused as he fiddled with the Metro Security Offices' phone roster. And just like that Grant had an idea. Maybe the simplest thing to do would be to just ask Kane to come up with a plan. *It couldn't hurt,* Eustace decided.

*   *   *

Danny had almost finished burning a copy of the parking lot surveillance files when Eustace called Kane.

"How's it going, partner?" Eustace asked. "You figure out what these guys are trying to smuggle in?"

They're not trying to smuggle anything in, you moron! Kane thought. *They're trying to — screw it. What's the point?* "It's going fine," he replied.

"That's good. I've got bupkis here. Do you have any idea how many fucking Metro stations there are? I'm gonna get tennis finger from dialing all these numbers."

Tennis finger? . . . . Crap, I forgot to tell him that we found the car.

"Yeah, that sounds rough. I'll tell you what. Why don't you take a break and Danny and I will handle the rest of them when we get back."

"Really?"

"Sure. We'll do the rest and we'll check out the bus station parking lots too. You can get yourself some lunch."

"Thanks, partner. I'll leave the list on your desk, you know, in case lunch runs a little long."

"OK, look I've got to—"

"Say, Kane, one thing I need to ask you. If you wanted to get us a piece of the Hopper thing, how would you do it?"

"Grant, they're not going to let us within ten miles of that investigation."

"Sure, sure, you're right, but, if, and I'm just saying 'if' you wanted to try, what would you do?"

"I'd find the guy making the threats before they do," Kane snapped. Danny pressed a button and the DVD popped out of the machine.

"Well, Duh!" Eustace complained. "How the hell am I supposed to do that?"

Kane glanced at his watch. "Think like the perp and anticipate him."

"Which means?"

Kane felt the seconds slipping away as he watched Danny struggled to shove the jewel case into his pocket.

"If I were going to kill somebody who was protected by the Secret Service I'd try to get to him through his family. Maybe—"

"Got it. I think Hopper's got a daughter. I'll check her out."

"Grant, for God's sake don't—"

"Later, Big Guy." The line went dead.

CHAPTER THIRTEEN

Carl Feeney parked the battered F150 next to a truly ancient International Harvester pickup and dipped his head as he neared the bar. He hadn't seen any cameras when he checked out the place but when you were plotting a murder you didn't take any chances. He gave the bill on his baseball cap a tug and pushed inside. It was a typical loser joint, cinder-block walls, sticky linoleum floor, bar to the right, tables to the left, pool table and bathrooms in the back, lighting just barely bright enough to distinguish between a glass of vodka and one of bourbon.

* * *

Feeney had arrived at this place and at this time by a circuitous route that he hoped was so tangled that the trail could never be traced back to him. He had started with a man he'd met near the end of his tour in Iraq, back when Bush was still President. They weren't friends. You didn't make friends with a guy like Clete Garrity. Someplace along the line life had flushed the humanity out of Garrity's soul like a shirt that had been washed so often that no discernible color remained. Feeney figured that making a living blowing the heads off strangers at five hundred yards would do that to a man. That's how Feeney thought of him now, not as Clete Garrity but as simply "The Sniper."

He'd tracked Garrity down through an old address they'd exchanged after a night of drinking at some base camp back in The Sand. Not that Garrity had shown any effects from the alcohol. Feeney had been sitting there, bleary-eyed, complaining about the pussies running the country while Garrity just nodded and popped another can.

"I've got a job I'd like done," Feeney had begun when he and Garrity reconnected. Feeney's eyes shifted nervously around. Garrity just stared at him.

"A job?" he asked.

"You know, a job, for a specialist."

Garrity gave Feeney a long look then moved his chin a millimeter left then right.

"If it's a question of money—"

"It's not," Garrity interrupted. "My time is otherwise committed."

Otherwise committed? Feeney almost asked what that meant but caught himself in time. "Is there anyone you can refer me to?" he said instead.

"I know a guy," Garrity said.

"Is he good?"

"He's a junkie," Garrity answered.

"A junkie? I need—"

"But," Garrity continued, "He knows a guy who's got the right credentials. The junkie could put you two together if the price was right."

"Why do I need this junkie? Why don't you handle the introduction yourself?"

Garrity gave his head another microscopic shake. "Can't. The guy knows me."

"Yeah, so?"

Garrity frowned. "People who know you can betray you. If they catch him, he gives them me and if they catch me I could give them you. Nobody wants that. The junkie makes the introduction and you don't know who the Operator is and he doesn't know who you are. You can't give him up and he can't give you up. More importantly, if they can't find you, they can't find me."

"But if this guy knows the junkie and the junkie knows . . . ." Feeney sputtered to a stop.

"Junkies OD all the time. Nobody thinks twice about it." Garrity took a long swallow of something, it might have been vodka or it might have been club soda. "Are you good with that?"

What was one junkie in the world more or less? Hell, he probably would be doing the guy a favor, putting him out of his misery.

"How much?" Feeney asked instead.

"Is the target a relative or somebody you're in business with?"

"It's—"

"I don't want to know any specifics. Is it somebody you know?"

Feeney hesitated briefly then answered. "No."

"Somebody in the government who's fucking with your business?"

"No."

"A cop?"

"No."

"Political?"

"Yes."

"State or federal?"

"Federal," Feeney said after another little pause.

"Somebody like a bureaucrat or higher up the food chain?"

"Higher."

Garrity considered that for a moment. "That's a lot of heat," he said in a distracted voice as if solving a math problem in his head. "The Operator's going to want at least a million, maybe more. Are you willing to spend that kind of money?"

"Absolutely."

Garrity was silent for a moment then nodded. "OK, my fee for the introduction is a hundred-fifty K payable if the Operator takes the job. If he turns you down we'll have to figure out something else. I get twenty-five K for my trouble no matter what. Agreed?"

"What about the junkie, after, you know?"

"That's included in the hundred-fifty. Loose ends are bad for both of us." Garrity pressed the glow-light button on his watch. "What's it gonna be?"

Feeney held out his hand and Garrity frowned and slapped it away. "Grow the fuck up," He snapped and handed Feeney a Go Phone. "I'll call you in a couple of days and tell you where and when to meet the junkie. What name do you want to use?"

"Ahhh, John Smith?"

Garrity's lips pursed into a thin line. "You'll be Joseph Green. He'll be Ray Black. Got it?"

"I'm Green. He's Black," Feeney repeated, fingering the burner phone.

"Don't use that for anything except talking to me. Nothing else, not even if your life depends on it. You got that?"

"Got it," Feeney said in a rush.

Garrity gave him another of his hard stares then stood. "I'll be in touch. Keep that thing on and charged up."

For three days Feeney carried the burner phone like a talisman. Last night it had rung. Garrity gave him the address of the bar and the junkie's description.

"You remember your name?"

"Joseph—"

"Don't say it!"

"Sorry."

"Never trust a phone. Do you remember both names?"

"Yes."

"That's better."

"Pick up some cheap clothes someplace for cash. Don't use Walmart. They video tape all their registers. Find some second-hand store that doesn't have any cameras. Don't forget to buy shoes too. And throw it all away when you're done. Wear a hat and sunglasses, the ones with yellow lenses so you don't trip over a chair in the dark and break your neck. Throw them away too after the meet. Don't drive your own car and don't rent a car. Borrow a car from somebody. Tell them your battery's dying or whatever. Stick some cotton balls in your cheeks to make them bulge out a little. On the way there buy two burner phones for cash and try to stay off the store cameras. Give the junkie one and you keep one. That's the only way you'll communicate with him. You got all that?"

"Yes."

"If you want to change your mind now is the time. Do you still want to do this?"

"I have to. The future of our country—"

"I don't want to hear that shit. I don't care. This is just business. Do you understand?"

"Yes. Anything else?" Feeney asked.

"This is my life here. I take my life very seriously. If you ever, and I mean ever, think about giving me up you remember two things: One, what I do for a living and two, you have a family. Are you understanding me?"

"I understand you," Feeney said, his guts suddenly empty and cold.

"All right," Garrity replied. "The Idle Hour Bar, two o'clock tomorrow afternoon."

"Got it." The line went dead. Feeney sucked in a shuddering breath and went looking for a bottle.

* * *

Feeney paused just inside the Idle Hour's front door and let his eyes adjust to the gloom. Garrity had told him that the junkie was a thin white man, about six-one with brown hair, a long face and big ears. Feeney peered into the shadows and spotted a cadaverous figure hunched over a table in the back. Feeney had briefly considered wearing a fake mustache but the one he bought at the costume shop looked so phony that he abandoned the idea. Instead he had stopped shaving the day he met with Garrity and this afternoon he greased his hair and combed it forward halfway over his forehead. It wouldn't fool anyone who knew him but in the bar's dim light it would make it more difficult for the junkie to pick him out of a lineup later, if it ever came to that, God forbid.

"Are you Mr. Black?" Feeney asked with his back to the light leaking from behind the bar.

"Yeah, Ray Black. Who are you?"

"Joseph Green." Black glanced toward the door then waved to the empty chair across from him.

Feeney stared at Black and was suddenly afraid. *What if this is a set-up? What if the place is bugged?*

"Let's sit over there," Feeney said, pointing to a table in the far corner. Black turned around, then shrugged.

"Did our friend explain what I want?" Feeney asked once they had moved.

"Hang on. They're not big on guys sitting around without buying something."

Not liking the lights above the bar Feeney handed Black a five.

"Coke," he said. Black frowned at the bill then stood up. A moment later he returned with a cola in a tall glass and made a show of shoving Feeney's change into his pocket.

"So, do you know what I want?" Feeney repeated.

"You've got a special job and you want the best."

"That's right. Can you put us together?"

"That's up to him. What's the pay?"

"Half a mil," Feeney said figuring that if the contractor wanted more he'd ask for it. The number seemed high enough to hold Black's interest.

"My end is ten percent," Black said. "In cash, in advance."

Black's face was lined and drawn, his eyes puffy. He barely moved his jaw when he spoke but Feeney caught a glimpse of the meth-rotted teeth behind his lips. Feeney laughed.

"Your fee is $50K, half when you introduce me and half when he finishes the job."

"All of it when I put you two together."

"You think I'm an idiot? You think I'm going to let you give me the phone number for one of your scumbag friends and then hand over fifty K?"

"I'm supposed to put you two together and just trust that you'll pay me?" Black replied.

"The man who told you to meet me has already vouched for me so let's stop screwing around. If you don't want to get fifty grand for making a phone call he'll find me somebody who does."

Black rubbed his hands on his thighs and stared down at the table as if it held a crystal ball.

"Here's how we'll do this," Feeney said a moment later. "I'll bring twenty-five K in cash. You make the call and I'll talk to your guy. If he takes the job I'll give you the rest of the cash."

"How do I know I'll get my money on the back end?"

"You can get twenty-five thousand and the promise of twenty-five more for making a phone call or you can sit here with your pockets empty while you try to figure out where your next meal is coming from," Feeney said with a sneer. He hadn't gotten rich without being able to read people. This guy was circling the bowl and he knew it.

"You think you can talk to me like I'm some punk!" Black demanded. "I put guys in the ground who would make you shit your pants. I won the fucking Bronze Star so don't treat me like some half-breed who's come to your house to clean your toilets!"

"Sorry, I didn't mean to come off that way," Feeney apologized. "The offer stands. Twenty-five in cash once your guy agrees to the meeting and another twenty-five after he takes the contract."

Black glared for a second longer then looked away.

"Fine," he said and downed the last of his beer.

Feeney passed Black the burner phone he had bought that morning.

"I've put my number in the address book. You call me when your friend's ready to set up a meeting. Don't use that phone for anything else."

"I'm not a moron," Black muttered and slipped the cell into his pocket.

Two days later Feeney got the call. They agreed to meet that afternoon but Feeney insisted on a different location and borrowed a different vehicle from the employee lot. He would have liked to have met at night but then he would have had to use one of his own cars. He picked a different bar even gloomier than The Idle Hour.

"Did you bring it?" Black asked once they had gotten a couple of beers. Feeney nodded toward the paper bag he had placed on the empty chair. "I want to see it."

"Help yourself," Feeney said, sick of the bullshit.

Black pulled the bag into his lap and peeked at the five bundles of bills inside. Squinting against the gloom he riffled three of the stacks to be sure they were hundreds all the way through not just hundreds on top with ones inside. Black put the bag back on the extra chair and hit a button on his phone.

"It's me. He's here. Pot's right." Wordlessly, Black handed Feeney the cell.

"Black tells me that you're looking for a contractor," the voice said.

"I am. When can we meet to discuss the project?" The caller laughed.

"We're not going to meet. I'm not going to see your face and you're not going to see mine."

"Then how's this supposed to work?"

"Take the phone someplace private and call me back in a couple of minutes."

So, Feeney thought, *this was it*. He was supposed to hand twenty-five thousand dollars to a junkie and walk away. If this was a rip-off then Black would disappear out the back door with the money and the guy on the other end would never pick up. Or he could grab his paper bag and walk out, end of story. He stared into Black's eyes but saw only hunger. *Fuck it!* Feeney stuck the burner phone in his pocket, hit the sidewalk and headed for the alley next to the bar. The contractor picked up on the fourth ring.

"Where are you?"

"In an alley. I'm alone. What do I call you?"

The Operator laughed. "I don't care — Donald Trump."

"I'll call you Donald. How is this going to work?"

"Who's the target?"

"High level. Political. Federal."

"Who specifically?"

There it was. If this was a setup, if it was a Fed on the other end and he answered that question he was going to go to prison for a very long time. Or, he could walk away and forget the whole thing. But then who would save America from becoming a police state? Fuck it! He had risked his life for his country before. He would risk it again.

"Supreme Court Justice George Hopper," Feeney said and silently counted off the seconds, listening for the scream of sirens and Federal Gestapo Agents yelling for him to get down on the ground.

"That's a big job," Donald said at last. "It's going to be very, very hard."

"Are you saying you can't do it?"

"I'm saying that it's very, very hard. . . . Still," Donald continued a moment later, "a man like me likes a challenge."

"So, you can do it?"

"I can do anything. But it's going to cost you. One and a half."

"I told Black half a million."

"I don't care if you told Black a dollar ninety-nine. I'm telling you a million and a half."

"How about we split the difference? One million."

"How about we don't."

"I can do a million and a half for the entire job but I've got other expenses here. Black, the guy who put Black and me together, other costs, you understand."

"I'm not some fucking Arab in a rug market, Mr. Green."

"I'm not saying you are. It's just that—"

"One and quarter and if you say anything other than 'yes' we're done."

"Yes," Feeney answered immediately. "What are the mechanics?"

"I'll give you a choice. You can pay me half now and half when the job is done but if we go that way I've got to know your real identity, where you live, and the names of your wife and kids. That way I can be sure that you'll pay the second half."

"What's the other option?"

"Payment in full in advance."

"What's the third option?"

"I hang up the phone and drop it into the garbage disposal."

Feeney thought about trusting a killer-for-hire with a million and a quarter dollars. Why wouldn't he just keep the money and laugh all the way to the bank? Then Feeney thought about some thug coming after his wife and daughter or telling the feds the name of the man who hired him to kill a Supreme Court Justice. Or he could forget the whole thing.

"What's it going to be?" Donald asked.

"How fast can you do the job?"

"You don't rush something like this."

"I want it done sometime in the next four weeks. It has to happen before they take their vote. How do I get the money to you?"

"Do you know about bitcoins?"

"I've heard of them. I'm sure I can figure it out," Feeney answered.

"I'll call you tomorrow with the transfer information. After that, destroy this phone."

"How will we get in touch?"

"When I call I'll give you a new phone number. Destroy this phone and get another one. Use it to call the new number. It'll be one that Mr. Black doesn't know about."

"All right. I can do that."

"Wait a minute," Donald said an instant before Feeney was about to hang up. "Why do you want that particular target taken out?"

"Have you ever heard of *The Weapon Shops Of Isher?*"

"What?"

"The right to buy weapons is the right to be free. As soon as the government takes away our guns the Secret Police will come for us. We have to be armed and ready when the New Gestapo shows up to take us all to the concentration camps."

Are you fucking for real? Donald thought.

"Yeah, OK, fine, you want to get ready to go to war with the government, but that's not what I meant. I was wondering why you picked that particular guy. Why not Lazzaro or Swanson? They're supposed to be sure bets to vote against you. It would make my job a lot easier if you'd let me go after one of them and you could be sure that you'll get the result you want. From what I've heard Hopper's a tossup."

For a moment Feeney considered telling Donald why he thought that Hopper was going to vote to take their guns away. But if this all turned to shit and they caught Donald he would talk and Feeney didn't want the Gestapo to know that a patriot had hacked Hopper's clerk's computer.

"We can't do it that way," Feeney answered.

"Why not?"

"Suppose you take out Swanson and the law gets struck down five to three instead of five to four," Feeney said, pretending that he didn't know how Hopper was going to vote. "That means we would have murdered a Supreme Court Justice for nothing, just on the off chance that we might not have gotten the decision we wanted. Even people who would normally be on our side would go nuts if we did something like that.

"On the other hand if we removed Swanson and the decision was four to four that means that if Swanson is replaced with a new justice like him, and with this president and this senate that's what would happen, then the next time this sort of law came back to the Supreme Court we would be sure to lose.

"But if we take out Hopper before anyone knows how he was going to vote then the law still gets knocked out and the guy who replaces Hopper will probably be somebody in the middle like him instead of somebody who's already against us like Swanson, and the new guy will think twice before he crosses us. Now do you understand?"

"I'm sorry I asked. Get ready to buy a shitload of bitcoins."

Feeney slipped the burner phone into his pocket and headed back to his borrowed car.

* * *

A week later Feeney transferred the bitcoins to some oddball Internet server in Belarus and picked up his new burner phone. After that all he could do was wait.

CHAPTER FOURTEEN

By the time Kane and Danny got back to the office Eustace had vanished leaving behind only a cryptic note: "Out on the case." Greg ground his teeth in silence, resenting the fact that Useless could get away with flitting around the city on his own while he, like an errant child, was not allowed out of the office without a chaperone. It had not always been that way but a succession of what Immerson called "problems" and Kane called "encounters with assholes" had led to Immerson's strict enforcement of the otherwise largely ignored travel-with-a-partner rule.

"So, Useless can wander around the countryside free as a bird and I can't get a sandwich without a babysitter? Is that what you're telling me?" Kane had snapped the first time Immerson had threatened to write him up.

Immerson angrily sucked in the edges of his cheeks while he struggled to pick out which of Kane's transgressions to deal with first.

"I told you not to call him that!"

"Useless is as Useless does," Kane snapped.

"There! Right there is why I can't trust you out in the world alone." Kane glared but said nothing. "Every other agent in this Division knows enough to at least pretend to be on his best behavior when I call them in here. But not you. You just can't help yourself. Until I can trust you to make it through the day without unnecessarily pissing off half the people you talk to, you only go out with a partner."

"So if we're out someplace and Eustace needs to take a pee do I have to go into the can with him?"

"Do you have a death wish? Do you want to lose this job the way you lost your last one?" Immerson asked in an almost compassionate voice.

"I'm a good investigator. I close cases."

"Closing cases in not enough! Jesus, Kane, you've got to learn how to get along with people, even people who aren't as smart as you are — especially people who aren't as smart as you are." Greg parted his lips but Immerson waved him into silence. "No, you've pissed me off enough already. Quit while you're behind. Get out of here before I write you up."

Teeth clenched, Kane stormed back to his desk. *No*, he decided, remembering that confrontation, *it would not be a good idea to complain now about Useless' Lone Ranger habits, besides it was almost quitting time.*

"Do you want me to work on sharpening the parking lot footage or should I go back to the video from the sidewalk cameras?" Danny asked, waking Kane from his reverie.

"Let it go until tomorrow. There's no point in putting in any overtime on it."

"I was thinking that maybe we might be able to pull up a scar or a tattoo or something on the guy who dropped off Brownstein's car."

"There's less than a one in a thousand chance that we'll get anything useful from the parking lot video," Kane said idly slapping his ballpoint against his palm. He looked up to find Rosewood staring expectantly at him. "The color of his hands was much lighter than the glimpse the camera caught of his face. That tells me he was wearing latex gloves so we're not going to see any tats. Between him walking hunched over, the hoodie and the sunglasses he could be the Elephant Man and we wouldn't know it."

"We still might catch something once he was out on the street," Danny suggested.

"He's a pro so the odds of that are. . . ." Kane shrugged. "It'll wait until tomorrow."

"Agent Kane, do you think it's him, the deputy who was with your nephew?" Danny asked in an uneasy tone. "Is that why you think he's a professional?"

"He's a professional because of the way he's put this whole thing together. Is he Mearle Farber? I sure hope so. Anyway—" Kane paused and pulled out his ringing phone. The screen said 'Martin Fouchet.' "I've got to take this. I'll see you in the morning." Kane tapped the "accept" icon. "Hi Martin."

"Greg, have you found out anything about Mr. Brownstein? Any leads?"

Kane considered a half dozen ways of politely ducking the question but found he couldn't ignore the combination of hope and fear in his friend's voice.

"Let's get dinner and I'll bring you up to speed. Pick a place."

"I'm attending a conference at the Jefferson on, well, the details don't matter. They have a five star restaurant—"

"Five stars? That means half the menu will be chopped liver, raw fish and snails. No thanks."

"They have a cocktail lounge that serves burgers and club sandwiches and the like. We could probably get them to bring you a steak. It's on me."

"That sounds better. See you at seven." Kane slipped the phone back into his pocket and turned to see Danny typing something on his computer. "Danny, go home."

"I just thought I'd get a start on the FR-2."

"Go home, call a girl, have some fun."

"I already told Diane that I had to work late. What are you going to do?"

"I'm going to have dinner with an old friend and give him some very bad news."

*   *   *

Perhaps in anticipation of a difficult meeting or maybe just because he was tired and frustrated and in need of a drink Greg left his car in the employee lot and took a cab to the Metro station. The Jefferson Hotel was barely more than a long block down Massachusetts from Dupont Circle and he found Martin Fouchet waiting for him in the black and white tiled reception room. Kane thought the professor looked pinched and lean as if he had been twisted and half wrung dry but Greg pretended not to notice.

"Hi, Marty," Kane said grasping Fouchet's hand and pasting on the best smile he could manage.

"Greg, thanks for meeting me. I — well, let's get a drink and something to eat." The professor led the way to a bar that looked like a 1950s men's club, all leather chairs and dark wood and walls hung with mahogany-framed maps. A waitress brought menus and ran through the bar's cocktail specials in an almost sing-song voice. When she came to one concocted of hot apple cider and spiced rum Kane waved his finger as if signaling an auctioneer.

"Just decaf for me," Fouchet said, "otherwise I won't sleep."

From the tightness of his lips and the lines around his eyes Kane figured his friend had other reasons than Brownstein's absence for not being able to sleep but he said nothing.

"Can I bring you gentlemen any food from the bar menu?" the girl asked.

Kane took pity on Fouchet and passed up the $38 strip steak in favor of the $21 burger and fries. The professor ordered a bowl of chicken noodle soup and a green salad.

"Have you found Mr. Brownstein?" Martin asked as soon as the waitress had stepped away.

"No," Kane said but trapped by the pleading look in Fouchet's eyes added, "He's disappeared."

Fouchet paused and seemed unable to assemble Kane's words into an understandable sentence. "Do you have any leads?" he asked finally.

Do you have any hope? Kane thought he meant.

"Here you go." The waitress, "Holly" her name tag said, reappeared before Kane could answer. "One Cider Me Timbers and one decaf coffee. I'll bring your meals in a few minutes."

Kane took a long swallow and felt the hot cider and rum warm a path all the way to his stomach and spread out from there. After looking into Martin's bleak face he took a second gulp.

"Marty, he's gone."

"You mean he's run away, left the country or something?"

"I mean he's vanished."

"Washington isn't the middle of nowhere. There has to be something you can do — surveillance cameras, cell phone records, something. How long can he hide without someone noticing him? What if I offer a reward?"

"I'm sorry, Marty. I didn't make myself clear. He didn't disappear. He *was* disappeared. Someone took him and put him someplace where no one is ever likely to find him again."

"And you have no clues, nothing?" Fouchet asked.

Kane tried to stall by taking another sip and was surprised to find his glass almost empty. He waved at Holly for another round.

"It was professionally done," Greg finally answered, looking back at his friend. "Someone who knew what they were doing wanted Brownstein to disappear and that's what's happened. I have no idea how we're going to find the perpetrator leastwise locate Brownstein's body."

"Body? You think he's dead?"

Kane took a breath then accepted a new drink from Holly.

"Marty," Kane said once she had left, "professionals don't run an operation like this for the heck of it. Somebody wanted Brownstein gone without a trace and that's what's happened."

"But why?"

Kane glanced away to collect his thoughts and found his eyes settling on a stylish blonde sitting alone on the far side of the room.

Noticing his attention she gave him the briefest of smiles then looked away.

"Does he owe people money, loan sharks or something like that?" Fouchet asked, his voice almost a whine. "I could pay them if it's money they want. I just need one signature from him."

Just as Kane dragged his eyes away from the blonde and back to his friend Holly appeared with platters and bowls.

"Marty," Kane said a moment later, "I'm not supposed to discuss open cases with anyone outside my department but, confidentially, I'll give you my opinion if you want it."

"Of course I want it!" Fouchet snapped.

"Congress gave HHS a mandate to identify potentially dangerous substances and keep them out of the country. As you well know they do that by adopting regulations that ban chemicals they think may be dangerous. Getting one of their prohibitions reversed in court could take years. According to Brownstein's deputy his department was only a couple of weeks away from approving a new set of regulations covering a whole new list of prohibited substances."

Kane realized that he was babbling like a school teacher and forced himself to stop. He caught the blonde glancing at him out of the corners of her eyes.

"Anyway," Kane said, forcing his gaze back to his friend, "With Brownstein AWOL there's no one to sign off on the final draft of the new regulations. It could be weeks, probably months, before his post is officially declared vacant, a list of replacement candidates is drawn up, they're vetted, the powers that be agree on his successor, and the new Director gets up to speed and signs the revised regs, assuming that he doesn't want to overrule the staff and make some changes to the list."

Kane took a bite of his burger and washed it down with the last of his cocktail. Martin stared at him expectantly. *Do I have to draw you a picture?* Kane thought, angry for no reason that he could justify.

"My guess is that somebody wants to import something on that new list, Marty, a lot of something on that list. Making Brownstein disappear buys them at least an extra couple of months to get their material into the country."

"You're saying that he's gone and that's the end of it?" Fouchet demanded, angry, as if Kane had told him that he was giving up on Brownstein's disappearance because he was too lazy to do his job.

"I'm saying that there's no physical evidence, no forensic evidence, no video, no cell phone records, no credit card records, no eye witnesses, no body, no nothing, zero. Nothing short of a really good session with The Amazing Kreskin and a ouija board is going to get us any closer to finding Brownstein's body," Kane snapped then wanted to bite his tongue. "I'm sorry, Marty. Sometimes I get—"

"It's all right, Greg. I understand. I'm grateful that you took this on at all. I was just hoping . . . ." Fouchet slouched back in his chair and closed his eyes. "Well, I can't have my people sitting around twiddling their thumbs while we wait for this to be all sorted out. Maybe we'll be able to find another way." *There's always Mexico*, Fouchet thought but he kept his musings to himself.

Marty lowered his eyes and they sat there in silence for perhaps a minute before the professor looked up and blinked several times, as if confused about where he was and how he had gotten there. A moment later he checked his watch.

"I've got a meeting with, well, it doesn't matter. And I probably should call my team, let them know that we're not getting the ACX as planned. Maybe someone will have an idea about another way to go." Fouchet dropped a pile of bills on the table. "Tell her to keep the change," he said then squeezed Kane's shoulder. "Thanks, Greg. I know you did the best you could."

Kane's eyes followed his friend all the way to the door and then drifted over to the blonde woman who, perhaps sensing his attention, lifted her head and looked back at him. He had two choices, leave or go over and introduce himself. If the collapse of his marriage had been more recent, if he hadn't been drinking, if he hadn't felt that old tingling in his pants, he might have given her a polite nod and called a cab. Instead he stood and walked across the room.

"Hello," he said, mustering a polite smile. "My friend just left and since we're now both alone I wondered if I might join you."

The woman's jaw was a bit too square for her to qualify as a classic beauty, more like the fresh-scrubbed but subtly hot girl-next-door. If Kane were describing her in a police report he would have said that she was five-feet six, a hundred-twenty-five pounds, thirty-five years old, blonde and blue, but that's not how Kane's brain was working right then. Instead he noticed the creamy hollows of her shoulder blades and the beginning of her cleavage and he imagined how the chill night air might raise her nipples against the thin silk of her dress.

"I don't know," she said with a sly smile. "Do you live in town or are you just visiting?"

Which answer does she want? Kane wondered but found no hint in her eyes.

"I live in D.C."

"And what is it that you do here, Mr. . . . ?"

"Kane. Greg Kane. I'm an investigator with Homeland Security."

"Really? Are you carrying a gun?" she asked with a lilt in her voice.

Two guns, Kane almost said. Instead he pulled his coat aside to reveal the Beretta 92 with which the Office armed its agents.

"I feel safer already. I'm Allison Varner." She waved at the chair across from her. "Please have a seat."

Kane found himself cataloging little things about her — that the blue diamonds inside the gold-hooped earrings looked real as did the gems in the gold bracelet encircling her left wrist, both of which meant she, or her husband, or perhaps her ex-husband, had money. He also noticed some things that were absent. There were no rings on her left hand, but married people sometimes took them off. She wore no pins or badges that might signify an occupation or political affiliation, though that was more a male affectation. Half the guys in the Office wore little American flag pins on their lapels. Kane refused to do it. If being a sworn agent of the Department of Homeland Security wasn't a good enough testament to his patriotism then some stupid lapel pin wasn't going to make any difference.

Kane's eyes were drawn to the soft folds in her pale blue and gold silk dress and he imagined what her body might look like if the cloth were suddenly to become transparent.

"Am I under investigation?" Allison asked.

"What?"

"The way you're staring at me I wondered if you think I might have committed a crime."

"Sorry. It's a habit from my job. They train us to be observant."

"And what have you observed about me, Agent Kane?" A vision of her breasts and the soft curves that flowed down to her hips filled his head.

"That you're a beautiful, educated, self-assured woman," Kane said in a clumsy attempt at gallantry.

Allison laughed. "You can tell I'm educated just by looking at me?"

"Your pattern of speech, your body language." Her stare forced him to go on. "You're at ease with the sudden attention of a member of law enforcement. Poor people fear the police. Middle-class people are usually deferential, eager to please. You're amused. That puts you in the upper-middle class or higher. An upper-middle class woman who speaks well and has money, or access to money, is almost certainly well educated."

"Do go on," Allison ordered, intrigued or vaguely irritated, Kane couldn't tell which.

Good sense would have told him to shut up at that point but Allison's smiling attention and the second rum punch dissolved his restraint.

"You were married but you're not married anymore." Allison's face clouded over but Kane pressed on. "Someone as attractive as you who's never been married either has no interest in attracting a man or very much wants to attract a man. You're neither which tells me that you were in a relationship that ended between one and two years ago." Kane's self-satisfied smile fled when he caught the pain in Allison's eyes.

"Brain cancer," she said, looking down at the now ring-less fourth finger of her left hand. "A little less than two years ago. When you've been with someone through all that being alone is . . . complicated."

"I'm . . ." *Sorry? An idiot?* "I'm divorced," Kane said. "Almost a year ago. She lives in Baltimore. I was a homicide detective," he babbled, feeling as if he had lost the ability to connect his mouth to his brain. "I took the job with Homeland Security to make a new start."

Allison looked up from her naked left hand but she could find no deceit or guile in Kane's face. *Perhaps he's safe,* she thought. *Cops are supposed to be hopeless womanizers. It had been weeks since. . . .* She waved at the barman and held up two fingers.

"We're a pair aren't we?" she said with a half-sad smile.

"What do you do?" Kane asked, anxious to veer the conversation in another direction.

"I work on the Hill," she said with a flicker in her eyes that told Kane that she hoped he wouldn't ask for any details. Just then their drinks arrived and they clinked glasses, both happy for the interruption. Kane noticed the barman make a note on his iPad. *She's probably billing the drinks to her room,* he thought. Kane wanted to ask what she was doing at this hotel, alone, when she lived here in D.C. Was she meeting a man? Had he stood her up? Was she on a secret mission for the unnamed congressman or senator or agency that signed her paycheck?

Allison put down her glass and forced a smile and through some sixth sense Kane knew that any of those questions would ruin things as surely as tipping a cup of spiders into a Waldorf salad, and the snake uncoiling in his pants was screaming at him not to do anything like that.

"Do you have a room here?" he asked instead.

"Yes," she said after half a second's pause.

"I've never stayed at this hotel. I'm kind of curious about what the rooms are like. Could I take a look at yours?"

Allison held his gaze for a long heartbeat. "Sure," she said then took as big a swallow from her glass as decorum would allow. Kane followed her, saying nothing, afraid that a single word might frighten her off, as if she were a rare bird suddenly landed on a branch just within his reach.

She slipped the key-card into the lock and he followed her inside. The instant he clicked the door closed behind them she turned to face him and no words were needed. After a quick, crushing embrace he stepped back and pulled her skirt up over her hips. When he yanked her panties down she bent her knees inward and then lifted one foot so that he could set them free. When he stood she twisted around offering him the zipper at the back of her dress. Then it was her turn to undress him and a few seconds later they tumbled onto the bed. After that it was all heat and sweat and noises without thought. When it was over she nestled against his shoulder, not sleeping, not fully awake. He caressed her nipples while she idly ran her fingers across his chest. He didn't speak, afraid that any words would break the spell.

His encounters since his divorce had ranged from unsatisfying to uncomfortable but tonight he felt like a man standing at the edge of a desert and scenting the distant rush of water on the wind. Once was not enough. Twenty minutes later ability caught up with desire and he slid his hands down her body and teased her thighs wide apart. This time he took her more slowly but more powerfully and it was after midnight before the fire in Kane's blood burned down leaving pleasantly warm embers behind. Spent, he collapsed against the headboard and encircled her shoulder, drawing her close.

"I've got a meeting in the morning," she said a minute later, apropos of nothing.

Kane turned toward her but in the darkness her face was a mask. He could barely make out the shadowed dips and planes of her features in the glow from the digital clock. He paused for a second and, finally understanding her meaning, he felt the warmth in his blood begin to go cold.

"I guess you need to get some sleep," he replied in a flat tone that made it clear that he knew her morning meeting was a lie.

"It's going to be a long day," Allison said as she pulled free from his arm and wiggled toward the edge of the bed.

"Yeah, me too." Kane rolled off the other side and went hunting for his pants. "Can I call you sometime?" he asked as he buttoned his shirt.

"Of course," Allison answered in a voice that didn't promise that she would answer. "Do you have a pen?"

Kane flipped the switch on the bathroom wall and in the spill of light through the half-open door he scratched out her number on the hotel pad. The question: *What the hell just happened?* screamed through his head.

"So, I'll call you," Greg said after he slipped on his coat.

"Or I'll call you."

"That would be good." Kane handed her his card embossed with the Homeland Security seal and his office phone number printed on the bottom. She dropped it on the night table next to the clock and he wondered if tomorrow morning it would end up in her purse or in pieces in the wastebasket.

Kane was halfway out the door when he stopped and turned back toward the bed. Allison was lying flat on her back, the sheet pulled up to her chin, her eyes gazing blindly at the shadowed ceiling.

"Did I do something wrong?"

"What?" She said, not trying to pretend that she didn't understand.

"You're treating me like a distant relative who's overstayed his welcome. What did I do?"

"My husband was the love of my life," Allison said. Kane had no idea what that meant so he just stood there and waited. "I'm not ready for a serious relationship."

"Neither am I."

"I'm not so sure that's true and I can't go through something like that again."

"I'm not asking you to go through anything."

Two seconds passed and she slowly twisted to face him.

"This could never be more than fun and games," she said as if cautioning a child against approaching a strange dog.

"I spend most of my life chasing criminals. I wouldn't have the time for anything serious even if I wanted it."

"If we saw each other again it wouldn't be exclusive."

"There would be other women in my life too. Jesus we just had sex. I didn't ask you to marry me."

"Just so long as you understand that there will be other men. Are you sure you're good with that?"

"Better than good."

"And no questions. No 'Where were you?' 'What's his name?' Nothing. The first time you start wanting something more than . . . this, that's it."

"Fine."

"Because there is no more. They'll never be any more."

"Just fun and games, got it," Kane snapped.

"All right, you call me and we'll see how it goes."

"Just so I'm clear, that means we're going to fuck again, right?"

"Yes, we're going to fuck again, and that's all we're ever going to do."

"Sounds perfect to me," Kane snapped then double-checked that he had his ID and his gun and then resisted the urge to slam the door behind him.

CHAPTER FIFTEEN

Grant Eustace knew that "smart" came in many flavors. There was "book smart" and "street smart", "Apple genius" and "common sense." Eustace had no illusions about his own place in that hierarchy. He knew that he was never going to be on Kane's level, not in a million years and that the word "clever" would never appear on his evaluation forms, but he did have one talent that was as valuable to a cop as diamonds and gold — cunning. As if he possessed some kind of crook-radar, Eustace could spot a wrong guy, a predator trying to blend in amidst the sheep, from thirty feet away. Half an hour ago his alarm had started going PING-PING-PING.

There was nothing overtly wrong about the target. His clothes were right — jeans, black sneakers, a worn, blue-wool jacket buttoned up to the top — but there was something about his body language, too focused, too determined, that sent a tingle up Eustace's spine.

It had started out as a simple reconnaissance mission intended only to familiarize himself with Mr. Justice Hopper's daughter, to get a feel for her in case Kane's theory about getting to the judge through his family might be right. According to a friend at the IRS Kathryn Hopper had had a varied career — cocktail waitress, Amway salesperson, telemarketer, receptionist, bartender and now she was the owner-operator of something called "Personal Essentials DC."

Eustace made a Google search and found that "Personal Essentials" was a franchise operation that hosted the equivalent of a migratory Tupperware party for cosmetics in bars and taverns instead of ranch-style living rooms. The parent company furnished Kathryn with a catalog of wholesale lipstick, nail polish, perfume, makeup, breath mints and whatever else a woman who spent four hours in a bar might have a craving for. She sold the stuff out of a suitcase, bar-to-bar, after paying a cut to the manager for allowing her to hang around his establishment. Eustace suspected that now and then her inventory probably also included a few joints, some special nose powder and a hit or two of meth. He figured that she was keeping the existence of her special merchandise secret from her father who was probably thrilled that she was at last earning enough money to be able to pay her own rent.

I bet he wonders if she's really his kid, Grant mused. *Maybe he thinks the wife might have slipped out the back door one afternoon while he was sending some punk to the slam but now that he's one of the Supremes he's too afraid of the answer to grab a sample of her DNA.* Not that Eustace was disappointed in Hopper. Human weakness was, after all, his bread and butter.

He found the girl by marking her car as "Identify But Do Not Stop" and waiting to see if some patrol unit with a plate reader passed her in traffic. It took a while but around 4:30 the system sent an email to his phone that her Civic had been spotted at a GPS location that corresponded with the address of a bar on Florida Avenue. It was not the sort of place you would expect to find the daughter of a Supreme Court Justice.

Eustace parked across the street and then, more out of habit than anything else, walked the neighborhood just to see if anything or anyone rang any bells. He spotted a junkie floating around, looking for something to steal, and a kid who made him for a cop from twenty feet away and quickly ran inside. Probably a lookout for a drug dealer in one of the apartments Eustace decided. And then there was the guy who set off his alarm — Caucasian, mid to late thirties, five-eleven, one-eighty, brown hair and heartless blue eyes. Eustace had seen eyes like that many times before, on punks and cons, bent correctional officers, on two-bit killers and pimps who would sell their own mothers for twenty dollars and a stolen watch.

The guy wasn't doing anything special, just wandering down the street and checking out the shop windows along the way. Eustace committed his face to memory and retreated to something called "Bean Town" where he took a seat by the window and ordered a coffee, black. Twenty minutes later he spotted Kathryn Hopper coming out of the Wilmington Tavern. She matched the stats from her DMV file, about five feet nine, thin, with long brown hair framing a long white face. She dumped a small suitcase onto her Civic's passenger seat and then got in on the other side. Eustace slurped the last of his coffee and jogged back to the department Malibu that he had parked three cars down. He followed Kathryn a few blocks southwest toward the Amtrak Station where she parked and then lugged her suitcase into The Caledonia Grill. "Best Crab Cakes In Town" a faded sign next to the door promised. Eustace had his doubts about that but he was getting hungry and he figured she might be in there for a while, plus it wasn't getting any warmer now that the sun had gone down.

Two hours later Hopper began to pack up her case and Eustace preceded her into the night air that now had fallen to under forty degrees. A flicker of motion caught his eye when she trudged back to her Civic. The guy was wearing a knit cap now and a pair of black gloves but it was the same man all right. Hopper started her engine and a cloud of white vapor spewed from the pipe. Eustace pulled out ahead of her and drove past the doorway where Mr. Blue Wool Coat had been huddled. Eustace wasn't surprised to see that the watcher was gone. If he was following the Hopper woman the guy would need to be back in his car, ready to pick her up at the end of the block. Eustace made a right at the corner, doused his lights and pulled into a bus stop. A moment later Hopper's Civic passed through the intersection still trailing a cloud of vapor that signaled a pin-hole leak in her head gasket.

Hopper had barely cleared the far corner when a pair of headlight popped up and a black Ford Fusion turned left on 3rd Street fifty feet behind her. Eustace made a U-turn, flicked off his lights, turned right on 3rd and pulled briefly to the curb before turning them back on. He marked the shape and height of the Fusion's taillights and stayed as far back as he could, occasionally pulling into a gas station or parking lot, then starting out again a few seconds later so as to appear to be a different vehicle entering the street.

Ten minutes later Hopper dragged her case into another bar but this time Eustace concentrated on the Ford, passing it when it pulled into an abandoned burger joint then circling the block and coasting without headlights into a loading zone fifty feet behind and across the street from where the Fusion sat beneath a weathered sign that read: "Blizzard Shakes!"

It was too dark to read the Ford's plate so after giving the driver ten minutes to relax Eustace disconnected the Malibu's dome light and slipped into the shadows. He headed away from the Ford until it was out of sight then he crossed the street and crept up the sidewalk on the other side. When he neared the edge of the abandoned burger joint he got down in a crouch and slipped from shadow to shadow until he got close enough to read the plate. *Lucky for me there's a full moon*, he thought and smiled as he memorized the digits. He watched the car for another half minute but he couldn't tell if anyone was inside. Slowly, he retraced his route up the deserted street back to the Malibu. He had parked it facing against the flow of traffic with the driver's door closest to the curb so that the body of the car masked his exit and re-entry.

Bent over he hurried past an alley next to a closed auto-parts store and duck-walked into the shelter of the car. Just as he was reaching for the door Eustace heard a faint squeak and then a puff of air brushed his cheek. As he turned toward the sound his life collapsed like a popped balloon when an ice pick slammed through his ear and into his brain.

The man who now called himself "Donald" muscled Eustace's limp body into the Chevy's back seat and quickly rifled through his pockets. "Homeland Security" — *Fuck*! he hissed when he saw Eustace's creds. *Now what?*

If he left the body here they might connect it to Hopper's daughter. If he drove it across town then he'd need some way to get back to his car without leaving any witnesses like cabbies or bus drivers and their associated surveillance cameras. As a compromise he dumped the Malibu as close as he could to the Capital Metro South station then walked the mile or so back to his Fusion.

He took Eustace's phone, watch, wallet and ring with him to make it look as much like a robbery as possible. The real questions were: How much did Eustace know about him and who had he told? Hopefully, the agent's phone with its call log, texts and emails would tell him if HS was running a formal operation on the Hopper woman or if Eustace had just been doing a routine check and something had spooked him. That would make sense since formal stakeouts were always handled by two-man teams and Eustace was clearly operating alone.

Well, Donald thought, *I've got two more weeks to run the operation if I need them. Let's just take this one step at a time.*

While Donald was planning his next move, back in the Metro Station lot, unnoticed, Grant Eustace was slowly and quietly cooling down to ambient temperature.

CHAPTER SIXTEEN

Kane showed up at work the next morning in an oddly disassociated state — vaguely tired, slightly hung-over, and guardedly excited. It didn't last. As he had expected Danny wasn't able to retrieve anything useful from the surveillance cameras around the bus-station parking lot where Brownstein's Volvo had been found. All they got was a grainy image of a broad-chested male in a hoodie and sunglasses and probably latex gloves.

Sandra Cray had given them a list of the forty-two substances that were on the new exclusion roster that her boss had been scheduled to sign two weeks from now. Most of them were beyond Kane's ability to even pronounce and he certainly had no clue which, if any, of them might be the motive for Brownstein's disappearance. And then there was the blurry image from the camera across the street from Brownstein's building of a man who might or might not be Mearle Farber, a mystery that teased Kane like a tongue worrying a loose tooth.

If it was Farber then he must have been paid to help Ryan Munroe escape. If so, then maybe Farber's old phone records and credit card receipts would give them some kind of a hint on where to go next. Kane could try to subpoena them and hope that Immerson didn't find out and have him fired for illegally working the Munroe case or he could call any one of the three agencies, City, State and Federal, who, theoretically, had jurisdiction over the presumed murder of two law enforcement officers and the escape of a man charged with both state and federal crimes. The question was, which of the multiple investigators was likely to give him the least amount of shit?

Kane had just brought up his address book when Immerson materialized in front of his desk. Usually these appearances were triggered by some real or imagined misbehavior on Kane's part but he could think of no one he had recently sufficiently insulted to trigger his boss's ire. Then he took a good look at Immerson's face and realized that they were in a whole different ballpark here. Worry and fear radiated off Immerson like heat from a stove. Kane shelved the smart-ass remark that was always simmering just below the surface and stood up.

"What's happened?" Greg asked.

"In my office." Kane followed him, drawing nervous stares from every agent they passed. Everybody knew something was up but, clearly, nobody knew what. Kane closed the door behind him without being told then stood in front of Immerson's desk, his hands clasped behind his back in something akin to "parade rest."

"Sit down." Uneasily, Kane sat.

"What was Eustace doing yesterday afternoon?"

Oh, crap, what jackpot has Grant gotten himself into now?

"I don't know," Kane said in as innocent a tone as he could manage. "He was gone when Rosewood and I got back around four." Eustace was, well, useless, but you still covered for your partner.

"Stop fucking around with me! What the hell was Eustace doing, God damn it!"

If Eustace had screwed up, punched out a citizen or gotten caught drinking on the job or whatever, Immerson would have been pissed but not enraged, not like this. He looked like he was ready to shoot somebody. Hell, Eustace could have been caught robbing a bank and Immerson wouldn't have been this upset. Kane studied his boss' face and now saw more than anger. There was sadness there as well. It wasn't something Eustace had done. It was worse than that, much worse. It was something that had been done to him.

"He's gone missing?" Greg asked. Immerson shook his head.

"No. Now, answer my question!"

Shit!

"He was helping us look for Brownstein's Volvo, checking the train and Metro parking lots. I called him when we found the car and told him that he could stop and go get something to eat. He's been kind of obsessed with the threats against Justice Hopper and he asked me how I'd go after Hopper if I wanted to kill him."

"And you told him that it was none of our business? No, where would the fun be in that? You decided that it would be a good joke to get him all wound up, didn't you?"

"No! . . . I mean I wasn't trying to yank his chain. We had too much work on our own case to have him screwing around with something that the Secret Service was never going to let us have a piece of anyway."

"What did you tell him, Kane?"

Greg took a breath. "He wouldn't let it go. He just kept grinding on it so I gave in and told him that if I'd wanted to get to someone like Hopper I do it through his family."

"Brilliant! Just fucking brilliant! And what did Eustace say to that?"

"He said that it sounded like a good idea and that he was going to check out the Justice's daughter. I tried to tell him not to be an idiot but he had already hung up. . . . How bad is it?"

Immerson paused and a look of profound sadness transformed his face.

"Homeland Security Agent Grant Eustace's body was found at seven-twelve this morning in the back seat of a department vehicle in a parking lot near the main Amtrak station," he said in a strained voice. "The cause of death appears to be a sharp object, probably an ice pick, being shoved into his brain."

It took Kane a moment to process Immerson's words and when he did he was almost drowned by a wave of guilt. Eustace was a man with a limited horizon and pedestrian goals, flawed and, if not the prisoner, at least the confidant of base desires, but beyond all that he was a cop and Kane's partner. When it came time to choose up sides, Grant Eustace had chosen to stand with the men and women who had sworn to protect the sheep and fight the wolves. A profound ache swelled in Kane's gut.

First Ralph Amoroso then his nephew and now Grant Eustace — the wolves were tearing his guys apart and it was all too much to bear. Almost physically sick Greg slumped down in Immerson's thinly-padded chair.

"Son of a bitch," Kane muttered, his shoulders hunched forward, his eyes closed.

"Did Eustace say anything else about what he was going to do yesterday?"

Kane opened his eyes. "No."

"Was he working on anything else?"

"No."

"Did he have a girlfriend he might have gone to visit? A bar he liked to hang out at? Is there anything you know about his life that might give us a clue what he was doing yesterday afternoon or evening?"

"No. What was the TOD?"

"Based on liver temp and lividity he was killed sometime between eight and eleven last night."

Kane's eyes went blank for a moment. "It wasn't anything in his personal life," he said.

"Why not?"

"Because Eustace was street smart. No run-of-the-mill punk was ever going to get close enough to shove an ice pick into his head. Whoever did this was a pro. Your average mutt, if he decides to kill a cop, he uses a gun. He doesn't think about how loud it is, who's going to hear it, how hard it is to hit a fatal spot, whether the target is wearing a vest, none of that. He just pulls it and starts banging away like some moron in the movies. And if he doesn't use a gun it's some punk-ass switchblade. Who carries an ice pick?" Kane paused a second then stared at Immerson. "Were there any defensive wounds?"

The boss shook his head. "None. And there was no blood in the car so he was killed someplace else and put into the backseat."

"He was killed near the car because he was too heavy for the doer to carry him more than a few feet. That kind of wound doesn't bleed much but it does bleed a little and there would be cast-off when he pulled the pick out. So, Eustace was parked someplace. It was dark. He was walking back to his car or getting into the car when somebody blind-sided him, killed him, and shoved his body into the back seat. That spells professional all the way — military, special forces, army ranger, something like that." *Dirty cop*, Kane thought, picturing Mearle Farber in his head.

"That doesn't get us any closer to finding out who did this," Immerson complained.

"Yes, it does, or at least we know where to start."

"How do you figure?"

"Grant wasn't visiting a girlfriend or getting drunk. He was working." Greg studied his boss' face but Immerson seemed confused. *Jesus, am I the only person around here who can add two plus two and get four?* "Hopper's daughter, he was following Hopper's daughter and he saw something or someone he wasn't supposed to and they killed him for it."

"If I tell the Secret Service that story they'll scream bloody murder and then order us to stay the hell away from Mr. Justice Hopper's family."

"So don't tell them," Kane said, standing.

"Where are you going?"

"Out to find out everything I can about Kathryn Hopper because one way or another something about her got Eustace killed."

"You can't go into the field without a partner." Kane looked at Immerson as if he had discovered a bug on his sandwich. "You've pissed off too many people too many times for me to let you run around out there alone. You've brought this on yourself Kane. I'll go through the transfer requests and get somebody in here to take Eustace's place in a day or two."

"Don't bother."

"Is that your way of quitting?"

"I've got work to do. I'll partner with Rosewood."

"Rosewood's got other duties."

"They can wait. He works hard and knows how to run the computers.

"He's not a field agent."

"He'll do until one comes along. If you don't like it, fire me."

Kane didn't bother closing the door behind him. Immerson considered his options but after a minute or so, no matter how he figured it, he realized that he didn't have any. He pulled Rosewood's file and confirmed that the kid had satisfied the firearms qualification requirements and then he started the paperwork to requisition Danny a gun.

CHAPTER SEVENTEEN

Just before lunch Ryan Munroe received an innocuous text message that contained the number "four." It could have been any number between one and five, each one of which corresponded to a different prearranged set of Metro stations, times, tracks, trains, and car numbers. The number four translated to the Potomac Avenue Station, the eastbound platform, 2:10 in the afternoon, the third car from the front. He had had to commit all of the details to memory. It wouldn't do to have the Gestapo search his place and find the list.

In the movies the spies met in public places and exchanged information while wandering around some park. That was a sloppy way to do it. The Feds could focus a directional mike on you from a hundred yards away and record every word. Cars were just as bad. They could be bugged and the cops could record a conversation by bouncing a laser off the windows. Besides that, in a park you were exposed and your escape routes were limited. If you were in the Metro once you hit a station you could disappear into the crowds or jump on another train. And unlike your car, they couldn't bug the train in advance.

There were hundreds, probably thousands of train cars in the Metro system and even if they could wire them all, given the ambient noise and the fact that Munroe's contact always used a different seat, they wouldn't be able to get anything useful. Inside a station you were almost invisible. Thousands of people poured in and out of them every hour. Once you were on a train you could turn your coat inside out, stick your green baseball cap in your pocket and put on a black knit hat and at the next stop emerge invisible, just another shape in the herd. On balance Munroe appreciated the system his contact had set up. When you were at war with the government you had to be careful. Not that it mattered, personally, to Munroe. The cops didn't need to record his conversations. He was already a wanted man and if they caught him he was dead meat. But that was not the case for his employer.

Munroe spotted his man at the rear of the car, two seats up from the door. The contact always looked the same, mustache, neat beard, dark hair under a black baseball cap, long-sleeved shirt and jeans, black athletic shoes. Because of the cold today he wore a black-nylon winter coat unzipped halfway to his waist. Munroe made a quick scan of the car but nobody seemed to be paying any attention to either himself or his contact.

"Give me an update," the man said, looking straight ahead, his lips barely moving.

"The contractor finished the job."

"I'm instructed to ask for the details."

"I leave operational matters to the man doing the work. All I care about is that it gets done on time."

"That's not good enough in this case. We have to be sure that we'll get the time we need. There are a lot of moving parts."

"The job is done. There's no link to my contractor. They're not going to find the subject, ever. That's all there is to it."

The contact frowned then looked toward the door.

"All right. I'll be in touch."

"Wait a minute," Munroe said, half ready to grab the man's arm. "I need to know when we'll get the material. I've got my own moving parts to line up before I can begin distribution."

"I'll give you two weeks' notice. That should be enough," the contact whispered with an expression that seemed to add: *for a low-life drug dealer like you.*

"It's not. I have people who're sitting on their hands waiting for product and not getting paid. I've shut down my business to get the network ready for this. I need to know when we're going to have something to sell. My guys can't wait forever."

The train pulled to a halt but the contact made no move to leave.

"You know how important this project is," he said.

Hell yes, Munroe thought. *Of course I know.* The big money was, as always, in drugs. People would buy drugs before they would buy milk for their kids. Hell, junkies would rather shoot up or coke up than eat, sleep or fuck. The big challenge was moving the cash.

Before the cops had grabbed him Munroe had mostly solved that problem by buying up bodegas and mini-marts, a few check cashing joints and, just before he was busted, a payday loan company. If a mini-mart took in $500 in cash you deposited $2,000 in the bank. Selling cigarettes and beer was a cash business. Short of comparing your inventory purchases against your sales tapes how were they going to prove anything? And Munroe even had a fix for that. He overbought cigs and beer from the wholesalers and ran the fake sales through his registers. Then he sold the extra inventory off the back of a truck. He wrote off the tax on the phantom sales as a laundering fee. Of course, he needed a place to store the additional inventory.

That's when he bought the farm and stocked the barn with steel shelves and a couple of forklifts. With more money he got more merchandise and with more merchandise he got more money. It only made sense to branch out — prescription drugs, both real and fake, more weapons, kiddie porn, whatever people wanted that the government wouldn't let them have.

He moved the money through the system as quickly as possible — cash to local banks, wire transfers from there to a bank in the Cayman Islands, hand-carried cashier's checks from the receiving bank to other Cayman banks — but the cash was like an incoming tide that never stopped.

When the cops grabbed him he still had ten million in currency buried in a hole he had dug in the wilderness of the Patuxent River State Park. As he was shoveling the dirt back in he couldn't help but think about Black Beard the Pirate and all the loot he was supposed to have buried on nameless Caribbean islands. Munroe wondered if he were hit by a bus or struck by lightning might someone a hundred years from now stumble over his stash of moldering hundred dollar bills. *That would be a hell of a thing,* he thought and smiled.

After he went on the run he used a front man to hire a lawyer who scoured the court records. His farm and his bodegas and the payday loan service and all his domestic bank accounts had been seized under the RICO statutes. They were all gone. He had made sure that the Cayman money had disappeared into a tangle of anonymous accounts. It was still there, waiting for him, but he was afraid to touch it. The way the government worked these days he figured that the NSA was tracking every wire transfer into U.S. banks out of the Caribbean, the Jersey Islands, Monaco, and the like. The instant he wired any of his money to a bank in the USA the G was going to know about it. Maybe the NSA would tell the FBI and maybe they wouldn't, but he wasn't going to take that chance any more than he was going to start digging up his buried stash.

For now, he was leaving his money right where it was. Some day maybe he'd use a false passport to disappear into Costa Rica or Crete or the South of France and then he'd make an annual trip to George Town and pick up a cashier's check. From there he could take a hop to Antwerp, Brussels or London and deposit it in a corresponding European bank and from there wire it someplace more easily accessible. By then maybe bitcoins would have the rough edges worn off and would be an even better alternative but for now Munroe thought the cyber currency was too risky.

Before they grabbed him he had stashed a million in cash in safe-deposit boxes under fake identities. Half of that had gone to Farber. His freedom was worth it. The money wasn't going to do him any good in jail. Now he was living on the fees his contact paid him, keeping the rest of his cash handy in case things turned sour and he needed to make another run for it. For now that was fine. He was too young to just lie on a beach all day. He needed something to do and freeing the country from the yoke of laws and rules, making it a place where the cream could rise to the top and the dregs would sink into the muck and people could do whatever they were strong enough to get away with was important work.

"We'll have product in quantity in twelve to sixteen weeks," the contact finally answered.

"Three months? What the hell am I supposed to do in the meantime?"

"My employer will continue to make payments on the same schedule until the first shipment is ready. Tell your man to keep a low profile. If we have new work for him we'll contact you in the usual way."

The train began to slow. The contact stood and without a backward glance edged toward the door.

CHAPTER EIGHTEEN

"Of course, the s-Methyl-6 groups could, theoretically, be attached to any one of, well, dozens of common, relatively common, industrial chemicals to form all sorts of nasty compounds." The chemist gave Kane a quick nervous smile. *Smoker*, Kane thought, noticing the pale yellow streaks in the valleys between his teeth where the drugstore whitening strips couldn't reach. There was almost no odor on his clothes and no nicotine stains on his fingers so he probably wore gloves. *Secret smoker. Probably less than five or six cigs a day or the gloves would be too much of a pain to put on every time.* When they first met Kane had noticed a faint industrial peppermint smell infecting the chemist's breath. A heavy mouthwash user, he probably kept a bottle in his desk and one in his car, no, probably Binaca in the glove box. The gold band on his skeletal hand was moderately well-worn so he had been married maybe ten or twelve years. *He doesn't want the wife to know he smokes.*

"Now, next on the list is dihydrophenyl—"

"Uhh, hold up a second, Dr. Lammerman." Kane held up his hand like a traffic cop. "Let's see if we can shortcut this process. Instead of going through every substance covered by the proposed new regulations can we just zero in on the most dangerous ones?"

"Well, they're all dangerous. If they weren't they wouldn't be on the list, would they?"

"Certainly some have a higher potential for harm than others."

"That depends on what you mean by 'harm.' Is your, ummm, suspect, looking for materials that have the highest potential for effecting mass casualties, creating abusive drugs, easy weaponization, making incapacitating agents . . . ?" Lammerman flashed Kane another of his nervous smiles.

"We don't have a suspect. We were hoping that we could figure out what chemical the individual wanted access to and then use that information to work backward to a pool of suspects."

"Oh," Lammerman said, in the tone someone might use after being told that his disease was incurable. "I'm afraid I can't help you then. Every substance on the proposed list is, by definition, dangerous. They all have the potential to create vast harm, which is exactly why they survived the comment process and ended up on the final list in the first place."

"Comment process? How does that work?"

"We're supposed to call it the 'comment process' but I think of it more as the objection process or perhaps the appeal process." Lammerman noticed Kane's tightly clenched hands and hurried on. "We post an initial list for public comment. Anyone can object to the inclusion of any item. We review the objections and then we certify the final list. When it's approved by Staff it goes to the Director. He either approves it or sends it back to Staff for further revisions. Director Brownstein had informally approved this list and was scheduled to sign the final draft when, you know, he disappeared. That's why I say that everything on the list deserves to be on the list."

"There must be some way to narrow it down."

Lammerman held up his hands in defeat. "There's no way I can filter the list without knowing what the . . . *person* is looking for. Of course . . . ." Lammerman cocked his head to one side. "Well, I could sort the list for you if that would help."

"Filter? Sort? What's the difference?" Kane asked, thinking, *I'm a cop not a scientist, moron!*

"Filtering," Lammerman began as if conducting a freshman lecture, "is the process of using some criteria, in this case degree of dangerousness, to separate out a subset of data that matches the desired criteria. Sorting is the process of reordering the data to group items by shared attributes." The chemist looked hopefully at Kane for some sign of understanding then leaned away from Greg's angry scowl.

"In English!" Kane snapped.

"Ahhhh, I could group the items based on the kinds of threats they pose."

Why didn't you say that in the first place? Kane wanted to scream.

"Which are?" he demanded.

Lammerman paused for a moment then picked up a marker and turned to the whiteboard behind his desk.

"(1) Waterborne mass casualties," he wrote. "Vector: Rivers, Municipal Water Supplies.

"(2) Airborne mass casualties. Vector: aerosol spray or fine powder in enclosed spaces — buses, trains, airplanes, sports stadiums, theaters and the like.

"(3) Contact contamination/illness. Vector: doorknobs, handrails, envelopes, product packaging."

"(4) Ingestion contamination/illness. Vector: food items — restaurants, food carts, supermarkets, catering companies.

"(5) —"

"Hang on," Kane called out. Lammerman paused with the Sharpie in mid-stroke and turned around.

"Yes, Agent Kane?"

"How many categories are we talking about here?"

"Oh, I don't know. Ten? Twelve?"

"And all the items on this list can be divided into any of a dozen different threat categories?"

"Yes, but not exactly."

"What does that mean?"

"Well, it's not that digital a result."

"What the hell does that mean!" Kane half-shouted while thinking *Kill Me Now!*

"An item isn't necessarily in just one category. It could be in two or three or even four." Reading Kane's confusion Lammerman rushed on. "Processed in one way a substance might be weaponized for distribution in water. Treated with a different process it might be incorporated in a powder that could be distributed as a semi-aerosol. There's a cross over you see. . . . Should I continue?"

Kane stared blankly at the board and tried to think. "Fine. Send me the final *sorted* list as an email," he said at last.

"Is there any particular order in which you'd like the threats grouped?"

"Surprise me," Kane snapped and turned away.

In the car with the windows rolled up and the radio on Kane found himself screaming, "Stupid, fucking, idiots! Morons! The whole fucking world is filled with morons!" and pounding his fist on the steering wheel. From the corner of his eye he noticed the driver in the next lane staring at him. Kane gave him the finger and hit the gas leaving the guy stuck at the light while Kane jumped the yellow.

Fuck! Jason's killer, that asshole Farber, was walking around out there someplace and Kane had no idea where. Brownstein had disappeared like some kid on a milk carton. Eustace was dead and the fucking Secret Service wouldn't let him within a hundred miles of Hopper's daughter. What else could go wrong? And then he thought about Allison Varner.

He had wanted to call her, had planned on calling her, had almost called her but . . . . *Shit, I don't need any more frustrations in my life*, he told himself, knowing that it was a lie. It had been a week. If he didn't call her soon . . . . Halfway back to the office he pulled into a Burger King lot and took out his cell.

"Hello."

"Allison, it's Greg Kane. Do you have any plans for dinner tonight?"

"As a matter of fact, I do." Kane waited. Nothing. *What did she expect him to say now — 'How about tomorrow night? How about the next night? Is there any time in the next month when you can squeeze me into your fucking schedule?' Screw that!*

"Sorry to hear it," he said in a tone that dropped about ten degrees. A heartbeat went by then another, then another. *Ball's in your court, sweetheart,* he thought.

Allison glanced around her office. Most of the staff were pounding their keyboards or on the phone. A couple of the interns were laughing, exchanging glances that had nothing to do with work, all of them as oblivious to her as if she were a desk or a chair.

"Nine o'clock," she said in a voice that caught in her throat.

"What?"

"Same place as last time. Nine o'clock," she said then hung up before she could change her mind.

"Son of a bitch!" Kane muttered and smiled. For a moment at least Lammerman and Jason and Eustace and Brownstein were all forgotten.

*   *   *

All the way back to the office something Lammerman had said nagged at Kane. *What was it? What was it?* For a moment he thought he had it and then it slipped away. As he was pulling into the employee lot he finally realized what was bothering him. The proposed regulations had been posted for public comment. Would the person behind Brownstein's disappearance have tried to get whatever substance they were interested in removed from the list?

Kane didn't think that a terrorist would draw attention to himself by asking HHS not to ban the chemical he planned to use in an attack but it wouldn't hurt to review the list of persons who had posted comments. And, Kane realized, there was another reason for reviewing the public comments — they might point to somebody who could give him a better understanding of the relative risks of the items on the list. God knew they couldn't be less helpful than Dr. Lammerman. That was something Danny could handle. As for Kane, he had a date to get ready for.

CHAPTER NINETEEN

Kane thought she might be waiting for him in her room but a call on the house phone produced only a series of unanswered rings. He located her, as before, in the bar. The fact that she was sitting in the same chair at the same table he found disquieting on some primal level.

"Hi, Allison," he said, hoping that his smile didn't look as uneasy as it felt.

"Hi, Greg. Have a seat." The glass at her elbow contained something cloudy and vaguely red and her face held the expression of a woman who had resigned herself to an uncertain fate. She finished her drink while he was pulling out his chair and waved to the cocktail waitress for a refill.

"Another of these," she told the girl.

"What can I get for you sir?"

"Screwdriver."

The girl tapped the order into her iPad and disappeared.

Allison stared at Kane like a gambler handicapping a horse for the next race. *Or a breeder evaluating a stud*, Kane thought. Tonight she wore a crisp, pale yellow dress, a gold bracelet and matching earrings. He couldn't see her shoes but he bet that they matched the rest of her outfit.

"Is something wrong?" Kane asked in response to her blank stare.

"No. Is something wrong with you?"

"Yeah." Kane barked a bitter laugh. "Lots of things, but that's life, right?"

If Allison had planned to answer her reply was smothered by the girl's arrival with their order.

"Is there anything else I can get for you?" She asked only because she was required to.

Allison shook her head and the waitress vanished.

"You look lovely," Kane said, more to fill the awkward silence than because of any real interest in flattery. Allison stared at him a moment longer and seemed to come to a decision about a question he had not asked.

"You're looking very dashing yourself," she said and gave him a somewhat reluctant smile. "Have you caught any bad guys lately?"

"Unfortunately, it's been the other way around." Kane frowned and downed half his drink.

"What happened?"

Kane knew he wasn't supposed to discuss work with civilians leastwise say anything depressing to a woman he was hoping to have sex with but almost against his will his frustration all came boiling out.

"My partner was murdered," he told her and took another gulp.

"That's awful. Do you have any leads?"

"I'm not allowed to know. Verboten. Don't go there!" He felt his control slipping away and waved the empty glass at the guy behind the bar.

"Because he was your friend? They're afraid that you're too emotionally involved?"

"With Grant Eustace? That would be the day! No, I was banned from the case because the Secret Service took it over and froze me out."

"I don't understand. Wasn't your partner with Homeland Security? Why would the Secret Service be involved?"

"Because my moron partner was off the reservation checking out a possible threat to Mr. Justice Hopper when he got himself killed and the Secret Service called 'dibs' . . . . Thanks." Kane handed the girl a bill and picked up his new drink.

"I . . . I don't know what to say," Allison replied once the waitress had left.

"Nothing to say." Kane looked at the drink then put it down without taking a sip. "I'd better slow down. You didn't come here to spend the evening with a complaining drunk. Sorry." Kane pushed the glass away. "So, how's your week been?"

How's my week been? Allison thought. *Compared to having your partner murdered? Boring? Drab? Empty? Numb?*

"Pretty ordinary, I suppose."

"What do you do?"

"Nothing very exciting," Allison said in an offhand tone and briefly glanced away.

"Come on. I told you about my job. Fair is fair."

She thought about dodging his question again, then gave in.

"I work for Senator Denning. . . . I'm his chief of staff," she added finally in response to Kane's stare.

"You're the chief of staff for a United States Senator? That doesn't sound like an ordinary sort of job to me."

"You'd be surprised. It's mostly just paper pushing."

"That sounds more like what I do." Kane laughed.

"I'm sure your job is much more interesting. What else are you working on?" Kane's eyes seemed to lose focus. "Nothing secret, just in general?" Allison asked to fill the silence.

Kane's thoughts seemed to return from wherever they had fled.

"Another case that's going nowhere."

"What can you tell me about it?" she asked and Kane found himself looking at a different woman from the one who had been sitting across from him only a few minutes before. Her expression of vague insecurity and cautious distrust had melted away and Kane felt himself responding to this attractive woman who now seemed sincerely, amazingly, interested in him. His blood began to quicken in his veins.

"It started out as a disappearance," he began, "but now I'm convinced it was a murder."

"Murder?" Her eyes seemed to glitter and she leaned forward in interest. "Who was the victim?"

"A mid-level bureaucrat responsible for keeping drugs and weapons of mass destruction out of the country."

"Oh, my God. Do you think he was killed by terrorists? Were they trying to pressure him to let them bring something in?"

"I don't know. I should but I don't."

"Do you have any suspects?"

"I can't get into any details. We have some leads that we're pursuing. That's all I can say, more than I should have said actually. Besides," Kane reached across the table and took Allison's hand. "I don't want to talk about murders and terrorists or any of that stuff. I came here to be with you. You are beautiful. You know I meant that, right?" Kane rubbed his fingertips across the back of her hand.

Until that moment Allison had been telling herself that she was just going to meet Kane and see how it went, that if he started getting clingy or needy or controlling or possessive or demanding or, or, or, then she was going to tell him, what? That he was the wrong man? That she wasn't ready for that? That she just couldn't be with someone like him? Maybe she was just going to tell him 'No.' But that was all a lie. From the instant that she had taken his call, deep inside she had known where this was going to end. Wordlessly, she stood and led him to the elevators and up to her room.

Tonight they took their time, more a growing heat than a flash fire. Once their clothes were off she retrieved a tube of gel from the dresser and they took turns massaging it into each other's skin. Something in the formula made it heat on contact and Kane felt as if he was being dipped in warm, scented oil that left a trail of sparks in its wake.

When they were finally done he caught his breath and noticed her staring at him, shadows filling the hollows of her eyes. It had been at about this point the last time that she had turned cold and seemed to want nothing more than to have him gone. Now he looked away, closed his eyes, and kept his mouth firmly shut. After a couple of minutes he heard her whisper: "Well?"

He felt like a man contemplating a fresh minefield.

"That was perfect," Kane said, figuring it was a safe answer.

"Any other thoughts?" Allison asked a few seconds later.

"Life is good." *Let her try to make something out of that*, he thought.

"Do you want to stay the night?"

There it was. A question with two wrong answers and no right ones. *Stall.*

"I hadn't thought about it."

"Well, do you?"

"I want to do whatever you want me to do," Kane said hoping that she would tire of trying to trap him into giving her an excuse to cut him out of her life.

She was silent for a full minute then, out of the blue, asked, "Do you ever think about simplicity?" Since the question totally confused him, Kane said nothing. "I do," she continued. "I think about it all the time. I want things between people to be simple, black and white, yes and no. No wondering, no complications. You just meet someone and you know exactly how it's all going to go." *What was she getting at?*

"Do you mean like Michael Corleone," Kane asked, totally lost, "meeting his wife on that road in Sicily where he took one look at her and knew, instantly, that she was the one? The thunderbolt?"

"Yes, wouldn't it be nice if things were that way in real life," Allison said in a wistful tone. "Then we could get all the nonsense behind us and live happily ever after." He heard the bitterness beneath her words like a sour aftertaste from a swallow of cheap wine.

"How would that work? What would you say if you turned around one day and saw some guy and you knew that he was the one? Would you take his hand and look into his eyes and whisper 'Thunderbolt' and if he said it back to you then, well, that was that?" Kane asked.

"Thunderbolt? No, that's how a man would do it. I'd go up to him and . . . ." Allison noticed a look of contentment mixed with desire on Kane's face and felt a little jolt of fear, suddenly wishing that she had never started this conversation. *I can't let this relationship go anywhere,* she thought and decided to turn the whole thing into just a silly joke.

"I'd say, 'Hey, sailor, buy a girl a drink?'"

"And you think that the guy would understand what that meant?"

"The right guy would. Of course, he'd have to be in the right place when I said it."

"In a bar I suppose."

"No, never in a bar, or a restaurant." Allison looked toward the window. "Or in a hotel room." Neither of them said anything for several minutes. Finally, Allison broke the silence. "I notice that you didn't bring a bag."

"No, I didn't."

"So, you're not planning on spending the night?"

"I guess not. Should I bring a bag next time?"

"That's up to you," Allison said, still looking away.

"There *is* going to be a next time, right?"

"Again, that's up to you."

"So, just to be absolutely clear, when, not if, we see each other the next time you're good with me bringing a bag?"

"Knock yourself out."

"I'm glad that's settled," Kane said.

"So, you're going now?"

"Not just yet," Greg answered, pulling the sheet from her body and pinning her beneath him.

CHAPTER TWENTY

Up until a week ago everything had gone according to Donald's plan. A million and a quarter dollars in untraceable, untaxable bitcoins had appeared in his account. *They should call them NOs,* he thought, *No rules, No records, No taxes, or maybe AMs — Anarchist Money.* He began planning the project immediately. It was always difficult to hit a high-profile target. Difficult but not impossible. Like every tough problem you just had to break it down into pieces and attack them one by one. There were only so many ways to kill a protected person and get away with it: (1) sniper shot; (2) bribe or become a guard; (3) bribe or become a member of the support staff; (4) bribe a relative or become a friend or some other person who had access to the target.

Sniper shots were possible with politicians who had to give speeches and cut ribbons and attend functions. Supreme Court Justices did none of those things and he had learned from his research that there were very few long-shot opportunities on the route between the court and Hopper's home. So, number one was out.

The idea of corrupting a member of the Secret Service protection detail was laughable. So forget that. There was no way that any of the clerks or staff at the Supreme Court were going to accept money to poison Hopper's tea and his housekeeper had been with him for almost twelve years so that was out. That pretty much left family and friends. The trick was to get Hopper out of his comfort zone, away from his usual protection detail, someplace where he was accessible, vulnerable. Hopper and his wife had divorced a dozen years ago just after he had been appointed to the Court. She was still in Denver. Before that they apparently had been staying together principally by inertia and she had no interest in uprooting her life and moving to Washington in order to be with him. So, the wife was out.

The daughter was another matter. She had entered UCLA while he was still on the 10th Circuit Court of Appeals but her college career hadn't worked out as hoped. Parties, drugs, and a loser boyfriend whom she followed to Chicago in her sophomore year had all conspired to screw up her life. Of course, members of the Court of Appeals couldn't afford to have drug-addicted children so after two expensive stints in rehab Kathryn followed her father to D.C. where he would be able to keep an eye on her. He thought. He got her an acceptance to George Washington University which agreed to give her credit for her first year at UCLA. But that didn't last.

The next three years were a succession of bad men and worse drugs, another stint in rehab culminating in an inconvenient arrest and messy headlines: "SUPREME CT. JUSTICE'S DAUGHTER CAUGHT WITH DRUGS." Hopper finally gave up, refusing to hire an attorney for her or even post her bail.

The Public Defender eventually got the charges reduced to misdemeanor possession and, for the first time in her life, Kathryn found herself completely on her own. Calls to Dad were answered politely but requests for money, loans, cars or any other material items were rejected. It took her two years to realize that she was really, actually, truly on her own. Her life over the next five years was a succession of low-level jobs — telemarketer, receptionist, waitress, bartender, then three years ago she started her Personal Essentials franchise where she actually achieved some moderate success.

The fact that she had finally managed to both stay clean and support herself paved the way to rebuild her relationship with her father. Over the past two years she had been a frequent visitor to his home and they had begun again to share birthday and holiday dinners and do the normal things that normal parents and kids did together. It wasn't exactly a scene out of a Norman Rockwell painting but it wasn't one from American Gothic either.

After researching Kathryn's history Donald watched her for two days. Slowly, a plan began to take shape. That's when things turned to crap. He didn't worry when the cop showed up. The girl already had a bored minder from the Secret Service. Donald had expected that and he was working out a way to deal with him. The problem was that the new Fed spotted him. Donald wanted the babysitter bored, complacent, just going through the motions, but now the Feds knew that someone might be watching her.

Donald had two choices — do nothing and hope that the guy couldn't identify him and wouldn't sound the alarm or take the fed out and dump the body someplace that wouldn't connect the murder back to the girl. He figured there was no more than a ten-percent chance of the second option actually working. Great choice — do nothing and be screwed or do something and probably be screwed. *Sometimes,* Donald thought, *life doesn't give you any good options, just less bad ones.* Well, if your only choices are driving off a cliff and crashing into a telephone pole, you choose the pole and hope for the best. An hour later Grant Eustace was dead.

A week later Donald was periodically and discretely checking on Kathryn Hopper and he didn't like what he found. The Secret Service now had two agents on her and they were taking their jobs seriously. Well, there was no help for that. Court decisions in big cases were often announced toward the end of the term which was in June. It was now mid-February. He would have to wait them out. With any luck in two or three weeks they would decide they were wasting their time and they'd cut the girl's protection detail back to a single agent. One babysitter he could handle and once he had the girl she would take him straight to the target.

Donald dialed Mr. Green's burner phone.

CHAPTER TWENTY-ONE

Greg felt Rosewood's eyes on him when he wandered into the bull pen tingling from too little sleep and too much sugar and caffeine. The kid was wearing a "Daddy, look what I did" expression.

"What have you got, Danny?" Greg asked, pulling a chair up to the side of Rosewood's desk. Danny's face morphed into a *How did you know I've found something?* look and for an instant Kane considered telling him never to play poker for money then let it go. After a second's pause Danny handed Greg a sheaf of papers.

"I went through the public comments on the proposed HHS regulations like you asked me," Danny began, "and I weeded out all the ones from companies located outside of our immediate area because it would take us too long to meet with them." Danny paused.

"Good thinking," Kane said. Pleased with the verbal pat on the head Danny smiled and continued.

"Next I excluded all the comments that came from lobbyists or trade groups because they would only lead us back to lawyers or PR people. Then I—"

"Danny," Kane cut in, feeling his grip on his temper starting to slip, "let's skip all the people that I don't want to talk to and go straight to . . . ." Kane looked at the top page of the printout, "EcoSafe Technologies."

"They're headquartered in the Virginia Bio-Technology Research Park," Danny said, disappointed that he had lost the chance to explain the brilliant steps he had taken to come up with a suitable candidate.

I can read, Kane thought and clenched his jaw. "Well, anyway," Danny continued a moment later, "They were founded by a Professor Elliott Bellingham. He was on the faculty at Yale." Danny smiled as if proud of Bellingham's Ivy League accomplishments. "I printed out his bio from the company's website." Danny pointed at the pages in Kane's hand. "I figured that he'd be a good person to talk to us about the excluded materials list, him being a Yale professor and all."

It had been Kane's experience that scientists were often the worst people to try to get a clear explanation about anything technical. Usually they gave you five minutes of mysterious jargon and then responded to your questions with "I can show you the math," secure in the knowledge that you would understand their hen scratching about as well as you could read Sanskrit.

Kane thought back to the half an hour he had spent on the phone with his friend, Marty Fouchet. He had called Marty in the hope that Fouchet might be able to give him some insight on the chemicals on the new exclusion list. By the end of the conversation it was all Kane could do to keep himself from running screaming from the room.

"If you'd like me to pick somebody else . . . ." Danny said, responding to Kane's frown.

Oh, shit. It's like dealing with a Golden Retriever, Kane thought, then forced his lips into a smile.

"No, Professor Bellingham will be perfect. Great. Good job."

Danny broke into a smile.

"I can make an appointment for us. When would you like to do it?"

"I'll handle it. I've got another job for you."

"Another job?"

"I need you to run a deeper search on that Baltimore County Deputy Sheriff, Mearle Farber."

"Shouldn't we talk about this outside?" Danny whispered.

"It occurs to me that since you turned up his picture on the Brownstein surveillance video now we can treat him like any other person of interest."

"But there's only a 61% chance that it's him. What if—"

"Sixty-one percent's good enough for me." Kane broke in. "When you checked him out before you had to tiptoe around. That didn't turn up anything useful. Now you can go after him full bore. Use his social to check for any credit cards, bank accounts, safety deposit boxes or cell phones. If you find any new accounts get those records too. Oh, and see if you can find any credit cards or bank accounts that might be linked to a debit card and if you do, pull those debit card records and check all the charges."

"What am I looking for?"

"Things that break the pattern." Kane could feel the gears turning inside Danny's head. "Charges that don't fit his normal lifestyle." Kane searched Danny's face for some sign of comprehension. *Nope, not yet.* "For example, suppose that every month there are ten charges at the same Safeway a mile from his home. That's a pattern. That's normal. Scratch those out. Every month there's an eighty dollar payment to Verizon. Normal, scratch that out. Then you run across a one-time charge to a Safeway thirty miles from where he lives. That doesn't fit the pattern. Find out what he bought."

"I don't think they keep detailed records that long."

"If he used his Club Card the list of his purchases is still probably somewhere in the computer. Subpoena it."

Danny thought about that for a moment and made a note. "OK, delete all the normal repeat purchases and follow-up on everything that's left. Got it."

"I especially want to know if he bought any burner phones. If he did, contact the manufacturer and get all the numbers for all the phones shipped to that store that were activated near the date of purchase. Then get the call history to and from each of those phones."

"That could be a dozen phones. I don't know if we can get a warrant for something like that."

"Not a regular warrant," Kane agreed. "A FISA warrant. This is a matter of national security, possible bio-terrorism, weapons of mass destruction. Issuing those warrants is the reason FISA was set up in the first place. A piece of cake. And don't forget gas stations," Kane continued while Danny furiously took notes. "We want the address of any gas stations he used outside of his own neighborhood. The same with any other vendors, restaurants, any purchases away from his home or work. Mark them on a map with the dates. I want to know where he went and when he was there. Pay special attention to patterns and repeats."

"Repeats?"

"Suppose that the fourth Saturday of every month at ten a.m. he always bought something at a 7-11 in Arlington. What was he doing there? What else is in that neighborhood? Is there a bank across the street? If so, did he set up an account there under another name? Make a list of what you find and we can have somebody canvas the neighborhood with his picture and see if we get a hit. Police work is mostly legwork, running down leads, talking to people, checking records. This guy lives someplace. He's got a credit card and a bank account in another name. He's got a car and an Easy Pass. He's got a new social security number. His life is like a sweater with a loose thread. All we need to do is find that thread, a name, a social, a VISA number and then one good pull will unravel it all. Do you understand?"

"Got it," Danny said, pausing long enough to give Kane another of his happy-puppy looks.

Oh, Jeez, Greg thought and flipped to the "Contact Us" web page for EcoSafe Technologies.

* * *

The Bio-Technology Park was near Richmond in a semi-futuristic glass building with patios and fountains and busy people in suits and lab coats buzzing about. *Did the Hollywood designers invent these kinds of buildings to populate their Sci-Fi movies or did the architects design them to look like the ones they'd seen in the Sci-Fi movies?* Chicken and egg Kane finally decided. There were about a hundred companies in the tech center, mostly start-ups. Eco-Safe's offices were on the fifth floor overlooking the fountain.

"Dr. Bellingham will be right with you, Agent Kane," the receptionist told him and went back to reading her magazine. From someplace beyond the wall behind her Kane heard a muted phone ring once then cut off. Greg was the only person in the small lobby and the receptionist didn't seem overworked. Their product was still in the design phase, Kane decided, no customers yet. He spent five minutes watching people scurry around the plaza below like little bugs in search of crumbs, then he heard a door open behind him.

"Detective Kane?"

The man was about six-two with receding hair streaked with gray, a thin, lined face, and brown-framed glasses.

"Agent Kane," Greg corrected him. "Homeland Security." Greg extended his hand.

"Of course. I'm Elliott Bellingham." Kane noticed that Bellingham's skin was as soft as a woman's and his shoulders seemed hunched as if he were carrying an invisible weight. "Let's go back to my office."

The door behind the receptionist's desk opened onto a long hallway that extended all the way to a distant glass wall. Apparently EcoSafe rented this entire portion of the fifth floor. Doorways studded both sides of the corridor and Bellingham led Kane through the second one on the left. The far wall was all glass from the waist up with Bellingham's desk tucked into the right-hand corner. Across from it was a small couch, a coffee table and two client chairs. Bellingham took one of them and waved Kane to the couch.

"Would you like coffee or tea?" the professor asked.

"No thanks." Kane gave the desk and the nearby bookcase and filing cabinets a quick scan.

"We run a pretty bare-bones operation here, Agent Kane," Bellingham said, misinterpreting Kane's gaze. "Actually, this is a lot fancier than my little cubbyhole at Yale, but then professors don't get the perks that CEOs do."

"When did you leave teaching?"

"About five years ago but it feels like it's more than that. It's a long road from a successful laboratory experiment to a mass-produced product." Bellingham looked vacantly toward the window then returned to the here-and-now. "But we're almost there. We hope to be shipping product in nine to twelve months, subject to EPA and Department of Agriculture approvals of course."

"What is your product exactly? I scanned your website but it didn't make a lot of sense to me," Kane said, feigning simple-minded confusion. It was an old interrogator's trick — let the subject think that you're stupid and then get him talking about something that he's an expert in. Once people are at ease they're more likely to give you the information you're really after. Cops make people nervous and Kane wanted the professor relaxed and talking.

"Our mission is to eliminate pests without poison."

"Pests without poison?"

"Maybe that should be our slogan," Bellingham said, smiling. "How much do you know about insects, Agent Kane?"

"Not a lot."

"Well, let me tell you, we humans are at war with the bugs. Not like in some horror movie with people fighting gigantic ants but at war just the same. The basic theme is the constant see-saw battle between human society and destructive pests. A bug, a beetle, a weevil, a fly, a what-have-you, attacks a commercial crop. We develop a poison that kills that insect. Then the bug mutates and becomes immune to our treatment. We develop a new poison. The bug develops a new mutation, and so on, but insects breed so much faster than we can develop new strains of crops or poisons that we're always only one or two generations away from disaster. The risk is even higher now that factory agriculture has specialized in only a few strains of most crops. A bug that's resistant to the standard pesticide protecting one of the major varieties of wheat or corn could bring the country close to famine in one season. Knowing all this it became clear to me that we needed to break that cycle, that we needed a better way."

As he spoke Bellingham's cheeks lost their pallor and his face became animated.

"What's that 'better way?'" Kane said, voicing the question he knew the professor wanted him to ask.

"You can't just kill the bugs," Bellingham said with utter conviction. "They breed too fast. You have to re-engineer them. You have to make it so that they kill themselves."

"You get them to commit suicide?" Kane asked, smiling, but Bellingham's frown made it clear that he wasn't amused.

"We make them sterile so that they die out."

"Didn't they try that with mosquitoes? They bred millions of sterile males and released them in the wild so that the females they mated with wouldn't be able to reproduce?"

"They irradiated them, the males," Bellingham corrected Kane. "The radiation made them sterile, and yes, they had some success but that process is expensive and it's only a stopgap measure, not a permanent solution. The key, Agent Kane is sterilizing the females rather than the males. Think about humans. You could sterilize half the males on the planet and the other half would just pick up the slack. But if you sterilized half the females the birth rate would be cut in half."

"So you. . . ?"

"From a purely biological point of view giving birth to a viable entity is a complex process involving many stages," Bellingham answered, slipping into lecture mode. "Each stage depends on very specific proteins with very specific components being folded in very specific ways. These proteins are expressed and folded by dozens of different genes. It's a chain Agent Kane, a very intricate chain, and if you disrupt just one link, assuming it's the correct link, the chain breaks and the next generation doesn't hatch."

"So, you make a chemical that destroys one of those—"

"No," the professor interrupted. "Chemicals don't work, not the way you're thinking. The key is in the gene, that is to say, the key is finding the right gene and removing it."

"So, you genetically engineer a new breed of insect?"

"No, you're thinking of gene manipulation, substituting a new gene for an old one or adding a new gene entirely. We don't add. We subtract. We target a gene that makes a protein that's vital for the subject insect to reproduce and then we remove or more accurately 'deactivate' that gene. We turn it off. Once it's switched off it doesn't make the protein. When the protein isn't made the insect cannot create a fertilized egg or cannot lay a fertilized egg or the fertilized egg cannot hatch, depending on which protein in the chain we choose to target."

Bellingham interpreted Kane's expression as confusion and continued in full lecture mode.

"We deliver our product as an aerosol spray like any other crop material. It's basically just water and a virus with a protein coat that's tailored to attack the specific insect we're after. Our method modifies a few sites in the virus DNA which avoids using recombinant DNA techniques. This is faster and similar to the way nature itself works and it's completely harmless to any other form of life, human, animal or insect. When the target insect comes into contact with our spray the virus replicates in its system and turns off the target gene. That's it. Nothing else. The insect eats the corn or leaf or whatever it normally feeds on and it destroys the farmer's crop as if our product wasn't even there. As far as the insect is concerned nothing has happened, until it mates and tries to reproduce. And then, again, nothing happens. There is no next generation. The modified parents eventually die and there are no offspring to take their place."

Bellingham smiled as if he had just explained the secret to a particularly difficult magic trick.

"But you can't be sure you'll get them all," Kane said. "Some of them may not be infected or new bugs might come in on the wind or whatever, which means that you'll have to spray every year and eventually enough of the bugs that survive will develop an immunity to your virus."

"No, no," Bellingham snapped. "That's the real genius of our product. It breeds true."

"What?"

"If by some fluke an infected female manages to lay a viable egg, let's say the virus arrived too late in the breeding cycle for example, or something else went wrong, the offspring will inherit the turned-off gene and also the virus itself. That means that any male that mates with that offspring will be a carrier and will himself deliver the virus to any other female he may mate with and all of the new female's offspring will themselves be sterile. The males will spread the virus to any uninfected females and all of them will become sterile. The few individuals that fall through the cracks will be destroyed by normal means. The percentage of insects that survive to breed is tiny. Millions of them are eaten by birds and bats and other predators. They freeze or fry; they drown. If you can cut the effective birth rate of, for example, a species of beetle to five percent of the normal population level natural predators will essentially wipe out the insect without any further human interference.

"You see, Agent Kane, this is the perfect solution. No poisons. Perfectly tuned to the target pest and nothing else. No effect on the crops themselves nor on the birds or other creatures that eat the target organisms. Pesticides are a nuclear bomb. EcoSafe is a laser scalpel. We only get rid of what we want to get rid of. I promise you, EcoSafe will change the world."

Bellingham searched Kane's face for some sign of, if not admiration, at least approval.

"Amazing stuff," Greg said at last. "A bit over my head," he added at the look of disappointment that washed over Bellingham's face. "How does your research tie into the proposed HHS regulations?"

During his lecture the professor had gotten to his feet and begun to pace. Wearily, he now slipped back into his chair.

"We're too small to build our own manufacturing operation. That would take hundreds of millions of dollars and, given the permitting process, several years. Once we perfected the formula in the lab we looked for a production facility that could manufacture the basic compounds to our specifications. We found one in India and then these regulations came out. I understand the government's concern. Yes, these chemicals could be used to deactivate vital genes. I understand why HHS classified them as something that might be used in the manufacture of a bio-weapon but the truth is that almost anything can be a weapon in the wrong hands. Gasoline, propane, castor beans, well, you see where I'm going. That's why we filed our protest."

Bellingham nervously drummed his fingers on his thigh.

"Couldn't you get an exemption or a permit or something?"

"The problem is the quantity. The manufacturer gave us a price based on a minimum purchase of at least two thousand pounds of material. It's just not economically feasible for them to set up their equipment for an order smaller than that, not at a price that would be acceptable to our customers. If we were only importing a few pounds for research purposes we could probably get a waiver but with such a large volume of material the government is worried that some of it might get diverted or stolen or misused."

"So, if that regulation goes through, you're out of business?"

"Five years down the drain unless and until an American manufacturer would agree to supply us at a cost our customers could afford to pay. I don't see that happening anytime soon." Bellingham frowned then seemed to brighten up. "Tell me, Agent Kane, has the HHS given you any indication if or when the new regulations will go into effect?"

"I have no idea. Months, at least, would be my guess."

Bellingham's mood brightened and he held up his hand. "I'll keep my fingers crossed."

"I imagine that when the regulations were announced you gave HHS's list a pretty thorough examination?"

"I don't know if I would say 'thorough.' We were mostly interested in how it would affect us, but we looked at it, certainly. Why?"

"If you had to guess, who do you think would want to import something on that list badly enough to kill for it?"

"If you're suggesting that we—"

"If I thought that EcoSafe would commit murder in order to bring a new kind of bug killer to the market I wouldn't be talking to you right now. I'd have fifteen agents in here with a search warrant hauling away all of your files."

Bellingham's face paled at the mention of "agents" and "search warrants."

"Well, good," the professor said at last.

"But given what was on the list who do you think might want the regulations stopped badly enough to kill?"

Bellingham paused, then stood and pulled a binder from the shelf. He opened it to one of the tabs and ran his finger down the page, making a few short notes as he went. Finally he returned to his seat and placed the binder on the coffee table in front of Kane.

"I can't tell you 'who,' of course, but those three items can be used to manufacture, respectively, stimulants, pain killers and hallucinogens. If you're looking for people who would be willing to commit murder I would think that drug dealers would fit the bill and a drug dealer with a top-flight lab and a skilled chemist would definitely be interested in any of those three compounds. If I were you, that's where I'd start."

Kane stared at the page and struggled to pronounce the names of the chemicals. The DEA ought to have a list of the likely players who would have the resources needed to manufacture drugs on that level.

"Can you make me a copy of this?" Kane asked.

Bellingham pressed a couple of buttons on his phone.

"Darlene, I need something copied for Agent Kane."

"Thanks for your help, professor," Kane said a minute later.

Bellingham smiled and shook Kane's hand. "My pleasure. Drug addicts are a plague on this nation. If I can do anything to help you stop them, just call me."

Kane left with the page containing the three circled compounds folded snugly in the shirt pocket over his heart.

CHAPTER TWENTY-TWO

Mr. Justice Hopper lived in a two-story red-brick house whose number had been removed. Like most Georgetown homes the front door opened directly onto the sidewalk making security especially difficult. To make matters worse only a seven-foot high red-brick wall separated the public sidewalk from the home's small, tree-shaded backyard. If the Secret Service could have had its way it would have moved Hopper to some fortified estate in Virginia surrounded by a barbed-wire topped wall with motion sensors installed every ten feet. But it couldn't so it had to make-do. Over Hopper's objections they built a twelve foot tall electrified fence around the inside of the patio guaranteeing, at least, that no one was going to crash into the house from the back yard.

A uniformed Secret Service guard was stationed next to the front door with a two-person team across the street in a windowless van. TV cameras fed the monitors inside with views up and down both sides of the narrow, tree-lined block. People were supposed to see the guard out front. They weren't supposed to know about the two armed agents in the van across the street. The neighbors figured it out pretty fast, of course, but the Service wasn't worried about the neighbors. They had all been vetted years ago when Hopper first bought the house and any new faces were checked out before they moved in.

On this particular evening, while Kane was home pounding on his electric keyboard and Danny was watching a new cable cop show called *Blue Heat*, SS Agent Craig Spangler was scanning the monitor fed by the north-facing camera and thinking about turning up the temperature on his electric socks. February nights in Washington were chilly and the agents couldn't use the van's engine to keep warm. "Get yourself some hunter's socks," his supervisor had warned him when he was assigned to the Justice's protection detail.

Already the shift had settled into a familiar pattern. By now Spangler and his partner, Agent Carol Hallstead, had learned the neighborhood's routine — the DOJ lawyer up the street who jogged obsessively, the young couple on bloated incomes from some tech company who practically lived in the brasserie at the south end of the block, and all the rest of the people who had a reason for being near Hopper's home. A plate reader at each end of the street identified all cars before they got close to the Justice's front door. Any vehicles that were stolen or had no business being in the neighborhood were immediately flagged.

"Pizza Boy at twelve o'clock," Carol called out. Twice a week an FCC Bureau Chief who lived around the corner had a pizza delivered and the kid from Sal's Sicilian Pies always followed a route that took him past Hopper's home. Carol switched to night-vision and confirmed the driver's identity. "It's Myron," she called out a moment later.

Something flickered on Craig's screen and he turned up the zoom.

"I've got a female with a large dog heading for us, east side of the street." Spangler played with the controls. "Black jacket, black pants, dark running shoes. Caucasian, about five-six, black baseball cap. No gloves. She's about fifty yards out." Spangler clicked his mike. "Voss, female and a large dog coming your way from the south. I don't recognize her. Stay sharp."

The uniformed guard bent forward and peered into the darkness. The woman was just a gray shape. The dog was clearer. Tim Voss loved dogs, not the little ones, rat dogs he called them. No, he liked big dogs, shepherds, labs, retrievers, but what the heck was that? Voss watched the pair approach. The animal had a rusty brown coat, short hair, and big, meaty shoulders. Voss squinted when they passed beneath the street lamp. *What the hell was some strange woman doing walking a dog like that past Hopper's house?* Voss clicked his mike.

"Craig, this doesn't feel right. That's a Rhodesian Ridgeback. Back in Africa they've been known to take on lions."

Spangler turned up the gain on the camera and zoomed in. He definitely had never seen that woman before and something about her coat seemed wrong.

"Carol, what's the temperature outside right now?"

Hallstead checked the readout on her panel. "Forty-six."

"That coat she's wearing looks thick enough for the arctic. . . . Voss, she could be wearing a vest."

The woman was now about forty feet away. Carol softly unlocked the van's sliding door and Tim Voss removed his Glock and held it out of sight against his side. As she neared his post the woman turned as if surprised, then gave Voss a friendly wave.

"Hello," she said smiling then dropped her leash. "Angriff!" she shouted and pulled an automatic from her pocket. The dog raced toward Voss who jumped back against the front door and started firing. The first two shots ricocheted off the sidewalk but the third one caught the dog in mid-leap. The woman was firing too and a bullet splintered the door a foot from Voss's head just before the dog's body crashed into him and he went down.

The woman ran forward and Voss struggled to raise his weapon but his hand was trapped beneath the dog's body. With a look of determined anger the woman aimed down at him but before she could pull the trigger Voss heard three quick shots and her head exploded. He looked past her to see Hallstead and Spangler running toward him. Voss pulled himself free of the eighty-five pound dead animal and scrambled to his feet. Hallstead kicked the woman's gun away even though one look was enough to confirm that she was irretrievably dead. Spangler unzipped her nylon coat.

"She was wearing a vest," he called out, then, "Oh, shit! — I've got grenades!" He pointed to two hand grenades clipped to her belt. "We'll have to get bomb disposal down here."

"I'll call the boss," Carol offered. "You OK, Tim?"

Voss stared down at the crumpled body and the hand grenades and muttered to no one in particular, "This is some really crazy shit."

* * *

It took two hours for news of the attack to reach Senator Arthur Denning. He had sponsored five different automatic-weapons bills, none of which had made it to a vote, and he had contributed $25,000 of his own money to the "Yes On Lyla's Law" initiative campaign. It was no secret where Denning's sympathies lay and friends in the law-enforcement community kept him up to date on any developments related to the "Gun Case."

Denning put down the phone and stared blankly at the wall. An armed woman with hand grenades had made it to Hopper's front door? *This was insanity. This had to stop.* Denning opened his cell's address book and selected a number.

"Roger, it's Arthur Denning," he said when the phone was picked up.

"Senator, what can I do for you?"

"Have you heard about the attack on Justice Hopper?"

"What? Was he hurt?"

"The Secret Service stopped it, but just barely. The woman got to his front door, Roger, with hand grenades, hand grenades! We cannot have these kinds of things in this country!"

"Absolutely not. What would you like me to do?"

"I need to be sure that Hopper is safe, that he's getting all the protection he needs."

"I'll set up a meeting with the Secret Service agent in charge of his security. He can give you—"

"No, I want my own man checking things out, someone I trust."

"That's going to be difficult. Secret Service isn't going to like that one bit."

"Jurisdictional pissing matches aren't my primary concern right now. The Secret Service is part of Homeland and you're the Principal Deputy Undersecretary. I don't think they're going to tell you 'No.'"

"I understand your concern, Senator, but I don't have the training for something like that. Let me see if I can find an experienced Secret Service agent in another division who could give you a more professional evaluation."

"Don't bother. You've got an agent in Homeland, a Gregory Kane. My niece knows him. It seems that he's made quite an impression on her. I'd like him to check out Hopper's security and give me a report."

"Kane? I've never heard of him. What division is he in?"

"I don't know but according to my niece he's got good skills, besides Kane's partner was killed running some kind of surveillance on Hopper's daughter so Kane's motivated to get into this."

Motivated? Roger Dawson thought. *This sounds like a shit-storm in the making.*

"First I'll need to find out if he's available. Let me pull up his file and see what other cases he's working on."

"I can tell you that. He's looking into the disappearance of some administrator at HHS." Denning waited but Dawson said nothing. "I'm sure his missing person's case can go on hold for a few days. . . . Roger?"

"Umm, sorry Senator. You know to get approval for this I'm going to have to call the Director."

"Call whoever you need to. Use my name if you have to. I'm counting on you, Roger, to make this happen."

"All right," Dawson said after a long pause. "I'll get this Gregory Kane authorized to review Hopper's protection arrangements and then give me a report which I'll forward to you. I'll brief him tomorrow as soon as I get the Director's approval."

"No, I want to tell him personally what I expect of him. You just get Kane clearance from the Secret Service and have him in my office tomorrow morning at ten o'clock."

"All right," Dawson said, defeated. "It's too late tonight but I'll call the Director and Kane's supervisor first thing in the morning."

"Good. Thanks, Roger. I knew that I could count on you. I won't forget your help."

Shit! Shit! Shit! Dawson thought as he hung up the phone.

CHAPTER TWENTY-THREE

When he entered the bull pen all eyes turned in Kane's direction and the sounds of clicking keys and muted conversations dwindled then died. Kane froze in mid-step and looked from face to face for some clue as to what had gone wrong. Danny's head shifted a fraction of a degree and Greg followed Rosewood's gaze to Immerson's office where the boss stood in the doorway, stiff and glaring.

"Kane!" Immerson jerked his hand like a kid grabbing a fly.

By the time Greg reached the office Immerson was already back behind his desk. A stranger who had been wedged into the corner chair stood. Greg automatically went into evaluation mode — fifteen-hundred-dollar suit, hundred-dollar tie, teeth that could only have been bleached that white with a five-hundred-dollar smile-center treatment.

This could only be bad news. Somebody well above Kane's pay grade wanted something from him and now, finally, with a plan for tracking down Mearle Farber, Kane was sure he wanted no part of it.

"Greg, I'm Sebastian Wren," the stranger said, smiling and extending his hand. *Some kind of political animal*, Kane decided, but with his leathery skin and trim physique Wren wasn't a standard bureaucrat or politician. *Law enforcement background of some kind*, Kane concluded.

"I'm the Special Assistant to the Principal Deputy Undersecretary for the Office of Intelligence & Analysis."

"It must be fun saying that at parties," Kane replied with a twisted smile.

"Kane!" Immerson's face had gone from pale to pink in a heartbeat.

"I mean, you meet a girl and she asks you what you do and you tell her that you're the Special Assistant to the Principal Deputy Undersecretary for the Office of Intelligence & Analysis for the Department of Homeland Security and she must practically wet herself."

"Shit!" Immerson muttered and sagged back in his chair. "Sorry Sebastian. Kane has an unusual sense of humor *that is often inappropriate*." Immerson said the last part with a hard glare that bounced off Kane with no apparent effect.

"It's okay, Frederick. I appreciate a man with a good sense of humor."

"I'm a laugh a minute," Greg replied.

"Kane . . . . oh, just sit down. Your expertise has been requested for a new assignment."

"Well, I *am* a whiz at balloon animals."

"Jesus, Kane, will you please give it a rest!"

"I think Greg is trying to tell us that he doesn't want a new assignment," Wren said, looking at Kane. Greg returned the tiniest of nods. "I get it, I do, but that's just too fucking bad. Your job is whatever your boss tells you it is and in this case the Deputy Undersecretary has given me my instructions and I've given Frederick his instructions and Frederick is going to give you your instructions and no matter how hard you try to make yourself *persona non grata* that's how it's going to be." Wren stared at Greg for a long beat then pretended to see some sign of surrender in the agent's face. "Okay, let me give you the rundown on your new job. You've heard about the incident at Justice Hopper's home last night?"

A woman showed up at the Justice's front door with a gun and two hand grenades? You call that an incident? Greg thought, but recognizing the *Don't fuck with me!* look on Wren's face he just nodded.

"A lot of people in Washington are very concerned about the threats on Justice Hopper's life, among them Senator Arthur Denning." *Denning! Shit — Allison! Oh, fuck.* "Do you know the senator?" Wren asked, reading the tightening around Kane's eyes.

"Never met him," Kane answered in a flat tone.

Wren thought that over for a moment then continued. "Senator Denning called Deputy Undersecretary Dawson last night and requested a personal briefing on the Secret Service's protection arrangements for Justice Hopper. Your name came up."

"Send somebody else."

"The senator specifically asked for you. What do you think about that, since you say you don't know him?"

Kane glanced at Immerson whose gaze looked like it might melt steel.

"I know someone in his office, socially. His chief of staff."

"His niece." It wasn't a question.

"His niece? Allison Varner?" Wren gave him a little shrug. *Fuck!* Kane mouthed.

"So you didn't ask for this job?"

"No."

"Maybe there was a little pillow talk about how much you wished that you could be involved in the search for your partner's killer? Maybe you hinted that it sure would be nice if somebody could pull a few strings to get you transferred over to Secret Service?"

Kane was half out of his seat before he got control and forced himself back down. Wren watched him with an almost amused smile.

"I never wanted any part of the Hopper thing and I don't want it now. That was Useless' dream, not mine, and look what it got him."

"Useless?" Wren turned to Immerson.

"Agent Kane's colorful nickname for his former partner, Grant Eustace."

Wren pursed his lips then shrugged. "Well, Kane, we're a long way past that now. It doesn't matter what you want or what you don't want. You've got the job, like it or not."

"You expect me to go over to the Secret Service and say 'Hi guys. I'm here to rate your operation and tell a U.S. Senator if you're screwing things up'? I wonder how well that's going to work?"

"I'm sure they'll give you every professional courtesy." Wren almost laughed out loud. "But first you've going to be briefed by Senator Denning. He's the one you're really working for, after all."

"I'm reporting to him?"

"Technically, you're reporting to me and I'm going to make your evaluation available to the senator but practically speaking, he's the boss." Wren glanced at his watch. "You're due in the senator's office at ten o'clock."

If this was all to keep Denning happy then if the senator should become unhappy with me. . . . Maybe there's a way out of this after all. Kane thought. Greg's sudden, twisted smile made Immerson's heart skip a beat.

* * *

Kane had never been in a U.S. senator's office before but it looked pretty much like he expected — a fancy lobby, a big room full of lots of earnest young people taking phone calls, opening letters and typing on computers and, finally, a formal office with leather chairs and heavy furniture and walls covered with photos and nineteenth-century landscapes. Kane had looked for Allison on the way in but she was nowhere to be seen. She probably had one of the smaller offices off the main work area Kane decided. *Was this her idea? Does she even know I'm here?* Given her fear of emotional intimacy he doubted that she wanted him in her office any more than he wanted to be here.

"Mr. Kane," the senator said, standing and offering his hand, "thank you for coming." Denning was coatless. Red and blue suspenders and an ochre and black bow tie adorned a starched, white shirt. His face was heavy beneath thinning black hair mostly turned to gray and his smile failed to reach all the way to his tired blue eyes. "Please have a seat."

"I think Allison has given you the wrong impression about me," Kane said, ignoring the proffered chair. "I'm not a security expert. I've never run a protection detail. I have no training in threat assessment. I'm just a retread cop who spends most of his time running down crooked vendors and corrupt paper pushers."

"Sit down, please," Denning repeated. Reluctantly Kane took the valued-campaign-contributor leather chair directly in front of the desk. "I assume you've done a little research on me," the senator began.

"I've been a little busy chasing real criminals."

"Not even a Google search?" Denning asked.

"I never made it to my desk this morning and I've never seen the appeal of viewing the world through a four-inch screen."

"You weren't even a little curious about me when you and Allison started dating?"

Dating? Fucking, more like, but saying that, Kane decided, would just be mean.

"I didn't give you a second thought then and to be honest about it, I still don't care."

"Not many people talk to me that way, Mr. Kane."

"One of the perks of being a cop is that I don't have to kiss anyone's ass."

"So, you like to tell it like it is and to hell with the consequences?" Kane just shrugged. "How do you know I won't take offense and call up my friend the Deputy Undersecretary and have him assign you to catching people who steal pencils from the stock room?"

"You're not that kind of guy," Kane said with easy certainty.

"Oh, really? What kind of guy am I?"

"I can tell you what kind of guy you're not. You don't spend a lot of time thinking about money. You don't have a big ego. You don't much care what other people think of you." Denning opened his mouth to ask a question but Kane cut him off. "You have a curious mind and you like learning how things work. You're a 'big-picture' guy. You would consider any act that was petty or mean as a failure of character."

"Have you ever considered a career in palm reading?" Denning asked in a sarcastic tone.

"You're thinking of retiring but you don't want anyone to know."

Denning's lips parted then he recovered and took a breath.

"I'd be interested in knowing how you came to those conclusions. I'm assuming my niece is partially to blame."

"Not at all. In fact, she never even told me that you two were related."

"Then how?"

"The money part? That's easy. You're wearing a $35 Casio watch. Your average plutocrat would rather die than have something on his wrist that didn't cost at least two or three thousand dollars. Plus that shirt is half a size too small across your chest which means it's off-the-rack, not the custom tailored model that someone in your position could easily afford if they cared about stuff like that."

"And the part about my ego, or lack thereof?"

"That picture of you and, what, a bunch of sixth graders at some park?"

"It's a summer camp for inner-city kids that I support. What about it?"

"You're wearing a dime-store Indian headdress."

"I sat in on their class on native Indian lore. So what?"

"You look like an idiot and you're laughing. Nobody with an ego would have put that thing on their head, leastwise allowed his picture to be taken wearing it, leastwise put it up on the wall of his office where everyone could see it."

"Maybe I hung it there because it's good for my image."

"Bull. You put it there because it pleases you to think about helping those kids and to remind yourself of what you think you're supposed to be doing here. That's not the act of an egomaniac. That's the mark of someone who thinks it's important to care about other people. And while we're at it, I'm guessing you paid for that camp yourself. Again, not the sort of thing that would be done by a guy who's obsessed with money."

Denning stared at Kane then took a deep breath. "Anything else?"

"Your tie totally gives you away. Half the people in this town think that wearing a blue suit with a red tie makes them look powerful which, for them, is the big prize. When you show up in a black bow tie with egg-yolk yellow dots on it you may as well carry a sign that says, 'Fuck you, I don't care what you think about me.' As for the curious mind—"

"Stop. I don't need to hear any more."

Kane spread his hands as if to say, *Fine, you asked.*

"Perhaps I should tell you a few things about yourself." Kane shrugged. "You also don't care what people think of you but for a different reason. You think most people are fools so their opinions don't matter. Unfortunately for you, even though you don't care what they think, you take personal offense at what you see as their stupidity. You think that because you're smart that ordinary people should just quietly stand aside and do what you tell them and that they're being petty and foolish when they don't. You're an angry man and part of you is afraid that it's never going to stop."

"I—"

"I'm not done. In spite of what my niece may have said, I wasn't sure you were the right man for this job. It's an understatement to say that Allison has not taken her husband's death well. Emotionally, she's a wreck and I have to take any opinions she might have about a man who's having casual sex with her with a huge grain of salt. In fact, I would be a fool not to be extremely distrustful of the motives and character of such a man. That's why I insisted on meeting you in person."

"Sorry I lived up to your fears rather than your hopes," Kane said with a sour expression. "No hard feelings. I'm sure Deputy Undersecretary Dawson will be able to find you someone more suited to your needs."

"You live by a set of what are, for you, unbreakable rules," Denning continued, purposely ignoring Kane's remark. "One of which is that decent people should be protected and that bad people should be punished. Oh, don't be so surprised, Mr. Kane. You're not the only one who can read people. In your case you can take the boy out of the parochial school but you can't take the parochial school out of the boy. One nice thing about being a U.S. Senator," Denning said in response to the surprised look on Kane's face, "is that I have a large and very skilled staff. Before I called Mr. Dawson I had my people, excluding Allison of course, do a thorough background check on you."

"Don't believe everything you read on the Internet," Kane said sourly.

"I believe one thing I read. You charged into automatic weapons fire to kill the man who murdered your friend."

"Meaning what, exactly?"

"Meaning that you don't run scared. I might have had my doubts about your character and your motives when you came in, Mr. Kane, but your complete lack of concern for earning my good opinion of you or for any damage I might potentially do to your career if you give me answers I didn't like has put them all to rest. Congratulations, Agent Kane. You've got the job."

"I don't want the job."

"Which is exactly why I'm giving it to you. Now, let's get down to business. Here's what I want you to do."

Kane frowned then, reluctantly, extracted his pad and began to take notes.

CHAPTER TWENTY-FOUR

When he left the senator's office Kane spent about six seconds deciding what to do next. The standard, color-inside-the-lines bureaucrat or, in Kane's view, moron, would have marched over to Secret Service headquarters, spent half an hour sitting on his ass until they had found somebody who was willing to spend the next half hour wasting his time with a bullshit briefing followed up with a prolonged orientation session which would not begin until well after lunch. *Screw that*, Kane thought and headed for the Supreme Court building on First Street N.E. Being polite and playing nice weren't going to get him anywhere. The bosses would just give him phony smiles and bury him in bullshit until he got tired and went away. If he intended to get anyplace he needed to force a confrontation. He'd either win it and get the cooperation he needed or lose which would dump it all back in Denning's lap.

Step One, get in their face and find out if Denning really had the juice to make this work. His Homeland Security creds got him past the regular Court Security Officers, then he ran into the Secret Service agent assigned to Mr. Justice Hopper. As expected, the man treated him like a yokel who had gotten separated from his tour group.

"Sorry Agent Kane," the babysitter, Agent Wellner according to his ID, told him in a tone that made it clear that he wasn't sorry at all, "The Justice is busy. You'll have to make an appointment with his secretary."

"No, I won't," Kane said. Wellner stood up straighter and took a step forward. "You're about six inches away from getting yourself assigned to foot patrol outside the Nigerian Embassy," Kane told him, refusing to back up an inch.

"I need you to leave now, Mr. Kane." Wellner said, opening his coat and showing his weapon.

"At eight-thirty this morning your Director authorized me to run a full review of Justice Hopper's security detail. Take a good look at my creds." Kane shoved his ID into Wellner's face. "The name is Gregory Kane."

"I don't care who you are. I don't have any—"

"Interest in saving your career? Idea of the proper response to what I've just told you? Clue as to the pile of shit you've just stepped into? Get out your phone and call your Director, now." Wellner hesitated and then raised his hand to his earbud. "No!" Kane shouted and waved his arm. "I told you to call your Director. Your supervisor has already proven his incompetence by not telling you about my assignment. If you don't want this little problem to escalate into a real crap storm get your Director on the line and tell her that Senator Denning's representative is very pissed that the Secret Service is obstructing his mission."

Normally the agent would have called in a couple of CSOs and had Kane tossed down the Courthouse steps but the words "Director" and "Senator Denning" made him pause.

"You stay right there," Wellner ordered then backed off ten feet and pulled out his phone. The call began with a few whispered sentences and was soon interrupted by delays as the agent was shunted to higher and higher levels of authority. Kane especially enjoyed watching Wellner's face lose its bland composure and grow redder and more irritated as the call dragged on. At the end Wellner was barely speaking, just uttering brief responses mostly consisting of "Yes, sir" and "I understand." Wellner finally hung up, composed his face into a rigid mask and, stiff-legged, walked back to Kane.

"Through that door," he said in a tight voice. "Tell the Justice's administrative assistant what you want. Whether the Justice will see to you or not is up to him."

Kane turned away without a word. Three minutes later he was ushered into Mr. Justice Hopper's office. Strictly speaking Kane didn't need to talk to Hopper in order to evaluate the Secret Service's security arrangements but only a fool would look at it that way. There were two basic parts to any protection detail: the protectors and the protectee. You couldn't evaluate one without understanding the other. What was the target's personality? Would he follow orders or fight you at every step? Did he appreciate his guards or resent them? Did he want to go out every night or have friends in or just sit quietly in his living room and read a book? Were there any circumstances under which he might try to give his protection team the slip? Did he have any guilty pleasures, a special food, a favored chef, season tickets to the symphony or a sports team, any habits that a hitter might be able to exploit? Was he bold or retiring, impulsive or methodical? When the chips were down, how was Hopper likely to react? These were things a good protection detail needed to know in advance.

Sure, Kane could have guessed the answers to these questions, assumed what kind of person Hopper was based on his occupation, but assumptions were risky and often wrong. Kane needed a feel for the man that he could only get from a one-on-one meeting.

"Mr. Justice Hopper," he began. "I'm Agent Gregory Kane, Department of Homeland Security." Hopper raised his eyebrows as if a peculiar creature had just wandered into view. "In light of the attempted break-in at your house last night I've been asked to make a thorough review of your security procedures."

Hopper stared at Kane for a count of two then apparently resigned himself to what he viewed as a waste of his time. He pointed to a club chair a few feet from his desk.

"Have a seat Agent Kane. . . . You don't need to call me 'Mr. Justice Hopper,'" he added before Kane had finished sitting down. "That's for out there," Hopper waved vaguely in the direction of the courtroom. "Most of my professional life people have called me 'Judge.' I see no reason to change that now." Hopper stared at Kane the way he might have looked at a new painting, trying to decide if he liked it and, if so, how much it might be worth.

"I'd like to get an idea of your schedule."

Hopper gave him another appraising look then began to speak.

"I get up around six-thirty, have breakfast at home and I'm here by eight. I eat lunch here in the building and generally leave around six. My housekeeper prepares dinner and I'm usually in bed by ten." Hopper spoke in a diffident tone as if unsure what Kane was really getting at.

"Is there anything that you eat that is unique, something that might be specially ordered just for you?"

"You think someone's going to poison me? No, everything Ardelia cooks is right off the supermarket shelf. And they make her shop at different stores on a random schedule. An agent accompanies her just in case."

Kane made a note. "Are you planning on attending any social events in the next thirty days?" he asked without looking up.

"The Secret Service has my full schedule," Hopper said, obviously irritated.

"How often do you see your daughter?"

"Kathryn? What does — just what are you getting at Mr. Kane?"

"As I said, I'm preparing a review of your security procedures."

"By asking questions that the Secret Service already has the answers to? What's really going on here, Agent Kane and what does it have to do with my daughter?"

As he had planned, Kane now had Hopper's full attention.

"How do you murder a high government official?" Kane asked.

"What?"

"You can't just walk up to him in the street or knock on his door. How do you get past his guards? How do you get close to him?"

"Why don't you tell me." *Good*, Kane thought, *he's pissed. He's almost ready to take this seriously.*

"You start with someone close to him, a guard, an employee, a friend, a relative. That's the weak spot."

"That wouldn't work with me, Mr. Kane, but you know that already. What are you really getting at?"

"The first thing you'd do is watch someone close to the target, get an idea of his or her habits and schedule, look for some way to use them against the subject. At least that was my thinking. About two weeks ago I said as much to my partner, Grant Eustace. He was kind of a glory hound, always looking for some big case that would put a gold star next to his name, maybe get him a promotion or a bump in pay."

"Was?"

"Grant decided to check out your daughter, nothing special, just watch her for a while, see where she went, what she did." Kane paused, guaranteeing that he had Hopper's full attention. "We found Eustace's body about seven the next morning stuffed into the backseat of his car. Somebody had jammed a steel rod, maybe an ice pick, maybe a thin screwdriver, into his brain."

"Is that what this is all about, revenge, about finding your partner's killer?"

Kane almost laughed. "Grant Eustace was an ambitious moron who put himself in the wrong place at the wrong time. He was my partner and it's bad business to let people get away with killing your partner but I wouldn't have gotten into this jackpot with the Secret Service over that. I'm here because your friend Senator Denning wants you kept alive and he wants me to assure him that the Secret Service is going to see that that happens."

"Senator Denning is not my friend. I don't even know the man," Hopper snapped.

"Well, he knows you. He's afraid the gun nuts are—"

"Stop right there!" If Hopper had had a gavel he'd have banged it. "I will not discuss or hear any discussion that is in any way related to any case before me. I specifically reject the term 'gun nuts' as applying to any of the parties in *Hoffkemper v. California*."

"Noted," Kane said, nodding submissively. "The point is, the woman who showed up at your house was an amateur, dangerous but crazy, the kind of person the Secret Service is perfectly capable of handling. Grant Eustace was killed by a professional within hours of the time he started watching your daughter. That waves a very big red flag. However you decide, whatever the Court's ruling is, you need to live long enough to cast your vote. If every time somebody doesn't like how a case is going they can change the result by killing the judge then this country is finished. So, here I am."

"I already have the Secret Service protecting me. What makes you so special, Mr. Kane?"

"I see things more clearly than most people. That's why I'm so popular." For the first time Hopper smiled. "So, how close are you to your daughter?"

"We talk on the phone or exchange emails two or three times a week. We have a standing lunch engagement every Wednesday. We used to use those occasions to try out new restaurants but after yesterday's . . . excitement I assume that we'll be eating in the building from now on. How could Kathryn possibly be used to do me harm?"

Kane had two or three ideas on how he might do it but he wasn't going to open that bag of snakes with the protectee.

"That's why I need to know everything I can about your daughter. What kind of person is she? What does she like? What does she dislike? What are her goals? What are her fears?"

"You want to understand her personality," Hopper said, then paused a moment before continuing. "You want to know how she would react to a threat or in an emergency. Do you think she's a target, that the person who killed your partner might do something to her in order to get to me?"

"It's a possibility we can't ignore. Now, tell me everything you can about Kathryn." Half an hour later Hopper started repeating himself. "I think I have enough for now," Kane said and put away his pen. "Thanks for your help, Judge. I'll see myself out." Kane stood and held out his hand.

"I don't want anything about my job hurting my daughter. She doesn't deserve that. As far as this case is concerned she's just . . . ." Hopper hesitated, suddenly lost for words.

"Just an innocent bystander," Kane said while thinking *collateral damage*. There was a brief flash of fire in Hopper's eyes but the judge bit his tongue. Kane nodded and turned toward the door.

"Protect my daughter, Agent Kane," Hopper called after him.

"It's my job to protect you, Judge. Hopefully that will be enough."

When he left the justice's chambers almost an hour after he had entered the building Kane found someone new waiting for him.

"Agent Kane, I'm Special Agent in Charge, Clark Millingham." Beefy, broad shouldered, built like an NFL free safety in a thousand dollar suit, Millingham stuck out a hand as black as India ink. *Well, they're taking me seriously now*, was Kane's only thought. *Time to play nice.*

"Pleased to meet you, SAC Millingham," Kane said taking the proffered hand. "Heck of a job you've got here." Kane gestured vaguely toward Hopper's office.

"It's what we train for. Is there anything the Service can do to help with your evaluation?" *Now you want to kill me with kindness,* Kane thought. *Well, let's see how long that lasts.*

"I want to talk to the daughter."

Millingham hesitated, trying to figure out where Kane was going.

"We've got a double team on her, 24/7. No one's getting near her."

"I appreciate that but I need to talk to her."

"What for?" Millingham asked his friendly tone now gone.

"For my report to Senator Denning." Kane smiled and waited.

"I'll see what I can do," Millingham said finally.

"No rush." Millingham fractionally relaxed. "I haven't had lunch yet. Two, two-thirty will be just fine. Do they have a cafeteria in this building? Hey, Wellner," Kane called to the scowling agent in the corner, "how's the food in this place?"

CHAPTER TWENTY-FIVE

Immerson wandered through the bull pen in a state best described as nervous euphoria, his emotions simultaneously being stretched in two opposing directions. On the one hand, with Kane temporarily somebody else's problem the office was the emotional equivalent of a placid, garden pond. On the other, dropping a bottle of nitroglycerin like Gregory Kane into the middle of a Secret Service operation was unlikely to end well and Immerson felt himself tensing in anticipation of the eventual explosion. At least Kane's errand-boy new partner seemed busy. Rosewood's desk was covered with stacks of folders and documents and Rosewood himself was industriously pounding away on his keyboard, apparently looking for more.

"Want to bring me up to date, Danny?" Immerson asked. The kid jerked around and for a moment a hand-in-the-cookie-jar expression clouded his face then, just as quickly, vanished.

"Uhhh, yes sir. I'm working on the Albert Brownstein disappearance."

"I assumed you were. Do you and Kane have any other open cases?"

"Uhhh, no sir." It came out half as an answer, half as a question.

Something's going on, Immerson thought but decided that he probably didn't want to know what.

"So, what's all this?" Immerson gestured toward the paperwork covering Rosewood's desk.

"Well, uhhh, we noticed a suspicious person near Mr. Brownstein's apartment before he went missing and Agent Kane thought he might have recognized him so I've been going through the suspect's credit cards and phone records from the time before he disappeared."

"The time before Brownstein disappeared?"

"No, before the subject disappeared."

"Wait." Immerson waved his hand, confused. "The 'suspicious person' that Kane recognized has also disappeared?"

"Yes sir."

"Around the time that Brownstein went missing?"

"No sir. About two years before that."

"This is someone who Kane knew from Baltimore?"

"Yes sir."

"You don't have to call me 'sir.' Just, 'yes' or 'no' without the 'sir' will be fine." Rosewood seemed confused but Immerson pressed on anyway. "Who is this 'suspicious person'?"

"He's a Baltimore County Deputy Sheriff, Mearle Farber."

"What would a Baltimore County Deputy Sheriff have to do with a missing HHS Director?"

"I don't know, s—." Danny sputtered to a stop.

"Have you located him?"

"Not exactly, but I think I might be closing in." He waited for another question but after a moment's pause Danny figured that he was supposed to keep talking. "Agent Kane gave me some tips about things I should look for and they've paid off. You know," Rosewood said, suddenly enthused, "Agent Kane really knows his stuff. I mean, he taught me more about how to track down people in one hour than any of the books I've read." Danny gave Immerson a smile then, chastened by his boss's silence, turned back to his piles of documents. "Well, anyway, this Farber had a Safeway Club Card that gave him a discount on gasoline. I checked his regular credit card transactions and nothing special popped up, but then I subpoenaed his Club Card records and I found a bunch of gas purchases at stations nowhere near his house or work," Danny pointed to a file on the upper right corner of his desk, "so I got the station's records for that time and date," his hand patted the next pile down, "and I matched the purchase amount on the Club Card to a credit card in the name of Benjamin Prentiss."

"Were you able to link Prentiss and Farber together?"

"Yes, I was," Danny said proudly. "I got Prentiss' driver's license and the picture matches Farber's."

"Do we know where Prentiss is now?"

"Oh, no. He went off the grid pretty soon after Farber went missing."

"And?"

"Oh, well, I've been going through Prentiss' credit card records," Danny patted yet another of his piles, "looking for links to bank accounts, email addresses and cell phone purchases. Prentiss paid his credit card bill by an automatic transfer from an account at the Eastern Federal Bank in Laurel. That account's dormant now but there were some pretty big deposits made to it. I think he was dirty and that's where he put his payoffs. And I'm following another lead. Agent Kane called it a 'thread.' I just have to find the link that ties Prentiss to the name he's using now. I think I'm getting close." Danny gave his boss a hopeful smile.

Good God, now I've seen everything, Immerson thought. Kane had managed to piss off just about every trained agent in the office and now he partners up with a wet-behind-the-ears kid and it's all cotton candy and rainbows. *I wonder how long this honeymoon's going to last?* he asked himself, then decided to just enjoy the peace and quiet as long as he could.

"Well, good work, Rosewood. Keep at it and let me know if you track this Farber down. Make sure you keep Kane up to date."

"Yes, sir — uhh, sorry. I'll email him my report before I go home tonight." Danny turned back to one of his printouts and began making notes.

It was a little past seven and Danny was just about to quit when he found the crucial link. At first he couldn't believe it. He just sat there and stared as if it might disappear if he looked away. It had started out as such a small mistake but Danny knew what that mistake meant right away. It was the loose thread Kane had told him to look for and Danny had pulled on it for all he was worth.

The Prentiss credit card had been used for some on-line purchases, nothing shocking, no shotguns or tear gas or anything like that, but the vendor had required an email login. Prentiss had used a Gmail account in some cryptic name. No big deal. But then Prentiss had wanted another, equally cryptic, Gmail account for something else and he'd had to give an existing email address to open the new one. He used the first fake-name email account to open the second one. That's where he screwed up. The records of the first account led Danny to the second one and the records of the second email address took Danny to a PayPal account and the PayPal account records led him to payment for a private mail box. The address on the private mail box matched the address on a newly issued VISA card in the name of Paul Conklin. A DMV check turned up a registration for a Toyota Camry and Paul Conklin's Virginia driver's license. When Danny accessed the driver's license he recognized the picture immediately, no question, none at all. The deadpan face on the Paul Conklin license belonged to Mearle Farber.

I've got you, you son of a bitch! Danny thought, then reached for the phone to call Kane.

CHAPTER TWENTY-SIX

Kane drowsed on the couch while his dinner of microwaved frozen lasagna congealed in the pit of his stomach. It had been a long day.

Millingham, or his bosses, had finally tired of the pissing contest and had arranged a meeting with Kathryn Hopper for mid-afternoon. Kane found her middle-aged, pale, nervous and anxious to please. He searched in vain for the free-spirited young woman who had turned her back on middle-class convention and decided that that girl was long gone. Instead today's Kathryn Hopper had the look of a two-time loser who was anxious to please her probation officer and was willing to do anything to avoid going back to the joint.

"My dad's all right, isn't he?" she asked thirty seconds into the interview. "He's not in any danger?"

"He's fine. I'm just doing a security assessment. Have you noticed—"

"Because if he needs anything from me, if there's anything I can do to help him, just tell me what it is and I'll do it," she told Kane with an almost desperate look on her face.

"Just answering my questions will help a lot." Kathryn gave him a quick nod and unconsciously wrung her hands. "Have you noticed anyone that you don't know in your vicinity more than once or twice?"

"You mean, like somebody stalking me?"

"No, not necessarily even paying any attention to you. Just there." Kathryn stared at Kane with confused eyes. "For example, you park your car and notice a blonde-haired man sitting in a car across the street, then, later, maybe when you're having lunch you see the same man at another table."

"Oh, no, no," Kathryn answered, enthusiastically shaking her head.

"How about seeing the same car more than once? You stop at a light and notice a silver Altima two cars behind you and then the next morning you see the same Altima parked down the street from your house. Anything like that?" Kathryn gave him another bobble-head response.

And that's how it went for almost an hour. It was like trying to get answers from a nervous golden retriever that desperately wanted to please you but was clueless about how to do it. If Kane had ever entertained any suspicions that the daughter might cooperate with somebody who was after Hopper he didn't any longer. Any harm to the justice from her would be either accidental or coerced.

By now the lasagna had solidified into a solid mass of acid and grease. Kane pushed away the almost empty bottle of beer and abandoned any thoughts of opening another. He lolled his head back and started to let his eyes slide shut when a shriek from his cell phone jerked him upright. The screen said: "Daniel Rosewood." Kane hovered his finger over the "Accept" button then sighed, dropped the phone on the cushion next to him, and closed his eyes. Whatever Danny wanted would wait until morning, Kane decided, and almost instantly he slipped into a leaden sleep.

* * *

Kane recognized the bar, Tommy's bar, the instant that he opened his eyes — the round tables, the warped plank floor; Sadie, weary, limp hair brushing her shoulders, laying down bottles of Rolling Rock with a *clack, clack, clack*. Kane looked around. Tommy had to be here. Tommy was always here. This place was his personal limbo between the real world and wherever it was that dead people ended up. Sometimes when Greg was awake he wondered if there really was somewhere else or if the dead just evaporated without a trace, but not here, not in Tommy's bar. While he was here Greg was sure that this was just a way station, a last-chance rendezvous for the living and a waiting room for the dead.

Kane rubbed his fingers across the table and drew little figure eights in beer-bottle sweat. Sadie turned around and seemed to look through him until Greg raised his hand, then she nodded and limped over to the bar. A minute later she thumped a Rolling Rock down in front of him and he handed her a five.

"Is my brother here?" Kane asked.

"Honey, he's always here," Sadie said in her lung-cancer voice.

Kane looked around. "I don't see him."

"He'll find you, don't you worry." Sadie held up the five and arched her brows.

"Bring one for Tommy and run a tab," Kane told her. Sadie shoved the bill into her apron and turned away.

Greg methodically searched the place starting at the pool table in the back. Tweaker and Fireplug were still playing a game that had neither a beginning nor an end. Beyond that was the hallway to the bathrooms, payphone, condom machine and the back door. At the jukebox, Slut Girl was pouring over the buttons as helplessly as if they were printed in Chinese. Big Jesse, Little Jesse, Denny and Phil surrounded a table full of empty bottles and plastic baskets of nachos and peanuts in the shell. Dapper Dave perched up on the last stool and watched Slut Girl's ass as she leaned over the Wurlitzer. Kid Billy, Babyface and Dumb Sally lined up along the bar from back to front where Studly the bartender poured a never-ending stream of bourbon and drafts.

Kane looked behind him toward the front door. A wash of gray light clouded the foot-square window in the top of the panel and he thought, again, about getting out of his chair and putting his face to the glass or maybe even opening the door and stepping outside, but he was overcome by a wave of fear. Somehow Kane knew that doing anything like that would break the spell that admitted him to this neutral ground and that once he tried to leave or even look beyond these walls he would never be allowed to return.

He heard a hollow *thunk* and when he turned away from the window he saw Sadie limping toward the gloom sheltering the back table. His brother was now sitting across from him. Tommy raised his beer, smiled and clinked the neck against the green bottle in Greg's hand.

"Happy days, little brother," Tommy said and took a gulp. "Ahhh, that hits the spot. I do miss a good beer."

"What do you mean, 'miss'? You live here. You can have all the beer you want."

"Did you ever watch an old movie and see all those beautiful people, smiling and dancing up a storm and wonder what they were thinking, Grego?" Tommy asked.

"They're not thinking anything. They're not really there."

"They're there for you, Greg."

"They're just a recording, a memory."

"Me too," Tommy said, smiling and taking another swallow. "This place," Tommy waved around the bar, "It's only here for you. Once you leave we all go back into storage like the refrigerator light going off as soon as you close the door. So, thanks for showing up." Tommy chugged down the rest of his Rolling Rock and waved the empty bottle at Studly behind the bar. Studly nodded and pulled a fresh one out of the ice.

"What's outside that door?" Greg asked, half turning around.

"Someplace else," Tommy answered.

"Can you go there?"

Tommy laughed. "Go there? I'm barely even here." Almost invisible, Sadie plunked another bottle on the table and then vanished like a shadow. "So, tell me, Greg," Tommy said, all humor suddenly gone, "why are you here?"

"I came to see you."

"Are you ready to listen to me this time, little brother, or do you just want to ask more questions that I don't have the answers to?"

"I always listened to you, Tommy, always."

"Until I died. Then you stopped."

"You said that you aren't real, that you're just a figment of my imagination." Greg reached across the table and grabbed Tommy's hand.

"I said that I was here for you. Maybe I'm me and maybe I'm just another part of you but I still have things to tell you if you're willing to listen."

Tommy seemed to flicker for an instant then solidify again.

"Whoa! Almost lost you there. Are you sleeping on the couch again, little brother?"

Greg found that his fingers were empty. Somehow Tommy's hands had disappeared into his lap.

"I'll listen, Tommy. What do you want to tell me?"

"What did I tell you the last time and the time before that?"

"I did what I was supposed to do. I took the classes. I saw the shrink. I'm under control."

"Said the man who swallowed a pill every time his tooth hurt."

"What's that supposed to mean?"

"Treating the symptom is a fool's game, Greg. You've got to cure the disease. Pull the tooth, little brother."

"I— what?"

"Let it go. You have to let it all go."

"What's that supposed to mean?"

"You've got this idea that you bought yourself a winning ticket and somebody's gypped you out of your prize."

"Stop speaking in riddles! For once can't you just say something straight out?"

"Complaining again. You don't hear me complaining do you, and I'm dead."

"And whose fault is that? I told you not take that call. I told you the roads were a mess. I told you to get yourself a fucking new set of tires! But, no, Mr. Nobody-Can-Tell-Me-Anything does whatever the hell he wants and leaves his son without a father."

"You filled in with Jason for me, Grego."

"Yeah, I filled in! What a great job I did!" Kane half shouted. "I raised Jason to want to be a cop like us and now he's dead too."

"You think you got Jason killed?" Tommy asked in a soft voice.

"If you're going to tell me I didn't, just forget it. I'm not a fool. I know what I did."

"And you think my getting killed, Jason getting killed, that that's unfair?"

"Of course it's unfair. All the bastards who get to live and you, oh, fuck it! What's the point?"

"See, that's your problem right there, Greg, that's the disease that you've got to cut out before it ruins you."

"What are you, some kind of shrink or mystic or something spouting all that inscrutable bullshit? Just say it straight out!"

"It doesn't sound like you're in any mood to listen to me, Grego. It sounds like you just want to bitch about how life's done you wrong. When people think like that it usually means they're planning on getting even somehow. Are you planning on getting even, Greg?"

"Tommy, I—" Kane began but then his brother shimmered. A lopsided grin split Tommy's face and before Greg could do more than shout his name Tommy flickered twice more and Kane's brother and the bar and everything in it disappeared.

*　*　*

Greg Kane opened his eyes with a start and looked blearily around his empty apartment. His phone displayed the words: "Missed Call — Allison Varner" at the top of the screen. Kane stared at the message but was too sick at heart to do anything but half-stagger from the living room and fall onto his bed. Mercifully, for the rest of the night he did not dream.

CHAPTER TWENTY-SEVEN

Now that they had all the "mine is bigger than yours" nonsense out of the way, Kane accepted the Service's offer of a briefing. Clark Millingham was nominally in charge but he was there mostly to keep Kane from bullying his people. S.A. Robert Dohenny was the direct supervisor on the Hopper Protection Detail and he ran Kane through the moving parts in textbook fashion.

Locations: (1) Home; (2) Work; (3) Other Venues; and (4) Transit;

Threats: (1) Short Range — Knife/Handgun; (2) Long Range — Long Gun; (3) Explosives; (4) Chemical Agents — gas/poison.

Human Factors: (1) Strangers; (2) Employees/Co-workers; (3) Known Third Parties — service personnel, journalists, attorneys; (4) Friends/Relatives.

Kane recognized it for what it was, a Dog & Pony Show to keep Senator Denning happy, but he took careful notes anyway, occasionally interrupting to ask a question. By the time the briefing finished at around ten-thirty Kane was convinced that the Secret Service had done a thorough and professional job of providing Hopper with world-class security and it depressed the hell out of him because it left him with a big problem.

In theory Kane's job was done. He had checked out Hopper's security arrangements and found that they were first rate. He could make his report and go back to looking for Mearle Farber, except for one thing — he didn't believe that Hopper actually was safe. He still thought that Eustace had been killed by a pro. A pro likely meant that serious money was behind the hit. The combination of a professional killer and financial resources meant that the operator wasn't going to be scared off by a solid protection team. Just the opposite. It meant that the hitter knew what he was up against and thought that he had a way around it. Maybe he was wrong. Maybe he would make a mistake and get himself caught or killed. But maybe not.

So, Kane asked himself what he should do — smile, shake Millingham's hand, and tell Denning "Mission Accomplished" or should he stick around a little bit longer just in case he thought of something that Dohenny and Company had missed?

"Agent Dohenny, what's the latest on Kathryn Hopper?" Kane asked as the supervisor was packing up his reports.

"We have her covered 24/7," Dohenny said easily, hoping that Kane would let it go.

"Covered how?"

Dohenny took a half breath and looked up from his materials.

"An agent is stationed overnight in her apartment. She's relieved in the morning and a fresh agent accompanies Ms. Hopper wherever she needs to go. When she finishes work we lock her and the night-shift agent back inside. The next morning we start all over again. She's never alone."

Dohenny turned away and zipped up his leather case, hoping that Kane was done.

"A single agent? Do you have a follow car?"

Frowning, Dohenny put the case down and turned back to Kane.

"As a precaution we detailed a second team to Ms. Hopper the morning Agent Eustace's body was found. So far we've detected no activity whatsoever in Ms. Hopper's vicinity. We're going to keep the second team in place through the end of the week. If nothing turns up between now and then we're going to reduce her detail to the primary officer starting on Saturday."

Kane got a faraway look as plans and schemes ran through his head. If, as he suspected, Kathryn Hopper was the weak link, a single babysitter wasn't going to be enough. A blitz attack would take out her minder and five seconds later she would be gone, all of which was bad. On the other hand if the Service continued to double-team Kathryn that might force the hitter to go to Plan B which could be much worse. Ten pounds of shaped C4 in a parked vehicle, triggered when the Justice's car drove past would kill not only Hopper but probably five or ten others as well including the Secret Service agents riding with him.

"Any other questions, Agent Kane?" Dohenny asked after two seconds of silence.

"No," Kane finally answered."

"So, you're ready to write your report?"

"Uhh, no, not quite."

Dohenny struggled not to frown.

"Is there something I can do to help you finish up?"

"Yes, I'm sure there is," Kane said then, again, seemed lost in thought.

"And what would that be?"

"As soon as I think of it I'll let you know." Kane hesitated, distracted by a trill from his phone. "I've got to take this," he said, tapping the screen. "Danny, what have you got? . . . . Stay where you are. I'll be there in fifteen minutes."

Kane slid the phone into his jacket and hurried away. Neither man bothered to say 'goodbye.'

* * *

Kane found Danny parked in a four-year-old Mazda 3 on T Street. He had stripped off his tie and shed his coat but he still looked slightly out of place.

"That's it," Danny said when Kane slipped into the passenger seat. Rosewood pointed his chin at the Capitol Mail & Shipping store across the street and four shops down. Danny's field trip here was wrong in so many ways that Kane didn't know where to even begin.

"Technically, you're not supposed to use a mail box as the address on your driver's license but if you're a criminal I guess you don't care," Danny said, nervously fingering the camera in his lap.

"Did you find something that makes you think Farber's going to show up here today?"

"No, I—, oh," he said, raising the camera. "This is just in case. It's got a 50X zoom so I can get his plate and a good shot of anyone he meets from a long way off." Danny smiled and turned back toward the mailbox store.

Greg kept his mouth shut and tried to think. The kid had worked his ass off and done an amazing job, an unbelievable job in tracking down Mearle Farber. For that, Kane could have kissed him. Then he jeopardized it all with this harebrained field trip. If Farber didn't show up Danny's coming here was a complete waste of time and if Farber did show and spotted Rosewood all Danny's work would be for nothing. Farber would instantly dump the Paul Conklin identity and they would be worse off than they had been before.

Kane knew what Danny was thinking — that he would come out here, get lucky and find Farber without being spotted himself, follow him, again without being noticed, and track Farber to his real address, and then call in the cavalry. Good God, it was like a kid's fantasy out of some old comic book. *Dumb, Dumb, Dumb.*

Ten seconds went by and when Kane didn't speak Danny turned to look at him. One part of Greg's brain told him, *People will never learn if you don't point out their mistakes.* Another voice wondered, *If Jason had been in this situation would he have acted any differently?*

"You did a terrific job, Danny," Kane said.

"Those tips you gave me really helped. We're gonna catch this guy, Agent Kane. We will."

Kane shot a nervous glance across the street. They had to get the hell out of here.

"Let's go over everything back at the office and figure out our next move." Kane reached for the door handle, then turned back.

"I'm really proud of you, Danny," Greg said. Rosewood gave him a smile that threatened to break his face.

CHAPTER TWENTY-EIGHT

Kane stalled on turning in his report, wanting to see if anything happened when the Secret Service reduced Kathryn's protection detail to just one team. He had uneasily waited through the weekend but nothing happened. Back at the office Rosewood wanted him to organize a surveillance team on Farber's mailbox but, fearing discovery, Greg had refused, instead ordering Danny to find another way. Now that Monday had passed without incident Greg realized that he had to let the Hopper thing go. Tomorrow he would turn in his report and get back to his real job. As if to mark the end of his detached duty tonight Kane had embarked on another date? assignation? hook-up? with Allison Varner.

"A penny for your thoughts," Allison said.

Kane's principal thought was that he wanted to strangle people who asked that question but he sensed that saying so would be a mistake. *What does she want to hear?* he asked himself and wiped his lips with his napkin to stall for time.

"I could tell you that I was thinking about how ravishing you look tonight, but you would dismiss that as an attempt to dodge your question with flattery. Or," Kane leaned a little forward, "I could say how lucky I was to be here with you but that would make you worry that I was developing a dangerous emotional attachment." *Was that a wry smile or a sneer?* "Or, I could turn it around and say that I was wondering what you were thinking. Which answer would you prefer?"

"How about the real one."

"Oh, you want the real one. Most women don't want the real answer to that question because they end up finding out that the guy's wondering what kind of underwear she's wearing or when his Viagra's going to kick in or if he's going to be able to get home in time to call the wife before she goes to sleep." *Well, there was no confusion about that look.* "In my case I was thinking that this was the best steak I've had in a long time. It has just the right amount of red."

"You're not nearly as funny as you think," Allison told him through clenched jaws.

"Gee, most people think I'm a laugh riot. Oh, you want to know what I really, *really* think. Fine. I was thinking that you're wondering if I had an ulterior motive in insisting that we have dinner together instead of just jumping into bed." The narrowing around her eyes told him that he was right and that she wasn't amused. "And yes, I did. I thought it might be nice to actually have a normal conversation before we climbed all over each other like wild animals."

"I don't think that's going to be a problem for you tonight," Allison said, stabbing her sea bass as if it was still squirming on her plate.

"Well, how about this then: I was thinking that you didn't tell me that you were Senator Denning's niece."

"I didn't tell you a lot of things," she said, briefly looking up from her dinner.

"Yes, and I wouldn't have minded not knowing if you hadn't talked your uncle into throwing me into a jackpot with the Secret Service. Pissing off people like that can really screw up a person's career."

"Since when do you worry about pissing people off?"

"I'm thinking about trying to avoid it. I've heard good things."

Allison glared at Kane for almost a full second before she broke into a smile.

"And that concludes the psychotherapy portion of our evening," Kane said and cut off another chunk of meat.

Allison concentrated on her dinner for half a minute then finally asked, "All right, what should we talk about?"

"That's a good question. Our jobs? Religion? Politics? . . . . Sorry," Kane said, reading the hurt look on Allison's face. "I wasn't making fun of you. Tell me something about yourself."

"Like what?"

"Anything. What you studied in school. What you like to do for fun. What kind of movies you like. The sort of normal stuff people talk about."

"On dates you mean, normal stuff people talk about on dates."

"Heaven forbid. . . . Fine, pretend I'm a woman, a friend of a friend, and we're having a pleasant lunch together."

Allison gave him a suspicious glance then shrugged her shoulders in surrender.

"I like to cook," she said.

"That's good. I like to eat. What else?"

Communicating with her is like trying to coax a nervous cat into taking a treat from my hand, Kane thought but somehow he kept her talking all the way through dessert. Kane heard music drifting in from the lounge and for a moment he considered suggesting that they go in and have a drink and maybe even share a dance, then just as quickly he abandoned the idea. She was starting to regret letting down her barriers and he sensed that one wrong word and this nervous cat was going to flee.

"Next time I can book the room," he said when the elevator started its climb.

"You don't like this hotel?"

"It's fine. I just meant that you don't always have to pay."

"I don't mind," she said in a voice that cooled five degrees.

You want to be in control, he thought. *You want to be able to throw me out and lock the door and call hotel security to kick my ass to the curb if it starts to look as if I might actually feel something for you.*

"OK."

Once inside she turned so that Greg could unzip her dress, but he gently turned her around to face him.

"There's no hurry," Kane said and, starting at her shoulders, began running the flat of his hands down her body, pausing at her breasts and then at her groin. Finally when his palms had reached her calves he raised them slowly until he had pinned her skirt above her waist with one hand while gently massaging her thighs outward with the other. He heard a catch in her throat and her breathing turned into a pant. Kane had just begun to pull her panties down, inch by inch, when a sharp *TRILL* shattered the mood.

"Don't answer it!" Allison ordered in a husky voice.

Kane fumbled out the phone and reached for the "Decline" icon then he saw that it was a text from Robert Dohenny: "KH kidnapped. Agent down" followed by a number.

"It's Hopper!" Kane told her, struggling to his feet. "They've kidnapped his daughter."

Allison froze then unconsciously pulled down her skirt.

"The ransom, they're going to want him to vote against Lyla's Law," she said in a worried voice.

"No, I don't think so." Kane hurriedly rearranged his clothes. "The decision's weeks away. They couldn't keep her captive that long."

"Then what?"

Kane looked at Allison in the dim light spilling through the windows, her skirt wrinkled and only halfway to her knees, her hair slightly askew, and he thought that he had never wanted a woman as much as he wanted her. In an instant she was in his arms. When he finally released her he could not have said how long the embrace had lasted. It seemed like both a second and a minute all at once.

"Remember where we left off," Greg told her and then turned away.

CHAPTER TWENTY-NINE

It was the fourth bar of the night and if Kathryn Hopper followed her usual schedule Agent Warren Emerson figured that they had two more to go before he could turn her over to the babysitter back at her apartment. He had checked out the room when they arrived and nobody set off any alarms. From his table against the wall he had a good view of both of the entrances and he watched every patron for signs of weapons or any unusual interest in Hopper's daughter. A trill of laughter marked Kathryn's goodbyes to a pair of women who were now admiring their new nail polish. A moment later she slipped into the empty chair opposite him.

"I need to visit the ladies' room," she told Emerson in a matter-of-fact voice.

He had laid down the ground rules on his first protection shift: She wasn't to leave the area where he had eyes on her for any reason. If she had to use the restroom then he would have a waitress make sure that it was empty, then he would go in with her to double check that all the stalls are unoccupied and then he would stand guard outside until she emerged. If he had to use the restroom himself the procedure would be repeated with the proviso that she would lock herself inside the ladies room until he was done and he gave her the "I'm back" knock.

"OK," Emerson said and walked her over to the bar. "Miss, would you mind making sure that the ladies' room is unoccupied?" He had badged the staff the minute they walked in and explained the procedure. The girl didn't mind. He tipped her a few bucks and she found the job no more trouble than delivering a round of drinks.

"Empty," the waitress said a few moments later and Emerson slipped three singles into her hand. He and Hopper went inside and he double checked the room then he returned to the corridor and planted his back against the wall next to the door. Emerson skipped his eyes between the men's room, the rear entrance down the hallway to his left and the bar's main room down the hallway to his right. About half a minute after Kathryn went inside one of the male customers entered the corridor. Emerson scanned him automatically — Caucasian, five-eleven, one-eighty, brown and blue, long-sleeved dress shirt, gray slacks, black wingtips. The guy gave Emerson a quick glance then hugged the far wall and slid by. A minute later, a cell phone to his ear, the man emerged and turned sideways so that he could clear Emerson without getting too close.

Just as he passed the cell slipped from his hand. Both Emerson and the customer turned to watch it bounce off the carpet and as soon as the agent's attention was distracted Donald slipped the stun gun from his sleeve and pressed it against Emerson's stomach just below his rib cage. It was an over-powered model that was guaranteed to produce an average of more than eight million volts over three seconds of use. The manufacturer bragged that it could incapacitate a man through five layers of clothing.

Donald kept the trigger down for a full three seconds then grabbed Emerson in a bear hug and bundled him through the woman's room door. Once inside he dropped the agent, bent over and shocked him in the throat for two more seconds. Donald was just straightening up when the latch on the cubicle rattled and Kathryn Hopper emerged. For an instant she was frozen by the image of Emerson on the floor then she took a breath to scream but Donald jammed the stun gun into her solar plexus and paralyzed her diaphragm. Now he had to move fast. He didn't enjoy killing but it didn't bother him either. Warren Emerson had seen his face and that meant he had to die. A gun was too noisy and a knife was too likely to get some of Emerson's blood on him but Donald had come prepared.

He pulled a plastic bag from his pocket, slipped it over Emerson's head and secured it tightly around the agent's throat with a piece of cotton twine. Donald wasn't worried about leaving prints. Earlier that evening he had coated his fingertips with cyanoacrylate, forming a barrier that sweat and skin oil could not penetrate. While Emerson thrashed in a vain attempt to draw a breath Donald gave Kathryn another jolt then slipped into the hallway to recover the dropped phone. A moment later he half-dragged, half-carried Kathryn out the back door. In a few seconds she was on his car's rear floor and they were heading into the heart of D.C.

Ten minutes later one of the nail-polish ladies pushed into the restroom and discovered Warren Emmerson's body. It was another fifteen minutes after that before the D.C. cops found Emerson's Secret Service ID and finally rang the alarm. By then Donald already had Kathryn Hopper safely tucked away. Part One of his plan was now complete.

CHAPTER THIRTY

It took Kane three tries to get through to Dohenny and when he finally connected the agent just rattled off an address and hung up. The Taft House was the sort of neighborhood bar and grill that you could find in any city in America, solidly middle class, reasonably priced and with a kitchen just big enough to serve a good burger and decent fries. When Kane arrived it looked like a war zone. The local cops had been posted at the exits with orders that no one without a badge was to enter or leave.

Inside two teams of agents were working their way through the patrons and staff with each person being separately interviewed by each team to make sure that nothing was missed. One squad of crime scene techs processed the ladies' room while the body still lay in the center of the floor awaiting clearance from the coroner's assistant. A second team had finished processing the rear door and was now working on the tables that had been occupied by the three patrons who left shortly before the body was discovered. The first team to finish their assignment would move into the parking lot where they would photograph every license plate and collect every cigarette butt and gum wrapper.

Kane found Dohenny in the corner nervously talking into his phone. The agent saw Greg and held up one finger.

"Yes, I've got a team on that. . . . No, no cameras in the bar. . . . Right, look Kane's here." Dohenny gave Greg a quick glance. "OK." Dohenny disconnected and slipped the phone into his pocket.

"What happened?" Kane asked, trying to tune out the frantic activity around them. Dohenny unconsciously wiped his sweating forehead and pulled out his notes. Kane recognized it as a defensive measure, a security blanket since Kane was sure that the details of tonight's events were burned into Dohenny's brain.

"The subject and Agent Emerson arrived at approximately eight-fourteen," he began, reading from his pad in a clinical tone. When he got to his description of the murder scene Kane interrupted Dohenny's report.

"Any prints on the plastic bag?"

"No."

"If his prints weren't found on the bag then we're not going to find them anywhere else. Nobody heard anything?"

"They had a basketball game on the flat screen behind the bar."

"Any obvious trauma to Agent Emerson?"

Dohenny shook his head. "Something like a blackjack might not have broken the skin. We won't really know until the M.E. takes a close look at the body."

"Any neighborhood cameras?" Kane asked.

"I've got guys walking both sides of the street. No ATMs or traffic cams in the area."

Kane's eyes glazed over for a moment then he muttered "Shit!" half under his breath.

"What?"

"This guy's no nut job. He's a pro and he's not going to make any stupid mistakes."

"Because he used a plastic bag and didn't leave any prints?" Dohenny asked.

"Because he used a piece of string to secure the bag around Emerson's neck." Kane read the confusion on Dohenny's face and continued. "Anybody but a pro would use tape to secure the bag. It's automatic, but a pro knows that a small length of tape is hard to carry unless you roll it up and then it's a pain to unroll, and tape will trap lint and threads and even skin cells. It's a CSI's dream, plus you can match the end you've got with the end still on the roll if the doer is stupid enough to keep it around. On top of that if this were some guy with standard military training he'd have slit your agent's throat instead of planning things thoroughly enough to bring the bag with him. The fact that he used a bag and then secured it with twine instead of tape tells me that we've got the real deal here."

"No one's infallible and from here on it just gets harder for him."

"How's he going to contact you?" Kane asked, suddenly changing the subject.

"What?"

"The girl has no intrinsic value. She's just a bargaining chip, so who does he negotiate with?"

"She's got the judge's numbers on her phone. We're setting a trap on all of Hopper's lines."

"Her phone is dead?"

Dohenny nodded. "He must have removed the battery and the SIM card. I figure the judge will get a call from some burner phone which will give us a chance to at least track the number back to the store that sold it."

"That'll be a dead end," Kane muttered, his mind already someplace else.

"We could get lucky."

"If our killer's phone was bought sooner than three months ago I'll eat my hat. No, my guess is that our guy's got a dozen of them stockpiled from mom and pop stores all over the East Coast." Kane stared blindly toward the door, then frowned.

"What?"

"Exactly. What? — What's he after? What does he expect to accomplish by taking the daughter?"

"You said it yourself. She's his bargaining chip. Hopper recuses himself from the Hoffkemper case and he lets the girl go." Kane shook his head. "Why not?"

"What if after he lets her go Hopper unrecuses himself?"

"Could he do that?"

Kane shrugged. "I don't know. I guess it would be up to the Chief Justice. But if you were doing this would you take the chance? Think about it. You go to all this trouble. You kill a Secret Service agent and you kidnap the daughter of a Supreme Court Justice and then you say, 'Promise me that you won't vote' and Hopper says, 'OK, I promise' and you just let her go and hope that Hopper is a man of his word? Does that sound like a good idea?" Kane nervously tapped his fingers against his thigh. "I don't see it. He's got something else planned, something that he thinks is absolutely going to take Hopper out of the case."

"His resignation from the court?" Dohenny suggested.

"Assuming he would resign and even if he did, that's still not 100%. The country would be outraged. Theoretically, the President could re-appoint Hopper to fill the vacancy once they had the daughter back. The Senate could confirm him in a day if they were pissed off enough."

"You think she's a lure," Dohenny said in almost a whisper. "You think he's going to use her to force Hopper to be someplace where he thinks he's got a shot at him."

"That's the only way this makes any sense," Kane said. "If—" Kane was interrupted by a tone from his phone. "It's Senator Denning," Greg told Dohenny, and tapped the 'accept' button.

CHAPTER THIRTY-ONE

Five minutes after he fled the bar Donald pulled into a shuttered gas station then climbed into the back seat and injected Kathryn with eight milligrams of Lorazepam. Next he removed all her clothing including her shoes just in case the Secret Service had fitted her with a tracking device. He covered her naked body with a blanket then dumped all her clothing into the trash bin behind the station. He had picked this spot in order to lead the cops in the wrong direction and now he turned around and headed back the way he had come. Fifteen minutes later he had Kathryn locked in the back bedroom of a crumbling house whose closest neighbor was one of dozens of abandoned bank foreclosures in the area. The owner of this house was also in foreclosure, approximately sixty days away from the hammer falling. He'd been happy to accept Mr. Smith's offer of a one month cash rental with no questions asked.

Donald propped Kathryn up on the bed and pulled a thin jumpsuit over her legs and chest then dropped a pair of cheap sneakers on the floor. This room had no heat and a heavy overcoat was hanging from a hook on the opposite wall. Donald checked her pulse and made sure that she had not vomited into her throat then covered her with a blanket and locked the door behind him. Days earlier he had placed a radio in the room with the volume turned up high then stood on the sidewalk and listened. Nobody was going to hear her screams.

There was no point in contacting anyone tonight. Let them stew for a while. The more anxious they were the more cooperative they would be. Besides, they would want proof of life and the woman wouldn't be in any shape to talk to them for another twelve hours. Donald made one more circuit around the property then locked up and climbed into bed.

* * *

Kane felt as if he was playing out a scene from a movie — the irate politician pacing his living room in the dead of night and demanding answers from his frightened subordinates, except that Greg Kane didn't work for Denning and the senator was more upset than angry.

"I don't understand how this could have happened without anyone seeing something," Denning complained. "Were they in on it, the people in the bar?"

"There's no evidence of that."

"Was the owner or the manager one of those gun-nuts? You can check for that, can't you, see if they're members of the NRA or the Aryan Brotherhood or something like that?"

Kane almost reminded Denning that no judge was going to issue a subpoena for the NRA's membership list but Greg bit his tongue. That wasn't the issue in any event. Everybody in the bar told essentially the same story and they couldn't all be involved. The evidence was pretty straightforward, one trained kidnapper with a well thought out plan. Sure, he might have had an accomplice, a helper, a driver, but that was irrelevant right now. All that mattered was that he, or they, had gotten away clean. All the authorities could do now was wait for the kidnapper to contact them and make his demands.

"The Secret Service is doing a thorough background check on everyone who was in the bar," Kane said with surprising tact. *Am I pulling my punches because of Denning's position or because he's Allison's uncle?* Greg wondered.

"A lot of good that does us now," Denning muttered. He took a sip of scotch and paced the room. "What happens next? What's our next move?"

"We wait for the kidnapper to contact us and go from there."

"You know what he's going to want, don't you? He's going to demand that Hopper vote to strike down Lyla's Law." Denning took another swallow of whiskey.

This guy's losing it, Kane thought. *He's smart enough to know better.*

"Senator, have you ever heard the phrase, 'You can't push a string?'"

"What?"

"When you don't control a situation trying to force things won't work. Right now we're not in control. The next step is up to him."

"Can you find him? Can you save her?"

How the hell am I supposed to know that? Greg thought.

"We'll know more when he contacts us," Kane said instead. Denning raised his glass and seemed surprised to find it empty. Angrily he slammed it down on the cherry-wood end-table and it shattered with a hollow, crunching sound. The senator stared at the debris like a man just woken from a dream.

"Crap!" He shook his head in dismay. "Sorry," he said, looking at Kane. "I've been acting like a damn fool. Let's sit down." Denning waved Kane to the sofa while he took the love seat on the opposite side of the coffee table.

"Just tell me straight out," Denning began in a tired voice, "did the Secret Service screw this up?"

Did they? Kane asked himself. *Should they have posted a second agent? Would that have made any difference?* In one sense, yes, because this particular scheme wouldn't have worked. In another, no, because this guy was smart and trained and he would have just tried something else and then they would have had two dead agents instead of just one.

"No," Kane answered after a second or two. "They played it by the book. Anyone can be gotten to if you want it badly enough."

"So, we just wait?"

"For now."

"Do you think he'll try to force Hopper to recuse himself?"

"I think he's going to try to kill him and this is only a scheme to get closer to his target."

"How's he going to do that? Surely the Secret Service isn't going to let Hopper anywhere near this man."

"We won't know anything until we hear his demands."

"Are you still seeing my niece?" Denning asked in a sudden change of topic. Kane just stared. "She's stopped talking about you. It occurred to me that you might have been upset that I dragged you into this Hopper thing and blamed her. It wasn't her idea you know."

"I never thought it was." Denning waited. "And, yes, we're still seeing each other."

"That's good," Denning said, giving Kane a sudden smile. 'Grieving is one thing but at some point you have to let it go. My wife . . . ." Denning paused then briefly looked away.

"Survivor's guilt," Kane said. "When I got out of the hospital the department made me go to counseling. They told me that sometimes people who live think that it's disrespectful to be happy after someone you care about has died, as if being happy is evidence that their death didn't really matter to you."

"Did that happen to you, when your partner was killed?"

"Me? No. I killed the son-of-a-bitch who murdered Ralph. I did right by him the same as he would have done for me."

Kane almost asked if Allison had gotten any counseling but then realized there was no point. If she had it hadn't helped and if she hadn't it was because she didn't want to let go of the pain. *Maybe she'll never let go of it*, he thought and wondered if he wasn't wasting his time with someone who was possibly broken beyond repair.

They stared at each other for a few seconds longer then Kane got up.

"I'll call you when we hear from him," Greg said.

"Good." Denning rubbed his forehead and looked away. Kane followed the senator's gaze to a picture of a much younger Arthur Denning and a smiling, brown-haired woman with sparkling blue eyes.

CHAPTER THIRTY-TWO

Danny Rosewood looked nervously over his shoulder knowing that he shouldn't be doing what he was doing but somehow unable to stop himself. He had tried to reach Agent Kane but all of his calls had gone to voice mail. Something was up, he could tell that much, but no one would give him the straight story.

"Ask your buddy, Kane," Jerry Helms had said and given him a nasty smile. For a second Danny almost asked the boss but stopped himself. He knew Kane wouldn't have liked that. *Well*, he decided, *partners trust each other. When there's something I need to know, Agent Kane will tell me.*

Danny had wanted to add Conklin's license number to the D.C. Police database with a "Report but do not stop" notation but Kane had nixed that idea.

"Why not?" Danny asked.

"If you had killed somebody and gone underground and gotten yourself a new identity you'd want to know if anybody had found you, wouldn't you?" Danny nodded. "If you knew all about the license plate database and the plate readers on patrol cars wouldn't you want to put a flag into the system so that you would be warned if anybody started looking for your new license number?"

"But that's an official police database."

"Farber was a dirty cop," Kane said as if he was talking to a five-year-old.

"So?"

"If I asked you to do something like that for me, could you?"

"Well, sure, but— oh." Danny said, finally getting it. "So, what should I do?"

"Find another way," Kane told him and hung up.

So, Danny had spent untold hours again going through all of Conklin's VISA charges and he found another way. This time, instead of focusing on unusual purchases, the outliers, he paid attention to the ordinary, repeated charges, food, gas, restaurants and the like. This quickly narrowed his search to a nine block area and he figured that Farber/Conklin probably lived someplace near the center. He briefly considered checking all the restaurants where Conklin's card had been used in the hope that he may have had food delivered to his home but, keeping Kane's paranoia about tipping their hand in mind, Danny let that idea go. Instead he started physically searching the target area. It took him several days but eventually he found his man.

Danny didn't actually have a plan, at least not much of a plan, nothing beyond driving the neighborhood and looking for Conklin's Camry whenever he could steal a few hours away from his desk. While Kane was on his secret assignment he spent his days driving in circles but one afternoon as he was grabbing a quick lunch at the Burger King he saw a silver Camry stop at the light. Danny swallowed without chewing and sprinted for the door. Just before the signal changed he caught a glimpse of the plate. The last three numbers matched. Farber was a block ahead of him by the time he got out of the lot which was probably the only thing that saved him from being burned.

Eventually Farber pulled into a row house near Brightwood Park. Danny glided by just as Farber was reaching into the back seat to retrieve a bag of groceries. The first two digits of the house number were 81 but Danny didn't get the rest. Heeding Kane's warning about spooking the target he resisted the impulse to park and take some pictures. Instead he kept going all the way to Missouri Avenue where he pulled over and tried to get Kane on the phone, again without success. Frustrated but excited he returned to the office and found the boss and another man standing next to his desk.

"Where have you been, Rosewood?" Immerson demanded.

"Just out doing some legwork, sir." Danny glanced at his other visitor.

"This is Special Assistant Sebastian Wren," Immerson told him.

Danny froze for a second.

"Mr. Wren," he said at last then nervously stuck out his hand.

"That's Supervisory Agent Wren," Immerson corrected him.

Wren smiled and took Danny's hand.

"Agent Wren will be fine. You look pretty busy there, Rosewood," Wren said gesturing toward the stacks of folders on Danny's desk. "What's all that?"

"That, oh, it's just, you know. . . data. Agent Kane said that finding someone is about getting all the information that you can and then looking for something that stands out, like a loose thread on a sweater that you can pull in order to unravel it."

"Have you found any loose threads?"

The Danny Rosewood of a month ago would have answered "yes" and happily explained every step in the process that had finally led him to their target, but some aspect of Kane's cynicism had by this time rubbed off on him.

The first week they had worked together something had come up and Danny had asked Kane, "Shouldn't we tell Mr. Immerson what we've found?"

"In due time."

"When will that be?"

"When it's too late for him to fuck up our investigation."

Danny just stared, too confused to know where to begin.

"Here's the deal," Kane said, irritated that he had to explain every little thing. "You tell the boss whatever you have to tell him in order to get what you need from him. Until you need something there's no point in confusing him with facts." Kane could see that the kid still didn't get it. He took a breath and tried again. "Look, whenever you tell the bosses anything there's always some finite chance that they'll find a way to screw up your case."

"But—"

"They might tell you to abandon a lead or chase a different lead or talk to somebody or not to talk to somebody. You never know. What you do know is that every time you tell them what you've done there's a chance they'll tell you that you were wrong and every time you tell them what you're going to do there's a chance they'll tell you not to do it. On the other hand if you tell them nothing then that possibility is reduced from whatever percent it might have been to zero. Zero is good."

"So," Danny began, struggling to digest this heretical doctrine, "never tell the boss what you've done or what you're going to do unless you have to?"

"Now you've got it," Kane said, pointing his index finger at Rosewood's chest. "There's only one exception to that rule."

"What's that?"

"It doesn't apply to me. You tell me everything and let me figure out if and what Immerson needs to know. Got it?"

"Ahh, yes, Agent Kane. I've got it," Danny agreed solemnly.

Now Danny looked from Wren to Immerson and back again.

"I'm still looking, sir. I figure Agent Kane will be able to give me some good ideas on where to go next as soon as he comes back from . . . well, whatever it is he's working on." Danny waited but neither man volunteered an opinion when that might be. "Is there anything else I can help you with?"

"We'll let you know," Wren said then turned away before Danny could offer to shake his hand again.

Once outside the office Wren hit the speed dial on his phone.

"Kane's gofer claims they haven't made any progress on the Brownstein case but he's holding something back. . . . No, sir, it's just a hunch. . . . Yes, sir. I'll give him a day or so to relax then I'll invite him out for a drink, man-to-man, well, man-to-kid, and we'll see if I can get him to open up." Wren switched off the phone.

Back at his desk Danny called up Google Street View and five minutes later found himself looking at Mearle Farber's front door.

CHAPTER THIRTY-THREE

For the first time in three years Mr. Justice Hopper missed work. The last time that had happened he had been the victim of a vicious bout of viral gastroenteritis. Today, it was a different sort of an attack. This morning he was closeted with his Secret Service team, two FBI agents with kidnapping expertise and Greg Kane. The first message from the kidnapper had arrived a little after nine, a text to Hopper's cell:

"Dad, I'm OK. He wants $1M to be paid in bitcoins. Sign in as Rumplestiltskin and reply as a comment here." The text was followed by a link to a story about a new high-tech watch on BusinessInsider.com.

"He wants money?" Dohenny said.

"That's good, isn't it?" Hopper asked, hopefully. "We can give him money."

Kane just looked at the tech guys.

"No luck. He bounced it through an anonymizing server and he turned the cell off the instant he hit 'send'."

No one even bothered to ask about monitoring the hundreds of thousands of people who might view the Business Insider article over the next few hours.

"He's stalling," Kane told Dohenny.

"That makes no sense. The longer this goes on the better our chances are of finding him."

"He's got a plan. This is all a head fake. How fast can we get our reply up?"

Dohenny looked at the tech.

"I've already signed in as Rumlestiltskin87. What's the message?"

"We need proof of life," the FBI agent told Dohenny.

"Judge we need a question that only Kathryn would know the answer to."

Eyes closed, Hopper tried to think. He answered a few seconds later. "When she was five she had a favorite doll that she took everywhere, 'Sally Sally'."

"Type this: 'Agreed — what was your favorite doll's name?'"

The tech's keys rattled and a few seconds later the Rumplestiltskin comment appeared at the bottom of the Business Insider page. A minute later Hopper's phone beeped with a new message: "Sally Sally. Sending transfer instructions at 6:00 p.m."

Dohenny looked at the tech but only got a brief head shake.

"What's his game?" Dohenny wondered aloud.

"It could be psychological," the lead FBI agent, Handleman, said. "He wants us on edge then he'll rush us with a short deadline once we're all revved up."

"He's running a game on us," Kane said but for the life of him he couldn't figure out what it was.

* * *

Donald filled a bowl with corn flakes and milk and carried it to Kathryn's room. He pounded twice on the door and called out, "Are you awake in there?"

"Yes," the woman answered in a shaky voice.

"Face the wall, your back to the door. If you see my face I'll have to kill you."

He entered a few seconds later. As ordered Kathryn's back was toward him and he placed the bowl of cereal and a plastic spoon on the dresser.

"After I leave you can turn around and eat your breakfast. If you're thirsty fill the bowl with water from the bathroom tap."

"What are you going to do with me?"

"That's up to your father. If he does everything I want I might let you live."

"Please don't hurt me. He'll do whatever you say."

"We'll see. I don't trust him."

"Why are you doing this?"

"Your father's a traitor to America. Men like him have to pay," Donald snarled and backed out of the room. Once outside he allowed himself a little smile. If the woman wasn't terrified before she was now which was exactly what he wanted.

* * *

Kane and the rest of the agents waited out the day but only accumulated more questions and no answers. Greg gave Senator Denning a progress report and then took a chance and asked him to transfer the call to Allison's desk.

"How's it going?" she asked.

"I wish I could tell you."

"You don't know or you can't say?"

"I meant that nothing about this makes any sense," Kane replied.

"Isn't that to be expected? I mean terrorists aren't the most rational people."

"This guy may be crazy but he's not stupid. Everything he's done up to now has been disciplined and professional. Suddenly he's turning this into a for-ransom kidnapping? If he was just after money there are a lot of richer people out there who are much easier targets. I don't know what his real plan is but I can tell you that the money is just a smokescreen. . . . Anyway, how are you?"

"I'm in the midst of preparing a very exciting press release on the patent-reform bill Uncle Arthur is sponsoring."

"What kind of paintings do you like?" Kane asked after a second of two of silence.

"Paintings?"

"You know, impressionists, old masters, abstract."

Allison paused for a moment trying to figure out how Kane's question fit into their conversation about kidnappings and high tech legislation.

"Why do you want to know?"

"I like impressionists. I know what you're thinking — what's a cop know about art?"

"No, I'm wondering if you're having a stroke."

"I'm going to need to clear my head once this kidnapping is over," Greg said, ignoring her gibe. "There's a new impressionist exhibition at the National Gallery."

"You're not making any sense at all," Allison told him.

Kane sighed, frustrated by Allison's confusion.

"I'm asking if you would go with me to the National Gallery when this is all over." Kane paused but she didn't reply. "Don't worry, it's not anything romantic. Think of it as pre-fucking exercise."

"I don't appreciate your snotty attitude, Greg."

"I figure looking at the nudes ought to get our libidos nicely revved up for the main event."

"You're on thin ice, Kane."

"So, you'll do it?"

The silence stretched for several seconds.

"Ask me again when you catch the guy," Allison finally told him and then hung up.

* * *

At three minutes after six an email appeared in Hopper's inbox: "Send money as instructed before six p.m. tomorrow. It will be used to defend Americans' constitutional rights. Sign the attached statement and release it to the press no later than six p.m. tomorrow." Two DOC files were attached to the email. The first contained the details for the transfer of one-million dollars in bitcoins. The second was a one-page text file titled "My Confession — My Pledge."

The tech printed out three copies then tore into the file's guts looking for user names, the Microsoft Word serial number, earlier versions of the text and anything else he could find buried in the file or the email. Kane grabbed one of the hard copies and began reading aloud.

"I have been planning on betraying the American People," he read, "by disarming them so that they will be easy prey for the secret police and the totalitarian government they keep in power. But now I realize that I must do the right thing. The so-called Lyla's Law is an unconstitutional scheme to turn a free and strong people into a mob of victims to be ground under the government's heel. I hereby promise that I will vote my conscience and do everything in my power to see that it is struck down and that I will vote to affirm the decision of the Court of Appeals in the case of *Hoffkemper v. California*. — George Hopper, Justice of the United States Supreme Court."

"Finally, it's starting to make some sense," Dohenny said when Kane finished reading.

"Not to me," Kane grumbled, skimming the sheet in the general direction of the coffee table. Dohenny stared at him and waited. "He's giving us too much time," Kane complained. "Why would he give us a full day to try to find him? He could have demanded that we do this tonight in time for the ten o'clock news or by nine tomorrow morning. Why is he stalling?"

"I'm grateful for small favors. Every extra minute is that much more time to track him down. — Anything?" Dohenny asked the tech.

"Nothing. He got into the file with an editor and stripped out all the identifying info in the headers. Even if I could tease out a serial number it's going to be a dead end."

Dohenny looked at Handleman but the FBI agent just shrugged. Hopper seemed frozen, his eyes locked on the page. Finally, he looked up.

"I can't sign this," Hopper said his expression somewhere between terror and tears.

"We're not there yet, Judge," Dohenny told him. "We've got almost a full day before we have to make that decision."

"This country can't work if people can blackmail the Court into deciding cases the way they want. A day or a year, it doesn't make any difference. I won't, I can't sign this." Hopper crumpled the page and tossed it halfway across the room. "I'll have to recuse myself," he said a moment later.

"Judge, we're not there yet," Dohenny told him.

"Don't you see? No matter what I do, I'm tainted. If he lets Kathryn go and I vote to affirm the Court of Appeals people will think that my vote was coerced. If Kathryn is . . . if we don't get her back and I vote to reverse the Court of Appeals then people will think that I did that to get revenge."

"Recusing yourself is what he wants," Kane broke in. "Everyone figures you're the swing vote. With you out of the way it's four to four and the decision of the Court of Appeals stands, which is exactly what he's been after from day one."

"How can I not recuse myself? No matter what I do my vote will be tainted."

"Not if we get her back before the deadline," Kane said.

"But—"

"Look, if we rescue her then no one can say that you voted against the law as a ransom payment and no one can say you voted in favor of the law for revenge. Once she's safe and sound everything goes back to where it was, the scheme didn't work and the kidnapper didn't get what he wanted."

"They kidnapped my daughter! No matter what I do people will think I voted out of personal prejudice or emotion," Hopper argued.

"Like you said, Judge, this is bigger than just you. There are only two choices here: one, you vote your conscience and some people maybe suspect you acted out of personal motives or, two, you don't vote at all and you send the country the message that the

Supreme Court's decisions can be rigged by coercing a justice on the wrong side not to vote. It's pretty clear which of those two options is the most dangerous."

Hopper seemed frozen for a moment then looked up at Kane. "Do you really think that you can save her?" he asked, more a plea than a question.

"That depends on whether or not we can discover what he's really planning because this," Kane waved at the wrinkled page, "is all a scam, a misdirect. If we can figure out why he was stalling then maybe we'd have a chance."

CHAPTER THIRTY-FOUR

"Your father's not cooperating," Donald told Kathryn late that night, his voice muffled by his mask. "Maybe he thinks I won't kill you, but I will."

"No! Please," Kathryn pleaded. "I can convince him. Please, just let me talk to him."

"So you can give him some clue where you are? I don't think so. Maybe if I cut off one of your fingers and send it to him he'd change his tune." Donald waved a pair of garden shears in front of her face.

"No! Please don't! Please," Kathryn begged and burst into tears.

"He better come across by this time tomorrow night or he's going to find out that I mean business." Donald stomped out of the room, slammed the door and tore off his mask. *That ought to motivate her to escape,* he thought. For a moment he considered driving past what he called "Point B" but decided against it. Either the occupants had left on their little trip or they hadn't.

Weeks earlier Donald had searched the tax assessor's records for the names of the owners of any houses that might work as Point B. Further investigation had narrowed the list. He identified the remaining targets on a Google map then hacked into the owners' Facebook pages. He was fully prepared to take over an occupied structure if necessary — a knock on the door, a jab with the stun gun, a pocket full of plastic bags, and in a few minutes the house would be his. But that turned out to be unnecessary. Mr. and Mrs. Irwin Wedemeyer were kind enough to post their plans for a week's visit with their daughter and new grandchild so he knew that their house was going to be empty. The day before he grabbed Kathryn it only took him ten minutes to defeat their bargain-basement alarm system.

Point B was on a street parallel to and one block north of Hopper's home. The last thing he did after disabling the alarm was to remove the nails from three of the boards on Point B's back fence substituting a couple of strips of strapping tape to hold them in place.

The day passed uneventfully. Donald kept Kathryn hungry and thirsty and scared out of her mind with threats of murder and amputation. Finally, the six p.m. deadline arrived. Donald turned on the news and quickly confirmed that Hopper had not signed the whacko "pledge" he had written up. *Good*, Donald thought, pleased that the target had reacted as expected. Time to move.

Kathryn was curled up on the bed, the blanket wrapped around her shoulders.

His mask back in place, Donald stormed into the room and half-shouted, "Time to show your father what happens to traitors! Put on your coat and shoes."

Kathryn stared at him dumbly and Donald took a threatening step closer. Whimpering, she hurried to comply.

"Where are we going?"

"The Gestapo thinks that they're real smart but they're not. They think they know where we are but we're going to fool them."

"What?"

"I'm going to take you right under their noses. They're going to find your body only two hundred yards from your daddy's house. That'll teach them that they're not so smart after all," Donald told her, playing the crazed terrorist for all he was worth. Kathryn's whimpers turned into a flood of tears. *I should have been an actor*, Donald thought. Half an hour later he pulled the Chevy he had rented to replace the compromised Fusion into the Wedemeyer's garage, put on his mask and released Kathryn from the trunk. Crying and stumbling, he led her to the guest bathroom on the first floor and locked her in. It took only a minute to release the packing tape and remove the loose boards from the back fence. Using a flashlight to make his way through the darkened house he dragged Kathryn from the bathroom to the kitchen.

"I think it's time to send your father a little present," he told her and pulled out the pruning shears.

"No! No! Please!" Kathryn cried and tried to pull away.

Donald drew her closer then froze as if listening to a distant sound.

"The gestapo's getting cute," he said, and pulled out a burner phone. Anxiously, he looked around the kitchen then dragged Kathryn to the stove. He quickly wrapped a length of nylon cord around her wrists then tied the end to the sink. "I've got to make a call," Donald said. "Don't go anywhere. I'll be right back." He raised the pruning shears and smiled, then hurried from the room.

The words *Oh my God! Oh my God! Oh my God!* screamed through Kathryn's brain.

Relaxed on the living room couch Donald opened an app on his smart phone that triggered a call to Hopper's number from a burner phone two blocks in the opposite direction. The pre-paid cell played a pre-recorded message as soon as Hopper picked up.

"Hello?" the Justice answered, glancing nervously at the tech hunched over his computer.

"You didn't do what I told you," a computer-generated voice shouted. "Do you think I wasn't serious? Do you think I didn't mean what I said?" The tech tapped furiously on his keys. "I'm going to kill her if you don't sign the pledge. You think you're smart but you're stupid. You have no idea of what I can do. You'll never catch me and even if you did it wouldn't matter because she'd still be dead."

The tech looked up and anxiously waved at Dohenny.

"I've got a hit," he whispered. "He's close! It looks like he's half a mile or less south of us."

Kane glanced at the Judge, frozen, holding his phone as if it were toxic. Over the speaker the computer voice continued its rant.

"I'm going to start sending you pieces of her just to prove that I mean what I say. Maybe then you'll do the right thing. I'm going to give you until ten tomorrow morning and then I'm going to start cutting. Don't think you can get away with anything. I'm watching you." The line went dead.

Everyone turned back to the tech.

"I've got him narrowed down to a couple of city blocks where two cell towers overlap," he said in an excited voice then began to highlight the target zone on a paper map.

Dohenny hit his speed dial and began assigning teams to the marked area. "We could use some more manpower if you're willing," Dohenny told Kane but Greg wasn't paying attention to him or anyone else in the room. "Kane? Kane?"

"This doesn't make any sense," Greg muttered.

"This is the break we've been hoping for."

"This is all wrong."

"What—"

"This isn't simply a mistake," Kane broke in. "This is a monumental blunder. He moves to within a few blocks of the judge's home and then he goes on a minute-long rant? He has to know that we would track that call. He has to."

"He's a fanatic and he's lost it. That's what people do when they get upset. They make mistakes."

"He's not that stupid," Kane insisted. "What was the point of the call anyway? Just to yell at us? Just to make threats and then give us another fifteen hours to track him down?"

"You're over-estimating this guy. You need to remember that criminals aren't geniuses."

"Our guy is a pro and he's smarter than this. We're missing something."

"Yeah, well when you figure out what that is you let me know. Until then we're going to tear that two-block target area apart."

A delay until six o'clock. Then an unnecessary and compromising phone call. Then another delay until ten tomorrow morning. What's he really after? Kane asked himself.

* * *

Kathryn strained her ears but heard nothing. Was he still in the living room? Had he fled? She tried to pick at the knots with her teeth but they were too tight. There was a knife block next to the stove but that was too far away. To the right of the sink was a tiled counter with three drawers underneath. If she stretched the cord as far as it would go she was just able to reach the top one. Praying that it wouldn't make any noise she wiggled the drawer open an inch at a time. Inside she spotted a silverware tray. One of the slots held four cheap steak knives with plastic handles. She pulled the tray to her side of the drawer and the tips of her fingers were just barely able to touch the closest knife. It took her almost two minutes of straining and struggling but eventually she was able to work it between her two palms and then twist the edge of the blade against the nylon cord.

Donald had quietly slipped into the garage and now was sitting behind the Chevy's wheel. An iPad rested on the passenger seat. Its screen displayed a wide-angle picture from the camera inside the middle button on Kathryn's coat. If he had had the choice he wouldn't still be here but the transmitter had a limited range and he didn't want the woman to hear the car starting up. He needed her to escape through the backyard and she was only going to do that if she thought he was still in the front of the house.

Donald peered into the screen. Yes, she had almost sawn through the line. A moment later her hands were free. She turned toward the living room and he held his breath. No, she was too afraid. Still gripping the knife she spun around and tiptoed toward the back door. He had made sure that it was unlocked and she slipped through it in a flash. There were no lights in the backyard but the moon was almost full and a couple of the windows on the house on the other side of the fence were aglow.

The picture jiggled as Kathryn ran across the lawn. She slowed for a moment then spotted the opening in the fence. Would she knock on the neighbor's back door or keep running? Terrified as she was Donald didn't think she was going to stop until she felt safe. As if she could read his mind she skirted the left side of the house and ran up the driveway toward the street. She was almost there.

Donald picked up the Push-To-Talk phone that was linked to its mate sewn into the hem of Kathryn's overcoat. The two units would function like a pair of walkie-talkies and would connect less than one second after Donald pushed the button. The call would last, of course, only for the instant between the time Kathryn's phone received the signal and the moment that the blasting cap and C4 it was connected to detonated, but for Donald's purposes that was plenty long enough.

He started the engine and made ready to flee the neighborhood as soon as he triggered the bomb sewn into Kathryn's coat.

CHAPTER THIRTY-FIVE

When she reached the street Kathryn instantly knew where she was. There was her father's house only a hundred yards away! A policeman was standing at the front door! She was safe!

Tim Voss was the first to spot her racing down the street still a couple of houses away. By the time he activated his radio she was almost even with the surveillance van and was running toward him at top speed.

"I've got a female heading for my position!" Voss shouted into his mike and then Kathryn entered the pool of lights set up in front of Hopper's home.

"Help me!" she screamed.

"It's Kathryn Hopper!" Voss shouted almost as loudly and ran toward her. Inside, Justice Hopper heard his daughter's cry and then Voss's message. He would recognize her voice anywhere.

"Kathryn!" he shouted and ran for the door. "Kathy!"

In the bouncing picture on Donald's iPad the Secret Service guard and the woman almost collided at the curb. For Kane time seemed to stand still and all the pieces that were spinning inside his head suddenly snapped together.

"No!" Greg shouted. Kane raced after Hopper and tackled him as he was reaching for doorknob.

"What are you doing?" Hopper shouted then hit the floor screaming, "Let me go! Let me go!"

Kane struggled to his feet and dragged the Justice back down the hall where Dohenny stared at them both in shock. Greg practically threw Hopper into the Secret Service agent's arms. "Keep him here!" he ordered and ran back to the front of the house. Outside Kathryn was hugging Tim Voss and sobbing, "I'm Kathryn Hopper. Help me! Help me!"

The picture on Donald's monitor had gone black when Kathryn embraced the guard. Now, hunched over the iPad he listened to the woman's cries and waited for Voss to lead her inside for her climactic reunion with the Justice.

"You're safe now, Ms. Hopper. It's all right. You're safe," Voss told her and turned just as the door flew open. For a second Voss froze and then Kane was on them. Barely slowing down he grabbed Kathryn's collar and dragged her toward the middle of the street.

"What are you doing?" Kathryn screamed. Kane ignored her as he fumbled with the overcoat's buttons, tearing them loose one after the other. On Donald's monitor the picture was a jumbled mess. The woman was spinning around, the camera wobbling and pointing in half a dozen directions. Donald caught a glimpse of the uniformed guard looking toward the lens and then disappearing off the screen.

"I want to see my father!" Kathryn shouted. As the last button tore away she slipped free of the coat and lurched toward the house. For half a second Kane found himself holding the empty garment then dropped it and ran after her.

"Shit!" Donald cursed and pressed the "Talk" button. The explosion threw Kane five feet forward and plastered Kathryn and Voss against the front door. Black, greasy smoke boiled from the shattered asphalt and the team in the van ducked as debris peppered its sheet-metal sides.

Ears ringing, blood dripping from his nose, Kane struggled to his feet and stumbled over to Hopper's daughter just as Dohenny, gun drawn, threw open the reinforced front door.

"Booby trapped," Kane shouted, his hearing gone. "Search her for any other bombs." It was like talking in a dream. Dohenny led Kathryn back into the street and forced her to remove her shoes and then her jumpsuit, finally covering her naked body with his coat. Kathryn cried hysterically but crying was better than dead. Shaking, shivering, wrapped in Dohenny's arms, she was finally allowed inside. Shell shocked, Kane and Voss and the two agents from the van watched the smoke curl up into the night sky.

A block away Donald eased out of the Wedemeyer's driveway and idled cautiously down the street. He was booked onto a redeye leaving BWI in an hour and a half and he cursed every foot of the drive there thinking about all the hard work and planning that had suddenly gone so wrong.

CHAPTER THIRTY-SIX

Dohenny stood like a man in the eye of a hurricane helplessly watching chaos swirl all around him. His best witness, Kathryn Hopper, was hysterical and even if she weren't she couldn't be questioned because the explosion had destroyed her hearing. If and when it would come back he had no idea. He wanted to summon the closest ambulance but couldn't, fearing that a fake unit staffed by more assassins might be parked around the corner poised for just such an opportunity. Instead he had to wait for a medical team that had been vetted by the Secret Service which meant that for the moment all he could do was treat everyone with basic first aid.

Kane was deaf and sporting a bruised face and skinned elbows and knees but was otherwise unhurt. Voss had been slammed backwards against the front door and probably had a concussion. Hopper's daughter's face was covered in blood and Dohenny guessed that her nose was broken. Luckily the booby-trapped coat had been lying on the ground when it went off and it had directed most of its blast more or less straight up. Dozens of ten-penny nails studded the limbs of the curb-side sycamore like porcupine quills.

Within minutes the D.C. police blocked off the street and a wall of uniforms surrounded the house. The ambulance finally arrived but the paramedics were thoroughly searched and their IDs confirmed before they were allowed inside. When they left with Kathryn Hopper a few minutes later Dohenny put armed men in the bus while Voss and Kane followed behind in a D.C. cruiser.

Dohenny refused to allow Justice Hopper to leave the residence, at one point threatening to have him physically restrained. Maybe that was part of the killer's plan — get the Justice running off to the hospital after his daughter and ambush him there. At this point anything was possible and Dohenny had no intention of letting Hopper outside the ring of armed men who now surrounded him.

Dohenny had already given Millingham a quick briefing and a new safe house was being prepared. Within the hour a new protection team would take Hopper to the secret location under heavy guard. What a fucking mess!

It took about forty-five minutes for Kane's hearing to return and he spent the time writing up a statement on a clipboard he borrowed from the admitting nurse. He had planned on giving it to whatever Secret Service agent showed up to debrief him but to his surprise his first visitor was not one of Dohenny's people but Allison Varner.

"You look like hell," she said, trying to smile but not doing a very good job of it. Kane didn't know what to say to that so he said nothing. "Are you OK?" she asked a moment later and stroked his torn-up palm.

"It's just a couple of bumps and scrapes."

"They told Uncle Arthur that it was a bomb of some kind." It wasn't exactly a question but it was close enough.

"They, he . . . whoever grabbed her, dressed Hopper's daughter in a bomb-vest, well, a bomb-coat, then let her escape, figuring that she'd run straight to her father and the blast would get them both."

"Oh my God! That's barbaric. How did you know?"

For a second Kane wondered if she meant him, personally, or all of them as a group, then decided it didn't matter.

"Just basic police work," he said with a shrug then winced as every muscle in this body throbbed in time with his beating heart.

"Do you have a concussion?" Allison asked in worried tone.

"No, I'm just banged up, that's all."

"But they're going to check you in, to be sure."

"I'm only staying long enough to give them my statement then I'm going home." Kane held up the clipboard then grimaced at a sudden, shooting pain.

"You're a mess," Allison said taking a mental inventory of his oozing scrapes and torn clothes. "Where's your car?"

"I don't know. Back at Hopper's place I suppose."

Allison stood then leaned forward and gently pulled Kane to his feet. "Come on."

"I have to be—"

"You can talk to them tomorrow."

"But—"

"Do you know anything that can help them catch the man who did this?"

"No," Kane admitted.

"Then it can wait."

I didn't see this coming, Kane thought and decided that some kind of maternal instinct must have kicked in. Allison looked as if she intended to half carry him like a football player being helped off the field. He waved her back and limped toward the door on his own, though he did let her hold his hand.

She brought him to her home, a two-bedroom condo not far from the Watergate and peeled off his clothes while the bathtub filled with steaming water.

"It looks like all the good stuff's OK," Kane said when his jockeys came down. Allison gave him a "Don't be a juvenile" look and helped him into the bath. Kane made little *ohh, ahhh, ohhh* sounds as jolts from his strained muscles competed with the delicious wave of heat flowing over his skin.

He closed his eyes for a few seconds then looked up and wanted to say *Take off your clothes and join me* but instead of desire her face showed only the concerned expression of a mother for an injured child, *That's the face of a care giver,* Kane thought, *the look she probably gave her husband a thousand times during his grim crawl toward death.* Greg closed his eyes and let the heat soak into his flesh. Later she handed him a pair of men's pajamas and let him slide into bed next to her. *Why does she still have her dead husband's clothes?* Kane asked himself though he already knew the answer. *He's not dead to her and she's not ready to let him go.*

"Don't get any ideas," Allison said just before turning out the light. "You're only here because I don't know what else to do with you. Your clothes are all bloody and your car's halfway across town."

"And besides, I'm a hero," Kane said, smiling.

"Oh, really?"

"Who do you think ripped the suicide coat off the Judge's daughter?" Kane answered, pleased with himself.

"What! You pulled a bomb off her just before it exploded?"

"All in a day's work," Greg said, closing his eyes and thus missing the terrified look that washed over Allison's face. After a few seconds of silence he opened them and saw her terrified expression slowly draining away, replaced by something akin to cold fury. Allison snapped off the light and, back toward him, curled herself into a ball.

I guess I'm not getting laid tonight, Kane thought then went cold when, almost silently, she began to cry. Kane tried not to hear her tears but that only enhanced his senses making every whimper and sob as sharp as the sound of breaking glass. Finally, her crying stilled but from the little shivers that rippled through the bed he knew that she was still awake. Eventually the darkness closed in on him and his mind slipped back into well-worn paths — *Danny was getting close to finding Farber's address. When they grabbed him could they make him talk? What had he done with Jason?* His nephew was dead, of that Kane had no doubt, but like a soldier vanished in some foreign land, Jason's body still needed to be brought home. *And who is Farber working for? Still Ryan Munroe? Was Brownstein's killing really about drugs or was it something worse?* Kane's brain burned through plans and options, ideas and schemes until, finally, consciousness slipped away.

*　*　*

Like a light being triggered in a darkened room Kane found himself suddenly back in Tommy's bar. In the shadows Sadie limped to the table where Big Jesse, Little Jesse, Denny and Phil were draining the last swallows from their mugs. On the other side of the room billiard balls made a ringing *CLACK* as Tweaker's break sent them scattering over the felt. Across the table from him Tommy raised his beer.

"Tommy," Greg said, "we're close, real close to finding out what happened to Jason." Kane smiled encouragingly but Tommy only frowned.

"And then what?"

"And then we'll make the bastard who killed him pay."

Tommy gave Greg a disappointed tilt of his head. "Will that make your life better?"

"He's your son. Don't you care about getting justice for him?"

"Are you doing it for Jason or for yourself?" Tommy asked.

Evil needs to be punished Greg wanted to scream but Tommy's placid expression smothered the thought. Tommy paused then took a swallow of beer.

"If you catch this man, will you finally be happy?" Tommy asked.

"I'll be *happier*," Greg said and lifted his bottle in a little salute.

"And what will you do after that?"

"Then I'm going to find Farber's boss and stop whatever scheme he's running."

"And then will you be happy?" Tommy asked in a soft voice.

"Life isn't necessarily about being happy," Greg snapped.

"You still aren't listening to me, Greg."

"What are you talking about?"

"A young man is on a horse, galloping down the road," Tommy said. "As he nears the bend a traveler at the side of the road turns toward him and shouts, 'Where are you going in such a hurry?' and the young man shouts back, 'I don't know. Ask the horse.'"

"What's that supposed to mean?"

"It means that you need to get off the horse."

"Jesus, talking to you is like dealing with some fucking fortune teller. Can't you just tell me something straight out instead of all this mumbo jumbo?"

"Do you remember when you got out of the hospital and they made you go to that anger-management therapist?"

"How could I forget twenty hours of concentrated bullshit?" Kane slugged down the last of his beer and waved the empty bottle in Sadie's direction.

"Do you remember the little book they gave you to read?"

"That Buddhist crap? Again, how could I forget? 'Practice mindfulness. Maintain a spirit of peace. Follow your breathing, in and out.' Jesus!"

A look of infinite sadness filled Tommy's eyes.

"That's not what the book said. That's what you wrote on the wall you built around yourself to avoid understanding what it said because you knew that if you could avoid listening to the book's message then you wouldn't have to change."

"Who are you and what have you done with my brother?" Kane asked with a sour grin. "Jesus, tell me something that makes some sense. Where's Farber? Where's Munroe? Why did they disappear Brownstein? What are they planning? Tell me what I want to know."

Tommy frowned then got a faraway look in his eyes. "All right, Greg. I'll tell you something important, something you won't let yourself know but something that you need to know if you're going to survive."

Finally, Kane thought and felt his hand gripping the bottle so tightly that he thought that the glass might break.

"The thing is, Greg, you're not really alive. You're a walking corpse. Every minute of your life you're consumed by your past and terrified of your future, and in between those two you're drowning in your frustration and your rage. You're a zombie, Greg, and anger and fear and regret have squeezed all of the real life out of you. You spend half your day imagining that if you can just run fast enough you'll be able to find happiness tomorrow and the rest of it convinced that if you struggle hard enough you'll be able to reach back in time and somehow fix everything that you think went wrong, and between wallowing in the past and dreaming about the future you've left no room to be alive today.

"But here's the good news. You can be reborn, Greg, you can live again, but only if you accept it that yesterday is gone and tomorrow doesn't exist and that all of your life is lived only in the here and now."

Kane stared dumbly across the table. He had hoped for some real answers, 'Go here' 'Do this' 'Do that' and instead all he'd gotten was the same hippy-dippy jibber-jabber that the so-called therapist had babbled at him two years ago.

"I don't understand a word you've said," Kane told Tommy, hopelessly disappointed.

"I know," Tommy replied in a voice of limitless sadness. "That's what's breaking my heart."

"Tommy—"

"Let the anger go, Greg, please. If you don't, no one can save you."

How the hell am I supposed to do that? Kane wanted to scream but before he could get the words out Tommy and Sadie and the bar and everything else disappeared.

Greg's eyes popped open and he found himself staring into the shadows above Allison's bed. Beside him he heard her breathing softly. *What kind of a welcome will I get when she wakes up and finds me next to her?* he wondered. *Will she still be upset? Will she be up for a little fooling around? Will—* then Kane stopped himself and a strange thought entered his mind. *You're alive,* it whispered, *in a soft bed, next to a beautiful woman who cares, at least a little, about you. Don't worry about tomorrow. Tomorrow doesn't exist. It's a myth, a fantasy, an illusion. Be happy in this instant. Enjoy the now.*

His questions forgotten, Kane allowed a smile to slip across his face, closed his eyes and slept.

CHAPTER THIRTY-SEVEN

To call the media coverage of the attack on Justice Hopper a firestorm would have been an understatement. As Carl Feeney watched the drama play out on Fox News he felt as if something soft and diseased had died in his stomach and the rot was spreading inch by inch through the rest of his body. Hopper's daughter kidnapped, fitted with some kind of a suicide vest and sent off to blow up the Judge in his own home sounded like something from an Al Qaida terror manual. And on top of that it hadn't worked. Hopper was still alive.

The TV showed endless videos of police blockades at both ends of his street. The Attorney General announced that the daughter had been sent off to some secret location surrounded by half a dozen armed bodyguards. The more he thought about it the more Feeney doubted that Hopper was even living at his home any more. The government probably had him stashed in some safe house and would be delivering him to the Supreme Court every day in an armored car.

Speculation over who was behind the plot was rampant. The media threw around phrases like "right-wing fanatics", "hate groups", "Aryan militias" and half a dozen other left-wing code words for patriots who were trying to keep America from becoming even more of a police state than it already was. What a fucking disaster! Judges were supposed to make their rulings based only on the law but if one of the other Justices was wobbling this cluster fuck might just tip him in the wrong direction. All that money for—

"Dad, I want to watch *Glamour Girls*."

Feeney pulled his eyes away from the video loop of greasy smoke boiling up from the street in front of Hopper's house.

"It's down to Kerry and Emma and that horrible Amber."

Feeney looked at his daughter, his incredible, beautiful daughter, upset about missing some mindless TV show and felt his heart melt. *This is why we do these things*, he thought. *Not for ourselves but for our children*. The fact that George Hopper's daughter had almost been blasted into wet hamburger at his orders did not enter Carl Feeney's mind. All he could think of was the clean and perfect world Robin would inherit if only he were able to protect her from the bleeding hearts and socialists who wanted to steal her birthright.

"Haven't you watched the story about those crazy people enough?" Robin asked. "Dad?"

Feeney stared at her, his heart almost stopped by her beauty and her innocence, then it seemed to miss a beat at the buzzing of the burner phone. Feeney tossed her the remote then mumbled, "I have to take this," and rushed from the room.

"Donald?" he whispered a moment later.

"Mr. Green? I assume you've seen the news?"

"It's a disaster! Whatever possessed you to—"

"You only specified the goal. Methodology was up to me."

"I figured you'd shoot him from some window half a mile away, not try to blow up his house with a suicide vest like some fucking Arab terrorist."

"That's enough."

"What are—"

"You're upset that the mission was a failure. I understand that, but that's enough."

Donald waited for five seconds and Feeney seemed to calm down.

"All right," Feeney said, "what's the next step?"

"There is no next step. I'd need ten men and rocket propelled grenades to get to him now."

"I paid you to kill him."

"You paid me to use my best efforts. No one can guarantee something like this. I got very, very close, as close as anyone could have gotten."

"So, that's it? Thank you very much, better luck next time? You were paid to do a job and you haven't done it."

Donald almost warned Feeney what happened to men who talked to him that way but held his tongue.

"Well?" Feeney demanded. When Donald answered all trace of human timber had disappeared and his voice was as flat and cold as if spoken by a machine.

"I'm keeping $250,000 for my expenses and inconvenience. I'll transfer the rest of the bitcoins back to you. Their value has gone up so you'll get almost the whole amount back. I'll text you the details on the transfer and then I'm going to destroy this phone. You'll need to do the same. Our business is over."

"Wait!" Feeney shouted. "What about Mr. Black?"

"What about him?"

"If they find him he can lead them to someone who can lead them to me."

"That's your problem."

"He can also lead them to you."

"That sounds like a threat," Donald said in a soft voice.

"It's a statement about something that's in our mutual self interest."

"How had you planned on solving that problem if my mission had been successful?"

"I thought I had it handled but I haven't been able to reach the other contractor. I think the mess you caused has him spooked."

"I'm sure he'll get around to Mr. Black eventually."

"You've got two-hundred fifty thousand dollars of my money. Earn your pay."

"You're skating on very thin ice talking to me that way, Mr. Green."

"Are you sure you want to wait for the other contractor to do the job? I heard that the Gestapo is offering a million dollar reward for information about that mess you caused. Do you want to gamble that Mr. Black won't try to make a deal, that he won't give you up for the money before he can be neutralized?"

The phone was silent for five seconds. "I'll take care of it," Donald finally growled then asked, "You still owe him money, don't you?"

"The job was never done. I don't owe him anything."

"But he thinks you owe him money, right?"

"I suppose," Feeney admitted.

"Good. As soon as I'm in place you'll call and tell him that you want to pay him off."

"Why would he believe that?"

"He's a degenerate addict. All he'll be thinking about is his next fix and how much dope that money will buy him. He won't be able to help himself."

"All right. What exactly am I supposed to say?"

"When I'm ready you'll call and arrange to meet him to deliver the cash."

"I'm not meeting with him."

"Don't worry," Donald said. "I'll have it covered," and then hung up.

Feeney dropped the cell into his top drawer and left his study. From down the hall he heard music swell and then Robin shouted, "Oh, my God, no! Not Amber!"

In spite of all the terror and heartbreak of the last two days Feeney smiled and at last felt the rats scurrying inside his stomach begin to slow.

CHAPTER THIRTY-EIGHT

Kane's cuts and scrapes were mostly hidden under his suit and his return to the office the next morning drew little notice. Other than a vague remark to Danny, Kane had shared the nature of his special assignment with no one and few of his fellow agents had cared enough about him to ask where he had gone. Even Danny and Immerson only knew that Kane had been tasked with reviewing Hopper's security procedures. On Kane's return the boss gave him a quick once-over and merely asked, "Are you all right?"

"Fit as a fiddle. Tight as a drum," Kane answered in almost a sing-song voice.

"Did you hit your head?"

"My head is fine."

Immerson gave him a questioning glance then shrugged.

"Are you all done with the Justice Hopper thing?"

"I gave my statement to the Secret Service first thing this morning."

"What about Senator Denning?"

"Him too." Kane scanned the bull pen and spotted Danny energetically running his mouse across his desk. "I guess I'd better check on the kid."

Immerson thought that he should probably say something encouraging like 'Good to have you back' but hesitated, unsure if Kane's obvious strengths outweighed his equally obvious flaws and then it was too late. Kane was already out the door.

"Hi, Danny," Greg said when he reached Rosewood's desk.

"Agent Kane!" Danny spun around and broke into a smile. "Are you all right? I saw that explosion on the TV. Were you anywhere near that?"

"Not too far away." Danny obviously had more questions but Kane cut him off before he could ask any of them. "Any progress on our guy?"

Danny gave Kane a "Mom, Dad, I got an A!" smile and started clicking his mouse. A picture of a row house with a green door filled the screen. "I found him. That's his house."

Kane placed his palms on the desk and leaned forward.

"You're sure? Did you take this picture?" Kane asked with an edge in his voice.

"It's Google Street View," Danny said and Kane relaxed. Danny running surveillance on an ex-cop like Mearle Farber was like sending a chicken out to spy on a fox.

"Does the boss know about this?" Kane asked, glancing over his shoulder toward Immerson's office.

"No," Danny said, not sure if that was the right answer.

"Good. We don't actually have any evidence on him for the Brownstein thing beyond some grainy video."

"We can still arrest him for helping that Munroe guy escape."

"That's not our case. It's not even a Homeland Security case."

"Are you saying that we should turn this over to the FBI or the Marshals?"

"Hell, no. We're going to grab this bastard ourselves. The FBI and the Staties can have him after he tells us what he did with Albert Brownstein."

"OK. When do we take him?"

Kane looked away from the monitor and into Rosewood's determined face.

"*We* don't. It's going to take at least six men to fully cover that house and we'll only get one shot at it. We're going to need a QRT." Danny gave Kane a confused look. "In Baltimore we call it the Quick Response Team. Like SWAT."

"Oh. Does Homeland have a QRT? I know the FBI has an HRT, Hostage Rescue Team. Should we call them?"

"No! I mean the paperwork . . . no."

"There must be a—" Danny paused and looked at Sebastian Wren striding toward them.

"Kane," Wren said, sticking out his hand. "I read your report on the Justice Hopper thing. Great job. Great job! The Principal Deputy is putting you in for a commendation." Wren noticed the confused look on Danny's face. "Your partner here saved Justice Hopper's life. Did you know that?"

"No sir."

"Well, he did. He figured out that the Justice's daughter had been outfitted with a coat filled with explosives and he ripped it off her at the risk of his own life before she and the Justice could be blown to smithereens." Wren patted Kane on the shoulder and smiled. Danny looked at his partner as if he had just been introduced to the Pope. Kane said nothing. "Well, what have you got there?" Wren asked, pointing at the monitor.

"Just a case we're working on," Kane answered when the silence became uncomfortable.

"The Brownstein disappearance? What's that have to do with it?"

"Just a lead we're checking out."

After another long silence Wren glanced at the clock over the bull pen door.

"Well, I'll leave you to it. Keep me advised. The Principal Deputy is very concerned about the possible WMD aspects of that case. If there's anything you want call me directly. After the job you did on the Hopper case I'll make sure that you get anything you need." Wren paused then turned to Rosewood and stuck out his hand. "Danny, that goes for you too. Is there anything we can do to help you?"

Danny shook Wren's hand. "No sir," then he glanced at the monitor. "Well, I was wondering, do we, Homeland that is, do we have a SWAT team?"

Kane forced himself not to clench his teeth and shout *Oh, shit!*

"A SWAT team? Why? Do you need a SWAT team?"

Danny glanced at Kane and quickly looked away.

"No, oh, no. Uhhh, we were just talking, well, I was talking. I saw this movie and there was this SWAT team in it and I wondered if we had one. I asked Agent Kane and he didn't know. He said the Baltimore PD has a QRT and I said that the FBI has the HRT so, well, anyway we were just wondering if we, you know, have something like that." Danny gave Wren what he thought was a casual smile. Kane kept his face as flat as one worn by a guy with a pair of threes who was trying to steal the pot.

"It's called the Special Response Team, SRT," Wren said. "Call me if you need one."

"Yes, sir, we'll let you know if we ever do."

For another second Wren looked questioningly at Kane then let it go.

"All right then. Congratulations again, Kane, on a job very well done. . . . Danny." Wren glanced a final time at the monitor then walked away.

"Do we have a SWAT team?" Kane muttered.

"It just slipped out. It was only a question. I didn't tell him anything."

Kane stared at the exit where Wren had disappeared then turned back to Danny.

"OK, nothing we can do about it now. Let's hope he's dumber than he looks."

"What should we do about. . . ?" Danny waved at the house on the screen.

"I'll make a call to the D.C. police. I'll get Immerson to back me up if I have to but I'm hoping I won't."

"When should we do it?"

Kane unconsciously sucked his teeth as he thought.

"Normally, we would stake out the place, make sure he's home, but this guy, he's got to be watching for strange vans parked near his house. If I were him I'd have a camera trained on the street, running a feed to an Internet site. . . . Let's keep it old school," Kane said after a few seconds pause. "One guy drives by after dark looking for lights and a car in the driveway. We do it again with a different car every half hour until we see something that tells us he's home. Then we come in hard through the front and the back doors and we leave guys outside in case he tries to crash out through a window." Again Kane looked around the room. It all seemed normal, ordinary, but he felt as if his every move was being watched.

* * *

Something was up with Kane and Rosewood. Wren was sure of it. He was just as certain that it had something to do with that house on the monitor, number 817. Unfortunately, he didn't know the name of the street. He could call tech support and have them hack Rosewood's hard disk but what reason would he give? Idly, he pulled out his phone then stuck it back in his pocket. Over the years he'd learned to let questions he couldn't answer percolate a while to give his brain a chance to chew them up and maybe spit out a better result. He decided he would give it at least until the end of the day. Maybe something would come to him. He could always make the call to tech support if he had to.

CHAPTER THIRTY-NINE

As the day wore on Kane was reminded again that most of police work was really paperwork. First, he had to get an arrest warrant allowing them entry to Farber's house. That meant an affidavit, an application, a draft warrant and almost an hour in the lumpy chair in the clerk's office waiting for the duty judge to review the documentation and question Kane about any factual issues that concerned him. When the warrant was finally signed Kane still had to recruit the manpower needed to serve it. If he had had any friends in the D.C. police that might not have been too difficult but, of course, he didn't. Kane generally considered himself ahead of the game if he was able to avoid actually making enemies.

After two hours of fighting the D.C. PD's bureaucracy Kane was only able to get the manpower he needed by reminding Captain DeJesus that in addition to aiding in the escape of a federal fugitive the target was also wanted on state charges of suspicion of murdering a police officer. Even then DeJesus was resistant. It took a call from Tony Canaro confirming Kane's story to finally get DeJesus' agreement to provide a six-man squad. Kane and Rosewood could go along but DeJesus made it clear that his man, Lieutenant Marty Bernard, would be in charge.

For a moment Kane thought about leaving Danny out of the raid but the kid had done good work and didn't deserve to be so brutally disrespected. Still, Kane resolved to keep Rosewood behind him at all times. It was a little after seven when Bernard and his squad assembled with Kane and Danny relegated to a couple of plastic chairs in the back of the room.

Bernard put up Google Street View images on a 60" plasma and slowly moved the POV down the block, stopping every thirty feet or so to spin the camera three-hundred-sixty degrees.

"All right, here's the target's house," Bernard said, tapping the screen with a rubber-tipped pointer then slowly zooming in on the front door. "As far as we know there's no connection between this unit and the houses on either side so the suspect's only points of egress will be the front and back yards. Desimone, Webber and Crane, you're Team Two. You'll position yourselves in the backyard at 794 Riverton."

Bernard switched to an aerial view and tapped the street in front of number 794 then drew a line from the curb, down the driveway, along the side of the building, into the backyard, then over the fence and into the rear yard of number 817. "You will wait on the 794 side of the fence until you hear my signal then you'll go over and into the backyard at 817. Webber and Crane will secure the rear of the house in case he comes out the back door or from one of the upstairs windows. Desimone, you will enter through the back door and clear the rooms at the rear of the house on the first floor."

Bernard paused and got nods and thumbs-up acknowledgments from the three men.

"Stottlemeyer and I will enter through the front door and clear the front rooms. Once the first floor is clear Desimone will hold position there while Stottlemeyer and I clear the second floor. If we still haven't found the suspect, two of us will search the basement. Kramer, you and Homeland Security agents Kane and Rosewood will cover the front of the structure to make sure that he doesn't jump out a window while we're clearing the interior. Does everybody understand their assignments?" In theory Bernard was talking to everyone but when he asked that question he never took his eyes off Kane.

"All right," he continued after a little pause to drive his point home. "The subject is considered armed and dangerous. He was a Baltimore County deputy sheriff who, with another officer, was transporting a prisoner wanted on weapons charges and suspected in the deaths of two federal agents. That prisoner went missing and the other deputy is missing and presumed dead. So what we've got here is a former law-enforcement officer who is suspected of murdering his partner in the course of helping a felon to escape. This is a very dangerous person who will not hesitate to kill any of us if we give him the chance. Do not give him that chance." Bernard gave his team a hard stare then looked toward the back of the room. "Agent Kane, do you have anything to add?"

Do I have anything to add? Kane thought. *You've as much as told them to shoot Farber down if he gives them the slightest excuse.*

The team twisted in their seats and Kane stood up.

"There's a mother out there whose son put on the uniform and climbed into a cruiser with this guy two years ago and was never seen again. Every day she wakes up and wonders, 'What happened to my boy?' If we kill Farber she's never going to find out. We need him alive because *she* needs him alive. You all know what I'm saying."

Kane looked from man to man and six blank faces stared back at him.

Shit! he thought. *I guess it will be what it will be.*

* * *

It was a little after eight and fully dark when the team was finally ready to go. Kane, Danny, Bernard and Kramer were seated in a black van around the corner and a block away from 817. Stottlemeyer was parked behind them in a blue Dodge Dart with a walkie-talkie lying on the passenger seat. Behind him in a third vehicle were Desimone and his two men.

"Make the pass," Bernard ordered.

Stottlemeyer carefully pulled around the van then made a cautious turn at the next corner. He kept his head pointed straight ahead while below eye level he held the transmit button down.

"I'm approaching the target." Stottlemeyer's voice was thin and scratchy over the speaker. "There's a light-colored Camry in the driveway. One light is showing in the first floor south-side window. No activity." There were a few seconds of silence then, "I'm off the block. Returning to base."

Bernard looked at Kane. He didn't need to ask the question out loud. Farber was probably there but they couldn't be sure. What time did he go to bed? Eleven? Midnight? They could wait and see if the light eventually went off. That would be a sign that Farber was home, unless it was on a timer, maybe automatically turning itself on at six and off at eleven. If they waited until the light went out then by the time they were inside Farber would have reached his bedroom on the second floor. That would give him enough time to grab a gun before they could clear the first floor and make it up the stairs, plus the stairs were a natural choke point and when climbing them the team would be exposed like tin ducks in a shooting gallery. If they went in now they stood a good chance of catching him in the living room, sprawled out in front of the TV. He'd possibly still have a gun but they'd be able to spread out and take him more or less by surprise.

Kane looked at Danny. The kid seemed all right, more excited, at least, than scared. *Screw it!*

"Let's do it," Kane said.

Bernard picked up the walkie-talkie.

"Team Two, move out for 794 then position yourselves by the rear fence and wait for my signal." Bernard released the button and shoved the unit into his pocket. "All right, everyone knows their assignments. Stick to the plan." He gave Desimone sixty seconds to get into position then motioned for Kramer to start the engine and move them out.

Thirty seconds later the van stopped in front of the adjacent home, number 815. Unlike raids in the movies Kramer did not slam on the brakes and screech the tires. Bernard gently opened the side door and the team exited as quietly as possible. Once outside they trotted toward the target. As they started to jog up the front walk Bernard clicked the transmitter and whispered: "Team Two — Go! Go! Go!"

Kramer held Kane and Danny halfway between the sidewalk and the front door while Bernard and Stottlemeyer waited on the porch for a count of five in order to give Team Two enough time to get over the back fence and across the yard. When Bernard heard Desimone's *CLICK* in his earphone he pointed at the door and Stottlemeyer smashed the steel ram into the lock. The door flew back with a crash and an instant later they heard a similar sound ring from the back of the house.

"Police!" Bernard shouted at the top of his lungs, already halfway through the living room. "Warrant! Police!"

Kramer, Kane and Rosewood pulled their guns and anxiously waited for the signal that one of the entry teams had found their man.

CHAPTER FORTY

Farber had briefly considered ordering a pizza but he didn't like scattering his new name and address around where somebody might sniff it out, so he threw a couple of hamburger patties into a pan and toasted some bread. It wasn't gourmet food but he wasn't a gourmet kind of guy so he figured that it all balanced out. He had just flipped them over and was debating slicing off a piece of yellow cheese when his phone rang, not the regular one he would have used to order a pizza if he had decided to go that way, but the other one, the one that only Ryan Munroe knew about.

The screen said "Blocked Caller" and for a moment Farber's paranoia made him wonder if he should answer it but what the hell was the good of having the thing if you didn't use it?

"What?"

"It's me." *It damn well better be you since you're the only guy who's supposed to have this number*, Farber thought, but he relaxed a little because he recognized Munroe's voice.

"What's the street number of your house?"

"Why do you want to know?" Munroe didn't know where he lived and he wanted to keep it that way.

"Just fucking tell me the number!"

Farber thought about it for moment then mumbled, "817."

"Shit! The guy called." Farber didn't need to ask *What guy?* "They're on to you. There's probably a SWAT team headed your way right now. Get out! Run!" The phone went dead.

Fuck! Farber turned the stove off and ran upstairs. He kept a "go bag" behind a false wall in his closet with clothes, a gun, a thousand bucks in cash, a clean phone, and the key to the safety-deposit box where he stored a hundred thousand more in cash, a clean ID and a virgin credit card. It took him only seconds to grab the bag and race down the stairs. He couldn't resist a peek out the window. A dark-colored Dart was rolling past, moving too slowly for his liking.

Farber grabbed his coat and ran out the back door. The yard was empty. He threw the bag over the back fence and scrambled over after it, cutting his palm in the process. The ground was soft from yesterday's rain and when he landed he slipped and muddied his knees. He couldn't worry about that now.

He ran down the driveway, keeping close to the side of the house. He couldn't see any lights from inside. Peeking around the corner the street looked empty. He turned right and headed up the block, then quickly crossed to the other side. He was almost to the intersection when the shadows lightened as a car turned the corner behind him. Farber hugged the bag to his chest and made a left on Polk. Once he was around the corner he took a peek back and saw a silver Ford Escape pull up next to the driveway he had just left. Three men in black uniforms with helmets and plastic face shields got out and jogged toward his back fence.

Fuck! How did they find me? He needed to get the hell out of here. He wanted to run but that would only draw more attention. He thought for a moment and decided that the Fort Totten Metro station would be the closest one, about a mile and a half away. He'd take the train someplace where he could hole up in a no-name, all-cash motel then get his money and new ID from the safety-deposit box tomorrow. After that he'd take a bus to the airport in New York or Philly or someplace far enough away that they wouldn't be running a facial recognition program on him. From there he could go anywhere he wanted. His new passport was pretty good. Maybe not the sort of thing that he might use to go to Russia or China or someplace like that but it wasn't going to set off any alarms entering Mexico or the Cayman Islands. Hell, he could be using an expired passport and he probably could still waltz into one of those countries.

By ten he had bought an anonymous room in a motel where credit cards were a rarity and nobody wanted to know your name. When he was finally able to sit down and take a breath he almost laughed. *Fuckers*, he thought, *I beat you, again.* Then he noticed he was hungry. And thirsty. Well, there were plenty of places in this neighborhood where a man could get a drink, and maybe a little more than a drink. The room looked lonely and suddenly he felt like celebrating. Hell, in a couple of days he'd be on a beach on some tropical island with money in his pocket. He'd be a brand new man.

CHAPTER FORTY-ONE

Shouts of "Clear!" echoed through Farber's house and after a couple of minutes Bernard waved Kane and Rosewood inside.

"He's not here," Bernard told them.

"Then we'd better get the hell out of here before he comes back and spots us."

"I don't think he's coming back." Bernard gestured for Kane to follow him. "It's still warm," Bernard said, pointing at the frying pan." Kane broke one of the meat patties apart with his fingers.

"It's still pink inside. He couldn't have left more than ten minutes ago." Kane helplessly looked around the room. An empty plate and a still cold bottle of beer were on the table and a block of yellow cheese and a knife lay on the counter next to the sink. Farber had been in the middle of cooking dinner when something spooked him. "Is there any way he could have spotted us?" Kane asked.

"I don't see how. We were parked around the corner and Stottlemeyer didn't even look at the place when he drove by. Who knew about the raid? Could someone in your office have tipped him off?"

"Nobody knew," Kane said, "just the judge who issued the warrant and your Captain."

"And your boss."

"No," Kane said and then looked at Danny.

"I didn't tell anyone," Rosewood volunteered.

Bernard thought about that for a moment. "Maybe he planted a camera at the end of the block and spotted the van."

Kane shook his head. "He'd have to have had four of them, two at each intersection, each one pointing in a different direction. They'd have to be wireless which means he would have had to climb the power pole or streetlight every couple of days to change the batteries. No way that's not going to be noticed. . . . We can check for cameras but we're not going to find any."

"Then either he's psychic or something spooked him," Bernard replied. "What do you want to do now?"

Kane thought for a moment then shrugged. "OK, let's have a look around, see if we can find anything that'll help us run him down. If his car has a GPS maybe that'll tell us something useful. Danny, check that out. I'm going to grab up any paperwork I can find." Kane turned back to Bernard. "Can you ask your guys to see if they can locate a cell phone or a laptop?"

"Sure."

An hour later they assembled back in the living room to compare notes. Kane had found a package of garbage can bags, two of which they had stuffed with old water bills, cable TV invoices, and other worthless documents together with the contents of Farber's wastebaskets. They had found no bankbooks, receipts for storage lockers, pieces of mail addressed to some other location, address books, or anything else of any obvious value. Kane had found three keys. One was a car key that started the Camry. One was to the padlock securing the rear access door to the basement and one a spare key to the house.

"Our shift is just about over," Bernard told Kane. "Unless Homeland wants to cover the overtime we need to call it a night."

Kane frowned and glanced around the living room as if he might find some inspiration in the worn couch or sagging club chair then, reluctantly, nodded.

"Yeah, OK, let's seal it up. I'll get a team in here tomorrow to tear the place apart in case we missed something. Thanks."

"OK, guys, let's wrap this up!" Bernard told his team.

Half an hour later Greg and Danny were in the parking lot behind their office. Greg had been quiet the whole ride back. Danny couldn't tell if he was angry or thinking or maybe both.

"What do we do now?" Danny asked.

"He can't have gone far," Kane said. "We've got his car. We've put his Conklin ID on the no-fly list and we've flagged his VISA card. He's only got the money he had in his pocket when he bugged out. He's not going anywhere until he can get a new ID and a new credit card."

"Wouldn't he have them already, as a backup?"

"I would if I were him. The question is if he had them on him or if he stashed them someplace. If he kept them in his house and anyone raided the place when he wasn't home he'd be screwed so he's probably stashed them somewhere. The question is where? I'd leave my back-up ID with a friend or put it in a storage locker or someplace like that where I could get at it if I was on the run. What about that mailbox store you tracked him to?"

"You think he might have left another ID in his mailbox?"

"Or in another mailbox he rented under another name." Kane glanced at his watch. "They're closed now. We'll check them out first thing in the morning. How long will it take you to get the GPS log from his Camry?"

"I've already downloaded it." Danny held up a flash drive.

"Can you print that out while I put together a press release?"

"Sure. What are you going to say, in the press release?"

"The headline at the top will be that the Office of Homeland Security is looking for Mearle Farber, AKA Paul Conklin on a matter of national security. Underneath that will be Farber's Baltimore Sheriff's file picture and Conklin's DMV photo and below that will be our phone number. I'm going to plaster this guy's face on every TV screen, newspaper and on-line media outlet on the east coast."

"Do you think it'll work?"

"I don't know. I guess we'll find out." Kane pulled out his building access card. "Let's get to work. If we're lucky we might just make the eleven o'clock news."

CHAPTER FORTY-TWO

The place was called "The Gentlemen's Lounge" but there was no lounging going on inside and the customers were certainly no gentlemen. Farber paid the ten dollar cover, got his hand stamped, and pushed through a curtain of clacking glass beads. In some places the girls worked poles but here they shimmied three times around a raised, U-shaped walkway, dropping their top for the second circuit and their panties on the third. They would pause when a customer signaled his interest with the wave of a folded bill. A single would get you a smile and a shake of her tits. For a twenty the girl would squat down in front of you for a few seconds and grin in a sad imitation of a bride on her wedding night before tucking your money into her elastic belt and moving on to the next guy down the bar. Some of the girls ended their final circuit wrapped in a fluttering tutu of currency. Other less popular women sported only a sparse belt of greasy ones and fives like the crown of a bedraggled tree two weeks after the first frost.

Farber ordered a scotch from the topless girl pouring drinks from inside the center of the "U". The label said "Cutty Sark" but Farber would have bet money that the contents were originally sold under the name "Old Walmart." Well, what the fuck did he care? Farber bought alcohol for what it did to him, not for how it tasted. He took a long sip and tried not to make a face.

The first girl was white and skinny with tits that looked like fried eggs hanging from a nail. Farber ignored her and checked out the place, searching for anyone who looked like a cop or seemed to be paying him too much attention. It looked like a typical crowd, part losers whose only chance at seeing a real, live naked woman was a place like this, bunches of young studs out to get loaded and leer at some ass along the way, and a few guys like him who were shopping for some companionship. Nobody rang any bells.

Skinny finished her tour and took over the cash register from the corn-fed blonde who had sold him his drink. The next one up looked promising — Asian, long black hair, small tits but everything was trim and well proportioned. He shook the ice cubes in his empty glass and Skinny poured him another shot. When the Asian girl reached his spot he waved a five and for a second she flashed him her pussy then turned away, her expression more a sneer than a smile. *Fucking bitch!* He banged his empty glass on the boards behind her but she didn't turn around. Skinny pulled it from his hand and poured him another two ounces of booze. Farber sipped and noticed that now it seemed more like a cocktail of razor blades and rubbing alcohol than something designed to be consumed by human beings.

The music changed into a tune with a beat that Farber's heart strove to match and he anxiously watched for the next girl on the tour. This one was black with firm breasts and wide hips and a bored expression that her fake smile and darting tongue were unable to conceal. And she was old, early thirties at least. He pointedly stared into the crowd of hollow faces when she reached his spot. As she neared the far end of the "U" at the finish of her routine the next girl climbed the steps. Farber leaned forward and stared down the runway past the sweating faces. Now, this was more like it. Eighteen, nineteen, he figured, maybe even younger, dancing her ass off on a fake driver's license and some desperate need to escape wherever it was that she had called home. Light brown hair, good firm tits. Something frightened and innocent seemed to huddle behind her baby blues. He liked her right away.

The guy to his left was a putz who smiled broadly then held up two ones. Jerk. Farber flashed her a twenty and she gave him her full attention. When she was halfway through her routine he held up another bill and gave her a "you and me" gesture. The empty look left her eyes and for a second she seemed frightened then she put the mask back on and moved along. Ten minutes later she replaced the black woman at the cash register and he waved her over.

"Let's you and me get together for a few minutes," he said, almost shouting to be heard over the throbbing music. "I'm thinking sixty." She gave him a nervous smile and started to turn away. "A hundred?" She paused and thought about it, her eyes picking at his untucked black shirt and muddy jeans.

"I'm not allowed," she mouthed.

"Two hundred," Farber said just loud enough for her to hear.

For a second she froze then glanced nervously at the exit sign at the back of the room.

"Meet me out back," she said then grabbed a bottle of Bud Lite and hurried down the bar. Farber stared after her and then pushed through the crowd toward the rear door. When he neared the hallway to the dancer's dressing room he caught the black woman staring at him like he was some smelly rat that had escaped its cage. He gave her a *Fuck you!* stare and pushed out through the back door.

The parking lot was full with mostly junkers, salt-eaten Tauruses, dented Sentras and F150s with an occasional Beemer or Infiniti thrown in as the exceptions to the rule. At the very back, looming over the quarter acre of sheet metal, were a couple of oversized pickups with full camper shells. Five minutes later the girl came out wrapped in a gray cotton bathrobe.

"Hi," she said, trying to pretend that she wasn't nervous. "You said two-hundred?"

"Sure."

"What for?"

"You think I'm a cop?"

"What for?" she repeated in a voice like a child demanding a treat.

"For a good fuck," Farber said and laughed.

"I don't do any rough stuff, and nothing, you know, back door."

"I wouldn't think of it."

She paused for a moment then glanced at the nearest camper.

"OK. I only get a fifteen minute break." Farber shrugged and she wiggled her fingers for the money.

"When were done."

"I have to get it now."

"When we're done," Farber repeated with an edge to his voice.

She stared at him for a moment then snapped, "Forget it," and started to turn away.

"OK, OK, half now, half when we're done." Farber held out five twenties. The girl stared at them for a second then stuffed them into the pocket of her robe.

"I'm Mary," she said after she unlocked the camper's door.

"Cliff," Farber replied and grinned. Once inside he locked the door behind them and his smile turned feral and mean.

Twenty minutes later Farber carefully stepped down to the filthy asphalt and pulled his coat tight against the bitter wind. A few seconds later Mary stumbled after him, and shouted, "Hey! Where's my money?"

"What money?"

"You owe me another hundred."

"Didn't anyone ever tell you to get your money in advance, you stupid whore?"

"Mister I got a kid. I have to—"

Farber raised his hand and she ducked back, covering her face with her arms.

"Shut up you fucking whore. I've already paid you more than you're worth."

Farber waited, part of him hoping that she'd argue and give him an excuse to slap her around but she just looked past him toward the club. Farber followed her gaze and saw the black woman standing in the open doorway, watching him. He stared for half a second then thought, *Fuck it! I don't need this shit now.* He squared his shoulders and strode back toward the building. Just to show her that he wasn't afraid of any black bitch he looked right at her and tried to force her back against the wall but then she showed him the ice pick in her right hand and he changed course, skirted the cinder-block wall and hurried around the building. He looked over his shoulder when he got to the street but the black woman had been smart enough not to follow him.

The streets were busy with people heading for the bars and flophouse motels, or looking for a good time.

The calls of the street whores, "Hey, baby, want a date?" rang from the entrances to alleys and the wide sidewalks in front of the all-night sandwich shops. *Like I would let one of those diseased animals near my dick*, Farber thought. A couple of blocks farther on he saw the flickering "a" in the neon script for the Belaire Motel and picked up his pace. A bunch of kids, laughing and swearing, surged out of Burger World forcing him to jog to his right where he almost tripped over a bum huddled under the grill's hot-air exhaust.

"Jesus!" Farber cursed and grabbed onto the wall to keep from falling. Frightened, the guy looked up and tried to pull away. Particles of grease had congealed on the bum's shoulders and the ragged baseball cap that bore a picture of an angry crow above the bill.

"Sorry," the guy said and pulled his legs tight to his chest. Farber cringed back as a cloud of body odor and jug wine and hamburger fat caressed his face like an invisible hand.

"Fucking bums!" he muttered and detoured around the man then called out over his shoulder, "Get a fucking job!"

CHAPTER FORTY-THREE

They didn't make the eleven o'clock news but Farber's "Paul Conklin" DMV photo got good coverage in the morning papers and on the drive-time broadcasts. Wren had promised that he would get Kane any resources he needed and Greg figured he would be a fool not to take advantage of the offer. By six a.m. they had a tip line set up and manned. By seven-thirty the phones were lighting up with calls from nut jobs, psychics, lonely old ladies, and citizens who thought that anonymously fingering their hated boss or faithless spouse would be a great way to get revenge. Farber was aware of none of this. He didn't stagger to the bathroom to pee out the last of the rotgut scotch until almost a quarter after eight, right on time as far as he was concerned.

He planned on arriving at the bank between ten and eleven, renting a car by noon, and being on a plane by five. None of that happened. After a quick shower he ran a disposable razor over his face and then unzipped the inside corner pocket of his go-bag for his safety deposit box key. And it wasn't there. A little ball of vacuum opened in Farber's stomach and he scrabbled his fingers helplessly around the compartment. No key. He dumped the bag on the bed and, with rising fear, worked his way through every item. No key. He went back to the bag itself, fingering every cavity, every zipper, every seam. No key.

Cold with terror he collapsed into the room's single chair and tried to think. The bank box held his new ID, his new credit card, his new passport and, except for a bit over the eight hundred bucks still in his wallet, all his cash. He couldn't get into the box without the key. He couldn't get a replacement key without identification in his new name. All the IDs in his new name were in the box. He had to have the key. *Where the hell was the key!*

Think! Think! Think! When was the last time he had seen it?

He had visited the bank three weeks before to drop off his latest payment from Ryan Munroe. Farber ran the morning back through his mind. As he always did when he went to the bank he had dressed in his blue suit, white shirt and dark tie. He gave the teller the slip with his new name, Harlan Boyce, and the box number. She pulled the signature card and compared it to the paper he had just signed. Of course the signatures matched. She smiled and grabbed her keys. That was one of the things he liked about that bank, no computers. It was like being back in 1970 — no photo IDs, no mag strips, not even a computerized database, just a name, a box number, a small steel drawer filled with well-worn signature cards and a key.

The woman had inserted her key and his into the locks and opened the little door, then she removed both keys and gave his back to him. He took the box to a little room, shoved the bundles of bills inside and closed it up again. A few moments later they repeated the process in reverse. She locked the door. Had she given him back his key? Yes, he remembered her handing it to him. He had held on to it until he was back in the car, then he must have done what he always did. He had to have slipped it into the little pocket he had sewn into the lining of his suit coat, the one that nothing could fall out of. When he was on the street he used that pocket to keep special items, the safety deposit box key, flash drives from Munroe with details of a new assignment, an emergency stash of flattened hundred dollar bills.

All right, he had put the key in the pocket. Then he went home, no, wait, he didn't go home. He was going to go home when the burner phone rang. It was Munroe calling him for a meet to give him new instructions from their mysterious employer. He remembered Munroe had made a joke about the suit, "A pig in a party dress" he said and laughed. Farber had smiled but inside he'd wanted to break Munroe's nose. *Then what? Think?*

He'd had to run around checking out some stuff for Munroe. He remembered that he had missed lunch. It was almost dinner time by the time he finished Munroe's errands and he stopped for take-out on the way home. When he arrived he was still pissed at Munroe over the remark about the suit and hungry and he had to pee. He'd thrown the suit on the bed, hit the head, then gone downstairs in his underwear and a bathrobe to eat the pizza he had picked up before it went cold.

Then what? Then what? TV? A few beers? When he'd finally gone upstairs the suit had still been lying on the bed. He'd put it into the closet! Had he taken the key out? He didn't remember, but, no, he couldn't have because if he had removed the key from the secret pocket the only place he would have put it would have been the go-bag and it wasn't there. So, it still had to be in the suit!

The cops would search the house. They'd go through everything, but would they find a key in a secret pocket of a suit hanging in the closet? Maybe. What were the odds? Farber thought about it, thought about the crime-scene guys he had known when he was on the job. They were pretty careful when they were running a room where they'd found a couple of bodies but an empty house where the guy was already in the wind? Eighty percent at least, he figured, eighty-twenty or better that they wouldn't find the key.

Farber glanced at the curtains. It was full daylight. No way he was going to be able to get back into the house now. He'd have to wait until dark, way after dark, three, four a.m. and then go in over the back fence, slip upstairs and get it from the suit. He wanted to be gone right now but there was no help for it. He wondered if the raid on his house had made the news and he turned on the TV. Ten seconds later his picture flashed up on the screen — "Armed and Dangerous." *Shit! Shit! Shit.*

He'd have to hole up in this fucking room all day. Had anyone seen him? The night-shift guy had been half in the bag and besides he didn't look like a big fan of current affairs. It was a risk that the night clerk might see the picture on the news and connect it to the guy in room 203 but less of one than showing his face outside right now.

OK, OK, Farber told himself. *Things could be worse. I'll just play it cool until it gets dark. Have a pizza delivered for lunch and shove the money through a crack in the door. When it's good and dark I'll steal a car, get the key, dump the car a few blocks from the bank and keep my head down until it opens. Maybe some cotton balls to puff out my cheeks and a fake mustache and a prayer that the old lady at the bank is half blind will do the trick.*

Sounds like a plan, Farber thought and switched the channel.

CHAPTER FORTY-FOUR

While Danny poured over Paul Conklin's credit card charges and phone bills for some clue that he may have previously missed Kane took Farber's picture to the Capitol Mail & Shipping store.

"Does this guy rent a box here?" Kane asked the fortyish woman behind the register.

"I don't think so," she said after a quick glance.

"Look again."

She pretended to stare at the photo then shook her head. "I don't know him."

"He rents box 1126."

"If you already know that why did you ask me?" she snapped.

"Why did you tell me that you don't recognize him?"

Angrily she grabbed the picture, squinted as if looking at it through a layer of frosted glass then said, "Oh, yeah, him," and dropped it on the counter.

"Open the box."

"Do you got a warrant?"

"Open it or I'll break it open and drag you in for obstruction of justice." When she didn't move and Kane reached for his cuffs.

"People have rights, you know!" she half-shouted then finally reached for her keys when Kane dangled the cuffs in front of her face.

"Open it!"

"Fascists!" she muttered as she unlocked the box. It was empty.

"Are you happy now?"

"I'd be happier locking you up for helping a cop killer."

"You'll change your tune when the People take their government back!"

Kane had a momentary urge to slap the sneer off her face but it passed.

"Your government thanks you for your cooperation," he said instead. "Have a wonderful day."

It was almost ten when he joined the crew that Wren had provided to search the 817 house. All they found were some fast food receipts, a water bill, and a coupon for 50% off a car wash and wax. There were no pictures, no bank statements, no nothing. They did find a laptop computer but the hard disk had been wiped. The techs promised to go through it anyway but Kane didn't hold out much hope that they'd turn up anything useful even if they could unscramble it.

He called Danny then Gene Boland, the agent who was running the tip line, and they both had nothing. Kane was back in the office by two. The tip line had yielded a few calls worth checking, but so far they had all turned out to be dead ends. Around three o'clock Boland told Kane that they had four more tips that looked promising and showed him the logs.

"How many guys do you have available?" Greg asked him.

"I've got three in the field. They should be freed up in fifteen or twenty minutes."

Kane leafed through the slips. "I'm not doing anything useful. I'll take this one," he said pulling a page out of the pile and returning the rest. Boland made a note and gave Kane his card.

"Call my cell after you eliminate it and I'll give you the next lead."

Boland's pessimism irritated Greg but then lots of things pissed him off, *So what's new?* he asked himself. The name on the call slip was "Evelyn Brouseau" with an address not far from Kalorama Park. About fifteen minutes later his phone said, "Arriving at destination on right" and he looked for a place to park. A long black sign with fancy pink letters bolted to the face of the building a few feet above a matching pink awning read: "Gentlemen's Lounge."

The door retreated a few inches in response to blows from Kane's fist and a black woman peered at him through the gap.

"We're closed. We open at five."

Kane held up his creds.

"Agent Gregory Kane, Homeland Security. I'm looking for Evelyn Brouseau."

The woman paused for a moment then pulled the door all the way back.

"I'm Evelyn Brouseau." A glass booth with a depression in the counter to allow money to slide in and out crouched against the left hand wall. "Let's go into the office."

Brouseau led Kane through a beaded curtain and across the deserted showroom. The floors were sticky, the carpet threadbare and stained. Bars, like sausage factories, Kane reflected, were never meant to be seen by the customers in the light of day. They climbed a flight of stairs and she ushered him into a small office. A window made of one-way glass looked out over the runway. Brouseau took a seat behind a cheap, scarred desk.

"I'm supposed to run the place when the boss isn't here. He usually gets in around eight. After that I watch the registers and I fill in on the floor when we're shorthanded." She glanced down at the runway. "The girls come and go. . . . You know how it is," she added a moment later.

"But not you."

Brouseau shrugged. "The money's good if you stay off the booze and the drugs. We're the employer of last resort for these girls. Most of them, if they didn't have a drug problem, an alcohol problem, an abusive boyfriend or father or a crack-whore mother problem, they wouldn't be here in the first place." A wistful look slid over her face. "Well, it's better than turning tricks on the street."

"Do you own a piece of the club?"

Evelyn gave Kane a fleeting smile.

"No. I'm just the hired help."

"That's why you still dance?"

"That's where the money is. I may not be a kid anymore, but," another quick smile, "I've still got what a lot of men want. . . . But that's not why you're here."

Kane handed her two pictures, one from Mearle Farber's employment file and the other from Paul Conklin's driver's license.

"Yeah, that's the guy," she said, tapping Conklin's picture after half a second.

"When did you see him?"

"Last night around eleven, more or less."

"You're sure?"

Evelyn paused, her lips coming to rest someplace between a smile and a frown.

"Did you ever hear the song, '*Private Dancer*,' Agent Kane?"

"Ahhh, Tina Turner?"

"Do you know the words?"

Kane shrugged.

"*You don`t look at their faces.*

"*You don't ask their names,*" she said as if reciting a poem.

"*You don`t think of them as human.*

"*You don't think of them at all.*

"*You just keep your mind on the money.*

"*And you keep your eyes on the wall.*"

"If that's how it works why do you remember him?"

"The men who sit out there," Evelyn nodded toward the runway, "are more or less creatures who come here to fulfill their animal needs, like werewolves under the influence of a full moon. That doesn't necessarily make them vicious or mean, just pathetic. But sometimes we get the other ones, the ones like him." Evelyn tapped Conklin's photo. "The ones who want to do more than just look."

"What did he want to do?"

"He took one of the girls out back, one of the new ones, young and stupid and desperate. The young and stupid part gets knocked out of them pretty fast until only the desperate part remains." She paused and for a moment seemed somewhere else, then her eyes clicked back into focus and whatever memory she had dredged up slipped away. "Anyway, he ripped her off and was working himself up to doing something more when I showed up."

"He was worried about you being a witness?"

"He didn't like the ice pick I showed him."

"How close were you to him?"

"About as far away as I am from you."

"You said that this happened out back?"

"There's a light over the rear door. I got a real good look at him before he took off."

"I don't suppose he paid with a credit card?" Kane said.

"That'll be the day. This is a cash business."

"Which way did he go?"

"The last I saw of him he was heading around the building, up toward the street. I couldn't tell you where he went once he hit the sidewalk."

Kane made a note and tried to think.

"Is there anybody who might have seen which way he went? A bouncer, a security guard, a street vendor? Anybody?"

Evelyn shrugged. "There are lots of people around here at night but nobody permanent, nobody who's always out front keeping watch."

"Regulars? Hookers? Maybe a cabbie who picks fares up here?"

"Sorry." She gave Kane another shrug.

Greg sighed and slipped his pad into his coat.

"Thank you, Ms. Brouseau. You've been very helpful."

"My pleasure. I hope you catch him."

Kane stood and she led him back through the club. He was halfway out the door when she stopped him.

"Agent Kane — what did he do?"

"In addition to his other victims he murdered a cop," Greg told her with ice in his voice.

"So, this is personal."

"I'm not going to let him get away with it if that's what you're asking."

"Good, good for you."

Kane tried to figure out the expression on Brouseau's face. Determination? No, he decided, satisfaction. As the door swung closed behind him he heard her begin to sing softly to herself: "You don't think of them as human. You don't think of them at all."

CHAPTER FORTY-FIVE

Kane knew that after dark he would need to have an agent canvas the neighborhood with Farber's picture. More hours lost. Halfway to his car he paused and scanned the street. Was there anyone here right now who might have seen Farber? Greg spotted a guy tending a coffee cart halfway down the block.

"Were you around here last night?" Kane asked, holding up his creds.

The vendor, a thin black man in his twenties, glanced at Kane's ID.

"No," he said, forcing a nervous smile.

"What time did you go home last night?"

"Seven?"

"You don't sound very sure."

"What time did it happen, whatever it is you're asking about?"

"Eleven."

Instantly, the man relaxed.

"No way, man. I was long gone by then." He handed the photo back.

"Who might be around here that late?"

The guy just shrugged and fiddled with his stack of paper cups. Kane put the picture back in his pocket and headed up the street. At the corner he mentally flipped a coin and continued straight on for another block. Over the next ten minutes he talked to a guy behind a card table piled with pirated DVDs, the mailman and a couple of hookers getting an early start on their evening's work. He was halfway past the alley fifty feet north of Burger World when he paused and peered into the shadows for signs of life. He spotted a Samsung refrigerator carton wedged in between two dumpsters and cautiously approached. A gray face peeked out of the end of the box then ducked back inside.

"Hello?" Kane called.

"Go away!" Kane couldn't tell if the voice belonged to a woman or a man.

"I'm looking for someone."

"I won't tell! You can't make me tell!" the voice, a female Greg decided, shouted back. He stared at the sagging cardboard for a second or two then turned away.

When he reached the intersection he heard a clattering sound and around the corner he spotted a hunched figure rummaging through a trash can. The man straightened, dropped three aluminum cans into a garbage bag at his feet and bent over to dig deeper into the bin, finally emerging with two empty Snapple bottles just as Kane drew near. He gave Kane a quick once-over then snapped him a little two-fingered salute.

"What can I do for you, detective?" he asked. The skin protruding from his fingerless gloves was a greasy black and the face above the once-beige trench coat was more gray than white. He looked to be in his mid-forties but life on the street wears a man down so his real age was anybody's guess.

"I'm looking for someone. Have you seen this guy in the last couple of days?" Kane gingerly handed over the picture. The man made a show of squinting at it and moving it closer then farther away as if a fog was obscuring the image. Finally, he looked back at Kane.

"What's he done?"

"I just want to talk to him."

The guy hesitated then studied the picture again. "Are you a friend of Starky's?" he asked suspiciously.

"Who's Starky?"

"Everybody around here knows Patrolman Starky," the man said softly but with an edge to his voice.

"I'm not with the D.C. police." Kane held up his ID.

"Homeland Security? You look like a cop to me."

"I used to be. Baltimore PD."

"I can't say I saw him," the homeless man said. His eyes flicked down, then he looked back up at Kane. "I can't say I didn't." When he returned the photo his grimy cuff slipped back and Kane noticed a tattoo of three stylized wings above a sword.

"Interesting ink."

"That's from another life," the man said and quickly pulled down his sleeve.

"My name's Greg Kane." Kane held out his hand. The homeless guy stared at it for a second then grasped it lightly with his stained glove.

"Randy Foy."

"What was your MOS?"

After another little pause Foy said, "I was just a grunt. A lowly 11B." He gave Kane a weak smile.

"82nd Airborne?"

"The 173rd. Courage and Strength," Foy said, his smile fading as he looked down at his stained coat and worn-out shoes. "But, hell, that was a long time ago." He looked back at the picture still in Kane's hand.

Kane knew what he wanted. By the hungry look in Foy's eyes a ten would spark a sudden improvement in the homeless man's memory. Greg slipped the picture into his pocket but when his hand came out it was empty.

"I didn't get any lunch," Greg said, ignoring the disappointed look on Foy's face. "Is there a decent restaurant around here?"

"Burger World down the street's OK."

"How about someplace a little nicer."

"There's a Denny's a block over." Foy pointed at the cross street and to the left.

"Let's get some lunch. My treat."

Foy uneasily ran his palm over his grimy coat. "I don't think—"

"It'll be fine. You're with me." Kane put his hand on Foy's shoulder and guided him forward.

When they walked into the restaurant the nineteen-year-old girl running the hostess stand lost her practiced smile but Kane just pointed to a booth by the window and told her, "We'll take that one." She froze for moment then grabbed a couple of menus and led them to their seats. Kane slid the plastic menu across the table to Foy. Randy seemed confused by all the choices and eventually defaulted to a double cheeseburger, fries and a chocolate shake.

"Afghanistan or Iraq?" Kane asked after the girl had taken their order.

"Afghanistan — Kunar Province mostly." Foy's eyes clouded over for a second then snapped back into focus. "Nothing like this over there," he said glancing around at the vinyl benches and Formica table tops. "How about you?"

"I never served," Kane said in an almost embarrassed tone.

"Then how come you recognized my tattoo?"

"In my job you run into a lot of guys with tattoos. It pays to learn what they mean. . . . And a lot of guys who claim to have served and never did. You get to learn how to recognize the fakes pretty fast."

"I wish I was a fake. I wish I'd never joined up," Foy said staring at Kane with sudden heat, then he looked away. "Do you want to know what happened to me? How I ended up here?" Not knowing the right answer, Kane just shrugged.

"Nothing," Foy said with a sudden, bitter smile. "I didn't get shot. I didn't get blown up. Not one damn thing."

Kane started to speak but then the girl brought their food. The way Foy tore into his burger Kane wondered when he had eaten last. When the shake was down to the dregs and all that was left of the fries were broken crumbs Foy looked back across the table and smiled.

"Thanks. That's the best meal I've had in a while. Man, I miss those shakes."

"Sure," Kane said. "My pleasure."

"You want to show me that picture again?"

Kane slid it across the table. Foy glanced at it and pushed it back.

"Yeah, I saw him. Eleven, eleven-thirty last night. I was up under the heat vent at Burger World. He passed me and went on up the block, away from the titty bar."

"Any idea where he was going? Did you notice if he turned down any of the cross streets?"

"Sorry."

"Well, thanks."

"You know," Foy said as if the idea had just occurred to him, "maybe I could look around for him. You know, walk the neighborhood, keep a watch out."

"Keep a watch out?"

"Sure. Twenty bucks?" Foy asked with a different kind of hunger in his eyes.

"I could get you into a program," Kane said. "Help you get off the sauce."

"Nah," Foy said, smiling. "That won't work."

"Why not?"

"Because you can't get straight unless you want to get straight, and I don't."

"Maybe some counseling—"

Foy waved Kane's words away.

"Do you have a pill that will make me forget, something that'll let me unknow what I know?" Foy's face grew hard then he forced himself to relax. "It's not what you think. I didn't get shot or get blown up, not me, personally. . . . Look," Foy said, struggling to explain, "you meet a guy, have some beers, find out where he's from, how he met his girl and then, boom, some asshole blows his arm off and he's gone and a new guy gets his bunk and he tells these stupid jokes and you find out that he likes olives on his hamburger and the next thing you know they're shoveling pieces of him into a body bag and then the guy who sleeps in the rack across from you and three down who looks like Opie and can draw like a son of a bitch goes out one morning and comes back without a face. And it never fucking stops. You just sit there and watch these guys get fed into the meat grinder day after day and pretty soon you don't want to know them. You don't want to talk to them. You don't want to hear about their girlfriends or how their little sister wants to be veterinarian or that their mom makes this great fucking blueberry bread pudding. You don't want to know anyone, but you can't shut them out. They just keep coming and they just keep dying, or worse, and it never stops."

Foy covered his face with his hands and shook his head as if that might drive the memories away. A few seconds later he wiped his eyes with a napkin and gave Kane an embarrassed little smile.

"So, thanks for the offer and everything, but what I was and what I am . . . fuck, it's like loving hot dogs and then taking a tour of the sausage factory. You can never go back to what you were before you knew."

"The booze will kill you, Randy."

"So what?"

"Randy, if—"

"Look, Mr. Kane, I know you mean well but you can only fight something for so long before you finally realize that you just can't win. So, thanks for the offer but I've given up. It's not so bad. Life is a lot easier when you're not chasing after anything, when you stop fighting it and you just take things as they come. When I'm loaded I actually feel pretty good. That's the only time the thoughts go away, the only time I can forget. So," Foy scraped up the last few fragments of fries. "What do you say? Twenty bucks and I'll keep my eyes open for this guy?"

Twenty bucks for eyes on the street? Kane thought. *That's a bargain. What the fuck should I care if he pickles another chunk of his liver on my money?*

"No fucking way!" Kane growled.

"Look, for ten I could—"

"Not ten, not five, not a penny! I'm not giving you any money for booze. Come on!"

Foy looked as if Kane had slapped him and Greg half dragged him from the booth.

"Is your manager around?" Greg asked the girl at the hostess counter. She looked from Kane to Foy then hurried away. A few moments later she returned with an Hispanic guy in a short-sleeved white shirt.

"Can I help you?"

"Agent Kane, Homeland Security," Kane said, showing his ID. "This is Mr. Foy. He's helping us with an investigation." Kane pulled out his wallet and began counting out bills. "Here's a hundred-twenty-five dollars." Greg shoved the money into the manager's hand. "I want you to start a tab for Mr. Foy. You feed him until this money runs out. Call me when it does. Give his waitress a 15% tip." Kane glanced at Foy then turned back to the manager. "No refunds. No take out. And if he brings in any friends they have to pay their own way. This money is only to feed him. It's just for food. Do you understand?"

"Ahh, I'm not sure we can—"

"Did you ever serve?"

"What?"

Kane pulled up Foy's sleeve and exposed the tattoo.

"173rd Brigade. Kunar Province."

The manager stared at the blue-lined wings then nodded.

"My dad was a marine at Lai Khe, in Vietnam." He picked up the hostess' pen and wrote down Foy's name and the word "Date" at the top of one column and "$125" at the top of another. "We'll run a tab."

"Thanks." Kane gave the manager his card then steered Foy toward the door.

"I'd rather have the money," Foy said anxiously looking back through the glass.

"I know you would, Randy, but I'd rather you stayed alive a little longer in case you change your mind. I'd really like you to change your mind."

"That's not going to happen."

"I guess we'll see."

"It's too late for me."

"Well, it's not too late for me." Kane noticed the manager watching them through the doors. "Good luck, Randy," Greg said and headed back to the street.

"Wait!" Foy called and jogged after him. "I lied," he said when he reached Kane at the curb.

"You lied about being in Afghanistan?"

"I wish. No, I lied about the guy in your picture. When I saw him I was just coming off a good high and I got the really stupid idea that maybe I could get a couple of bucks out of him for another bottle. It took me a block to catch up to him and when I got there he punched me then he threw me against a wall. He scared me. Some soldier I am. One day I'm in Afghanistan fighting the Taliban and the next some civilian shoves me and it scares the piss out of me. I would have told you, eventually, after I drank up your money. Sorry," Foy said, looking down.

"Where was he going the last time you saw him?"

"I'll show you." Foy checked the traffic then jogged across the street with Kane following behind. A hundred yards farther up he took a right and then pointed toward the end of the block. Kane's eye was drawn to the "Belaire Motel" sign with the "a" flickering excitedly in the dim afternoon light.

CHAPTER FORTY-SIX

Half a dozen questions raced through Kane's head, the foremost of which was "Is Farber still there?" closely followed by "How long is it going to take me to get a team down here?" Just as Kane pulled out his phone he heard Foy mutter, "Shit!" and looked up to see a D.C. patrol car pulling to the curb. The window whirred down and the cop in the passenger seat glared at Foy.

"Did you forget what I told you, Randy? "

"I just—"

"You just earned yourself a trip to the station." The door cracked open and Foy took a step back. Before the cop could get out Kane pushed Randy behind him and pulled out his creds.

"Agent Gregory Kane, Homeland Security. This man is my CI."

The cop, the black plastic bar on his chest said "T. Starky," glared at Kane's ID.

"He never told us he was working with HS."

"He wasn't supposed to." Kane glanced from Starky's unhappy face toward the Belaire Motel then back again. "How would you guys feel about helping me take down a wanted felon?"

"Wanted for what?" Starky snapped.

"He killed a cop."

"Are you shitting me?" Starky half-shouted, his eyes turning mean.

"A Baltimore County Deputy Sheriff working prisoner transport. The mope was paid to break the guy out. You two interested in helping me take him down?"

Starky glanced at his partner then turned back to Kane.

"Where is the son of a bitch?"

"Holed up in that motel." Kane pointed down the block.

Starky popped the lock on the back door. "Get in."

Kane shook his head. "We can't take the chance that he'll spot your unit. We go in on foot. After we get the room number and a passkey one of you will need to cover the back in case he decides to go out the bathroom window. The other two of us will go in the front. He's armed and dangerous." Kane pulled a paper from his coat. "I've got an arrest warrant."

"Fuck your warrant. The son of a bitch killed a cop."

"I need him alive." Starky looked like he had bitten into something he thought was chocolate and it turned out to be shit. "I need him to rat out the guy who paid him to kill the cop. . . . Are we clear?"

Starky hesitated then nodded. "Yeah, fine, we don't kill him — unless he makes us. What about him?" Starky pointed at Foy.

"He did his job. He found this asshole for us. He stays here. . . . Randy," Kane said, turning toward Foy, "You clear out. We've got this now."

Kane expected Foy to nod or give him a wave or just leave but he did none of those things. For a moment he just stood there then he began to mumble "Oh, shit. Oh, shit. Oh, shit. Not again. Oh, shit," and tears began to trickle down his cheeks.

"Randy, it's OK. We'll be fine."

"No! That's what they always said. 'We'll be fine.' 'Everything is fine.' And when they came back they didn't have any legs!" Foy buried his face in his hands and began to cry.

"What the hell is wrong with him?" Starky growled.

"Have you ever seen your best friend blown up by an IED?" Kane half shouted back.

Starky was quiet for a moment then his face hardened. "I did my time in The Sand."

"So, now you know what's wrong with him. . . . Come on, let's go get the bastard."

The three men, the driver's name was Jerry Danaher, jogged up the street and Randy Foy, his nightmare repeating itself, could only stand there and watch them go.

Staying out of sight of the rooms as much as possible they slipped into the manager's office. Starky took the lead when they went inside.

"Hey, Oscar," Starky called to the clerk. Oscar did not look pleased to see him.

"Officer Starky, is there a problem?" Oscar asked in a nervous tone.

"You've got a guest who is a very bad man. He's not the kind of guy you want in your fine establishment. He's bad for business. Real bad. But this is your lucky day. We're going to get rid of him for you. No charge. . . . You got a picture?" Starky asked Kane. Greg handed over Farber's photo. "What room is this piece of shit in?"

Oscar looked at the picture and for a fleeting second thought about lying and saying that the man wasn't there but one look at the three cops drove the idea from his head.

"He's in room 203."

"Good. Grab your passkey."

Oscar held out a plastic card but Starky waved it away.

"No, you're coming with us."

"You take the key."

"We wouldn't want you to give this guy a call once we're out the door, would we?" Oscar frowned. "You come along with us just so you're not tempted to do something stupid." Starky waved Oscar from behind the counter. "Which one is 203?" Oscar pointed out the window toward the second door from the end on the upper floor. "You got it, Jerry?"

"Give me ninety seconds to get under the bathroom window." Both uniforms pressed timer buttons on their watches and Danaher headed for the back of the building. At sixty seconds Starky nodded to Kane. "Let's go."

They moved out in a line close to the wall then up the stairs, Kane in front, then Oscar and Starky bringing up the rear. When they neared number 203 Kane took the passkey and pushed Oscar out of the way. Faint music and the words ". . . . seek medical attention in the event of an erection lasting more than four hours" drifted from the room. Greg gave Starky a nod and the cop crouched under the window on the opposite side of the door and checked his watch. A few seconds later he looked up and flicked his finger at Kane.

Greg slipped the mag card into the slot. It made a slight *CLICK* and then the LED blinked green. Kane twisted the handle and slammed into the room with Starky barreling in low behind him. Events seemed to melt together and it felt as if the seconds were ticking off both slow and fast at the same time. The covers on the empty bed were rumpled and out of the corner of his eye Kane spotted an automatic on the night table. A burly, shirtless man with a sagging belly materialized in the bathroom doorway at the same instant that Kane registered the sound of the front door slamming against the wall. The guy had heavy cheeks and a full day's beard and he looked more angry than surprised.

"Police!" Kane shouted at the top of his lungs, "Down! Down! Down!" He pointed his Beretta at Farber's pallid, hairy chest. The suspect glanced longingly at the pistol only five feet away. Suddenly there was a blur to Kane's right and Starky smashed his Sig Sauer 40 caliber into the back of Farber's head. In an instant Starky had pinned Farber's neck to the greasy carpet with his right knee. Kane holstered his weapon and grabbed Farber's right hand while Starky snagged the left. Kane pulled both wrists high up Farber's back and Starky snapped on the cuffs.

"What was that?" Kane asked once they were both on their feet.

"You said not to kill him. You didn't say we couldn't bust him up a little. Besides, he was going for that gun," Starky pointed to the nine millimeter pistol next to the lamp. "We'd have had to shoot him in another second or two." Starky smiled and when Farber started to groan he mashed his foot on the back of the prisoner's neck. "You want to give a shout down to Jerry so he can come on up here and join us?"

Five minutes later they had Farber dressed and re-cuffed. For a moment Kane thought about calling Danny and having him cancel the search but he changed his mind. If they wanted any chance of Farber leading them to whomever hired him to kill Brownstein his capture had to remain a secret. Kane threw the prisoner's wallet, phone, keys and gun into a pillowcase and stuffed everything else he had with him into Farber's go-bag.

"You want to follow us to the federal lock-up?" Starky asked as they walked Farber toward the door.

"I've got a unit down the street. I'll transport him."

Starky gave Kane an angry glare.

"What is this, 'Wham, bam, thank you, ma'am?' We bust this guy for you and you screw us out of the collar?"

Kane thought for a moment then pulled out his phone.

"What's your sergeant's name and number?" Starky frowned then grunted, "Max Kirov" and recited the number while Kane dialed. "Hello, Sergeant Kirov? . . . This is Agent Gregory Kane, Homeland Security Office of Special Investigations. I ran into a situation with a wanted federal fugitive. Two of your officers helped me take him down. . . . Yes, officers Starky and Danaher. The suspect is wanted for the murder of a police officer and aiding in the escape of a man being held for the murder of two federal agents. . . . . Yes, a real piece of shit. Anyway, I wanted you to know where your men have been for the last half hour and to tell you that Homeland will be sending you a letter of commendation to be put in both their jackets. I really appreciate the cooperation. . . . Absolutely. Their help was invaluable. I'll make sure they get credit for the collar. . . . He's right here." Kane handed Starkey the phone .

"Yeah, sergeant, he's in cuffs. . . . No, Agent Kane has a federal warrant so he's taking custody of the guy. . . . We'll be back on patrol in five." Starkey handed the cell back. "Sorry I went off on you."

"No problem. Thanks for the help."

Starky looked at Farber and frowned. "I just wish we could have shot the son of a bitch."

"Don't worry. I've got something worse than that planned for him." Kane gave Farber an evil smile but received only a blank stare in return. *You just wait*, Kane thought. When they returned to the cruiser they found Randy Foy still standing there, watching.

"You see, Randy. Everything's fine," Kane told him while Starky secured the prisoner in the back seat. Farber looked out and spotted Foy and gave him the stink eye. "Don't worry. He can't hurt you. He's never getting out."

"I'm not worried," Randy said, "not about him. . . . Did he have a gun?"

"They all have guns. It's fine. It's just part of the job."

"That's what my sergeant used to tell me. 'It's the job.'" Foy gave Kane a helpless, wounded look.

"The thing you've got to remember, Randy, is that it's no longer *your* job. Not anymore. Never again. You did your part. Now you just have to let it go."

"How can I do that? How am I supposed to do that?"

"I'll tell you a secret, something that my brother told me to help me with my own problems." Foy stared at Greg, confused. "Are you listening?" Greg waited and finally Randy nodded. "OK, here it is. You can't reach back in time and fix everything that you think went wrong. You can't live in yesterday and dream about tomorrow because that leaves you no room to be alive today. Randy? . . . Randy are you listening to me? Here's the most important thing Tommy told me: You have to accept that yesterday is gone and that tomorrow doesn't exist. We live our entire lives only in this one instant. Everything happens only in the here and now. The past is dead, Randy. It's dead and gone. Do me a favor, OK? Please, remember that and let it go."

Foy stared at Kane as if he had been speaking in some secret code for which Randy held no key.

Of course he doesn't understand how to do that, Kane thought. *Neither do I. Physician heal thyself.*

"That's OK, Randy. Don't worry about it." Kane patted Foy's greasy shoulder and headed back to the cruiser and his prisoner.

CHAPTER FORTY-SEVEN

Starky and Danaher wedged Farber into Kane's backseat and used the belt to strap him down tight. "That ought to hold him," Starky said testing the second pair of cuffs that secured Farber's manacled wrists to his belt. Kane read Farber his rights from a card then shook Starky's hand.

"Thanks. I'll get your cuffs back to you tomorrow."

"No problem. They're doing what they were made for." Starky glared at Farber. "Rot in hell, asshole!"

Kane waited until they had left then turned toward his prisoner.

"Anything you want to tell me, Mearle?"

"I'm not talking. Go fuck yourself."

"Not today," Kane said and pulled out his cell. He scrolled through his phone list and muttered: "Tony . . . Tony . . . Tony Canaro!" In the rear view mirror Greg saw that he had Farber's attention. Kane tapped the entry and a moment later the line was answered.

"Tony, it's Greg Kane. . . . Yeah, I'm doing great. Better than great. Guess who I've got cuffed in the back seat of my car? . . . . Not even close. Remember the deputy who went missing with my nephew Jason? . . . . Yeah, that's him, Mearle Farber. So, you want to guess again who I've got locked up in my car? . . . . Yes, fucking way! After killing Jason and letting Ryan Munroe loose he's been hiring himself out as a hit man. . . . God's truth. I've got an arrest warrant on him right here in my pocket. The thing is, Tony, I think BPD has jurisdiction of this case, I mean, he killed a Baltimore County Deputy Sheriff and he aided and abetted the escape of a BPD prisoner. So, I was wondering Tony, if I was to turn him over to you, do you think you could find a cell for him?"

"Hey, you can't do that!" Farber shouted.

"Shut up, Mearle. I'm on the phone here. . . . Sorry Tony, you were saying? . . . . I don't know, an hour, maybe a little longer if the traffic is bad. Will that be enough time for you to do up the paperwork?"

"Hey, you've got a federal warrant on me. You've got to take me to a federal lockup!"

"Shut the fuck up! Don't make me use the Taser on you, Mearle. . . . Yeah, Tony, Farber says he doesn't want to go back to Baltimore. . . . Yeah, too fucking bad, right? So, have you got a place for him? . . . Good, that's real good."

Kane paused then turned to watch Farber while he talked to Canaro.

"You know, Tony, we don't want any mix-ups," Greg said with an evil grin. "We want to make sure the booking sheet is right, so I think you should sign him in as 'Baltimore County Deputy Sheriff Mearle Farber.'"

"You son of a bitch!" Farber shouted and lunged forward as far as the belt would allow. "You can't do that!"

"You know, he seems upset but hell, Tony, we need to be accurate here. . . . No, gen pop will be fine. He doesn't need any special treatment."

Farber started thrashing at his bonds. Kane just smiled and then gave him a wink.

"So, Tony, make sure you note that he's got to be kept available for his interview with U.S. Attorney's office. They're going to want to talk to him so we might as well clear it on his intake form right up front."

"You can't do that! The trustees process those forms. If they think I'm talking to the feds those animals will kill me!"

"What's that, Tony? . . . Really? You think there might be a problem? . . . I've got an idea. Let's move him around if there's any trouble. Give him a tour of the facilities if things go bad for him at Kenilworth. . . . Yeah, I think so too."

"Bastard! You fucking son of a bitch!" Farber screamed.

"Tony, he's freaking out back there. I'm going to have to hang up now. I might have to tase him. . . . Yeah, I will. I'll see you in a little while." Kane clicked off the phone.

"You can't do that. Putting me in gen pop that way is the same as killing me. It's flat out murder."

"Oh, you'll be fine," Kane said and started the engine.

"You're bluffing. Well, it won't work. I'm not going to talk."

Kane turned east. It took him almost twenty minutes to get to the 295 then he merged into traffic and headed north.

"What do you think? Stay on this or take the 95?"

"Fuck you!"

"Yeah, at this time of day they're both going to be a bitch. You know, I think the 95 might be the better bet."

"This is coercion. Even if I talked nothing I said could be used in court."

"Talk? I thought you were exercising your right to remain silent." Farber glared into the rear-view mirror and struggled against the belt.

"Hey, there it is," Kane said a few minutes later. "I-95 north, six miles ahead." Kane glanced in the mirror. "Hey, nice teeth, Mearle. Are they real?"

"Of course they're real."

"Too bad."

"What's that supposed to mean?" Farber tried to snarl but Kane could hear the fear in his voice.

"Oh, come on, Mearle. You know how it works. The old cons always want a 'Welcome to Gen Pop' blow job but they don't want their dicks bitten off so they have to take precautions. They usually only knock out the top four teeth, though I have seen them get a little over zealous and take out the bottom ones too." Farber's face went white and he involuntarily clenched his jaws. "Of course, that might be from the lack of proper tools. I hear that they usually just smash the guy's mouth into the edge of the sink two or three times to get the job done. I guess it's not an exact science." Farber tucked his chin in as far as it would go against his chest and looked wildly around.

"There we go," Kane said, pointing. "I-95 North. It won't be long now."

"What's it going to take?" Farber asked.

"What's what going to take?"

"Stop fucking playing games with me. What do you want from me to turn this car around?"

"Are you saying that you want to waive your right to be silent?"

"Stop screwing with me and tell me what it's going to take to turn this car around."

"I haven't thought about it. I'll tell you what. Why don't you tell me everything, starting with you killing my nephew and ending with you doing a rabbit last night and then we'll see what we see."

"I'm not talking without a deal."

"Suit yourself. . . . Jeez, this traffic is a mess." Sweat began to drip down Farber's face and a sour smell filled the car. Kane cracked the rear windows a few inches on each side.

"I'll talk but I'm not waiving my rights. None of this is admissible in court. You got that? This is all under duress."

"Admissible, not admissible. That's for the lawyers to figure out. I'm just a cop. . . Hey, it looks like it's thinning out a little." Kane hit the gas and plunged into a gap in the fast lane.

"Shit! Stop the fucking car. Stop! I'll tell what you want to know!"

"Stop? Here? Are you nuts? Why don't you just quiet down and enjoy the ride, while you still can."

Farber began to suck in air in rapid gulps.

"Hey, settle down or you're going to hyperventilate. I'm not stopping to give you first aid."

Farber looked wildly around like an animal stuck in a trap.

"It wasn't personal," he said in almost a whine. "I didn't have any choice. What was I supposed to do? Munroe offered me half a million bucks, tax free!"

"Well," Kane said, "if it was tax free. . . . So, where'd you dump the cruiser?" Farber tugged impotently at the cuffs and Kane waited him out. He knew that getting the answer to that first question would be like pulling the keystone from an arch. After that it all would come flooding out. Half a minute went by. Kane kept his eyes on the road, not even looking at Farber in the mirror.

"I sank it in Liberty Lake where it turns into the Patapsco River," Farber said in a breathy voice. "I can show you where."

"Where's the kid's body?"

"In the trunk. He didn't suffer," Farber said in a rush. "A quick one to the head. He didn't feel a thing."

Kane's heart went cold and he wanted to put his weapon against Farber's forehead and pull the trigger. Instead he clenched his teeth and grasped the steering wheel so tightly that his knuckles turned white. A full minute passed before he could bring himself to speak.

"Are you still in contact with Ryan Munroe?" Kane said in a voice like gravel falling through a grate.

"Burner phones, sometimes we meet someplace. I don't know where he is or how to find him." Farber looked nervously out the window as Kane passed a lumbering semi. "For Christ's sake pull over. I'm doing what you asked."

"There's plenty of time to turn around if you tell me what I want. Who ordered the hit on Brownstein?"

"What? Who?"

"So much for your cooperation. I've got you on tape so stop fucking around."

Farber licked his lips and in response Kane pressed a little harder on the gas.

"All right. All right! It was Munroe. Who do you think?"

"Why did he want Brownstein killed?"

"He wanted him disappeared. Why? He's got some deal with somebody who's developing a new drug. The guy needs some chemical that Brownstein was going to make illegal so he had to go."

"What did you do with him?"

"I made him disappear."

"Stop fucking around. Where'd you put him?"

"I put him in a cave."

"A cave? Where?"

Farber licked his lips and looked out the window. Kane waited him out.

"A place off highway 211 in Virginia, about ten miles east of I-81. You get me a deal and I'll take you to him. Otherwise good luck finding him or the kid."

"Deals are up to the U.S. Attorney. Let's get back to the guy who wanted Brownstein out of the way. Who is he?"

"I don't know. I've never met him. He only talks to Munroe. Mr. X is what I call him."

"You said it was a new drug. What kind of a new drug?"

"What am I, a chemist? All Munroe told me was that this guy had invented some hot-shit drug and that he was going to manufacture it in big quantities but he needed to import some chemical or whatever in order to make it."

"What do you mean, 'big quantities'?"

"Big. Like boxcars full. The guy promised Ryan a distributorship from here to Philly, sort of a test market. Once it caught on Munroe figured he could wholesale it to people he knows in New York, maybe even go nationwide. He's got big plans. He said Mr. X would manufacture, we would wholesale, and the gangs and the mob would handle retail."

"When and where is Munroe getting his next delivery?"

"Like he would tell me something like that. Besides, I told you that the guy who's going to manufacture it hasn't gone into production yet. Munroe said that it was going to be two or three months before we got any product."

"How does this drug work? What does it do?"

"What does it do? What does any drug do? It gets you high. It fucks you up."

"Cut the bullshit! Is it a painkiller, hallucinogen, go sleepy, sex enhancer, amphetamine, what?"

"I don't know. All Ryan said was that it was supposed to get people high. Mr. X told him that the customers were going to be the same people who bought H, speed, coke, weed and oxy. Ryan said

Mr. X called it a 'broad spectrum recreational product' whatever that means."

Kane slowed a bit and tried to make sense of what Farber had just told him. Speed freaks and heroin users were looking for different kicks. Junkies wanted to go all soft and floaty. Tweakers wanted a knife-edge, high-voltage kick. How could one pill give both of them the jolt they were looking for? Kane glanced in the mirror. Farber was anxiously calculating the declining mileage between themselves and Baltimore. Kane was running out of time and there was one more big question he needed answered.

"How did you find out we were coming for you?"

"What do you mean?" Farber said, trying to sound confused.

"What do I mean? What the fuck do you think I mean. Your dinner was still hot on the stove when we crashed your place. Somebody warned you. Who was it?"

"Ryan, who else?"

"Munroe? How'd he find out?"

"How do you think? Somebody, Mr. X, talks to Ryan. Ryan talks to me. That's it. It's like a fucking underground cell. All I know is that somebody told Ryan that you were on to me and that I had to run, so I did."

"When did you get the call?"

"When? About two minutes before you kicked in my front door. I saw your guys going over the fence into my back yard."

Two minutes? Kane thought. That ruled out a leak from the judge who had issued the warrant and also from the D.C. police. Both had known Farber's house was blown hours before the raid.

"Tell me exactly what he said, word for word," Kane ordered.

Farber made a "you're a pain in the ass" face, then pursed his lips as he tried to remember.

"Fine," he said. "I picked up the phone. I knew it was Munroe because he's the only one who has that number. He said, 'What's your address?' something like that." Farber paused. "No, wait. He said 'What's your house number?' I told him '817.' He said, "The guy called me. They're on to you. Get out now!' I grabbed my go-bag and went over the back fence. I didn't even make it to the end of the block before your guys pulled up and headed for my back yard."

Kane turned the exchange over in his mind.

"Munroe didn't know where you lived?"

"*Nobody* knew where I lived. How the hell did you find me?"

"He didn't ask for your full address, just the house number?"

"I wouldn't have given him the full address. I almost didn't give him the number." Farber twisted in his seat as a road sign slipped by.

"Hey! We're almost into town. I held up my end of the deal. Get me the hell out of here."

Kane glanced at Farber in the mirror. In uniform or out he was a thug, a brute, an animal wearing shoes. He might last a day, maybe two or three in general population at the main jail but eventually they'd find him curled up on the floor bleeding out through twenty round little holes in his chest, exactly what he deserved. On the other hand, if Ryan Munroe remained ignorant that Farber had been grabbed maybe Mearle could lure him to a meeting. Probably not. Munroe gave new meeting to the word "paranoia" but it was worth a try. And if they got Munroe maybe he would lead them to Mr. X. Kane took the ramp into downtown Baltimore.

"Hey, you fucker!" Farber shouted, throwing himself against the belt. "We had a deal! We had a fucking deal!"

"Relax, I'm taking you to the federal building. You're the FBI's problem now."

"You can't use any of that stuff I said against me. That was under duress!"

"Tell it to your lawyer."

"I will. And I'm going to tell him how you—"

"You have the right to be silent. Shut up!"

Farber glared at Kane for a moment then, when he saw that they were heading away from the BPD building, he smiled, laid his head back against the seat and closed his eyes.

* * *

Special Agent Leonard Franks glanced at his watch and noted, unhappily, that it was still a little over an hour until quitting time. It had been a perfectly tedious day filled to the brim with reports, meetings and then more paperwork. He had just moved his mouse into the next vacant box on the form when his land-line beeped.

"Franks."

"Hello. This is Homeland Security Agent Gregory Kane. I understand that you were the primary on the Ryan Munroe case a couple of years ago."

"Yes, I was," Franks said, sitting up a little straighter. "How can I help you, Agent Kane?"

"Do you recall the names of the two Baltimore County deputies who were transporting Munroe when he went missing?"

What the hell? Franks paused for a moment then answered: "Mearle Farber and Jason Kane. Kane? Any relation?"

"He was my nephew," Greg said and struggled to keep his voice from breaking. "Mearle Farber murdered him."

Franks' skin began to tingle and he waved for another agent to tap the call.

"How do you know that?" Franks asked, stalling for time.

"Because Farber admitted it to me."

Franks stood up and motioned for his team.

"Where are you now, Agent Kane?"

"I'm in the lobby of your building. Mearle Farber is my prisoner. I'm here to turn him over to you. Will you please come down here and lock up this son of a bitch," Kane said in a voice barely his own, "before I change my mind and take him out and shoot him in the head."

Franks pulled on his coat and started running for the elevator before Kane had even hung up the phone.

CHAPTER FORTY-EIGHT

Ray Black paced his tiny room and went over everything again but he still ended up with the same frustrating results.

The day after the meeting with Mr. Green he had called to ask for his money. Green had not picked up. Then he called the operator he had introduced Green to. Donald also didn't pick up. Black called several times more over the next few days but all he got was the automated "The person you are calling is not available" message. Weeks later that changed to "The number you are calling is no longer in service." Screwed again.

When did my life turn to shit? he asked himself for the hundredth time, but unlike the previous occasions this time his answer was *When I took my first hit of speed.* It didn't matter that it had happened while he was still in uniform, when he was on a mission where falling asleep would likely mean getting dead. Damn, that stuff made him feel invincible and there's nothing a warrior loved more than feeling like Captain America.

Dozens of times in the last couple of years the words "I've got to get myself clean" had drifted through his brain but they were merely fleeting notions, like the gaze of someone driving through a city in which he never intended to stop and put down roots. On the few occasions when he might have been ready to give up the stuff Black had been too broke or too fucked up to actually do anything about it.

After his meeting with Mr. Green, Black had twenty-five thousand dollars in his pocket. *I've just set up somebody I don't even know to be murdered,* Black realized as he looked around the filthy tavern. *They're all hopeless losers,* he thought and then he caught a glimpse of himself in the mirror behind the bar. He was a fucking loser too, worse than them, he realized. At least they weren't supplying killers for hire.

As he stared at the face of the man he'd become, a man whom he didn't recognize and one he didn't want to know, Black promised himself, *I'm not going to be this guy anymore.* The next morning he signed himself into the New Beginning Treatment Facility. It cost him fifteen thousand dollars but he figured the chance of turning Mr. Black back into First Sergeant Arnold Demeter was worth it. He hit a bad spot a few days after he finished his rehab and felt the speed tempting him like a departed lover suddenly appearing on his doorstep and begging to be let back into his life. Then he saw the news about the attempted murder of Justice Hopper and his guts knotted. *Was that the hit Mr. Green had wanted done? Had he gotten himself in the middle of the attempted murder of a Supreme Court Justice? Fuck! Fuck! Fuck!*

The day he had made the introduction Black was so strung out that he hadn't really thought about who was going to be the target or how that was going to affect him. The only thing on his mind was the money and the drugs it would buy. *Shit!* What had happened to his brain? It was a half million dollar job. It had to be somebody big. And the hit had failed.

The whole government, the FBI, Secret Service, U.S. Marshals, they were all going to be on this like flies on shit. They were all going to be looking for him. If Black needed any incentive to stay clean that was it. He was so frightened of spending the rest of his life in prison that even the thought of getting juiced made him sick to his stomach. He immediately started checking the neighborhood for cars he didn't recognize, ducking into front doors and out the back ones. Was anyone watching him? Was he being followed? He had just started to relax, then he heard a buzzing from inside his kitchen drawer.

What the hell? Black yanked it open and saw the burner phone rattling around between the can opener and the cork screw like a big black roach.

"Hello?"

"Mr. Black, have you seen the papers?" Green asked.

"What?"

"I told you half up front and half when the job was finished. A deal's a deal. Where do you want to meet to pick up your second installment?"

Black's brain was spinning. *The deal was that the second half would be paid as soon as the operator took the job, not when it was over. And besides, Donald had missed. The target was still alive. Why would Green want to pay him when the operation had failed?*

"Meeting?" Black mumbled. "When?"

"When do you want your money?" Green thought Black sounded like he was stoned out of his mind. *Fucking stupid junkie.*

"I'll call you back," Black said and dropped the phone like it was radioactive.

Nobody pays money they don't have to for a job that went bad. There is no Santa Claus. *Jesus, they're going to kill me,* Black thought. The words "loose end" kept shooting through his brain. What was he going to do? What could he do? He could run. They probably wouldn't be able to find him. Probably. Maybe. But running was a coward's play. Screw that. He might be a burned-out recovering junky but he wasn't any fucking coward! *Well, if I'm not going to run then I'm going to fight,* Black decided. The problem was that he was all alone. The operator was a pro and Black had nobody to watch his back. He needed help. How the hell was he going to get anybody to stand up for him?

Black paced the floor and twisted the problem around and around until he finally came up with an idea. It wasn't a good idea. In fact, it scared the piss out of him. It was risky and dangerous and even if it worked it would screw up his life forever. And what if he was wrong? What if Green wasn't out to kill him? Another twenty-five thousand in cash would give him a shot at a new job, a whole new, and better, life. Maybe he wouldn't have to jump off that cliff after all. *Money? Fight? Escape?*

Hell, he could set up a money drop and see what happens. There were ways he could reduce the risk. If it didn't work he could always fall back on Plan B. An hour later Black called Green and told him where to leave the cash.

* * *

"You called it," Feeney told Donald. "He couldn't resist the money."

"How did he sound?"

"Like a junky with shit for brains."

"So the meet is on?"

"He wouldn't go for a face to face. He wants me to tape the money to the back of the dumpster behind the Idle Hour bar."

"I don't like that. When are you supposed to leave it?"

"I figured you'd need time to scout the place so I stalled him until two tomorrow afternoon. I told him I would have to get the money from three different banks in order to keep each cash transaction under the ten-thousand dollar federal reporting limit. . . . Are you there?" Feeney asked after several seconds of silence.

"For a brain-dead addict that's a half-smart plan. He can sit back and watch the alley if he's worried or even pay somebody to pick up the package for him." Donald was silent for several seconds. "Before you make the drop call and tell him that you had to get the money in twenties in order to keep the banks from getting suspicious. Make up six stacks of fake bills, each about an inch thick. Put twenty dollar bills on the tops and bottoms and seal them all in an oversize, yellow, padded envelope. And tape it closed real good to discourage anyone from peeking inside. If anybody but him leaves that alley with it I'll be able to spot it and follow them."

"What if he doesn't show up?"

"Oh, he'll show up all right. The only thing on a junky's mind is getting high. To get high he needs money. If you're supposed to leave the money at two I'll guarantee you he'll be there to grab it before three."

"What if he rips the package open and realizes it's a fake?"

"You're a regular question box, aren't you?" Donald sighed and forced himself to take a breath. "Look, I know what he looks like and he's not getting out of that alley alive. If he sends someone else you can bet that he'll be nearby because he won't want them getting greedy and running off with his cash. Satisfied?"

"All right, all right. I just want to make sure that we've covered all the angles. I'll call you when I've delivered it."

"Don't bother. I'll be in place, watching, hours before you get there."

Feeney hung up and went searching for latex gloves and a pair of scissors.

* * *

Donald checked out the Idle Hour's garbage bins just after dawn. There were only two ways in and out — down the dead-end alley along the back side of the building and through the bar's back door. Donald jogged to his car and retrieved his tools. He quickly drilled five angled tap holes through the back door and into the jam then he dipped a handful of four inch steel screws in cyanoacrylate and screwed them home. Just to guild the lily he injected the rest of the "super glue" into the crack between the door and the jam. Nobody was going to open the alley door until the owner got a contractor down here to cut the thing free. OK, Mr. Black was going to have to enter and leave the alley from the street if he wanted to get his money.

Donald moved his car then returned on foot to do a careful search of the neighborhood. He found the place he wanted across the street and two buildings down. Weathered planks faced a gate across a passage along the side of an old bakery. Years ago they had probably used the walkway to hand-truck sacks of flour to the basement where the ovens were located.

Donald scanned the street then cut the chain and pushed the screeching gate out of the way. The boards hid him from passersby and the gap along the hinged edge was wide enough to give him a good view of the entrance to The Idle Hour's alley.

Donald slipped out and retrieved a can of 3-in-1 Oil from his trunk. It took a bit of effort but he was eventually able to swing the old gate open and closed without making any noise. He peered through his monocular and confirmed that no one was going to get in or out of the alley without him being able to check them out. Donald put a square of foam rubber on the filthy concrete and settled in to wait for Mr. Green to leave the package and then for Mr. Black to make a grab for it.

Two seconds after Black entered the alley Donald would be out of his bolt hole and halfway across the street. He figured he would be on Black from behind while the junky was still hunched over the dumpster. After that events would dictate how things went. If possible Donald planned to hit Black in the back with a five second burst from his stun gun, then jab him with a mixture of enough heroin and speed to kill three men. If worse came to worst and Black spotted him and turned to fight, Donald had a suppressed .22 that would be no louder than an old man's cough. A couple in the chest to slow Black down and three in the head to finish the job. Junkie dead in an alley. The cops would call it a Public Service Murder and head straight for the donut cart.

Donald took a long pull from his water bottle and leaned back against the brick wall to wait for his prey.

CHAPTER FORTY-NINE

Before calling Green to set up the money drop Black cased the area around the Idle Hour in a way not very different from Donald's investigation and Black came to a similar conclusion. He identified four surveillance locations with varying degrees of desirability where Donald, or someone like him, might hide. The abandoned bakery was number one on Black's list. A five story apartment house bordered the bakery's rear parking lot and the window at the end of the apartment building's fourth-floor hallway afforded him a good view of the side passage and the gate. Black had identified similar surveillance points for each of the other three potential locations and planned to visit them in turn until he either found someone watching the Idle Hour or he convinced himself that Mr. Green didn't have any surprises planned. That hope vanished the instant he spotted Donald crouched behind the gate.

Black knew that for the first hour or so a sentry was usually careful but as the watch went on he lost focus. After a meal or a piss break he would sharpen up a little and then slowly begin to zone out until he neared the end of his shift when he'd start paying attention again. The money delivery was set for two p.m. so around twelve or twelve-thirty a pro would start watching in earnest. Black had spotted Donald a little after eight so he figured that by eleven Donald would both be bored with all the waiting and not yet revved up for the main event. That's when Black planned to make his move.

The apartment house had a weed-filled strip of dirt between its back wall and the chain-link fence separating it from the bakery's parking lot. Black had filled a knapsack with things he thought he would need including a gun, heavy gloves, and a pair of baseball shoes he'd picked up the day before at a Big 5 sporting goods store. The preferred method to get past a chain-link fence was to use a pair of three-foot long bolt cutters to snip a line of links and then slip through the tear but people tended to notice a guy carrying bolt cutters and each snip made a noise. The cleats on a pair of baseball shoes would securely grab onto the links and if you were careful you could climb a steel fence in a few seconds and barely make a sound. Donald could only see the first few feet of fencing directly behind his position. The section near the property's eastern boundary was completely out of his view.

At ten-fifty Black slipped out of the apartment house's back door and put on the spiked shoes and his gloves. As casually as he could he walked over to the fence then turned to study the windows along the building's back wall. As far as he could tell no one was watching. Why would they? An overgrown strip of dirt backed up against a decaying parking lot wasn't a very attractive view. Still, you never knew what people would do. Black took one final look at the apartments then climbed the fence. For a second he hesitated at the top then slipped his right leg over and dug the toe cleat into a link on the other side. The steel made a little rattle as he brought the other leg over and began the climb back down.

Once on the ground the spikes made a dull *clack, clack, clack* against the decayed asphalt. Should he stop here and change shoes? No, he was too exposed. Instead Black varied his pace so that the noises sounded too irregular to be footsteps. When he reached the Bakery's back wall he took a deep breath and pulled off the spikes. If Donald had heard anything and chose this moment to peek around the corner Black was screwed. Fifteen seconds later he had returned the spikes and gloves to the backpack and finished tying the laces on his sneakers. After another deep breath and a quick look around he removed his Sig Sauer, zipped up, and strapped on the backpack.

Foot by foot he worked his way to the edge of the building. In the movies the cops always poked their heads around corners like nervous birds, which was really a bad idea. The human eye is attracted by swift motion. Any sudden movement is likely to be noticed, which was why snipers were trained to approach their targets at the rate of inches per minute instead of inches per second. Black pulled a dentist's mirror from his pocket and slowly extended it just beyond the corner of the building. It showed him Donald sitting crosswise in the passage with his back against the wall, his head turned to the right so that he could watch the street through the gap between two of the planks.

Black muffled his gun underneath his coat, cocked the hammer with the barest of clicks and sucked in one last, deep breath. *OK, go time!* With the Sig stretched out in front of him in the traditional two-handed grip Black swung around the corner and fast-walked down the passage. Donald sensed him almost immediately. *This son of a bitch is fast!* Black thought even as Donald was grabbing his own weapon from the concrete where it had lain.

Black fired three shots without even thinking, pure reflex. The first caught Donald in the stomach. The recoil walked the barrel up so that the second hit round hit him high on the chest and the third drilled a nasty hole through the middle of Donald's forehead. Black kept walking. The body had blocked the gate but it reluctantly slid aside when Black hauled on the latch. He noticed that there was no blood on Donald's stomach or chest and realized that the operator had been wearing a vest. If the third shot hadn't hit Donald in the head it might be Black who was dead right now instead of the other way around.

Black pulled out a well-used painter's drop cloth and draped it over the body. If no one in the apartment building had seen the shooting he figured there was a good chance that the body would remain undiscovered for at least several hours. He only needed it to stay hidden until Mr. Green made the promised money drop at two.

Black shoved the gun into his waistband then squeezed through the gate and pulled it closed behind him. He took a quick look around but no one seemed to be paying him any attention. He paused half a second to wipe his prints from the rusted pipe and then headed for the corner. He had parked a stolen car half a block down. He intended to abandon it a quarter of a mile away and then walk to the public lot where he had left his Toyota. He wanted to dump the gun and everything else but he couldn't, not yet. By one o'clock he was back, parked down the street from the bar, waiting.

Green arrived promptly at two. Even if Black hadn't recognized him he couldn't miss the big, yellow envelope Green carried into the alley. Black started his engine and waited. Luckily Green wasn't a professional criminal. He cruised along oblivious to the cars around him. Black had no trouble following Green to a large construction company's corporation yard a few miles outside of town. Green parked the well-used RAM pickup he had driven to the bar and went inside. Anticipating a long wait Black had brought a sandwich and bottled water. It was almost six-thirty when Green finally emerged. This time he slid into a silver Ford Expedition with chrome rims. Black snapped a picture of the plate and, later, another of the sprawling house where Green parked the Ford and then went inside. A few dollars to an Internet database gave Black the registered owner's name, Carl Feeney. Another payment to a different site rewarded Black with an image of Carl Feeney's driver's license.

Got you, asshole! Black thought when the picture matched the man he had met weeks before. Within an hour Black's gun, his shirt, coat, the backpack and all the rest of it were at the bottom of a large body of water. He allowed himself a short break for a decent meal and a good night's sleep before diving into the shit again.

Tomorrow he would start Plan B.

CHAPTER FIFTY

While Ray Black contemplated Plan B and drove white-knuckled past the corner where his old connection still offered little packets of short-term invincibility Gregory Kane inched his way back toward D.C. and wondered who had betrayed them. As usual the Beltway was jammed with idiots darting in and out of openings barely the size of a sixties-era Cadillac and viewing any hundred-foot-long stretch of open asphalt as an invitation to kick it up to seventy and trust their brakes to save them from disaster.

The list of suspects was short but not sweet. Danny? No, Kane refused to believe that. Besides Danny was the one who had found Farber in the first place. Kane tapped a button on his phone and set it to speaker mode.

"Danny, are you alone?"

"I'm at home. My girlfriend is here. Where are you?"

"Did you tell anyone that we'd found Farber?"

"You mean before the raid? No, nobody."

"Not even your girlfriend?"

"That's against the rules." Kane waited. "No, I didn't," Danny said a second later. "Why?"

"Are you absolutely sure? Think hard."

The phone was silent for a couple of seconds. "I'm sure. Why?"

"Because Farber got a call that we were coming."

"How do you know that?"

"I'll fill you in later. The point is that someone tipped him off."

"Maybe it was somebody on the D.C. PD," Danny said after another second's pause.

"Outside of the D.C. PD and the judge, who knew that we were interested in a house with the number 817?" Kane asked.

"Supervisor Wren knew," Danny said uneasily. "But he didn't know the street name or why we were looking at it."

"He didn't need to," Kane said.

"Maybe he told someone."

Who could Wren have told? Kane wondered. *His boss, the Principal Deputy? Did he have a secretary, an assistant? Had someone hacked his computer?*

"Maybe," Kane said finally.

"Where are you? The boss was asking for you."

Kane thought about the three calls from Immerson that he'd ignored. "I'm stuck in traffic. I'll see you in the morning." Kane disconnected. Nothing had changed. He had to find the leak and he had very little time. How long could they continue to pretend that they were still looking for Farber? Once they were past the weekend how long before somebody at Homeland found out that Farber was already in FBI custody? Two days? Three?

Kane dialed Ron Franks' cell.

"I'm a little busy right now Kane," Franks said instead of "hello."

"Is Farber cooperating?"

"We're negotiating."

"You can't give him a pass. He killed a cop."

"And we'd like to recover the body."

"I know where it is, more or less. It'd be some work but we can find it without him."

"Kane, you've already told me all of that. Look, I don't have time—"

"I've got to identify the leak in my office before anyone finds out that we've got Farber."

"What does that mean?"

"On Monday morning I'm going to drop a juicy tidbit in someone's ear and see where it ends up."

"No, you're not. We need Farber to lure Munroe into a trap. If you tell people you've got a lead on him then Munroe will panic and he won't come within miles of the meet."

"Once you spring your trap on Munroe I won't have any bait to catch my mole."

"Kane, I'm warning you. Do nothing. Nothing!"

Kane thought about arguing but knew it would be waste of time. At this point Franks was like a dog with a bone. *Fuck it!* He'd do what he had to do and worry about it later.

"How long can you keep anyone at Homeland from finding out that you've got him?" Kane asked.

"As long as I have to."

"How long is that in days?"

"Three days," Franks said after a long silence. "Maybe four."

Maybe two, Kane thought.

"Call me when you've set up the meet with Munroe."

"Take it easy. Farber's refusing to cooperate until the U.S. Attorney signs off on a deal so nothing's going to happen before Monday. I'll keep you in the loop," Franks said in the same voice people used when they told you that the check was in the mail.

"I didn't make myself clear. You need my cooperation. If you don't call me by eleven Monday morning with all the details of the deal you're giving Farber then I'm going to tell my boss that I caught Farber and where he is."

"The hell you will. If you interfere with our getting Munroe I'll have your badge."

"In your dreams."

"If you fuck this up, Kane, I swear I'll destroy you."

"You'll destroy me?" Kane said, feeling his control slip. "For catching a wanted criminal and reporting the arrest to my boss?"

"I can—"

"You can go play with yourself!" Kane shouted as something inside him snapped. "Jesus, how stupid are you? I don't work for you. I'm the hero who caught the guy. You're the asshole who let the best lead to a wanted fugitive slip away. One word from me and you'll be at the bottom of the crapper trying to figure out which way is up and we both know it." Kane took a breath and tried to calm himself. "So, what time Monday morning are you going to call and give me your report?" he asked finally.

Franks didn't answer and Kane waited him out. "I'll call you when the U.S. Attorney signs off on Farber's deal," he finally said in a voice like ice.

"Which will be when?"

"I should know something by eleven on Monday."

"What a coincidence. If I haven't heard from you by eleven-fifteen I'm telling my boss everything."

Too angry to speak Franks hung up.

Well, I never figured we'd be pals, Kane thought.

* * *

Kane was at his desk by eight on Monday morning. Danny arrived at ten after and Greg motioned him over.

"Did you find any trace of Farber?" Danny asked then glanced around to see if anyone was watching.

"Nothing beyond the hot lead you're working on." Kane didn't like lying to Danny but anyone with good interrogation skills could read the kid's face like a book.

"I'm — What?"

"You worked your tail off over the weekend and came up with something unusual when you went back through Farber's credit cards."

"I did?"

"You called me at home and as soon as I heard about it I told you to follow up."

"And did I?" Danny asked.

"Of course, and you know what? I think with a little luck it just might break the case. Of course it's too soon to get everybody all excited so you can't tell anyone about it."

"Sure," Danny said. "I get that. We can't say anything until we find out if it's going to get us somewhere."

"Exactly," Kane said, patting Danny on the shoulder.

"Is there something I should be doing, you know while we're waiting to see if the new lead is going to pan out?"

"Good question. Somebody told me about a new drug that's coming out. He called it a 'broad spectrum recreational product.' It's supposed to appeal to anyone who uses heroin, cocaine, and amphetamines. Have you ever heard of anything like that?"

"I—"

"Kane!" Greg looked up and spotted Immerson standing in his office doorway. "Get over here!"

"Check it out will you? I'll be back in a minute."

By the time Greg entered the office Immerson was seated behind his desk. Kane closed the door without being asked.

"Where were you Friday afternoon?"

"Out running down tips. Didn't Boland tell you?"

"It's not his job to report your whereabouts to me. It's yours."

"Oops. Sorry," Kane said, though he didn't look sorry at all.

Immerson frowned, shuffled a few papers then looked back at Kane.

"Did you turn up anything?"

"Yes and no."

"What's that supposed to mean?" Immerson snapped.

"I found a stripper who said that Farber might have been in her club on Thursday night but it was dark and the guy paid cash and she had no idea where he went when he left." Kane shrugged.

"And then what?"

"I canvassed the neighborhood and eventually I called it quits but by then it was late and the traffic was so bad that I just went home. I checked with Boland's team over the weekend and they had nothing. I called Danny and he's still pushing paper. I came in early this morning," Kane said earnestly.

"You need to get me your FR-2."

"Absolutely."

Immerson looked at Greg for a count of two then shook his head. Kane just stood there with his hands behind his back and tried to look innocent.

"Oh, get out."

A moment later Kane pulled up a chair next to Danny's desk.

"I couldn't find anything on the phrase 'broad spectrum recreational drug,'" Danny said.

"Do you know anybody in the tech department at the DEA?"

"I can make some calls." Danny clicked a few keys and pulled up the Homeland directory then migrated down the section listing the liaisons for ATF, ICE, DEA, FBI and the rest of the Federal alphabet soup. "You know," Danny said a moment later, "you could ask Professor Bellingham. He hates drug addicts."

"How do you know that?"

"He called, while you were on that Justice Hopper thing."

"What did he want?"

"He asked if we needed any more help. He said that he thought that drug addicts were a scourge on the nation and that he would do anything he could to stop them. I told him that we were still investigating but we would call him if we needed anything. So," Danny suggested, "maybe you should ask him if he's heard of some kind of broad spectrum drug."

Kane felt a slight tickle at the back of his brain.

"When Bellingham called did he ask for me or for you?" Greg asked a moment later.

"It buzzed at my desk but he could have asked for you and they transferred the call to me because you were, you know, out in the field."

"No, if he asked for me and I wasn't here they would have just sent him to my voice mail," Kane said absently.

"When the operator told him you were out he might have asked to speak to me, well speak to your partner."

"He's a civilian. How would he even know I have a partner?"

"In the movies investigators always have partners."

This isn't the movies, Kane thought.

"How do you answer your phone?"

"What?"

"How do you answer your phone? 'Hello', 'Special Investigations', 'Rosewood'?"

Danny paused for a second. "I guess I just say, 'Hello' I mean, it's ringing at my desk so they already know who I am."

Like a half-remembered melody something was nagging at Kane but he didn't know what.

"I want you to think hard." Danny straightened in his chair. "I want you to repeat your conversation with Bellingham word for word, starting with 'Hello.'"

Danny looked confused, then closed his eyes and began to speak. "I said 'Hello' and he said 'Agent Rosewood?' and I said 'Yes' and he said 'I understand that Agent Kane is out of the office today' and I said, 'Yes, can I help you?' and he said, 'I was wondering if I can give you any more help with that list of proscribed substances' and I said 'I don't think so but I'll ask Agent Kane when he comes in' and he said 'I hate to think that this is all about drugs. Drug addicts are a scourge on this country. I'll give you any help I can to stop them' and I said—"

"That's fine," Kane interrupted and seemed lost in thought. *Why and how could Bellingham have known Danny's name?*

"I don't understand."

"You said 'Hello' when you answered the phone."

"Is that wrong? Should I have answered 'Agent Rosewood'?"

"How did he know your name?"

"Well, I guess the receptionist—"

"Receptionists don't give out personal information. If someone calls for me they either get me or they leave a voice mail or they ask for someone else. They're not supposed to say, 'Agent Kane is out of the office. Would you like to speak to his partner, Agent Rosewood?'"

"Maybe she made a mistake," Rosewood said, trying to be helpful. Kane just looked away. Someone at HS was talking to Ryan Munroe. Someone at HS had told Bellingham the name of Kane's partner. *Was it the same someone,* Kane wondered, *and if so how did Elliott Bellingham fit in?*

"I want you to track down everything Professor Bellingham has ever published — scientific papers, commencement speeches, press releases for his company, letters to the editor, everything. Get it to me ASAP. I need to read it before I leave this afternoon."

"Uhhh, OK," Danny said. "Why?"

"Because I'm going to take your advice."

"What advice is that?"

"I'm going to ask Professor Bellingham to help us with our case. With any luck he'll have dinner with me tonight and I think it would be a good idea to know as much about him as possible. Don't you?"

"Sure. I guess," Danny said though he didn't have a clue what Kane was getting at.

* * *

At twelve minutes after eleven Kane got a call from Leonard Franks.

"The U.S. Attorney has approved the deal," he said instead of 'Hello.'

"Which is?"

"Farber serves twenty-five years in a medium-security federal prison under another name. In return he takes us to the two bodies and he helps us get Ryan Munroe."

"When's he going to do that?"

"The paperwork won't be finished until later today. He won't give us squat until everything is signed." Franks was clearly irritated by the delay.

"You know he probably has a safe word set up with Munroe. If he doesn't use it you're SOL," Kane said as if talking to a slow child.

"I have done this kind of thing before, Kane. We told him we'd trim three years off his sentence if he gets us Munroe. He won't deliberately screw us."

"Keep me posted."

"You're on the top of my list. . . . Don't fuck this up Kane."

"You too," Greg said and hung up.

Kane spent the rest of the day trying to concoct a true but misleading report of yesterday's activities then he began plowing through the pile of printouts Danny had dropped on his desk. Bellingham's academic papers were mostly composed of acronyms scattered across sentences apparently designed to torture the English language. After scraping away all the jargon, compound clauses, graphs and statistics, the science generally seemed to follow the path Bellingham had outlined in their first meeting.

As far as Kane could tell the research had been broken into several phases: (1) find crucial links in the reproductive process of the target species; (2) discover the proteins whose presence or absence was vital to the functioning of that targeted process; (3) locate the genes that either produced those proteins or produced other proteins that suppressed hostile factors; (4) determine an effective method for deactivating or removing those vital genes.

Bellingham had produced separate papers describing each stage in the process via a series of experiments. He had started with simple bacteria then advanced to fruit flies and had lastly moved on to mice.

A year after the mouse studies were completed he took a leave of absence from the university and founded Eco-Safe Technologies. That was five years ago.

Kane set the scientific papers aside and leafed through the rest of the pile.

"Where did he get the money for his company?" Kane asked Danny a minute later.

"I don't know. Maybe he funded it himself. He's pretty rich, or at least his family is."

"How rich?" Kane asked as he leafed through the file for Bellingham's bio.

"Well, originally it was timber money and then they invested in railroads, to haul the wood I guess. According to Wikipedia, Bellingham's father was supposed to be worth around two-hundred million and the professor is an only child."

"Timber and railroads. That's old money. Send me the link to his Wikipedia page and see if you can find anything else on his background."

Kane flipped through the remaining printouts and sorted them in chronological order, oldest to newest. The first was an interview published fifteen years ago in the university's alumni magazine — advancing science, unlocking the mysteries of life, making the world a better place, blah, blah, blah. After that the sources became increasingly less prominent — an article in a short-lived science-for-the-masses magazine *Tech & Science Frontiers*, a letter to the editor of *Modern Biology* and six years ago an opinion piece titled "Overpopulation & Species Collapse" in the on-line magazine *The New Patriot* published by the Save America Foundation.

In it Bellingham had argued that treating diseases suffered by the carriers of "defective" genes would result in wide-scale genetic contamination that would, in the end, lead to a wave of epidemics and the potential collapse of humanity itself. Bellingham's thesis was that diseases arising from genetic causes should not be treated but rather the genes responsible should be deleted from the host population or the carriers should be sterilized or the carriers should be allowed to die from the disease as a way of ridding future generations of the defective genes.

"Feeding fertile people who cannot feed themselves," Bellingham wrote, "only results in increasing the population of people who cannot feed themselves and thus exacerbates the famine condition instead of solving it. Similarly, treating a genetically-caused disease that would otherwise kill the host only results in even more people being afflicted with that condition. In both cases common sense dictates that the subjects should either be allowed to live or die in accordance with the laws of natural selection or, at minimum, should be rendered incapable of spawning a new and larger generation suffering from the same ills."

Kane tried to imagine the representatives of a charitable organization telling a starving village in the Sudan they could only be fed or given typhoid medicine if they volunteered to be sterilized. He was pretty sure that Bill Gates wouldn't be on board with anything like that.

And now I understand why Bellingham's no longer teaching classes at Yale, Kane thought.

* * *

Kane's dinner with the professor was at a fish restaurant called "The Shorebird" about five miles south of Richmond just off the I-95. It was neither particularly fancy nor a chain outlet featuring a Wednesday-night special of all-you-can-eat popcorn shrimp. Bellingham was waiting near the hostess desk when Kane arrived.

"I'm sorry we couldn't meet closer to your office," Bellingham apologized once they were seated, "but we're at a crucial phase in our work right now."

"It's not a problem. It gave me an excuse to leave early." Kane flipped through the menu then looked up. "What's good here?"

"You can't go wrong with the crab."

After the busboy had delivered their drinks and a basket of fresh bread and the waitress had taken their order Bellingham glanced around and then asked softly, "How can I help you, Agent Kane?"

"To be honest, I'm not sure you can. I'm probably grasping at straws here but I was wondering if there's been any, I don't know, chatter in the scientific community about any new designer drugs?"

"Designer drugs?" Bellingham asked. "I'm in the insect-killing business. Wouldn't the DEA or FBI know more about something like that?"

"You're probably right. As I said, I'm grasping at straws." Kane focused on buttering a piece of bread then looked up at the professor. "I was thinking that you must subscribe to all those scientific journals and that maybe there were some articles about, I don't know, people figuring out what part of the brain responds to what kind of drugs or that someone has noticed that some new drug stimulates the brain in some new way. You see what I'm getting at?" Kane asked, seeming both hopeful and confused.

"Well," Bellingham began, then paused. "I think I understand what you're asking but that's a question that should be directed to a grad student or a research house. It's more or less a standard process. You have an idea for a line of research and you institute a publication review to see if anyone has done something like that already and what they found and if they're still working on the problem. You don't want to reinvent the wheel after all."

"Could you refer me to someone who could do that kind of a study for my office?"

"I'll email you a list of names and a few commercial firms that do that sort of work."

"Great. You see, that helps me already," Kane said smiling. "Who knows. Maybe someone's published something that might lead us back to one of the chemicals on the new HHS list. At least that might give us a place to start."

Bellingham began to say something but stopped when their dinners arrived. "How is your investigation going?" he asked once the waitress had left.

"We're not getting anywhere on the drug end of things. If we were I wouldn't be asking for your help." Kane looked around as if concerned that someone might overhear. "But we've made some progress on the missing HHS administrator."

"You've found him?" Bellingham asked, leaning forward.

"No, nothing like that, but we've got a good lead on a person of interest. Of course, I can't get into any details but we may be getting very close to grabbing him up."

"Do you think he can lead you to the body?"

"Officially, the HHS administrator is only missing but, well, who are we kidding? Nobody thinks that he's on the beach in the Bahamas. As for leading us to him, I think we can apply enough leverage to our target to get his cooperation. Of course, we have to catch him first."

"Are you close? When do you think you'll be able to find him?"

"Two days? Three?" Kane wiggled his hand from side to side. "You can't be sure of anything in my business. You just take it one day at a time."

"But you have a good lead?"

"Let's just say that I'm very optimistic about our chances."

"Well that's good news." Bellingham held up his glass as if for a toast.

"Yeah, but that's only step one. We still have to find out who hired him and then figure out what chemical they're interested in and then keep them from getting it, though that's going to be the DEA's problem not mine. They're welcome to it."

"You're not interested in stopping drugs?" Bellingham asked.

"The idiots want drugs," Kane said and stabbed a chunk of potato. "You can't stop them. You get rid of oxy and they start shooting heroin. You get rid of speed and they start snorting coke. It's like trying to hold back the tide. Prohibition didn't work for alcohol and it doesn't work for drugs."

"You'd let people buy them legally?" Bellingham asked.

"If they want to kill themselves then let them. At least that would take the profit out of it."

"You don't mind it if addicts die?"

"They're dying now and making those animals in the cartels billions in the process," Kane said, spearing the last piece of his sole. "Do you disagree?"

For a moment Bellingham seemed lost in thought. "It's a serious problem," he finally answered. "Something needs to be done. I agree with that. . . . More bread?"

Kane tried to draw the professor out with a couple more gambits but Bellingham seemed to have tired of the subject of drug addicts. He spent the rest of the evening commenting on the wine and the difficulty of finding scallops that hadn't been treated with STP. For an instant Kane thought about asking the professor why someone who wanted to use genetic tools to exterminate insects had spent a year and a half applying his techniques to mammals but quickly discarded the idea. If his hunch about what Bellingham was up to was correct Greg didn't think he'd get a truthful answer anyway.

Kane went home, not sure if his long drive to Richmond had accomplished anything until he showed up at the office the next morning and found Sebastian Wren standing next to his desk, waiting for him.

CHAPTER FIFTY-ONE

Wren pulled up a chair and both men sat down.

"My boss wants an update on the case. What have you got on Farber?"

"It's all in my FR-2," Kane said, pulling a sheet of paper off his desk.

"Come on, Kane. Cut the crap. You're too good an investigator not to have something better than just running down calls off the tip line."

"I don't know what to tell you."

Wren scowled and waved Danny over. Danny looked uneasily at Kane then rolled his chair to the other side of Kane's desk.

"Rosewood, your partner was just telling me about your new lead." Danny shot Kane a nervous glance. "Good work, by the way. What's your time line on it?"

"Well, uhhh," Danny began and looked helplessly at Greg.

"Jesus, give the kid a break," Kane said. "OK, fine, we do have something, sort of."

"What does that mean?"

"We can't officially have this information without a warrant which hasn't come in yet. Once we have the warrant then we'll have the information."

Kane was saying that they'd gotten a lead by hacking into some database without a warrant and that they couldn't admit that they knew what they knew until the warrant officially arrived.

"When do you expect to have the warrant?"

"I'll make the call right now."

Kane pulled out his cell and headed for the far corner of the room. Wren half stood to follow him then thought better of it. He looked at Danny who returned a weak smile.

Franks answered on the fourth ring.

"I've got a bite," Kane said.

"What?"

"I put my bait in the water and this morning I got a bite. In a couple of hours Farber's going to get a call on his cell from his boss warning him not to visit his girlfriend."

"What girlfriend?"

"Her name is Giselle. He's been seeing her for about a year. He's planning on holing up at her place until the heat dies down. I've got her address and we're going to stake out her place and grab him the minute he shows up."

"You made her up," Franks said.

"If Munroe asks, Farber met her at a diner. She's a graphic artist. A little heavy and very lonely and eager to please. Just Farber's type. She lives on Glasner Avenue. Make sure he sticks to the story."

"And how is this supposed to help me?"

"It's going to get you Munroe. Here's the story. Farber was going to stay at Giselle's place until things cooled down enough for him to skip town. Since he can't do that with us watching her he'll need Munroe to get him cash, a clean ID and a credit card."

"We've already tried that. Munroe told him to sit tight and he'd see what he could do."

"Now you've got a reason to try again. When Munroe calls to warn him about Giselle being burned, have Farber say that if Munroe doesn't come up with the money and an ID then if he gets caught he'll tell them who Munroe's employer is."

"How would Farber know that? Munroe probably doesn't even know."

"Farber was a cop. He has cop skills. He figured that someday he'd need insurance in case things went wrong so he made it his business to find out who was paying Munroe. How he did it isn't important."

"Why should Munroe believe him?" Franks demanded.

"Have Farber say that he knows that the boss is 'The Professor.'"

"The Professor? Who the hell is The Professor?"

"He's Munroe's boss."

"How the hell do you know that?"

"Attention to detail and superior abilities."

"You've got a hunch," Franks scoffed.

"Just have Farber follow the script," Kane told him.

"And then what?"

"And then I'll tell you who the professor is," Kane said and hung up.

"It took a bit of convincing," Kane told Wren a moment later, "but we got a telephonic warrant. Why don't you get a cup of coffee and give Danny some time to legally access the data."

Wren frowned then got up. "I'm going to get a cup of coffee."

"Now what do I do?" Danny asked once Wren was gone.

Kane handed him a folded piece of paper.

"I did some trolling in social media last night thanks to those programs you loaded on my laptop. Type that into a blank screen and print it out for Wren. How you got it is a trade secret."

Danny made a confused face then started typing. Five minutes later Kane handed Wren the printout containing Giselle Edwards' name and address.

"How did you connect her to Farber?" Wren asked.

"Good police work," Kane said and winked, hinting that he had done something illegal that he didn't want showing up in the file.

"All right," Wren said. "You're going to stake her out?"

"If you'll get me the manpower."

"Tell Immerson what you need. I'll see that you get it. Good job."

Wren stood and Greg and Danny followed suit. "What do we do now?" Danny asked once Wren was gone.

"I'll tell the boss that we need to have a team stake out Giselle Edwards' home."

"But she has nothing to do with Mearle Farber."

"We need Wren to think that she does."

Just before lunch Farber got a call on his burner phone.

"They're on to your girlfriend, Giselle," Munroe warned him. Franks was listening on an earphone as Farber responded, following the script they had printed out for him.

"Well, you'd better get me some cash and a clean ID," Farber threatened a minute later, "because if they catch me I'll give them the professor."

"Who?"

Franks thought Munroe sounded honestly confused.

"The professor. Your boss."

"How would you know that? I don't even know who he is."

"I used to be a cop, remember? Anyway, how I know is not important. You just tell him that he'd better get me what I need if he wants to stay off the fed's radar."

Munroe thought that over then said, "I'll make a call" and hung up.

* * *

Kane had just started briefing Giselle's surveillance team when Franks called. Greg excused himself and retreated out of earshot.

"Munroe went for it," Franks told him, clearly excited. "He claims he won't be able to get Farber a good ID until tomorrow night. We still have to work out the details of the meet."

"They're stalling," Kane said.

"Of course they're stalling. And, yes, they're planning to kill Farber as soon as he shows up. Your turn. Who's the professor?"

"Elliott Bellingham," Kane told him after a moment's hesitation. "He used to teach at Yale. Now he runs a company call Eco-Safe Technologies in Richmond."

"A Yale professor is Mr. Big? Are you kidding me? What's he a professor of, International Drug Dealing?"

"Microbiology, DNA, genes, things like that."

"And one day he woke up and decided to become a criminal mastermind? Are you insane?"

"He's got a plan to save the world."

"Better living through chemistry?" Franks taunted. "Do you have any actual evidence on this guy?"

"We will once you connect him to Munroe."

"So this is another one of your hunches."

"I call it logic, deduction and superior intelligence. Besides, it worked, didn't it?"

"That remains to be seen. . . . Fine, what's your plan?"

"Bellingham's going to be talking to Munroe. He may or may not meet with him. You'll have to stake out Bellingham's home and office, tap all his phones and intercept every cell transmission to and from both locations. Then you'll have to backtrack them to the phones on the other end."

"The judge is going to have a heart attack when he sees our warrant request."

"Bellingham's suspected of planning to import tons of prohibited chemicals to use in the manufacture of toxic substances. That's a WMD case. That means you're in the FISA court. A FISA judge will give you a warrant for anything you want."

"Fuck! You want me to blanket intercept a Yale professor's home and office phones under a FISA warrant based on your suspicions? Do you have any idea what'll happen if you're wrong and the professor finds out what we've done? The word 'shit-storm' doesn't begin to describe it. It'll be on the front page of every paper in the country. We'll be subpoenaed to testify in front of a congressional committee. You're gambling with our jobs here."

"And what do you think will happen if this guy sells a few million doses of a designer drug and people find out that we knew what he was up to and we didn't do anything because we were afraid it might hurt our careers? You want to talk about a shit-storm, think about that."

"God damn it, Kane, what kind of a jackpot have you gotten me into? I'm screwed if I do and I'm screwed if I don't! You know what I *should* do? I should give this case back to you then you can go get the FISA warrant. Your guys can sit on this professor. How about that?"

"That's not going to work. Remember I told you that I have a leak? I've got it narrowed down to either Sebastian Wren, the Special Assistant to the Principal Deputy Undersecretary for the Office of Intelligence & Analysis or his boss, Roger Dawson, the Principal Deputy Undersecretary for the Office of Intelligence & Analysis. I can't take a piss around here without Wren and Dawson finding out."

"Are you kidding me? The Special Assistant to the Deputy Undersecretary?"

"Or his boss."

"I couldn't even fantasize about getting a warrant on either of them without the approval of the Attorney General."

"That wouldn't work. Even if I had enough hard evidence to convince the AG Wren's boss would hear about it before you were out of the building."

"Shit! Shit! Shit!"

"Relax. This guy's dirty and we're going to be heroes. We just have to get him to lead us to Munroe and then grab them both."

"You haven't left me any way out. Was that your plan all along?"

"My plan is to give you the biggest bust of your career. You can thank me later."

"Yeah, sure I will. Crap!" Franks was quiet for five seconds then Kane heard him sigh. "All right. I'll get the warrant and I'll put a tracker on his vehicles too."

"No, don't do that. He's smart. He might check. If he finds a tracker he'll know we're on to him and then he'll know that the meeting with Farber is a set up. If that happens he'll never go near Munroe and we'll lose them both. You're going to have to tail Bellingham the old fashioned way. Besides, I doubt that he'll meet with Munroe face to face. If you can record him giving orders on one of his burner phones that should be enough, especially if you grab Munroe and are able to convince him to testify."

"Did you think that plan up all by yourself, Kane? Because it stinks. Bellingham might not call. If he calls we might not be able to detect it or decrypt it. He might not say anything incriminating, and the chances of the call actually getting us close enough to Munroe to grab him are crap, not to mention that Munroe will probably never cooperate even if we do capture him."

"Do you have a better idea?"

"No," Franks growled and hung up.

Kane pocketed the phone and returned to the conference room to finish setting up his phony stake-out. After that, all he could do was wait for Franks to get his warrant and then for Bellingham to take the bait.

CHAPTER FIFTY-TWO

Carl Feeney weaved through the parking lot and tried to hold the pizza box level. Distracted, he almost dropped it when the corner caught on a passenger-side mirror that seemed to dart into his path. It had been two days since he had left the dummy package of money for Ray Black. Had Donald just killed the addict and left town? Shouldn't he at least have called and confirmed that he'd taken care of the problem? Feeney had carefully watched the news but there had been no report of a man being found dead in the Idle Hour's alley, but then a junky dying from an overdose wasn't really news, was it?

Feeney juggled the pizza and dug into his pocket for the Expedition's remote.

"You owe me money," a voice said from behind him. Feeney spun around, bumping the box against the driver's side window and sending it flying. "You're lucky that was only your dinner," Black said, pointing toward the pizza upside down on the ground. "That could just as easily be you lying there."

"How did you—"

"Find you, Mr. Carl Feeney of 191 Shiloh Lane where you live with your wife, Cynthia, and your daughter, Robin? What you should be asking me is what's going to happen next?" Black just stared.

"What's going to happen next?" Feeney finally repeated.

"You're going to pay me the twenty-five thousand you owe me and another twenty-five as a penalty for sending your friend to kill me."

"What? I left the money—"

"Shut up! I'm not in the mood for any of your bullshit. Do you read me?"

Feeney looked from Black's scowling face to the gun tucked into his belt and nodded.

"Did you or did you not ask me to find you a hit man for a big job?"

Feeney stared at the gun then nodded.

"Answer me when I ask you a question!"

Feeney nervously looked around to confirm that no one was near.

"Yes."

"Did you promise to pay me fifty thousand dollars if I connected you to a hit man and he agreed to take the job?"

"Yes."

"Did I connect you with a hit man and did he agree to take the job?"

"Yes."

"How much did you pay me?"

"Twenty-five thousand."

"So, you owe me money, right?"

"Yes."

"Here's how it's going to be. You're going to put fifty-thousand, in cash, in this locker at the bus station." Black handed Feeney a key. "And then we're never going to see each other again. Agreed?"

"Yes," Feeney said, his eyes darting back and forth between the nearby cars and the gun in Black's belt.

"Was there something you wanted to ask me?"

Feeney licked his lips then said, "What about, you know?"

"Your friend who was supposed to kill me when I picked up the package?"

Feeney tried to hold Black's gaze then gave him a slight nod and looked away.

"I told you to answer me when I ask you a question."

"Yes," Feeney mumbled.

"I'll tell you what," Black said, smiling. "I'll answer your question if you'll answer one for me. Deal?"

"What do you want to know?"

"Was Hopper the hit you hired him for? Was your operator the idiot who set off that bomb in D.C.?"

Feeney studied his shoes for a count of five then mumbled, "I didn't tell him to do that. It's all your fault!" Feeney complained. "I asked you for a professional not a lunatic. If you had found me a sniper instead of some crazy man then Hopper would be dead and you'd have gotten your money."

Black gave his head a disappointed shake and laughed. "You asked me to find you a guy to murder a Supreme Court Justice and now you're complaining that he wasn't Mr. Normal? Psycho is the price of admission for that job." Black waited for some response from Feeney then shrugged. "OK, my turn. You can forget about your guy. He's out of the picture. Permanently. So if you have any ideas about asking him to take another shot at me you can forget them. Was there anything else you wanted to know?"

Feeney tried to think but his brain wouldn't work.

"You've got until five p.m. tomorrow to leave the money. After that I'll come to your house and we'll have another talk. Maybe I'll tell your wife and daughter what kind of a guy you really are. Do you want that?"

"You'll get your money," Feeney promised.

"You're damn right I will." Black glanced at the tomato sauce leaking into the asphalt. "You better buy yourself another pizza before the family starts wondering if something's happened to you."

Feeney paused for a moment then headed back the way he had come.

* * *

It had taken Feeney several hours and not a few lies to get his hands on fifty thousand dollars in cash. Sure, he could have walked into First Federal and handed the teller a withdrawal slip and told her to give it to him in hundreds but all that was going to do was guarantee him a meeting with the manager. *Why do you want all this cash, Mr. Feeney? Are you in trouble Mr. Feeney? Do you want me to call the police Mr. Feeney?* And the transaction would be remembered. So he pulled the money from different accounts in different banks over several visits.

Feeney glanced at the clock over the ticket counter — 1:27 p.m. He just wanted this whole nightmare over with. He took a quick look around but no one seemed to be paying any attention to him. The bank of lockers was along the back wall. The blue, plastic cover on the end of the key said "319." Feeney shoved a handful of quarters into the slot then opened the door. The locker was empty. He pulled the manila envelope from under his coat, slipped it inside then re-locked it. For a moment Feeney wondered what he was supposed to do with the key then realized that Black must have kept another copy. Feeney angled toward the trash can to the left of the front door but just before he reached it two men grabbed him from behind and two more, shouting "FBI! Don't Move! FBI!" leapt in front of him and pointed guns at his head.

Feeney froze and found himself unable to think. *What was happening? FBI? How? What did they want? Did they know?* His stomach seemed suddenly full of ice and his legs had lost their hold.

Rough hands pulled his arms behind his back and he felt cold steel crush his wrists.

"You're under arrest for murder!" one man shouted and Feeney felt like a puppet whose strings had been cut. Sound faded in and out. ". . . you say can be used against you in a court of law," he heard before he lost focus again. A sea of faces were staring at him in worry and surprise. Two of his captors began to drag him toward the door. He tried to twist around and ask them what this was all about and where they were taking him but all his strength had fled.

*　*　*

"I understand that the arrest went as planned," the man in the gray suit said once they had taken their seats.

"The subject was taken into custody at one-twenty-nine this afternoon. They found fifty thousand dollars in cash in the locker and the key still in his hand. We have it all on tape."

"Has he made a statement?"

"Not yet, Mr. Harrington, other than to claim that this is all some terrible mistake."

"Perhaps when he learns that Sergeant Demeter is cooperating," Harrington glanced at his client sitting next to him, "Mr. Feeney will realize that his position is hopeless and agree to make a deal."

Assistant U.S. Attorney Karen Swerner frowned at Harrington's use of Demeter's former rank as a subtle way of trying to sanitize his client. "We'll see," she said and shot a quick look at the man formerly known as Ray Black.

"In any event," Harrington continued, "I believe that we've fulfilled all of the terms of the immunity agreement." The lawyer began to tick off the deal points on his fingers. "Sergeant Demeter got Mr. Feeney to admit on tape that he hired Glenn Phillips to murder Mr. Justice Hopper—"

"He never admitted to hiring Glenn Phillips."

"He admitted to hiring a man he called 'Donald.' Sergeant Demeter identified the body of the man he had introduced to Feeney and your office determined that the real identity of that corpse was Glenn Phillips. If I may continue?" Harrington took Swerner's silence as consent. "Sergeant Demeter's information was confirmed both by Mr. Feeney's statements and his payment of the money. Sergeant Demeter will testify against Mr. Feeney as agreed. Since the man who referred Mr. Feeney to my client is still at large we'd like Sergeant Demeter admitted to the Witness Protection Program right away."

"Actually, we know the location of the other member of the conspiracy," Swerner said and picked a piece of paper from her desk. "Cletus Garrity contracted the H1N1 virus and was admitted to the Val Verde County Hospital in Del Rio, Texas a little over three weeks ago. He suffered a pulmonary failure that antibiotics were unable to control and died four days later. So it seems that your client no longer needs witness protection."

"Maybe he does and maybe he doesn't," Harrington said, "but he's getting it anyway. A deal is a deal."

Swerner frowned then snapped, "Fine."

"Then I think we're done."

"What about the reward?" Demeter asked. Swerner and Harrington stared at him. "The million dollar reward for turning in the guys who tried to kill the judge."

Swerner glared at Harrington who paused for half a second then turned to his client. "Arnold, you're not getting the money."

"But—"

"Arnold, you participated in a plot to murder a Supreme Court Justice. As part of that plot a Secret Service agent was killed and a woman was kidnapped. No court is ever going to say that you deserve a reward for what you've done. You should be jumping up and down and thanking God that you're walking away Scott free and getting a new identity instead of spending the rest of your life in a federal penitentiary. . . . Was there anything else?"

Demeter glanced down at his hands that no longer had the shakes then back up at Harrington and Karen Swerner.

"Thank you," he said and readied himself to begin his new, and what he hoped would be better, life.

* * *

Carl Feeney glanced around his cell. "So, this is what America has come to," he thought as he waited nervously for his lawyer to arrive. "This is the reward I get for being a patriot."

CHAPTER FIFTY-THREE

Kane felt like a commander who had been racing to ready his troops for battle and then, suddenly, found himself with nothing to do but wait. Franks' team was setting up the surveillance on Bellingham and preparing for Farber's promised meeting with Munroe. Kane had gotten his boss to detail a team to handle the phony surveillance on Farber's fictitious girlfriend though Kane, Farber and Munroe all knew that nothing would come of it. The only person who thought that there was some purpose to the operation was Immerson himself. A few minutes ago Kane had finished his last project, reading everything he could find on Sebastian Wren and his boss, Roger Dawson.

After graduating from Princeton Wren had applied to the FBI and started his career as a lowly field agent. Within two years he'd managed a transfer to the Office of Professional Responsibility, the FBI's equivalent of a police department's Office of Internal Affairs. After three years in OPR Wren received a posting to FBI headquarters in D.C. The Department of Homeland Security was created in late 2002 and in late 2003 Wren made the transition to HS where he steadily moved up the executive ladder. If and when his boss, the Deputy Undersecretary, moved on Wren was on the short list to take his job.

Wren's boss, Roger Dawson, grew up in Rhode Island. His father was an executive in a commercial casualty insurance company that had been founded a hundred years before by one of his ancestors. Dawson, like George Bush (43) attended Phillips Academy in Andover, Massachusetts then Yale, though Dawson was more than ten years too late to have crossed paths with the former president. Dawson did a brief stint as a junior executive in the insurance industry then followed the path blazed by generations of well-born but not well-heeled New England gentlemen and secured an appointment with the CIA. Melding a combination of family connections, decent intelligence, social skills and political correctness Dawson made the jump to HS's executive ranks upon its creation halfway through Bush's first term. The most recent rumor was that Dawson was planning a run for Rhode Island's 1st Congressional seat once the current occupant announced his plans to run for a soon-to-be-vacant U.S. Senate position.

Kane stared at the clock. It was four minutes after two. He could check on the teams watching Giselle's home but what was the point in that bit of theater? Calling Franks would be counterproductive to say the least. That relationship was frayed almost to the breaking point as it was. Danny was doing something on the computer, his fingers tapping madly away. Was there any point in asking him what it was? Kane couldn't think of one. He looked again at the clock. It was still four minutes after two. *Fuck it!* Kane picked up the phone.

"Allison, it's Greg. Can you meet me in the lobby of the National Gallery in twenty minutes? . . . I'll explain when I see you. . . . Good. Thanks." Danny glanced over just as Kane stood up. "I've got a meeting out of the office," Greg told him. "If something comes up call me on my cell."

"OK," Danny said and turned back to his keyboard.

Kane figured it would be faster to take the Metro and half-jogged from the Archives station down 7th to Constitution. Allison was there ahead of him in a black and white outfit that was supposed to make her look like a prim and proper executive assistant and, as far as he was concerned, failed completely. He thought about hugging her but knew that such a public display of affection would upset her. He stopped a polite foot and a half away and smiled.

"Thanks for meeting me," he said.

"Is someone else after Justice Hopper?"

"Let's walk and talk." Kane looked around the foyer then led her into the West Gallery. "I was kind of out of it the last time I saw you. How have you been?"

"I'm fine. What's this about?"

"Remember when I talked about our taking some time off and looking at the paintings? This is it. It's about us spending a little time together. Catching up."

"You called me away from work so that we could catch up?"

"You agreed to it, remember?"

"What is this, a date?"

This was not going well. Kane had not expected it to but he had hoped he might be wrong.

"Some things are going on at the office, an investigation, and I don't know where it's all going to end up."

"Is it something my uncle can help you with?"

"Let's go in here," Kane said leading her into one of the galleries along the south side of the corridor. "Remember when I told you that I liked the Impressionists?" Kane pointed to a painting of small boats pulled up on a beach.

Allison glanced at the canvas and then looked back at Kane. "Where is this coming from?"

Greg took a breath. "The last time I saw you I had almost been blown up. It wasn't a situation that was conducive to conversation. The time before that we were just about to make love and I had to run out because a Secret Service agent had been murdered. This afternoon I had some free time and I thought it would be nice for us to get together and look at some beautiful art and talk like two normal people. That's not so terrible is it?"

"I have a job," Allison said, glancing at her watch.

"The Senate is in recess. Your uncle won't even be back in town until tomorrow." Allison forced herself to look at the Monet then uneasily turned back to Kane. "Look, I was almost killed doing a favor for your uncle. Are you telling me that it's too much trouble for you to spend an hour with me wandering around one of the finest art galleries in the world?"

Allison paused for half a second then let her shoulders slump. "Fine."

For the next five minutes they exchanged polite conversation about the artists, each picking out paintings they especially liked.

"You can have a copy made you know," Allison said when Kane expressed his appreciation of "The Bridge at Argenteuil."

"It wouldn't be the same. I'd pay someone to make me something that Monet might have painted but didn't," Kane said.

"Any artist good enough to do that you couldn't afford."

"This is nice," Kane said a moment later, looking at her and getting a confused glance in return. "Just doing something for the pleasure of it. I've been trying to dial it back, let things go. It's supposed to make you happier."

"Are you trying to tell me something?"

"Someone gave me a book a while ago, about Buddhism. I thought it was all BS but, now I don't know. I'm not so sure."

"Buddhism?"

"The idea," Kane said with sudden enthusiasm, "is that yesterday is gone and that tomorrow doesn't exist. That we have to stop being tortured by the past and expecting to be happy in the future and instead we need to find the joy in each second today." Allison stared at Greg as if she suspected that he was cursing her in

Chinese. "So, this," Kane gestured at the paintings, "is about enjoying the moment."

"Forget the past and live for today. Is that it?"

"It's—"

"Tradition? Honor? We should just throw them away?"

"I'm just saying—"

"We have a debt to our families, to our loved ones, not to forget them. We owe them that."

"Remembering someone and trying to live with them in the past are two different things," Kane said fighting to keep the disapproval out of his voice.

"So, because I won't pretend that Brian never existed I'm a fool who's living in the past?"

"I'm just saying that it's a bad idea to have your emotions all tangled up in the past and in the future because then you can't be happy in the only place where you're actually alive, which is now."

"By 'now' you mean my being here with you. Do you actually think you can tell me how to live my life?"

"I'm not telling you how to live your life. I'm just saying that obsessing over something that's already happened and that you can't change is a bad idea."

"Who are you to lecture me? If I want pop psychology I'll call Dr. Phil," Allison said, turning away.

"Wait!" Kane reached for her arm but she shook him off.

"Don't touch me." She glared at Kane for a moment then held up her hands. "That's it. We're done."

"Allison, please. I care—"

"Don't!" she half shouted. "Don't you dare tell me that you care about me." Kane took a half-step back and held up his hands in surrender.

"I was only trying to tell you about something that seemed to be helping me. I know you're afraid of getting hurt again and I just want you to be happy."

"My happiness is not your concern." Allison started to leave then turned back. "I know what you mean by 'living in the now.' You mean replacing Brian with you but that's not going to happen. I'm never going to turn my back on my husband. Not for you. Not for anyone."

"You can't hang on to someone who no longer exists. No matter how much you wish it wasn't so he's gone and you can't get him back."

"He's not gone unless and until I say so and that's never going to happen."

Allison's heels made an angry clicking sound as she stormed away.

CHAPTER FIFTY-FOUR

"None of this fits," the man called "Mr. X" said when Munroe reported Farber's demand. "Less than a week after they find Farber's address he claims to know who I am and insists on a meeting? What if he didn't get away at all? What if they caught him and covered it up and this is all a scheme to lead us into a trap?"

"He used the safe word," Munroe answered.

"He could be cooperating with them. We're in the dark here. We need information."

Munroe wanted to ask about Farber's cryptic reference to "The Professor" but he knew that it would be a bad idea. If it had been nonsense Mr. X would have laughed it off and told Munroe to sever all contact with the former deputy. If the reference meant something, as Munroe suspected it did, Mr. X wasn't going to let him in on the secret. That led to a further question: *How would Farber know more about Mr. X than I do?*

Farber's claim that he got the information by using his law enforcement skills didn't wash. Farber had been a deputy sheriff who spent most of his time transporting prisoners and serving eviction orders. He sure as hell wasn't some Sherlock Holmes. So, where had he gotten this "Professor" crap?

Mr. X was worried. That was pretty clear. Mr. X distrusted phones and they usually communicated through an intermediary but now they had been forced into in almost daily telephone contact. It was pretty clear that Mr. X or The Professor or whomever was worried and that worried Munroe as well. Mr. X had promised to cut him in on a multi-million dollar drug empire and now all of that seemed as if it might be at risk.

"What do you want me to do?" Munroe asked.

"Stall him. Tell Farber that you won't be able to meet him until late tomorrow night. Say that you'll call him an hour in advance with the location. That should give us enough time to get some answers."

Munroe didn't ask where those answers were going to come from. He knew his employer had a source who was feeding him info. How else would he have learned about the raid on Farber's house?

"I want you to grab that agent, Kane," Mr. X said.

"What?"

"If this meeting with Farber is a setup Kane will know all the details. Tie him up and take him somewhere safe and question him."

"How am I supposed to do that?"

"Surprise him inside his home. Incapacitate him before he knows what hit him. I'll get you his address."

"It's not that simple," Munroe complained.

"I'll give you a hundred thousand dollars. Be creative. Do it tonight."

* * *

Kane lived on the fourth floor of a six story apartment building halfway between Trinidad and Brentwood Park. The lobby door was locked but Munroe figured that he could get past it pretty easily. The main questions were, first, if he could get into Kane's apartment; second, how he was going to quietly disable a trained agent and, third, how he was going to get Kane out of the building without being seen. He started with the last question first. How did people remove a body in the movies? In a rolled-up rug. It was as good a way as any.

Munroe checked Google for D.C. carpet cleaners and then sign makers. Using an ID that wasn't linked to his real address he rented a white panel van and then visited a sign shop on the way back from the rental lot. It took them about fifteen minutes to create an eighteen by thirty plastic stick-on that read "Montpelier Carpet Care — Cleaning & Restoration." A final stop at Walmart got him a hand-truck and a six by eight foot Arabian-style carpet. A few minutes with Photoshop produced two invoice forms with the heading "Montpelier Carpet Care" and the company's real address and phone number. The first document was a work order for the delivery of a newly cleaned carpet to Gregory Kane in apartment 4C. The second was instructions to pick up a stained carpet from Gregory Kane at the same address.

It was almost three-thirty when Munroe arrived at Kane's building. He set the rolled-up carpet vertically on the hand truck and pressed the buzzers for all of the apartments on the third floor. If anyone asked who he was or what he wanted he had a clipboard with a work order bearing the notation "Deliver with customer-supplied house key." No one asked any questions. One of the third-floor occupants just buzzed him in. Dressed in a khaki shirt, brown pants and a brown baseball cap Munroe wheeled the rug into the elevator and pressed the button for the fourth floor.

Now came the tricky part. Given a minute or two a skilled burglar could pick a garden-variety residential lock but most thieves just jimmied the door or used a bump key. A set of twenty bump key blanks that would fit a wide variety of residential locks could be purchased over the Internet for fifty dollars. High-end bump-proof locks were available but most apartment houses didn't want to spend the money to retrofit an entire building. Kane could have done that himself, of course, but most single guys, especially cops who figured that they could take care of themselves, weren't that worried about their personal security.

The lock on Kane's door was an old Yale. Munroe pulled the Yale bump key off the ring, slipped it in, then simultaneously gave it a firm tap and a twist. Nothing. The timing between the rap, or bump, and the twist had to be just right. Munroe did it again. On the third try the pins bounced above the cylinder just as Munroe applied the torque and the lock turned. Munroe took a look down the deserted hallway then wheeled the rug inside. A quick check confirmed that the apartment was empty. He stuffed the rolled-up carpet in the back of the closet then entered the bathroom. The floor was some kind of vinyl but Kane had placed a towel in front of the toilet, apparently to insulate his feet from the cold floor while he peed.

Munroe ran a fine wire from the back of the toilet down into the water at the bottom of the bowl and secured it with a dab of super glue. He equally spaced six more fine, bare wires under the towel then joined them near the edge of the porcelain and ran that single wire to the rear of the tank. He attached the wire from the bowl to one terminal of a stun gun and the wires from under the towel to the other. He taped the stun gun to the backside of the tank then locked down the switch. Lastly he dropped a handful of salt into the water. Now he just needed to test it.

The stun gun was rated at eight million volts. Munroe dropped an insulated wire into the bowl and set another one on top of the towel. Then he moved the two free ends toward each other. When they were about an inch apart a surge arced through the towel and electricity sparked across the one-inch gap. Munroe was not surprised. The manufacturer had promised that the jolt would penetrate several layers of clothing with enough voltage to incapacitate a man. Munroe quickly pulled the ends apart then filled the sink with water to which he added another handful of salt. Once the towel was dampened with the salt water he laid it back across the bare wires.

The final step was making sure that he would know if and when his trap had been sprung. Munroe scanned the bathroom and spotted a Kleenex box on the shelf next to the medicine cabinet. He cut a flap in the back and inserted a wireless camera. The pinhole lens fit neatly behind the hollowed out center of one of the "e"s. The battery wouldn't last more than twelve hours and the broadcast range was only five-hundred feet but that was enough. Munroe took one more look around then grabbed his clipboard and hand-truck and returned to the van.

He drove around the block then pulled into a new space across from the entrance to the building's underground garage. Along with his address Mr. X had provided him with Kane's DMV picture and the make and model of his car. Munroe settled in to wait. Around a quarter after six he spotted Kane's black Mustang and he scrunched down in his seat. As soon as the car disappeared into the garage Munroe got out the hand-truck and headed for the building. This time he punched the buttons for the fifth-floor units and, again, a helpful tenant buzzed him in.

He dithered a minute in the lobby pretending to be checking his iPad then rode the elevator to the fourth floor. Once there he slipped into the stairway and called up the view from the spy camera. The bathroom was dark. Now he just had to wait and hope that the building wasn't full of health nuts who enjoyed climbing the stairs. He had a scare around a quarter to seven when he heard footsteps descending. Luckily there was no one in the fourth-floor corridor and Munroe returned to the landing as soon as the tenant had passed by.

Inside the home Kane pushed the half-empty pizza box aside and chugged down the last of his beer. *So*, he thought, looking around his empty apartment, *now what?* It had been a disaster of a day. Franks had sent him a text telling him that they hadn't gone live on Bellingham's phone surveillance until four that afternoon. Some problem with the warrant application.

For about one second he thought about trying to fix things with Allison then snorted. *Yeah, that'll work.* Kane eyed the empty bottle and decided that one more beer wouldn't hurt him. He found a basketball game on ESPN, put his feet up on the coffee table and half watched the screen. Around ten after seven he felt the beer demanding to be set free. As he settled in front of the toilet and started to unzip, Kane noticed that the towel was damp. *Jesus, was the plumbing leaking? After the day he'd had that's all he needed. How much is it going to cost to get a plumber up here at night? Would the landlord pay for that? Ten to one the manager would try to blame it on him. Fuck. Well, maybe it wasn't that bad. Maybe it was just a washer.* The beer became more insistent. *Well, pee first, check the pipes second.*

Kane aimed slightly toward the side of the bowl, closed his eyes and let go. A fraction of a second later he felt as if he had been dipped waist deep into molten lava. Because of the minerals and other waste products it contained human urine was highly conductive. The stun gun's eight million volts were only slightly diminished during their trip through the salt water in the bowl and then up the stream of urine and into Kane's penis. The charge roared through his groin and then down his legs and out through his heels. One second Greg was standing in front of the toilet and the next he was lying half conscious on the floor, fighting to draw a breath.

As soon as the monitor showed Kane entering the bathroom Munroe hurried down the hall and slipped the bump key into the lock. He paused for a couple of seconds until Kane toppled off the edge of the iPad's screen then he rapped the key and managed to turn the tumbler on the first try. Munroe abandoned the hand-truck just inside the door and raced into the bathroom where he found Kane shuddering on the floor in a puddle of his own urine.

Munroe pulled out another stun gun and gave Kane a three-second jolt in the side of his neck then dragged him out of the bathroom. A few seconds later he had Kane's ankles, wrists and mouth wrapped in duct tape. Munroe searched Kane's pockets and removed his cell, wallet and creds. A few seconds more and Kane's knees were taped together and his arms were secured tightly to his chest. *Jesus, this guy stinks!* Munroe thought. He removed the carpet from the closet, rolled Kane up inside it, then wrapped bands of tape around the rug's top, bottom and center.

It took all of Munroe's strength to stand the rug up against the wall and then get the hand-truck's blade under the bottom. Another two lengths of tape secured it to the hand-truck's steel frame. Had he forgotten anything? The camera! Munroe pulled the stun gun from behind the toilet tank and then grabbed the Kleenex box. He stuffed them into a paper bag from the kitchen along with the roll of tape. Carrying it wouldn't look right but he couldn't leave them behind. He briefly considered dropping the bag down the garbage chute but that was the first place the cops would search once Kane went missing.

Munroe did a final check of the apartment, carefully wiping down anything that he might have touched. Getting Kane and the rug out the door was a pain and a half but he did it, wiping his prints from the knob as he left. Everything went smoothly until he reached the lobby and realized that he couldn't simultaneously open the front door and push the hand truck through it. He was looking around for something to wedge under the jam when one of the tenants showed up.

"That looks like a two-man job," the man half joked.

"It's heavier than it looks."

"Here, let me hold it for you," the guy volunteered.

Munroe spun the hand-truck around, pulled it through the opening and then across the street to the van. After half a minute's more pushing and straining he manhandled Kane into the back and then he was gone.

CHAPTER FIFTY-FIVE

Kane couldn't tell if he was awake or stuck in a nightmare that wouldn't end. He remembered a horrifying pain then spasms then a searing jolt and then nothing. He couldn't see. He couldn't move. He almost couldn't breathe. His body was a mass of throbbing pain. He seemed to be lying down. Had a bomb gone off? Was he trapped in the rubble of what used to be his apartment building? For a moment he panicked and thrashed violently but accomplished nothing. He could barely even draw a breath. Was he awake or asleep? He could feel pressure on his arms and the weight of his body against something hard. A faint chemical smell tickled his nose. Even in his dreams in Tommy's Bar he'd never experienced such strong physical sensations.

His brain slowly began to clear and Kane decided that he wasn't dreaming. The floor beneath him vibrated and rolled him slightly left then right. He was in a vehicle he concluded. Someone had grabbed him. It wasn't hard to guess who. The van took a hard left and Kane rolled against the right-side wall. He had no idea of how long they'd been traveling or at what speed but he started counting "one-thousand one, one-thousand two. . . ." just the same. At least it gave him something to do.

Months earlier Munroe had rented a self-service storage locker in Arlington as a bolt-hole in case something went seriously wrong. He had picked the place because it was completely automated. He arrived at a little after eight and swiped his RFID card across the scanner. The gate rolled out of the way and Munroe headed for his unit which was at the end of the third row of stucco buildings. At twenty by thirty feet it was the largest size they offered. People who had lost their homes had been known to camp out in their lockers jammed in between their living room set and their old bicycles, though officially the management prohibited the practice.

In reality, if you were quiet and kept any smells and smoke to a minimum you could pretty much do anything you wanted except manufacture meth or grow weed. Those activities were disallowed not because they were against the rules but because there was no gas service for the former and insufficient electrical power for the latter. Munroe's unit was at the end of the row and the next two spaces up the line held only furniture and office equipment. Kane could make as much noise as he liked and no one was going to hear him.

Munroe rolled up the door and pulled the van inside. Along one wall he'd set up a couple of pole lamps, a table, two aluminum chairs, a cot, a small fridge, and an induction hot-plate. *All the comforts of home*, he thought as he opened the van's doors and dragged out the rug. He heard a faint grunt when it hit the concrete floor.

It took half a minute to unroll his captive and then manhandle Kane into one of the chairs. Munroe wished he had bought a model that had arms so that he would have had supports that he could fasten Kane's wrists to. Well, they would just have to stay taped against his chest. He juggled his prisoner like an unruly sack of meat and then ran another length of tape around each of Kane's ankles and the chair's front two legs. One final strip around the agent's chest and the chair's aluminum back and he was done.

Throughout the process Kane watched Munroe with hate-filled eyes. When he was done Munroe ripped the tape from Greg's mouth.

"You can scream all you want," he said, smiling. "No one's going to hear you. . . . Go ahead, give it a try."

Kane looked around the bare room then shouted, "Hello! Can anybody hear me?" Hello!" Munroe opened his hands as if to say, "I told you so."

"Now that that's out of your system we can get started. Here's how it's going to be. I'm going to ask you questions. Eventually, you're going to answer them. Every time you refuse to answer you're going to be punished." Munroe held up his stun gun and triggered a blaze of sparks. "If you lie to me, you're going to be punished." More sparks. "You're too smart to believe me if I told you that I was going let you go so I'm not going to bother lying to you. I will promise that if you tell me what I want to know then when we're done I'll give you something to eat and drink and I'll let you take a piss before I put you out of your misery. Nothing is going to save your life but this can go easy or it can go hard, depending on how cooperative you are." Munroe paused for a second but Kane just stared at him. "OK, let's get started. Do you have Mearle Farber?"

One school of thought was that prisoners should say nothing, not the name of their dog, not the time of day, not the color of their hair. Nothing. The theory was that the first answer you gave was like boring a hole in a dam and that with every subsequent response the structure would be further weakened until it eventually collapsed. The problem with that strategy was that it vastly accelerated the interrogation and the amount of pain the prisoner would suffer. If Kane's hunch about Bellingham was correct and if Munroe was reporting to him then the FBI might pick up a phone call passing between them. It was a thin chance but it was something, provided that he could survive long enough to be rescued. Kane needed to play for time which meant that he had to draw out the interrogation with a mixture of truths, half-truths and outright lies.

"Don't you read the papers? We've been beating the bushes for Farber for almost a week."

Munroe cocked his head as if deep in thought. "Somehow, I don't believe you," he said and jammed the stun gun against Kane's stomach and pressed the button. "Try again," Munroe ordered when Kane had stopped screaming. "Do you have Mearle Farber in custody?"

"Absolutely not," Kane said truthfully. Technically, it was the FBI who had Farber. Munroe raised his eyebrows but didn't trigger the gun again.

"Do you know where Farber is now?"

"No."

"Do you have a plan to capture Farber?"

"Hope springs eternal," Kane said with a weak smile.

"I consider that nonresponsive." Munroe jammed the gun into Kane's stomach for a two-second burst. Greg screamed and tried to bend forward but was restrained by the tape. *Stall, stall, stall,* he told himself, grimacing and gasping for breath.

"Give it a rest. I didn't hurt you that much," Munroe told him. "Let's try this again. Do you have a plan to capture Farber?"

Greg eyed the gun but knew that he needed to make Munroe work for every answer. If he gave up information too easily Munroe wouldn't believe the lies he told later on down the road.

"Our plan is to keep looking until we find him." Munroe didn't even bother speaking. He just hit Kane with another jolt.

"What's your plan for finding Farber?" Kane hesitated and Munroe raised the gun.

"All right! Wait! . . . Farber's got a girlfriend. We're staking out her place in case he shows up."

"What's her name?"

Kane hesitated then eyed the gun and spit out, "Giselle."

"How did you find out about her?"

"I don't know. My partner—"

Munroe jammed the contacts against Kane's shoulder and pressed the switch.

"Stop lying."

"My partner," Kane repeated, breathing heavily, "is the paperwork guy. He pulled Farber's credit card statement and found something that led him to the woman."

"What, specifically?"

"I don't know." Munroe gave Kane another jolt. "I don't *know*! A charge at a restaurant, a piece of jewelry, whatever. It's not important. He's a kid! I tell him to find me something and he comes back with an answer. How he does it isn't my concern."

Munroe gave Kane a long look then slipped the stun gun back into his pocket.

"Who am I working for?" Munroe asked.

"Don't you know?" Out came the gun. "Jesus! If I knew that I'd have already arrested him."

"You'd need evidence first. Who do you suspect who my boss might be?"

"Someone who wants to manufacture a new kind of drug," Kane answered.

Munroe raised the gun. "You can do better than that." Kane lowered his head and Munroe gave him a five second burst. Kane screamed then slumped against the tape. After half a minute Munroe threw a cup of water in Kane's face and slapped him awake. "Who do you think might be my boss?" Kane shook his head and slumped in his chair. "All right, we'll do this the hard way." This time the gun snapped and hissed for a full ten seconds and Kane lost consciousness. Two minutes later Munroe asked again, "Who do you think might be my boss?"

Kane looked around blearily then seemed to pass out. Another jolt provoked almost no response. Munroe slapped Kane's face but got only a few mumbled words in return.

"Who's my boss!" Munroe shouted followed by another slap.

"Bugs," Kane muttered. "Sterilize the bugs."

Another slap had no effect and further use of the stun gun elicited only groans until the battery ran down. Munroe checked Kane's bonds then slipped outside and made a call.

"He claims they don't know where Farber is," he said as soon as the line was answered.

"Do you believe him?"

"I don't know."

"What do you know?"

"He's a tough guy. All I managed to get out of him was something about bugs."

"What about bugs?"

"He was out of it, babbling. 'Bugs, sterilize the bugs.' That's all he said before he passed out completely."

"Could he be faking?"

"Anything's possible but I ran the stun gun's battery dry. It's going to take half an hour to get enough of a charge in it to go back to work on him."

Bellingham tried to organize his thoughts. He'd half-convinced himself that as long as the authorities didn't have Farber he was safe but Kane's cryptic comment about sterilizing bugs sounded like a reference to him. Did Kane know something or was he just suspicious or was his comment merely the ramblings of an addled mind? And if Kane did know something, or thought he knew something, had he told anyone? He was a policeman and until he had some real evidence Kane might have kept his suspicions to himself. Bellingham struggled to control his fear. He needed answers and he needed to protect his identity. He had worked very hard to keep Munroe from learning who he was. His only option now was to get Munroe out of the room and finish Kane's interrogation himself. He had been so close. All he needed was a few more months. He had gambled that Kane had nothing but now it seemed as if he might be wrong.

"Hello? Are you there?" Munroe called.

"You're at your safe house?"

"Yes."

"I need to question him myself. With some luck I should be there in about ninety minutes. Don't do anything until I arrive." The line went dead.

CHAPTER FIFTY-SIX

Ron Franks smiled as Raylan Givens blew away yet another inbred, hillbilly drug dealer. *Damn, I wish we could do that*, he thought as Marshal Givens swiveled and blasted scumbag number 2. At the crack of the pistol Franks' wife snuggled a little closer against him. Then his cell phone rang. Without being asked she disengaged herself and hit "pause" on the remote.

"It's work," Franks said.

"I recognize the ring. I'm going to go pee."

"What's up?"

"We've got activity at the house. Calls between a burner phone and an unregistered cell in Alexandria."

"Do we have an address?"

"The caller hacked the GPS chip. All we've got is the cell tower location. The content is interesting though. It looks like the guy in Alexandria has got somebody under forceful interrogation. He's apparently using a stun gun. They're trying to find out if Farber is in custody. Whoever they're working on told them 'no' but they don't necessarily believe him. The subject also said something about sterilizing bugs. That seemed to upset the guy in the house."

"That's what his company does," Franks said, his brain racing. "It makes some kind of chemical that sterilizes bugs."

"Well, it got our guy's attention. He's going to the Alexandria location to question the prisoner himself."

"Follow him and don't lose him," Franks ordered.

"It's a long way from here to Alexandria. I wish we'd put a tracker on his car."

"If we had put a tracker on his car he probably would have found it and then he wouldn't be going anywhere. Call the team set up on his office and have them meet you on the I-95."

Franks hung up and called Kane's cell. It rang four times and went to voice mail.

"Shit!"

"What's wrong?" his wife called from the kitchen.

Franks pulled out his notepad and dialed the number Kane had given him for Danny Rosewood.

"Hello?"

"Agent Rosewood? This is FBI Special Agent Ron Franks. When's the last time you talked to your partner?"

"Agent Kane? Uhhh, sometime after lunch today. He said he had to meet someone. Why?"

"I just called him on his cell and it went to voice mail. Do you have another number for him?"

"No. That's the only one he has as far as I know. Is there something wrong?"

Kane said he could trust Rosewood but as far as Franks was concerned Kane's partner was only a voice on the phone. He wasn't even FBI. But somebody was being tortured for information about Farber and Kane wasn't answering his phone. Two plus two still made four.

"Can you run a GPS trace on Agent Kane's phone, find out where it is?"

"I can do that from my office. Why? Is he in trouble?"

"He could be," Franks said after a slight hesitation.

"What kind of trouble?" Rosewood asked, the concern clear in his voice.

"Bad trouble. How fast can you run the trace?"

"Give me fifteen minutes."

"Call me back as soon as you've got an address and I'll send agents to his location."

Danny hung up without saying goodbye and ran over to the bookcase where he had left his wallet, keys and gun.

"What's going on?" Diane asked, half a turkey sandwich in one hand and a Snapple in the other.

"Gotta go," Danny called out, pulling on his coat. "Agent Kane's in trouble."

Diane was wearing her pink slippers and pink flannel pajamas with the ducks on them and Danny thought she was the cutest thing he'd ever seen. Halfway across the room he stopped, ran over, kissed her, and then raced for the door.

"Be careful!" Diane shouted after him.

* * *

The trace on Kane's cell came back to his apartment. Danny figured that if he drove full out that he could get there faster than any agents Franks might send. When he arrived he buzzed the building's manager.

"Open it," Danny ordered after his pounding on Kane's door drew no response.

"Do you have a warrant?"

"There's no time for a warrant. Open it."

"The master key's in my apartment. Maybe I should call a lawyer—"

Danny turned and kicked the door as hard as he could, just like they did in the movies. It exploded inward but he hadn't expected it to hurt so much and when he went inside he limped. It took only a few seconds to confirm that the place was empty. He found Kane's cell phone, wallet and gun on the floor of the closet next to the bathroom. He debated for a moment then stuck the gun in his belt figuring it couldn't hurt to have a second weapon. Danny pulled up Franks' number from his call list.

"Where's Kane's phone?" Franks asked him.

"I'm at his apartment. His phone, wallet and gun are here but he isn't."

"Does he know anyone in Alexandria?"

"I don't know. Why?"

"We got a lead to a cell tower there. I think it may have something to do with your partner. Does that ring any bells at all?"

"No," Danny said after a moment's thought. He quickly scanned the address list in Kane's phone but nothing matched. "What's happened?"

Franks hesitated. At that moment he was a few minutes away from linking up with his men. Rosewood was closer to Alexandria than he was.

"All right, get out your pen. I'll give you our best guess about where Kane might be."

"What's happened to him?" Danny demanded.

"Here's what we know," Franks said and began to explain.

* * *

Franks' men used a rolling tail to stay on Bellingham all the way onto U.S. 1 then followed him west toward the Alexandria National Cemetery where they had to fall back or risk being spotted. Somewhere between Highway 1 and the cemetery Bellingham got far enough ahead of the lead car to duck out of sight and then switch off his lights. By the time they turned the corner the street ahead was empty. Two of the trailing cars went north on parallel streets while Franks headed south in case Bellingham had doubled back.

The professor didn't think he was being followed but by this time security had become second nature to him. Driving with his lights off and taking refuge several times in shadowed driveways he was able to work his way into the blocks of apartments behind the cemetery west of Four Mile Run. He pulled into the guest parking lot of a twelve story apartment house and waited until the road was clear. Finally he headed out, again without lights, moving north for half a mile then parked briefly before turning his headlights back on. Ironically, it was Bellingham's attempt to avoid surveillance that revealed his location.

Danny had been cruising the western edge of the cell tower zone and noticed a pair of headlights blink off. Nothing about that was unusual but it was something and so far all Danny had was a lot of nothing. He made a left and headed toward where the lights had disappeared. He had almost reached the southern end of the search zone when he noticed a pair of taillights suddenly appear in his mirror. He made a quick U-turn but they too soon vanished. Danny slowed at the next intersection but the cross street was empty. Certain now that he would never find Kane Danny continued straight on then stopped for a red light. As he was sitting there a black Audi A6 crossed in front of him on the green. He only caught the last three numbers on the plate but they matched Bellingham's car. Danny flicked off his lights and turned left, driving with one hand and dialing with the other.

"I've got him," Danny said when Franks answered.

"Has he spotted you?"

"I don't think so. I'm not using my lights." Danny gave Franks his location.

Shit! Franks thought. *I hope he doesn't kill someone.* "Keep feeding me your position. We'll be there in a couple of minutes."

The Audi made another turn then pulled into the driveway of a public storage facility. It paused briefly then the gate opened and it drove through. Danny parked on the street and ran up to the entrance. The gate was steel, eight feet high with a keypad mounted inside a steel casing ten feet back toward the curb. On the other side of the fence the Audi turned right at the end of the main aisle and disappeared.

"He's driven into a storage yard," Danny told Franks and gave him the address. "You need a key code to get in."

"Don't move. We'll track down the owner. I'll be there in about three minutes."

Three minutes? Danny looked at the deserted rows of lockers. *Screw that*, he thought and parked his Mazda as close to the fence as he could. It wasn't easy with his sore foot but he managed to climb onto the hood and then to the roof. From there the top of the fence was about chest high. *Thank God they don't have barbed wire*, he thought and tried to swing himself over. Most of him made it but on the way down his coat caught on the steel and he tumbled the eight feet to the ground landing on his ass. When he looked up half his coat was flapping in the breeze like a flag.

Danny struggled to his feet. His hands were scraped and his butt hurt but nothing seemed broken. *Where was his phone?* Danny stared at the remains of his coat. *Crap!* It hurt like hell but on the third try he managed to jump high enough to grab the dangling sleeve. The coat tore free and fluttered to the ground but his cell was no longer in the pocket. He spent half a minute wandering around in the dark looking for it then gave up.

Danny glanced back through the fence at the deserted street then turned and scanned the rows of silent buildings. *Stay or go?* Agent Kane was in trouble. *Screw it*. He still had both guns. He wasn't waiting for anybody.

* * *

Bellingham parked one row short of the target and walked the rest of the way. Munroe was waiting for him outside the closed door.

"He's awake. I left him alone like you asked." Munroe rolled up the panel and led the professor inside.

"Is your device all charged up?"

Munroe pointed to the stun gun on the table. "All set."

"Wait outside and shut the door." Munroe frowned but complied.

"Hi, Professor," Kane croaked when Bellingham approached the chair.

"I need some answers, Agent Kane."

"You need a hell of a lot more than that. I can't even begin to count how many years you're going to spend in a federal prison."

Bellingham held up the stun gun. "How did you know it was me?"

"I read your bio."

"Explain," the professor ordered.

He's basically a teacher, Kane thought. *He likes to talk and I need to stall for time.*

"The first time we met you told me that you hated addicts. Fine, nothing unusual about that, but then you called Danny and told him again how much you hated addicts. Not drugs, addicts. You weren't upset about drug dealers or the availability of drugs. You hated the people who took the drugs. That got me thinking. After that it was obvious."

"You're stalling."

"You wanted answers. I'll shut up if you like."

"What was so revealing about my CV?" Bellingham snapped.

"Well, not just your CV. Those articles you wrote were what really told the story. It wasn't hard to connect the dots." Bellingham frowned and sparks arced across the stun gun's contacts. "Don't get your panties in a twist," Kane said with a warped smile. "I'm getting to it. OK, one you hate drug addicts. Two, you wrote that drug addicts should either be allowed to die or be sterilized. Three, your initial research was into finding a way to make insects sterile. Four, you elected to extend your research beyond insects, to mice, mammals. You wouldn't have done that if all you were after was a better way to kill bugs. You had your eye on sterilizing people all along. My guess is that when the university realized that you were developing chemicals that might be used to make humans sterile you were asked to retire but by then it was too late. You'd already figured out how to do it."

"That's all supposition," Bellingham said.

"Supposition? Really? Look around. You're in bed with a wanted killer. You've kidnapped a Homeland Security agent. That seems like pretty solid evidence to me."

"Not if you aren't around to testify." Bellingham turned away.

"Wait. Isn't this the place where the mad scientist explains his great plan and attempts to convince everybody that they're all wrong about him?"

"Since you're going to be dead in a little while there's no point in trying to convince you of anything."

"Doesn't a condemned man get a last request? At least satisfy my curiosity. I'm right about you, aren't I?"

Bellingham paused, then turned back to Kane.

"No, you're not, at least not entirely."

I knew it, Kane thought. *Your ego is too big for you to just walk away. You can't resist the chance to tell me how brilliant you are, how right you are.*

"OK, smart guy, where did I go wrong?"

"The delivery mechanism is more complicated than you think. More elegant."

"It's a drug that gets people high. What's elegant about that?"

"It gets them high but it is not physically addicting. That's key. There are no withdrawal symptoms, no tremors, no shakes, no hallucinations. People will be free to stop taking it anytime they want."

"So what?" Kane demanded.

"That's an absolutely vital element. The compound will only affect true emotional addicts. The occasional user, the teenage experimenter, the temporarily depressed individual will suffer no physical withdrawal which means that they can easily quit if they want to. That was a moral imperative. I'm not out to kill stupid children who swallow a pill that somebody gave them at a party. I'm not a monster."

"Kill? This stuff is going to kill people?"

"Only if they take it hundreds of times. And technically it doesn't kill them. It just shortens their life expectancy. A hard-core addict who took a hundred doses over six months would likely die within another two years. A hundred doses over a year would extend that to death in four or five years. Two hundred doses within one year and, statistically, they'd be dead within nine months. It's not a straight line calculation."

"You're planning on killing thousands of people?" Kane asked.

"I'm not killing anyone. I'm *allowing* defective people to reduce their life expectancy by choosing to take illegal drugs. At most, I'm giving them the opportunity to choose to shorten their lives in exchange for sensory pleasure. It's not really very different from selling sugar, bacon, alcohol and cigarettes to an obese diabetic. I'm just affording them an opportunity to exchange a long boring life for a short, happy one. Are people criminals who sell overpowered motorcycles to teenaged boys?"

"Are you going to put a warning label on this stuff? Will there be a little skull and crossbones on each pill?"

To Kane's amazement, Bellingham smiled.

"You know, that's not a bad idea. For some people it would probably make the product more attractive. And it's not thousands, or hundreds of thousands of people. There are millions of addicts in the United States. Within five years after I begin distribution I expect that that number will be reduced by at least fifty percent. Within ten years I hope to have it down to under ten percent of current levels."

"You're hoping to kill millions of people over the next ten years and you think you're not a monster?"

"Most of them are not going to die. The majority of the decline in the addict population will be from the elimination of addictive genes from the reproductive pool."

Kane thought about that for a second. "The same way that you were going to get rid of the bugs," he said, almost talking to himself.

"The product has a duel, cumulative purpose. Only fifteen or twenty doses will be sufficient to sterilize the majority of the users, given a standard normal curve. If they don't exceed that dosage then the only effect, other than their inability to have or father children, will be a slight reduction in life expectancy, two or three years at most. It's only the heavy and continuous addicts who will significantly reduce their life span, and their lives are such a hellish nightmare already that that would probably be a blessing." Bellingham babbled on, oblivious to Kane's disgust. "If we sterilize the addictive personalities who take repeated doses eventually their genes will disappear from the population leading to a natural and material reduction in the number of addicts in the gene pool as a whole."

"You're insane."

"I'm the most sane person in this room. Have you seen the statistics on the number of crimes committed by drug addicts? I'm going to save our country from millions of burglaries, hundreds of thousands of auto accidents, thousands of murders, and thousands of criminal drug gangs. The list of crime and pain and financial loss directly arising from drug addicts is almost beyond measure. I'm going to end that and most of that result will not be from people dying. No, it will be from people not being born with defective genes in the first place. You're a policeman. If you had an ounce of sense, if you cared about the victims of crime instead of a bunch of loser drug addicts you would be helping me."

"You killed Albert Brownstein. You're a murderer."

"One man died so that thousands can live. How many people died building the Hoover Dam or the Golden Gate Bridge? In any great enterprise there is always, inevitably, collateral damage."

Bellingham stared at Kane as if looking for some sign of agreement.

"Is that how you'll justify murdering me?" Kane asked, thinking of Ronnie Dubois dismissing his killing Lyla Masterson as "collateral damage."

"Dying is your choice, Agent Kane. If you would only recognize the value, no the *necessity*, of what I'm doing your death would no longer be required."

"My choice, hmmmmm," Kane said. "Well, hell, if I've got a choice, sure. Where do I sign?"

"Somehow I don't think you're being sincere. For what it's worth, I regret that it's going to be necessary for Mr. Munroe to kill you."

"Well, if you're sorry about it, that makes all the difference, *asshole*!" Kane shouted.

Bellingham frowned then turned as the door clattered up to the ceiling.

CHAPTER FIFTY-SEVEN

When he reached the end of the row of lockers Danny looked left then right. In the shadows at the end of the next row down he caught the faintest glint of light. Half jogging, half limping he moved toward it then paused when he realized that he was looking at a strip of chrome on Bellingham's black Audi. He made a hunched pass around the empty car then inched forward to the next aisle. The lockers on both sides seemed deserted. Carefully, listening at each door, Danny worked his way up one side and then down the other but he heard no sounds and saw no glimmers of light. He crossed the back of the next row and then peeked up the other side.

At first this aisle seemed as empty as the last but as he was about to turn the corner he caught a hint of movement in one of the shadows near the last locker on the far side. Danny ducked back. After a second or two the shadow resolved into a man-shaped form staring out toward the street. A line of light leaked from beneath the nearest door. Danny watched the man for several seconds. All his attention was focused on the storage yard's main entrance. *He'll see Franks' car!* Danny realized. *He'll kill Agent Kane and then he'll escape! I have to do something.* The back fence was twenty feet to Rosewood's left. *I have to get as close to him as I can without him seeing me.*

One foot at a time Danny crept back to the fence then worked his way forward until he was directly behind Munroe. His gun held two-handed, straight out in front of him the way he had been taught Danny moved forward as quietly as he could manage. When he was six feet away the man heard some rattle or scrape and started to turn around.

"Don't move!" Danny ordered barely above a whisper. "Federal agent." For a second Munroe froze then slowly continued his turn. "Stop or I'll kill you!" Danny hissed, the fear clear in his voice.

"I rent a space here," Munroe said. "I was just taking a break. I can show you my access card." Munroe's hand dipped toward his pocket.

"Stop or I'll shoot!"

Munroe paused then pulled his hand back.

"Sure officer. No problem."

Danny looked wildly around for some other threat but saw none.

"Open that door. We're going inside. You first."

"Whatever you say." Munroe took a couple of steps forward and yanked the door up above his head. A wash of light spilled out and Danny squinted against the glare.

"Hands above your head. Get inside." Looking past his prisoner Danny spotted Kane fastened to a chair with silver tape and another man standing next to him. "Raise your hands!" Danny shouted, "Federal agent."

As soon as the door went up Kane heard the shouts and saw a figure in the darkness behind Munroe. It was only when the second man stepped into the light that Kane realized that it was Danny.

"Are you all right, Agent Kane?" Danny called.

Don't look at me! Kane wanted to scream. *Keep your eyes on your prisoner*, but he was afraid that saying anything would distract Danny even more. The kid was doing it all wrong. He needed to get both men face down on the floor then cut him loose. Instead Danny just kept walking Munroe deeper into the room.

"I'm fine," Kane said, "Get them—" but it was already too late. Munroe's hand darted toward his belt and before Danny could decide whether to shoot him or yell at him Munroe had his pistol out and pointed at Kane's chest.

"Drop your gun or I'll shoot your friend!" Munroe shouted. Wild-eyed Danny looked from Munroe to Kane and then back to Munroe. If he pulled the trigger the man might still have time to kill Agent Kane.

"Shoot him!" Kane shouted.

Danny lined up the barrel but held his fire. His whole life he had been taught that decent people didn't shoot a man in the back.

Munroe took a quick glance over his shoulder. "Put your gun down or I'm going to kill your friend." Danny hesitated.

"Don't do it!" Kane ordered.

"One. . . Two . . ."

"All right! All right!" Danny shouted and squatted down, gently laying his pistol on the floor." At this point in the movies the gunman would turn around and motion for the cop to put up his hands or some such silly thing. In real life it never happened that way. Munroe instantly swung around and fired. Danny had been beginning to stand and shoved off on his bad ankle but only managed to move far enough for the bullet to hit him in the shoulder instead of the center of his chest. Munroe saw Danny's body jar with the impact and then the stain blossom on the agent's sweatshirt. Munroe took a second to make sure that Danny's gun was far out of his reach and then he turned to Bellingham.

"We've got to get out of here," Munroe yelled.

For a second the professor seemed frozen then he dug into his pocket for his keys. Suddenly he jerked his hand out and shouted, "He's not—"

Kane's gun wobbling wildly in his hand Danny fired off six shots as fast as he could pull the trigger. Four missed completely. One nicked Munroe's arm. More by luck than skill the last one struck Ryan in his heart and he was dead before he hit the floor.

In a daze Danny pointed Kane's Beretta at Bellingham and struggled to his feet. The professor dropped his keys and hurriedly raised his hands.

"Cut me loose!" Kane ordered and nodded toward one of the shelves where Munroe had stacked a plate, a cup, a fork, a spoon and a cheap, stainless steel knife. Danny staggered over, grabbed the blade and a few seconds later sawed through the tape around Kane's wrists. As soon as his hands were free Greg took the knife and cut through the rest of his bonds while Danny struggled to remain conscious. Once out of the chair Kane retrieved Danny's gun.

"Face down on the floor!" Kane shouted, pointing the weapon at Bellingham.

"There's no need—"

"On the floor now or I'll shoot you dead!" Bellingham made a face and lay on the concrete. "Where's your phone?" Kane called to Danny, not taking his eyes off the professor.

"Lost it," Danny said in almost a whisper.

"Professor, reach into your pocket. Very slowly take out your phone and slide it over to me."

The burner made a skittering sound as it slid across the concrete.

"I'm a federal agent," Kane said in answer to the "What is your emergency?" question. "My partner has been shot. He needs an ambulance immediately. . . . Danny, where are we?" Danny shook his head and tried to think. "Danny! What's the address!" *Address? Oh, right.* Danny recited the location he had given Agent Franks. "Did you get that?" The 911 operator repeated it back. "Tell the paramedics that their call is a federal agent who's been shot in the line of duty."

Kane checked Bellingham then moved back to where Danny was leaning against the wall. His arm had dropped and Kane's gun was now pointing at the floor.

"Danny, don't close your eyes. You have to stay awake. You're going into shock." Kane grabbed a towel from the shelf. "Press this against your shoulder as hard as you can."

Behind him Kane heard a screech of tires and lights stabbed into the room. Four men with drawn guns raced inside shouting, "FBI! FBI!" Kane recognized Franks and shouted back, "He's been shot! I've called for a bus," then he turned back to Rosewood.

"Danny, stay with me!"

Danny gave Kane a glassy stare, smiled and collapsed at Greg's feet.

CHAPTER FIFTY-EIGHT

"I've got a bus coming," Greg called out then knelt next to Rosewood and put pressure on the wound. "Get somebody outside to flag it down and lead it here." Franks waved at one of his agents who ran toward the front gate. "And do me a favor and hook that guy up." Behind him Greg heard the sound of cuffs clicking closed.

"Royatt," Franks called to one of his men and pointed at Danny. Reluctantly Kane let the FBI agent take over first aid. "Are you hurt?" Franks asked once Kane was back on his feet.

"I'll be all right." Greg looked around the room in a daze. "That's Munroe over there." Franks looked at the body then back at Kane. "The kid shot him dead. Saved my life." Greg turned his gaze to Bellingham. "That's the bastard who's behind all this." Kane walked over and the professor took a step back.

"I'm invoking my right to be silent."

"Fine. Just listen. Right now, right this minute, you're at a fork in the road. If you pick one path you can have a show trial, give interviews, and tell the world everything you were trying to accomplish." Bellingham tried to keep a poker face but Kane saw a hint of smile creep across his lips. "The other choice is a trip to Gitmo and solitary confinement."

"You can't do that!"

"You were going to manufacture a weapon of mass murder. That makes you a terrorist."

"I'm an American citizen. I have the right to a trial. I have—"

"The right to be silent so shut up. Here's the deal. You make one phone call and you get the interviews and the show trial. You don't and you're going to find out a lot more about the Patriot Act and solitary confinement than you ever wanted to know."

"I'm not going to incriminate myself," Bellingham insisted. Kane laughed.

"Incriminate yourself? That guy," Kane pointed at Munroe, "was killed in the commission of a crime. That triggers the felony-murder rule which means that anyone who was part of that crime, namely you, is himself guilty of murder. We've got you dead-bang on murder right here. Then there's my kidnapping and attempted murder. Then there are your phone calls with Munroe. You've got them on tape, right?" Kane asked Franks.

"The wiretap went active today."

"It was a—" Bellingham started to say then shut his mouth.

"A burner phone?" Franks finished the professor's sentence for him. "We were set up outside your house and recorded both ends of your conversations. How do you think we knew you had Kane locked up here?"

Bellingham tried to look unconcerned but failed miserably.

"Well, there you go, not that we need all that other stuff. My testimony alone is enough to send you to a federal prison for the rest of your life. So, you're toast no matter what you do or you don't do. This is your fork in the road and you need to ask yourself if protecting your snitch is worth keeping the world from hearing your message. Well, is it?"

* * *

The barely audible buzz began just as he was pouring his first cup of coffee.

"What's that?" Susan asked.

"Work." His suit coat was draped over one of the dining room chairs and he pulled the cell from the inside pocket on his way out of the room. His wife had long ago become accustomed to calls at odd hours and turned back to her breakfast of oatmeal and herbal tea.

"Yes?"

"We're OK," the professor said. "We questioned Kane and he's got nothing."

"You're sure?"

"No man lies under that kind of pressure. Farber is our only loose end. My man will silence him tonight."

"Any idea how he found out about you?"

"No, but after tonight it won't matter."

"What about Kane?"

"He's dead."

"Dead!" he hissed. "You were only supposed to find out what he knew!"

"And we did. Did you think we would kidnap and torture a federal agent and then just let him go?"

"I never agreed to anything like that."

"Please. You knew we killed Brownstein. You knew what was going to happen to Kane when you gave me his home address."

"Jesus!"

"Farber will be the last one, then it's smooth sailing. I'll tell you what. You keep a close watch on your people and let me know if they find out anything about Farber and I'll give you a five million dollar bonus when we go into production. And that's just the beginning. There'll be more money from this product than you ever dreamed of. Are we good?"

"I'm not a murderer."

"We've only done what we had to do. So, are we good?"

Bellingham heard a sigh then, "Yes. We're good, but Farber has to be the last one."

"He's the final loose end. We won't need to kill anyone else. Call me at six to confirm that your people don't have any idea where Farber is."

"All right."

The phone went dead. He stared at the display for half a second then went back to finish his breakfast. Twenty minutes later, just as he was reaching for his coat and keys, the doorbell rang. He opened it to find two men in white shirts and dark suits. He knew they were federal agents before they even spoke. They might as well have been carrying a sign.

"Secretary Dawson, I'm FBI Special Agent Ronald Franks. This is Special Agent Amos Royatt."

"Would you like to come inside—"

"Please place your hands on the wall and spread your legs," Franks ordered. Dawson just stared at Franks as if he had started speaking in pig Latin. Franks pulled Dawson through the doorway, spun him around and pushed him against the wall.

"What's this all about? I'm—"

"Roger Dawson, you are under arrest for the murder of a federal official, conspiracy to murder a federal agent, kidnapping of a federal agent and conspiracy to kidnap a federal agent," Franks patted Dawson down for weapons. "You have the right to remain silent. Anything you say can and will be used against you in a court of law. You have the right to an attorney. . . ." Franks' voice seemed to fade away and then, as if someone else had taken control of his body, Dawson was wracked with sobs.

With snot dripping off Dawson's chin, Franks cuffed his hands behind his back and he and Royatt half led, half carried Roger Dawson to their car.

CHAPTER FIFTY-NINE

Allison felt a shadow cross her desk and looked up to see her uncle frowning down at her.

"We need to talk in my office."

"What's happened?" she asked once they were behind closed doors.

"Are you still seeing Agent Kane?"

"No." She almost asked if something had happened to Kane but resisted the impulse. Not having to deal with him being blown up or shot or whatever was a big part of why she had broken things off.

"I just got a call from a friend at Homeland Security. Agent Kane's partner has been shot."

"Is he . . . alive?" she asked, finally settling on the alternative of life rather than death.

"They think he'll make it. Infection is always a risk but he's young and healthy so he should be all right." Denning studied Allison's face but couldn't interpret her expression. *Sadness mixed with determination?* "We need to go visit him."

"Was Kane's partner helping you with something?"

"He was shot in the course of saving Agent Kane's life."

"So, someone was trying to kill Greg and his partner stopped them? Why were they. . . . no, never mind. Was Greg shot too?"

"No. He's banged up quite a bit but basically OK."

Allison nervously fluttered her fingers then looked up. "Well, all right, I'll cancel your ten o'clock and I can take the meeting with the Department of Transportation people."

"Eric can handle that. We're both going."

"I don't see why I need to go."

"Why did you break up with Kane?"

"What does that have to do with anything?" Allison snapped.

"You're family, Allison, and I care about you, very much."

"And I care about you. Look, Greg just wasn't. . . . we weren't a good match, that's all."

"Brian's been dead for two years."

"Don't you think I know that?" Allison said, her eyes beginning to glimmer with faint tears.

Denning stared at her then sighed. "No, honey, I don't think that you do."

"Why is everybody nagging me about this? It's nobody's business! Go, go visit this agent and let me do my job."

"Your job is coming to the hospital with me."

"I don't want—"

"Kane almost got himself killed doing a favor for me and as much as you don't want to admit it there was something between you and him as well. We have an obligation and we always pay our debts. Get your coat."

* * *

Greg paced the hallway and periodically glanced at the woman who had introduced herself as Danny's girlfriend. She seemed very young but then Rosewood seemed young too. *Maybe I'm just getting old*, Greg thought.

"We were watching TV when Danny got the call that you were in trouble," Diane said when she caught Kane looking at her. "He just grabbed his gun and ran out. I told him to be careful," she added as if suggesting that Danny might not have been hurt if he had taken her advice. "But I guess that's part of the job, isn't it?" she added with a quick, nervous smile.

Kane stared at her and didn't know what to say. Most cops went their whole careers without firing their gun outside the range. Looked at that way this was a once in a lifetime event, but he couldn't promise her that it would never happen again. You didn't get to control things like that. *Look at me*, he thought.

Behind them the elevator dinged and Kane saw Allison and Senator Denning heading toward them. The thought *Maybe she's changed her mind* flashed through his head then died when he noticed the pinched look on her face.

"Senator," Kane said, holding out his hand.

"Agent Kane. We heard about your partner and rushed right over. Is he going to be all right?"

"They say he'll be fine. The doctor's in there with him now. Oh, this is Diane . . . ."

"Diane Odermatt," the girl said and accepted the Senator's hand.

"She's Danny's . . . friend. Diane, this is Senator Denning and his niece, Allison Varner."

"Pleased to meet you," Diane said and glanced down the hall. "Ummm, I'm going to get a cup of coffee. I'll be back in a few minutes."

"I heard that you had something of a close call," Denning said to Greg.

"He saved my life." Kane glanced at the door to Danny's room. When he turned back Allison looked like she was going to be sick.

"We're very glad he did," Denning said. "I understand that this lunatic you caught was planning on flooding the country with some kind of toxic drug. What's wrong with people?" Denning asked, not expecting an answer. "Anyway, please take care of yourself, Agent Kane. We can't afford to lose men like you. If you ever need anything make sure you call me."

"Thank you, senator," Kane said. He risked another look at Allison but she wouldn't meet his eyes.

"I assume you haven't had a chance to listen to the news this morning?" Denning asked.

"No, I've been a little busy."

"The Supreme Court's going to announce their decision in the gun case next Wednesday. I wonder if you saving Justice Hopper's life has had any effect on the result."

"It's not my job to worry about things like that," Kane replied because that was what he was supposed to say.

Denning looked at his watch. "I've got a committee meeting in a few minutes. I just wanted you to know how much I appreciate everything that you and your partner have done." They shook hands and Denning and Allison turned to go.

"Allison, could you stay for a minute?" Kane asked, his tongue running ahead of his brain.

"I have to—"

"No, it's fine," Denning interrupted. "Stay here and talk with Agent Kane. Petty cash will cover your cab fare back." The senator hurried off before Allison could object.

"Thanks," Kane said once Denning was gone. "I just wanted to—"

Behind him the door opened and a young Asian doctor stepped out. "He can have visitors but only for a few minutes," he said and then rushed off. Danny waved at Kane through the open door.

"Could you wait for me for a minute? Please?"

Allison glanced at Kane's partner. He looked like a teenager costumed in bandages for a high school play. He smiled at her.

"All right," she agreed and paced across the hall. Kane went in and closed the door behind him. A moment later Diane returned with a cardboard cup filled with a coffee-like substance.

"Greg just went in," Allison said. "I don't think he'll be very long." Diane sipped at the coffee and made a sour face.

"At least it's got caffeine." She gave Allison a weak smile. "Are you and Agent Kane . . . together?"

"No," Allison answered, a little too quickly and too emphatically Diane thought. "He handled an investigation, of sorts, for my uncle. I work in his office, my uncle's office, so I . . . he brought me along."

"Oh," Diane said, hearing more than Allison intended to say. "Well, he seems like a great guy. Danny just worships him."

"He's a very good investigator I'm sure."

"Oh, that's not why Danny likes him, I mean, he respects his abilities and all but it's more than that. When Agent Kane's old partner died Danny wasn't even technically an investigator. He was in tech support but Agent Kane saw Danny's potential and he picked him out of all the people in the office to be his new partner. He trained him, taught him things. He believed in Danny.

"You know," Diane said, lowering her voice almost to a whisper, "the FBI agent told me that Danny was the only one that Agent Kane trusted. It's true," Diane said as if Allison had given some sign of disbelief. "Agent Kane told the FBI that if anything happened to him, if anything went wrong, that Danny was the only person he should tell. And he was right," Diane said, tears suddenly beginning to slide down her cheeks. "When Agent Kane needed help Danny was the one who found him. Danny was the one who saved him." Diane let out a little sob and hunted through her purse for a tissue.

Allison watched the girl wipe her face and all she could think was, *What's wrong with you? Being Kane's partner almost got your boyfriend killed.*

"Are you and Danny engaged?" Allison asked, anxious to change the subject.

"Well," Diane said with a little smile, "not exactly, but we're going to get married — I know we will. We've talked about it. Danny wanted to make sure that he would pass his probationary period but now that he's proven himself I think we'll make it official."

Proven himself? Allison thought. *By getting shot?*

"Aren't you worried about him having such a dangerous job?" Allison asked in an almost accusatory tone.

"It's important work," Diane said defensively. "It's what he's always wanted to do."

"But what about you? What if the next time he's not so lucky? Do you want to be married to someone who you know might go off to work one morning and never come home?"

Diane noticed that Allison's face had gone pale and her mouth was tight and pinched.

"My mother's friend, Irene, was married to a lobbyist," Diane said. "Safest job in the world, right? One morning he was sitting outside a Starbucks, typing something on his iPhone, when some old guy got confused and hit the gas instead of the brake. He plowed his Buick across the patio and all the way through the front window. He killed Irene's husband and a woman who was texting to her son. Whoever I marry there's always the chance that he might walk out the door one morning and never come home. That's why it's important to marry the right person, so that you get the best life you can."

You're so wrong! the voice inside Allison's head shouted. She struggled to control herself and instinctively grabbed the girl's arm. "Diane, listen to me. I've been through this. I lost my husband. You can't imagine what that's like. I think about him every day. You never want to go through something like that. Never!"

"I'm so sorry," Diane said and gave Allison a hug.

"It's all right. It's just that you seem like a nice person and I don't want you to be hurt the way I was, I mean, marrying someone and then losing them so soon."

Diane took half a step back and looked confused.

"Do you regret marrying your husband?" she asked a heartbeat later.

"What?"

"Knowing what you know now, if you had a time machine and you could do it all over again would you still marry your husband or would you pick someone else?"

"I loved Brian!" Allison almost shouted.

"I understand but you said that I shouldn't marry Danny because he might be killed, that I should find someone safer, so I wanted to ask if you would do that. If you had the chance would you have broken up with your Brian and married someone else who you thought was safer?"

"No!" Allison said, almost in tears. "He was the love of my life!"

"Danny's the love of my life," Diane answered barely above a whisper.

Almost in horror Allison stared at the girl then, sobbing, fled.

Better to have loved and lost than never to have loved at all, Diane thought. Then another old homily slipped into her brain. *Do as I say, not as I do.*

A moment later Greg opened the door.

"He's all yours," he said then, seeing the tracks of tears on Diane's cheek, his smile quickly faded to concern. "Don't worry! Danny's going to be fine, one-hundred percent. Good as new."

Diane sniffled, gave Kane a massive hug, then ran past him into Danny's room. Kane followed her with his eyes then reached in and closed the door. When he turned away he saw that the corridor was empty, that Allison was gone.

CHAPTER SIXTY

The paperwork required to document Bellingham's case was worse than Kane had even imagined and the following Monday afternoon found Kane still typing and printing and filing. From time to time he'd glance up from the monitor and more often than not he'd catch Fred Immerson staring at him as if Kane were some strange and potentially dangerous dog that had wandered into Immerson's yard. Kane knew that Immerson was making up his mental list of Kane's triumphs and mistakes and that the final tally had not yet been determined.

On the positive side Kane had caught Brownstein's and, presumably, Grant Eustace's killer and had thwarted a plan to distribute massive quantities of a toxic drug. And he had discovered a traitor and a criminal in their own organization.

The negative entries on Kane's ledger were equally serious. He had lied to Immerson about his investigation, not once but several times, lies that not only struck at the heart of the rules that governed the Office but evidenced at least a lack of trust and at most a lack of respect for Immerson himself.

Even worse than that Kane had been party to the arrest of a senior Homeland Security official. Yes, the man was a crook and a traitor but those sorts of transgressions were always better handled privately and quietly. Instead the public had now learned of the man's crimes and that led them, inevitably, to wonder how many other Homeland Security officers, and by extension, how many government officials of all types, were despicable criminals who should not be trusted to do the nation's work. And the worst of Kane offenses was that he had done all this through the offices of their prime competitor, the FBI.

Immerson wasn't so much interested in punishing Kane for these past transgressions as he was worried what new mischief Kane might create in the future if some similar situation should arise. But any action against Kane, a transfer or demotion or tasking him to inventory the supply of paperclips in the Bismarck, North Dakota office, held its own risks.

Kane had a powerful ally and protector in Senator Arthur Denning who could be expected to make substantial trouble for anyone who messed with him. And then there was Sebastian Wren to consider. On the one hand Wren would naturally have the same concerns about Kane's organizational soundness as Immerson himself but on a personal level Kane had done Wren a good turn. Upon Dawson's arrest Wren had been provisionally tapped to fill Dawson's position and unless Wren got caught screwing a coke whore on his desk during business hours his appointment was almost certain to be made permanent. Wren might feel a residue of good will for Kane and thus block any attempt at retribution for Kane's bureaucratic misdeeds.

When all was said and done, Immerson decided that the scales were evenly balanced. Kane would get neither a commendation nor a rebuke but instead would be allowed to go along as he had before in the hope that if he were someday again faced with a similar situation that he would display a better sense of discretion. That was a faint hope indeed Immerson knew but there was nothing to be done about it now.

"Kane!" Immerson shouted across the bull pen and waved Greg to his office. Kane closed the door behind him and took his usual chair.

"I've been reading your report on Rosewood's actions," Immerson began. "Let me get this straight. He went over the fence at the location without waiting for backup?"

"Yes."

"Then he fell off the top of the fence and lost his phone?"

"Yes."

"He accosted this Ryan Munroe, a man suspected of already killing two federal agents, and failed to immediately cuff him or even search him for weapons?"

"Yes."

"When Munroe first reached for his weapon Rosewood had a shot and he didn't take it?"

"Yes."

"He gave up his gun when he still had a chance to shoot Munroe?" Immerson asked, shaking his head in disbelief.

"Yes."

"Quite a list of mistakes, wouldn't you say?"

"Yes it is," Kane agreed.

"He was your partner. You're the man who was almost killed as the result of his failures. What do you think I should do?"

Kane frowned. *Was it anger or regret*, Immerson wondered.

"Here's how I see it. Danny was never in the military and except for some firearms classes he never had any law enforcement training. He's never been in combat or been shot at or been in any real physical danger. As far as I know he's never even been in a serious fist fight. He found himself alone in a very dangerous situation. It would have been the easiest thing in the world for him to stay at the front gate and wait for back up. But he didn't.

"When he spotted Munroe he could have gone back to the front gate and reported to the FBI when they eventually arrived. But he didn't. When Munroe told him to put down his gun he could have done nothing, waited to see if Munroe actually shot me and then shot him in return. Instead he did a very foolish thing that he thought, wrongly, would protect me.

"After Munroe shot him he could have given up or tried to crawl away or played dead. He had never been under fire before, certainly never been shot. He was in pain, bleeding. He must have been terrified. What did he do? He pulled out a backup gun and killed the son of a bitch and saved my life. It was the bravest thing I've ever seen. I think you should give him a medal."

"What if he screws up again? The next time you might not be so lucky."

"He's trainable. I'll teach him what he needs to know."

"All right," Immerson said after a moment's thought.

Kane stood but before he reached the door Immerson called after him, "I think you're right, Kane."

"About what?"

"That was the bravest thing I've ever heard. When you see Rosewood you can tell him that he's passed his probation. He's got the job if he still wants it."

"Oh, he wants it," Kane said. "You can take that to the bank."

Greg's phone was ringing when he got back to his desk.

"Kane."

"Mr. Kane, It's Ernie Ramirez . . . the manager at Denny's. You asked me to run a tab for that homeless guy, Randy Foy."

"Oh, sure. Is there a problem?"

"You said to call you when the money ran out. I think he's only got one or two meals left on the tab you had me run. What do you want to do?"

Kane ran a fast mental calculation. If Randy was eating a meal or two a day, plus tip and tax, well, the timing was about right. *Now what?* Should he just keep on feeding this guy? For how long? A month? A year? And then what?

"Mr. Ramirez, can I call you back in a few minutes?" Kane took down Ramirez's number and hung up. After his last dream about his brother Greg had dug out the little Buddhism book they had given him in the anger management class and he had been reading a few pages at odd moments every day. Kane rummaged for it in his top drawer and then began flipping pages and making notes. Ten minutes later he called Ramirez back.

"How long are you going to be at the restaurant?" Kane asked.

"Another couple of hours I guess."

"Good, I'll stop by."

Forty-five minutes later Kane handed Ramirez an envelope.

"The cash is for you. Add it to his account. And there's a note in there for him. I'd appreciate it if you'd give it to him and ask him to read it. Can you do that?"

"Sure, I guess."

"Thanks," Kane said. After he left Ernie opened the envelope. It contained five-hundred dollars in twenties which he duly added to Foy's account. *He's lucky I'm an honest man*, Ernie thought, then picked up the note. He knew that he shouldn't read it, but he did anyway:

"Randy,

"I know you're hurting. I read somewhere that denying our pain only makes it worse. I didn't listen then but now I'm starting to believe that they were probably right. They warned me that the more I tried to push my anger into a corner, to ignore it, to deny it, the stronger it would get, that it was like a seawall raised against the waves and that by fighting against them it would inevitably be broken.

"They told me that to be free of my anger I had to accept it, smile at it, and let it pass through me and wash itself away. I'm trying to do that and it seems to be working. I'm asking you to do me a favor — try to do the same thing with your memories. Stop fighting them. Stop trying to drug yourself into forgetting them. Accept them as part of you. Acknowledge them. Own them and then let them drift away when they're ready to go and, most of all, remember that the past is dead but that you are not.

"I believe in you.

"—Gregory Kane"

Ernie read the note a second time but it seemed like mumbo jumbo to him. Well, it was none of his business. When Randy came in for dinner half an hour later Ernie told him that his friend had filled up his account with more money and he gave Randy the envelope and watched him read the note. After a minute the homeless guy stuffed the paper into a grimy pocket and walked over to his regular table without saying a word.

As the weeks went by Randy Foy slipped from Kane's mind. Greg had told the manager to call him when Randy's account again ran low but Kane never heard from Ernie Ramirez again.

CHAPTER SIXTY-ONE

On the following blustery, rainy Wednesday morning the Chief Clerk of the Supreme Court released a bound pamphlet containing the Court's Bench Opinion in the matter of *Hoffkemper vs. The State of California*.

The attorneys were accommodated first and then hundreds of copies were made available to the horde of reporters. While those endowed with speed reading skills madly flipped pages, more seasoned journalists focused on the name of the Justice who authored the opinion. Upon one reporter's announcement that the decision had been written by Mr. Justice Wheeler jubilation spread among the citizens opposing Lyla's Law and dread reigned in those supporting it as Justice Wheeler was generally considered to be leaning toward finding the statute unconstitutional.

Those interested in only the headline now jumped to the end to see if the opinion of the Court of Appeals had been affirmed or reversed while the rest scanned the decision for the details of the reasoning behind the ruling.

The opinion commenced with a recitation of the facts and the case's judicial history ending with the finding of the Ninth Circuit Court of Appeals that the law's provisions were unconstitutional as being in violation of the provisions of the Second Amendment. For the next several pages Wheeler summarized the arguments of the parties, pro and con and then, finally, got to the heart of the matter.

"The Constitution is a living document that must be read in a reasoned, reasonable and intelligent context against the background of the society that exists at the time each case is decided. When the Fourth Amendment was adopted there were no tape recorders, movie cameras, telephones, emails, automobiles or a thousand other such devices yet on many occasions this Court has been called upon to determine if, without a search warrant, the government's recording of a telephone call, reading of an email, emplacement of a camera in a private residence, or the search of an automobile is or is not a violation of the Fourth Amendment. To do so we have had to understand the intentions of the Founders in enacting that provision and apply those intentions facts of the case.

"When the Second Amendment was adopted 'arms' were single-shot, black powder, muzzle-loading rifles and America was a rural, agricultural society. There were no machine guns, multi-round clips, armor-piercing bullets, or the like. Nor was the country anything like the highly urbanized nation we have today.

"In the case at bar we must determine if it would have been the intention of the drafters that any citizen at any time should have the unrestricted right to freely possess and carry these modern weapons amongst crowds of thousands of people no matter how fearsome or dangerous those firearms might be. In short we must interpret a more than two-hundred year old rule in the context of modern technology and an urbanized society, both unimagined and unimaginable at the time the Second Amendment was adopted.

"The Respondents have argued that the language of the Second Amendment is absolute. Under their interpretation we would be living in a society reminiscent of the Wild West where armed men roamed the streets at will, immune to any governmental restrictions on their ability to carry loaded firearms. If that were the case then today we would be in an even more extreme position than the residents of Tombstone or Dodge City were a hundred and fifty years ago.

"In the days of Wyatt Earp and Billy The Kid at worst the weapons were single-action six-shooters with black-powder bullets while the modern-day gunslingers that the Respondents contend should be free to walk the public streets will be carrying semi-automatic pistols holding fifteen rounds or more or armor-piercing military-assault rifles with fifty shots in the clip. The notion that the Founding Fathers ever intended or would have ever countenanced such a proposition verges on the surreal.

"As the Petitioner has pointed out, even though the First Amendment absolutely prohibits the government from making any law limiting the freedom of the press it is clearly constitutional for the government to prohibit the publication of falsehoods, private information without the consent of the owner, child pornography and numerous other classes of printed materials, the apparently absolute language of the First Amendment notwithstanding.

"The Second Amendment is no less sacrosanct than the First. As such the right to bear arms is subject to the same level of reasonable interpretation and limitation in support of a compelling state interest as are the rights to the freedom of speech, freedom of the press and freedom of religion. If the government can constitutionally prohibit shouting 'Fire!' in a crowded theater in spite of the right of freedom of speech, prohibit having multiple wives in spite of the right of freedom of religion, prohibit the publishing of pictures of naked children in spite of the right of freedom of the press then the government can similarly constitutionally prohibit citizens who are not members of law enforcement, the military, or a recognized militia from owning high-capacity weapons so long as the prohibitions imposed are reasonable and are adopted in support of a compelling state interest.

"Given the frequency and lethality of the shootings of innocent citizens, not to mention members of law enforcement, with such high-capacity, rapid-fire weapons and the obvious danger they pose to the general public, we find that such a compelling state interest exists in this case. The so-called Lyla's Law does not violate the provisions of the Second Amendment.

"The decision of the Court of Appeals is reversed."

The vote was six to three with Mr. Justice Hopper siding with the majority. He did not write a separate opinion and said nothing at all beyond "I concur."

The Respondents promised to place a measure repealing Lyla's Law on California's November ballot. Pollsters gave it a fifty-fifty chance of being successful.

When he heard the decision Kane wondered if saving Justice Hopper's life had made any difference at all. Even if Hopper had died it still would have been a vote of five to three in favor of the law. Or would it?

Kane had to wonder what had made Mr. Justice Wheeler apparently switch sides. Had the attacks on the life of one of their own affected the Court's thinking? If Carl Feeney hadn't dispatched an assassin to murder Hopper would the result have been six to three to uphold the law or perhaps five to four to strike it down?

Kane figured that no one would ever know.

CHAPTER SIXTY-TWO

Upon the announcement of the Lyla's Law decision the atmosphere in Senator Arthur Denning's office was euphoric. Perhaps because of her inevitable association of the gun case with Gregory Kane, Allison Varner politely deflected all references to the matter and tried to pretend as much as possible that it did not exist. That evening, worn down and vaguely sad, she ate her dinner at the coffee table while the evening news filled the TV. When the picture of the Supreme Court building appeared she turned off the sound. Random images of angry crowds, robed men and talking heads flashed by. Eventually, a video of a smiling man and woman holding a three-year-old girl appeared. Thinking that the gun case coverage has run its course she turned on the sound.

"We just want to thank all of the people who worked so hard and so long to make this possible," the woman said. "Even though Lyla is gone, this law bearing her name will stand as a shield to help protect our daughter, Ellen, and all the other children in this state."

"Ms. Masterson, the opponents of Lyla's Law have vowed to begin an initiative campaign—"

Allison jammed her finger back down on the mute button. *Masterson? Those were Lyla's parents? After Lyla had been killed they had chosen to have another child, another little girl?* Allison thought. *How could you do that?* She wanted to scream. *How could you abandon Lyla that way? How could you have another child as if Lyla was replaceable like a failed car or a broken washing machine? You should have . . . .*

Suddenly confused, Allison couldn't finish the sentence. *Never had another child? Lived your lives in perpetual grief? Crawled into a hole and ceased to exist?* a little voice in the back of her mind asked. None of those things made any sense, she knew. *But how could you face the pain of possibly losing another child?* Allison demanded. *What if this girl, this Ellen, was shot or hit by a car or fell off her bicycle? Or got cancer like my Brian?*

One and out? the tiny voice demanded. *One terrible thing happens and you become so paralyzed by the fear of it happening again that you stop living?* it sneered. *Yes! Yes!* Allison shouted at her traitorous self. *Once bitten, twice afraid?* the nagging voice asked. She had heard that voice, faintly, once or twice before, but she had always been able to silence it, to drown it out. But now it had come back louder than ever.

I can't! I can't! she shouted at herself. Images of bombed-out buildings and bodies lying in the street flickered across the TV and Allison mashed the power button until her finger hurt. She found a bottle of bourbon in the cupboard and poured an inch of it into a glass. She didn't usually drink the stuff but all the scotch seemed to have disappeared. This was Brian's bottle, still at the same level it had held the last time he went into the hospital. Knowing that they would not allow him any whiskey he had made himself a farewell drink. He liked it over ice. He said that bourbon was one of America's great contributions to the world.

Before she finished her glass Allison's head began to spin and she lay back and closed her eyes. For no reason that she could name she began to cry.

CHAPTER SIXTY-THREE

Allison woke up with sore joints and a nagging headache and vowed never to drink bourbon again. She looked into her closet and the task of picking out her wardrobe for a day at the office seemed overwhelming. After unsuccessfully working her way down to the end of her closet she took a step back then picked up the phone and called in sick. When she wandered out toward the kitchen she spotted the bourbon bottle still on the counter. That was something that she definitely had to get out of the apartment. She found an empty cardboard box, put the bottle in it, then checked behind the bar for any other surplus items. Soon several ancient, half-empty bottles of flavored liquors were packed in the carton as well.

Feeling for the first time in weeks as if she had accomplished something, Allison attacked the kitchen. She pulled all the items off the shelves and quickly filled the trash bin with stale crackers, moldy bread crumbs and chipped plates. With liquid soap and a scrubby sponge in hand she next went to work on the shelves themselves. As Allison scrubbed her energy returned and upon finishing with the kitchen she decided that the bedroom needed a good cleaning too.

Soon she was running low on soap and had filled all the wastebaskets. At the very least she would need to load up on cleaning supplies, garbage bags, and cardboard boxes. After finishing her shopping she stopped for a quick lunch then went back to work. Her closet proved to be a treasure trove of surplus dresses that no longer fit or whose styles were hopelessly out of date, sweaters she had received as gifts from Brian's mother and would rather die than wear, scuffed shoes, and worn-out stockings. Those items that still had some life in them went into a box for the Salvation Army and those hopelessly frayed found themselves stuffed into one of the black plastic bags.

Halfway through the afternoon she had worked her way almost to the end of the rack and ran into Brian's brown, wool suit. He had hated that suit, the product of an impulse buy that he instantly regretted. Well, maybe the Salvation Army had a client who needed a decent suit for a job interview. Allison carefully folded it into the bottom of a fresh box. The suits all came with vests but while Brian never wore them he was too thrifty to just throw them away. Into the box they went. Then she came across the drawer filled with Brian's underwear, handkerchiefs and socks. What was she supposed to do with old jockey shorts? Some people used them as cleaning rags but the thought creeped her out. They ended up in one of the plastic bags.

Brian's shirts were a problem. They were all folded and starched. He had loved those shirts. Well, whoever got the suit would need the rest of the outfit. She picked out two shirts that went with the brown suit and then three ties that also matched. And so it went. She paused for dinner but the cleaning seemed to energize her soul and she moved on to the other rooms. When she finally stopped around midnight, too tired to even think, the bedroom floor and half the hallway were hip deep in boxes and bags.

She woke the next morning just before ten and felt as if she had spent the previous day breaking rocks. She glanced at the legends neatly printed on the boxes in Magic Marker — "Suits", "Dress Shirts & Ties", "T-shirts & sport shirts", "Pajamas." What was she doing? That was all that she had left of Brian. She could see him still, his silly smile, the way he tilted his head when he was confused. A few cardboard boxes? No, Brian wasn't some collection of old sweaters and ragged sweat shirts any more than he was in some hole in the ground. That grave didn't hold her husband, just the container he had come in. He still lived inside her and he always would.

She arranged for some men to come over and cart the boxes and bags away and after they were done she fell into a dreamless sleep. When she awoke early that afternoon, she called Greg Kane.

CHAPTER SIXTY-FOUR

When Greg Kane opened his eyes he found himself standing inside the entrance to Tommy's Bar. Kane turned toward their customary table and saw his brother, smiling and raising a beer in a friendly toast.

"Hi, Tommy," Greg said, suddenly finding himself in his usual chair with no memory of crossing the intervening space.

"Hi, yourself. You got Jason's killer," Tommy said. Kane found himself beginning to smile but stopped when Tommy added, "Why is he still alive?"

"What do you mean?" Greg asked though he knew exactly what his brother was getting at.

"You could have shot him in that motel room. Those city cops would have backed you up one-hundred percent. So, why didn't you?"

"I needed him alive to get the guy who hired him," Kane replied almost apologetically.

"Sure, if he was any other mope and you were any other cop, but he was the guy who murdered my son, your nephew. Why didn't you kill him when you had the chance?"

"I don't know," Kane answered, looking away.

"Sure you do."

"Why don't you tell me?" Greg shot back, his gaze fixing on Tommy's face then shying away.

"I asked you first. . . . Come on. You need to say it out loud."

"What do you want me to say? That I was afraid?"

"You weren't afraid. Say it."

"Fine, I was a pussy. I was weak."

"That's another lie. Haven't you learned by now that you can't lie to me? Come on, say it!"

"Because I'm not a murderer," Kane answered softly, still looking away.

"Now you're talking like a damn lawyer. He killed a cop, your blood. That's a capital crime. The penalty for that is death. Shooting him wouldn't have been murder. It would have been justified. What was the matter with you? Didn't you want to make him suffer? Weren't you angry?"

"I—" Kane began then stopped. He thought about Farber, about how much he hated him, but that hate was now a memory that had lost its sting, like a photo of an old tragedy or the echo of a voice long since stilled. Without his noticing, somehow the fire inside him had begun to flicker out. "No," Greg said at last.

"You're not? Then how do you feel?"

Kane thought about that for a moment then answered, "I feel free."

"It took you long enough," Tommy said and waved Sadie over for another round.

Greg followed her path and noticed a new face at the table next to the door, a little girl, nine or ten years old, in a pink dress with pink tennis shoes.

"What's she doing here?" Kane asked. Tommy followed Greg's gaze.

"She's here for you," Tommy said.

The little girl caught Kane's eye and waved.

"What do you mean, 'She's here for me?' Kids shouldn't be in a bar. Where are her parents? Who is she?"

"You know who she is."

"What does she want?"

"Go over and ask her."

Greg stared at the child for a long heartbeat then struggled out of his chair.

"You hang in there, Greg," Tommy said. "Just remember what I told you and you'll be fine." Tommy raised his bottle in a toast, smiled, then shimmered and disappeared.

Kane gawked at the empty chair then turned toward the little girl. Lyla smiled and waved at him but when Kane tried to take a step his feet were stuck to the floor. He strained and managed to pull one free. Lyla's mouth was moving but Kane couldn't make out the words. He staggered forward another step then she waved one last time, said something else he couldn't hear, and then everything disappeared.

Kane awoke like a drowning man gasping for air. It was gone, all of it, Tommy's bar, Sadie, Big Jesse, Little Jesse, Denny and Phil, Tommy and the little girl, all vanished too soon. Kane felt as if something beautiful had been irretrievably lost, as if he had started some vital work but had been thwarted with important business still left undone.

CHAPTER SIXTY-FIVE

Around four a.m. Kane finally slipped into a fitful sleep but then woke up again at half past five and gave it up. He arrived at his office about an hour later and tried to catch up with his paperwork but the dream nagged at him like a half forgotten song. Half the time he wondered what Lyla had been trying to tell him and the other half he thought that it all had been merely the product of his wounded brain finally starting to recover and that these hallucinations with Tommy were merely the new Gregory Kane trying to heal the old one. But then the expression on Lyla's face and her little wave would overwhelm him and he would worry at the dream's meaning all over again. Eventually, in the war between emotion and logic, emotion won out.

Danny had returned to work on restricted duty and when he appeared at about half past eight he found Kane waiting for him.

"You're in early," Danny said. Kane waved his partner over to his desk.

"I'm taking a few days off," Kane said and handed Danny a bureau form. "Do me a favor and give this to Immerson for me." Danny saw the words, "Request for Paid Time Off" at the top of the sheet. "I'll only be gone for a few days. I just need to clear my head," Kane said in answer to Danny's unasked question.

"Uhh, sure thing Agent Kane. Is there anything you want me to handle while you're away?"

"Sit down," Kane ordered and Danny quickly pulled up a chair. "I don't want to be bothered, no calls, nothing. I'm going to turn off my phone so don't get upset if you can't reach me."

"But what if there's an emergency?"

"I'll check my voice mail and text messages every night. If it's important enough I'll call you back and if not, it can wait." Danny stared while he struggled to work through all the scenarios of things that might go wrong. "OK," Greg relented, "here's the name of my hotel." Kane handed him another sheet. "Do not give this to anyone, especially Immerson. I'm trusting you to keep this to yourself. If there's an emergency and I don't return your message you can call me at the hotel. OK?"

"You got it, Agent Kane." Danny looked at the address on the printout. "Symington, California? I've never heard of it. What are you going to do there?"

If Kane actually understood what he expected to accomplish he would have said nothing but he was acting on instinct now with no plan or logic involved. The chances were good that if Greg had owned a dog or cat he would have described his plans to it in the hope that his scheme might make more sense when spoken aloud. Hell, he probably would have explained himself to a talking parking meter if that was his only option but Danny was there so Kane told him instead.

"I know that doesn't make any sense but it's something I feel like I need to do," an embarrassed Kane admitted when he was finished.

"Oh, no, Agent Kane. I think it all makes total sense."

Maybe you should explain it to me, Kane thought and smiled.

"Well, anyway, I'll be back on Monday, Tuesday at the latest, and don't give anyone that phone number."

"Sure thing, Agent Kane. You can rely on me."

"I know I can, Danny. And from now on, forget that 'Agent Kane' stuff. Call me 'Greg.'" Kane glanced at the clock and hurried to his feet. "I've got to get out of here before the boss shows up and tells me that I can't go."

"Have a good trip, Agent — Greg," Danny called after him.

CHAPTER SIXTY-SIX

"I'm sorry, Agent Kane is out of the office. He's expected to return early next week. Would you like to leave a message?"

Allison's first call to Kane had immediately gone to voice mail and now this. *What was his partner's name? Roswell? Rosewell? Rosewood.*

"Can I speak to his partner, Daniel Rosewood?"

"Hello," Danny answered a minute later.

"Umm, Danny, this is Allison Varner, Senator Denning's niece. I saw you at the hospital. Do you remember? I was in the corridor with your fiancé. You waved to me."

"You're Agent . . . Greg's friend. Diane told me that she talked with you. How I can I help you?"

"I've been trying to reach Greg but his phone just goes to voice mail. Do you have another number for him?"

"He's on a break for a few days. He doesn't want to be disturbed."

"I understand but I really need to talk to him."

"Have you left him a message?"

"I, umm, it's not the sort of thing I want to talk about in a voice mail. I need to speak to him directly."

"Gee, I'm sorry Ms. Varner. I'm under strict instructions not to give out the phone number of his hotel. I gave Agent Kane my word not to give it to anyone, not even our boss, but if you left him a message I bet he would call you back."

"Thank you, Danny. I'll work it out." She hung up.

Now what? It had been so difficult to even make the call and now it was all for nothing. She stood at the window and looked out at the lengthening shadows then wandered from room to room. The apartment seemed different now, bigger, emptier. She picked up the phone then put it back down. She tried to imagine what she would have said if she had succeeded in getting Kane on the line. *Hi, how are you? How have you been? Would you like to have dinner when you get back? Maybe we could have a drink?*

Allison thought back to the first time they had been together. How odd it seemed, as if the Allison now and the Allison then were two different people. She picked up the phone and managed to catch Danny Rosewood before he went home.

"Danny, it's Allison again. I know that you can't give me Greg's number but can you tell me where he went? It's very important."

What was it that Agent Kane had said? *Don't give anyone the hotel's phone number.* Of course that meant that he couldn't tell anyone the hotel's name either. But Greg hadn't said he couldn't tell people *where* he was going.

"He went to Symington, California," Danny answered.

"Symington, California? I've never heard of it. What's he doing there?"

Looked at one way, Agent Kane probably wouldn't want him to say, but looked at another way Danny thought that maybe he should tell her. So he did.

CHAPTER SIXTY-SEVEN

By the time he had packed and dealt with all the airport nonsense, flown across the country, and checked in at the Best Western he booked over the Internet Greg was too tired to do anything beyond grabbing a quick dinner and watching an HBO movie on the room's TV. When he woke the next morning he reminded himself that he was on a vacation, of sorts, with no schedule or deadlines and he treated himself to a long, hot shower and a lazy breakfast before setting out on what, in the cold light of day, seemed to be a fool's errand. Perhaps, he thought, this trip was evidence that his brain had not really healed itself after all.

Kane plugged the address into the rental car's GPS and about twenty minutes later spotted the white and black marble sign: "Fairhaven Acres Memorial Park." He took a left and pulled into the lot fronting the caretakers' building. At first Kane was surprised by the number of vehicles but then realized that the media frenzy surrounding the Supreme Court decision would have spilled over into every aspect of Lyla Masterson's life including this one.

A white gazebo flanked the beginning of a path that wound through the grounds and inside it Kane found an index to the graves. The edges of the page holding Lyla's name were worn from frequent use. According to the plastic-covered map she had been laid to rest in plot 843, just past Sunrise Hill near the beginning of Serenity Glade.

When Kane reached the top of the slope he noticed a trickle of people wending among the markers, pausing in ones and twos for a few moments at one particular spot. Greg ducked back under the greening branches of a big-leaf sycamore and waited for them to leave. Where Washington had been gray and battered by storms here the breeze felt soft on his face and bore the fragrance of eucalyptus and bay. Kane gladly waited, enjoying the morning sun that warmed his skin. After about fifteen minutes the last of the other visitors turned away and Greg walked down the slope.

The headstone was black marble with the name "Lyla Masterson" inscribed in gold leaf. Above it a laminated photograph of a smiling child in a pink dress had been set into a depression chiseled into the stone. Below her name and the dates of her birth and death were the words:

GONE FROM LIFE TOO SOON
BUT HER DREAMS LIVE ON
IN ALL OF US

Kane stared at the marker but heard and felt nothing beyond the rustle of the breeze and the distant screech of a stellar jay. A part of him wanted to ask if she really had appeared in his dream and what she had wanted to tell him but he knew that only a fool or a lunatic would believe something like that. For a moment he wished that he could whisper the thoughts racing through his head but then realized that even if Lyla were standing before him that they could not be translated into words.

What am I doing? Kane berated himself. *The only part of Lyla Masterson here is the memory of her in the minds of her visitors. The child herself is irretrievably lost.* Kane stared at the headstone a moment longer and knew himself to be a fool.

For a second the breeze picked up and brought Kane the sound of footsteps moving down the path behind him. Time to go, Kane knew, and put this madness behind him. He turned away from Lyla's marker then froze when he saw her standing in front of him.

"Hey, sailor," Allison said, "buy a girl a drink?" and before he could answer she was in his arms.

CHAPTER SIXTY-EIGHT

The conference room was in a basement and furnished with a couple of dozen folding chairs, a card table and an ancient coffee machine. A random group of fifteen or so people dressed in everything from jeans to business suits, polyester to silk, populated the room. The meeting was just about to begin when a lone man slipped through the door and took a seat in the back.

A woman dressed in a blue and black blouse and gray slacks stood and walked to the front of the room.

"I'm Irene Goldin," she said.

"Hi, Irene," everyone except the last-minute visitor replied.

"We'll get started in a minute but first I want to ask, do we have any new people here today?" For a moment no one answered but when Goldin's eyes settled on the late arrival the man hesitated then uneasily got to his feet. Everyone swiveled in their chairs to face him.

"Umm, I've never been to one of these meetings before," he said, nervously fingering the cuff of his grimy shirt. "To tell you the truth I didn't want to stop drinking. I didn't think I could keep from going insane without the booze, but someone told me that there was a way that I could have a better life and that he believed in me, and I didn't want to let him down, so I've been trying to stop. It's been eleven days since I had my last drink and I don't know if I can hold out much longer. I feel like I'm hanging off the side of a building by my fingertips and that any second I'm going to fall."

"You can have a better life," Goldin said. "We're all proof of that. We've all been where you are. The first step is letting go of the past and learning to live one day at a time. We know that's harder than it sounds but we'll help you. Before we go any farther, it's customary to begin by telling us your name."

"Sorry," the man said, dipping his hand into his pocket and rubbing his fingers over the letter that was now his constant companion. "I knew that." He paused a moment and looked at the people who seemed to think that he still had some value and that maybe he still had a chance at a decent life.

"My name is Randy," he said, "and I'm an alcoholic."

— The End —

ABOUT THE AUTHOR

David Grace has written fifteen novels. To see a list of his other books and to read free excerpts from them, visit his website

www.davidgraceauthor.com

Print editions of his novels are available from Wildside Press and Amazon.com